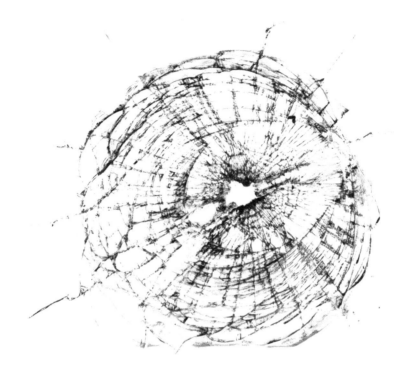

A September Day and Shadow Thriller
HIT AND RUN

Book Five

AMY SHOJAI

FURRY MUSE
PUBLISHING
P.O. Box 1904
Sherman TX 75091
(903)814-4319
amy@shojai.com

September & Shadow Pet-centric Thrillers
By Amy Shojai

LOST AND FOUND

HIDE AND SEEK

SHOW AND TELL

FIGHT OR FLIGHT
Introducing Lia, Tee, and Karma

HIT AND RUN

WIN OR LOSE

Chapter 1 (34 Years Ago)

Latana Ojo lied better than anyone she knew.

She'd never outgrown the make-believe games that filled her days with technicolor drama, a stark contrast to the black-and-white drudgery of the Ojo's hardworking New York lifestyle. Her older sister's recent marriage to a wealthy landowner many states away left Tana on the hook for helping in the family business every day after school. Their restaurant catered to high-class clientele with five-star cuisine, but Tana wanted more than a future of dowdy hairnets, clunky shoes, and shapeless aprons that Momma wore working her magic in the kitchen.

She yearned for glitz and romance. Her upcoming birthday would be the first chance to spread her wings, wear makeup and high heels, and even a sparkling tiara. Her girlfriends didn't understand, and thought Tana should be satisfied with the fantastic party her parents were planning. And the fifteen skinny pimply neighborhood boys chosen for her *quinceanera* court, one representing each year of her life, bored her to tears.

Then she met the elderly but oh-so-stylish Anita Page when the actress returned to New York for some family business. Papa got Ms. Page to sign a picture for the restaurant, which he framed and hung on the wall by the cash register.

Tana burned with inspiration. She'd be an actress! Not a film star, like Ms. Page, but a theatrical performer, singing and dancing for adoring audiences. She'd escape her parents' insular life here in Little Spain, wear glamorous costumes, elegant hairstyles, and fancy jewels, and make a name for herself on Broadway. Of course, she'd be choosy when handsome, dashing actors romanced her. Ms. Page attained fame as one of only a handful of Latinas performers, and Tana would too.

Actors lied and got paid to do it. They recreated themselves into whatever they wished. After all, Ms. Page had been born Anita Evelyn Pomares, with grandparents from Spain, just like Tana. So she'd change her name, and transform her dream into reality.

Tana's own striking blue eyes, honeyed hair, ageless grace, and husky voice rivaled the film star in her prime. Ms. Page noticed it, she said so herself. When Tana confided her dream, Ms. Page smiled with encouragement, but said she'd need an agent to protect her from vultures, whatever that meant. And she autographed a fine lace handkerchief.

She knew her parents wouldn't agree, so Tana never mentioned her dream. She found an agent, but he only considered girls eighteen and older. One little lie would smooth the way.

Tana practiced for a week what to say and how to act. She knew what to wear. Her *quinceanera* dress made her look and feel sophisticated and stylish, but she couldn't wait until October's gala party. Two months was a lifetime away. Momma and Papa didn't need to know she borrowed the dress for this most important interview. They'd understand, once she got famous. Success had no need of forgiveness.

She faked a sick stomach to stay home from school and get the night off from work. She'd interview with the agent and be home before her parents knew any better. Tana wore a touch of makeup she'd stolen from her sister while helping her pack for her honeymoon, and the new white satin pumps chosen to go with her dress. The beautiful long white lace swished around her ankles, and the blue sash matched her eyes. She considered but left behind the tiara, fearing that might be too much.

The agent beamed. He told her she looked like a princess. She blushed, and at his prompting she sang part of a song and danced a bit. But he interrupted before she finished her prepared monologue. He praised her audition, but said he wanted more. Something special to prove she was serious. And he showed her what he meant. Right there. On top of the desk.

He ruined her dress. Ruined her dream. Ruined her.

So Tana killed him.

She'd lied to everyone about everything ever since.

Chapter 2 (Present Day)

Angela Day twisted her wedding ring as she perched on the edge of the chair and glanced around the bank lobby. She'd unzipped her parka, and the boots covering her jittering feet still dripped melted snow from the latest December flurries. An oversize bag sat between her feet. The newspaper article from the Chicago Tribune, carefully folded, peeked out from the bag. She got the local paper the rest of the week, but always picked up the Chicago paper on Sundays. The story jolted her memory—a name, a single name she'd heard him say—and might mean nothing, or everything. For days, it niggled the back of her mind, an echo barely heard, insistent, insidious. Inevitable.

Peter had always talked her down whenever she got her back up. He didn't want her to ask upsetting questions that stirred things up. She twisted the ring again, missing him desperately. Peter died six months ago. Now Angela had nobody to talk her down. Only memories, nothing to fill her days, nothing to stop the questions tormenting sleepless nights.

The bank teller waved and Angela clutched her bag to her chest and followed him into the vault. She signed the safety deposit box log—her throat clogging when she saw the last signature. The box belonged to her dead son, Chris. Her husband had been the executor of his will. But Peter never looked in the box, fearing what he might find in a dead cop's private files. She had had to jump through several hoops this morning to gain access to the box, but Angela couldn't let fear rule the rest of her life.

She presented her key, then sat at a private carrel. The teller placed the small metal box before her and left. Angela took a deep breath before opening it.

A thick bundle of papers and file folders stuffed it to the brim, nearly overflowing the deposit box. She removed and paged open the first file. Angela caught her breath and gently picked up a small photo. Her insides quivered. Chris stood proud, beaming, beside his somber bride. On the back, in his familiar scrawl, he'd written: *When you're ready, the answers are here.* Her chest tightened. She set the picture aside.

Angela leafed through stacks of newspaper clippings, some dating back decades. She scanned the headlines, and none made much sense. She set each in a neat stack, until she came to the most recent. There! That was the same name, and the same face, featured in the news story stuffed in her purse. She fished it out, unfolded it and spread the two accounts side by side.

The earlier piece profiled Clear Choice Laboratories, a Chicago company credited with solving a number of high-profile cases by identifying incriminating evidence. A picture of the lab owner, Brad Detweiller, grinned with a cocky smugness while accepting grateful congratulations from Detective Christopher Day.

In the more recent paper, a much older Detweiller hid his face from the camera. He dodged questions about a recent lab error that caused a conviction to be thrown out. The news report suggested an indictment might be forthcoming. After scanning the notes more thoroughly, the speculation echoed much of the concerns raised by Chris's safety deposit box research.

Angela shivered, and blew out several short breaths, trying to calm herself and regain control. She rubbed her arms, looking around to be sure she remained alone. She'd always assumed her son's murder had had something to do with his wife's shady past. His note on the wedding picture supported her assumption. Angela still resented how September had disappeared after Chris's death. But how was Detweiller connected?

Maybe she was reading too much into this. Chris wouldn't poke a known hornet's nest without police backup, she argued with herself to calm irrational worries. If he considered this a private family matter, and Detweiller helped him out in some way, Chris might have confided in… Pulling out her phone, she searched the contacts, and called a longtime family friend, then left a message when prompted.

She shifted in her chair, unable to get comfortable as she read through Chris's notes from the earliest to the latest. Chris expressed surprise and then outrage. Highlighted phrases painted a dark story of a decades-long conspiracy that victimized dozens of innocent children, including his wife. Angela's breath quickened. His investigation proved Detweiller played a role, but Chris died before he was able to expose the crime. Had Detweiller killed her son to silence him?

Angela gathered up the files with shaking hands and carefully replaced them in the box. At the last moment, before calling the attendant, she slipped the wedding photo into her purse.

"Who else has access to this box?" Angela watched as the teller secured the box and handed her back the key. "It belonged to my deceased son. It's been nearly two years." She steadied her voice. "His widow moved away—"

The woman checked. "The listing includes a Mrs. September Day, but she has never accessed the box."

"Yes, that's my daughter-in-law."

Zipping her parka, Angela hurried out to the parking lot, squinting up at the gunmetal clouds. Once in her car she started the engine and turned the defrost blower on high. As she waited for the ice to melt, Angela pulled out the picture again, tracing the face of her son with one gloved finger. "I know you loved her. You saved September, wanted to heal her." She bit her lip. "And they killed you for it."

Angela had wanted to love her daughter-in-law, but prickly September kept everyone at a distance. Chris had finally broken through the woman's brittle exterior after gifting her with a dog. What was his name? Dakota, that was it. The German Shepherd died trying to protect Chris from whoever wanted to keep this horrible secret.

She rocked back and forth in her seat. It was time for the truth to come out.

On impulse she pulled a pad from her purse and wrote a quick note, then tore off the cardboard backing and folded it around the picture to protect it. She should have done more when she had the chance. But maybe it wasn't too late. Maybe she could still get justice for her son.

Her car slipped and slid in the slushy back streets as she drove to the post office. She bought a card and envelope. Angela slid the note and picture inside along with the safety deposit key. After googling the location on her phone, and scribbling the address with shaky hands, she added postage and sent the card on its way.

Her phone burbled. She took a deep breath before answering the familiar number. "Thanks for returning my call. You're a good friend, and I need your professional advice. Before he died, did Chris talk to you about his safety deposit box?"

Chapter 3

September relaxed and breathed again once she pulled into the unloading zone at DFW Airport. "We made good time. We can get breakfast once y'all check your bags with the curbside service."

Combs smiled from the passenger seat and shook his head. "You don't have to come inside. We've got this." He turned halfway in his seat. "Melinda, help your brother get his stuff together. Willie, listen to your sister." Combs turned back to September with a crooked grin as the pair unloaded luggage with the usual sibling squabbles. "Gotta love child labor, right?"

She laughed wistfully and touched his hand. "You'll have a great time. The kids need a break, and so do you. Disney in December heals lots of hurts, ya know."

"Going to miss you." He laced their fingers together and leaned in for a quick kiss that warmed her from the inside out. He'd invited her to go, too, and she'd been tempted. But Detective Jeffrey Combs needed time with his kids. And she needed to finish up with the contractors rebuilding her house.

"Text me pictures, okay?" With his ex-wife's health in decline, his petition for sole custody meant major changes for Combs as a single parent. She told herself that concentrating on his family's new normal took priority over any other relationship complications.

She'd recently begun practicing yoga to manage stress. It had the added benefit of increasing flexibility, which helped reduce pain from old injuries. Thankfully Shadow tempered September's PTSD, and she'd not had a major meltdown in months. At the thought, she glanced at the big black dog in the rear of the car. The German Shepherd immediately stood up, shook himself, and yawned, his tail beating a tattoo against the now closed rear hatchback window.

Melinda tapped purple fingernails on the passenger side glass until September rolled down the window. "Dad, are you coming?" The girl tossed her long, curly red hair with impatience. "Kiss her goodbye already, let's go."

September blushed and laughed, and the teenager grinned. At least the kids liked her, maybe more than that. Her throat grew thick watching the two kids—an emotion she'd never expected to feel. Surviving a killer's attack together during the tornado ten months ago had forged a bond closer than many families shared. Maybe by next Christmas September could say yes to a family trip together.

Willie joined his sister at the window. "Take care of Kinsler, okay? I'm gonna bring him a Mickey toy so he'll forgive me for leaving him."

September stuck out her lower lip. "Nothing for me?" When his face fell, she laughed. "Willie, I'm teasing. Lia and I will take good care of your dog, I promise." She leaned closer and whispered. "Dogs always forgive, even without toys. He loves you bunches, even more than chasing squirrels."

Shadow woofed at the squirrel reference, and Willie laughed, but looked relieved.

September and Shadow temporarily shared an apartment with Lia Corazon at the young woman's boarding kennels. Once the contractors finished rebuilding her tornado-damaged house, she'd move back into the Victorian on Rabbit Run Road before Combs returned home. The renovated home would have plenty of room for the future September wanted more than anything.

"Daaddee, c'mon already. Bring the tickets! Willie already got your bag, too. We'll wait for you by the bag checker." Melinda grabbed her brother's arm and tugged him away.

September turned to Combs. "Going to miss you bunches. Be safe. You're really important to me. We've got plans, you know." She coughed to cover the sudden catch in her voice.

"I love you, too." He folded her into strong arms, kissed her hard and got out of the car. "I'll see you in two weeks, and call and text as often as I can." His spicy aftershave lingered when he slammed the door, the thumping sound so final it made her heart hurt.

He walked around the car to her open window, and bent to stare into September's cat-green eyes. Combs stroked the white streak in the coffee-color hair, and she leaned into his hand. "We've still got a date for New Year's Eve. I'll give you your Christmas gift then." He cupped her cheeks with both hands, and she closed her eyes as he kissed her once more, slow, soft, sweet, before he pulled away, leaving her rosy warm and breathless. "Drive safe, September. You know your mom won't be happy if you're late."

And just like that, the warmth fled, and her shoulders hunched. Today's departure gave Combs a reason to bow out of her family's early Christmas gathering. Mom insisted, since in alternate years her siblings spent the holidays with their spouses' families. She halfway believed he'd planned it that way, and couldn't blame him. Mom expected September at ten o'clock sharp to help with dinner preparation. Her brother Mark and three sisters, kids in tow, would arrive with potluck by eleven; dinner would commence a half-hour later, and the interminable gift exchange start an hour after that.

She'd rather go to Disney World. Maybe she could still snag a ticket...

Combs checked bags as Willie chattered about plans for his eleventh birthday celebration at the Magic Kingdom. Melinda practiced the studied indifference perfected by thirteen-year-olds everywhere. September raised a hand to wave, but Combs didn't see, and the trio disappeared into the busy DFW terminal.

Alone. And this time, not by choice.

For so long, she'd locked herself away from the world. Hell, it had taken her years to change, to learn to trust anyone. Her cat Macy gave her a reason to live, and her dogs—first Dakota and especially Shadow—taught her to love again. And now Combs offered the promise of a future. A normal life.

So she wasn't really alone. She actually had good friends now, and a big family waiting for her. "Baby-dog, ready to go home?"

He woofed, and jumped from the rear cargo area onto the back seats. The notch out of the tip of one ear, and the white slash of fur down one side of his face added character to his regal bearing. Badges of honor, hard won victories from saving her, and others.

Shadow nosed her hand when she reached behind her seat. "Yes, I'm nervous about today's gathering. You know what Mom's like. But I'm getting better, right?" She turned, put the car into gear, and navigated out of the airport.

Shadow watched the North Texas landscape speed by, particularly interested in the pastureland dotted here and there with Longhorn cattle. He pushed his nose into the window's narrow opening to sample the breeze. September double checked to engage the child locks. The dog had an uncanny ability to open car door windows, and she didn't want him becoming a furry black missile on Hwy 35. Since he'd taught himself the behavior, she'd put the action on cue. In the past, the skill had come in handy.

Training and experience had matured Shadow far beyond his true age—he'd be two years old in February—although he'd turn into a play maniac given half an invitation. He continued to meet the world with tail-waving joy. September had never met a dog so eager to learn, or as stubborn at knowing (and proving) when she was wrong. After nearly losing Shadow more than once, she wrestled with giving him the freedom he deserved while keeping him safe.

Because Shadow didn't want her protection. He wanted to live, love, and play. By her side. Wags and kisses—and protection—provided free of charge. And he wanted her to live, play, and love him back. That simple.

And that hard. Especially in her large and complicated family.

Twenty minutes later, they drew near her parents' house. September slowed, but drove past the empty driveway. She didn't want to spend any longer one-on-one with her mother than absolutely necessary… And she still had fifteen minutes until she was expected. She made a face. September preferred the company of dogs and cats, and found them much easier to understand than most people. Combs excepted, of course. Lately, Mom had been even more prickly than usual. "What do you think, Shadow? Wanna go get the mail?"

His tail thumped on the seat. Shadow didn't understand the words, other than the "go" word. But going anywhere with her made them both happy.

During the house renovations she'd rented a post office box, but only checked mail a couple of times a week. Most bills she paid electronically, but for the first time in ages, she'd ordered holiday gifts. This year, she had a reason to celebrate, instead of looking over her shoulder for lurking bogeymen. If the gifts had arrived, she'd be able to add to today's pile rather than having to deliver them for Christmas proper.

September parked in the deserted parking lot in front of the small brick post office. Shadow stood, waiting eagerly for the door to open, and woofed with disappointment when she left him behind. "Be right back." She'd only be gone a few minutes. If the packages came, she'd need both hands to ferry them to the car. Shadow's imposing presence, not to mention his battle-scars, kept strangers to a cautious distance with no need to lock the new car.

The bright blue sky and mild forty-degree temperatures made September yearn to ditch the family obligations and take Shadow for a tracking run. It had been two weeks since their last case reunited a missing cat, lost at a rest area along Hwy 75, with its family. Vacation with pets meant extra precautions. She made a note to post additional holiday safety tips on her blog. This time of year meant a reduced workload for her, but an increase in business at Lia's boarding kennel. They made a pretty good team, with September's innate caution tempered by the younger girl's impulsive enthusiasm.

September zippered her light jacket against the breeze. Her dark hair needed a trim and fell into her eyes, but she'd decided to let it grow out. She pulled on her blue bump cap that helped keep hair at bay. She'd rolled her eyes at the gift from Mom, who insisted wearing a bright blue knit-covered hardhat during house construction could address safety with style. September had been surprised to discover how much she liked the bump cap, and often enjoyed wearing it. Besides, Mom would see it and that could ease the perennial tension that stalked their relationship.

She trotted to the building and pushed inside. She heard thumps and soft conversation from the back of the building when she keyed open her box. A wad of mailings, mostly advertisements, stuffed the box, plus two numbered keys for larger lockers. *Yes!* That meant packages.

September tossed the ad fliers into the trash. She stacked the three Christmas cards and tucked them into her waistband to open and read in the car. Then she collected boxes from the lockers, balanced them in her arms, and teetered her way back to the car.

"Wait, Shadow." Before opening the rear hatchback, she reminded him to stay in place. "We got mail baby-dog! Fun presents for the kids. Maybe something for you, too." September opened the large boxes quickly and sorted through the bright gift-wrapped packages. She kept one package for Shadow and climbed back behind the wheel before handing the loosely-wrapped gift to him on the back seat.

He sniffed the gaudy wrapping, nose-poked it, and grinned with delight when it squealed. September laughed out loud, watching him brace the package under one paw to rip the paper off the new bear-toy. "You destroyed your last one. Hope this one lasts longer." He settled down with the fluffy brown stuffie between his paws, clamped his jaws around the toy, and half closed his eyes in bliss. She figured the new toy would help keep him occupied during the long day ahead.

"Let's see who sent cards." September hadn't sent any cards in forever. Until recently, she'd wanted to keep her location a secret. And she could count on one hand the number of her friends.

She examined the return address before opening each, smiling at the messages inside. The first, from Doc Eugene, featured dogs and cats as holiday angels. After caring for Shadow and Macy-cat, he'd become part of her extended family. September made a mental note to buy some cards and send a few back. No, probably too late for this year.

The next two, postmarked from South Bend, Indiana, raised goosebumps on her arms. She cautiously opened the first, and laughed with relief. "It's from Teddy!" She held the envelope out for Shadow to sniff, and he woofed in recognition at the scent. The old man had surprising computer skills he'd shared with her on more than one occasion. "I sure miss him. Says he's staying with his son's family while he finishes his latest contract job." After Teddy's wife Molly died, he'd left town and hadn't been back.

Still smiling, she tore open the last card, and then dropped it, hissing with shock. Inside the generic card, a photograph. Sandwiched between thin protective cardboard. Of a much younger September looking frightened, and Christopher Day beaming. Their wedding day.

The back of the picture had a note in his familiar writing: *When you're ready, the answers are here.*

"What answers, Chris? When I'm ready for what?" Her skin tingled, and she grasped the steering wheel to steady sudden dizziness.

A thin sheet of flowered stationary fell into her lap, along with a small key. Without reading, September knew the sender. Only one person witnessed their wedding. September forbade pictures, but Chris's proud Mom found a way.

She covered her mouth with one shaking hand and picked up the note in the other to read silently: *I know who killed Chris and it's not what you think. You need to know the truth. Please come.*

Two years ago this coming Wednesday, on December 18, Chris and their dog Dakota were murdered by her stalker Victor Grant. Once his attempts on her life landed him in prison, she'd felt safe for the first time in years.

If not Victor, then who killed Chris—and why? And, oh God, if the killer remained at large, everyone she loved remained at risk. Her family, Shadow and Macy. Combs, and his kids.

Her mouth soured, and she squeezed her eyes closed as her vision turn dark. September pressed both fists to the sides of her head, fighting against hyperventilation as the doors of the car squeezed closer and closer. Her heartbeat thrashed, a beat-beat-beat in her ears that shut out everything.

Shadow pushed forward between the seats. He nose-poked her shoulder, insistent, relentless, until she responded. She reached back with one hand to accept his demand for contact. She clenched her other fist and the key gouged her palm. She concentrated on the biting pain in one hand contrasted with Shadow's icy wet nose against her other. Slowly, the black sparklies at the edge of her sight receded.

This wasn't the first time she'd been ambushed by the past. She'd survived each hit, then run away as fast and as far as possible. But this time, she'd run toward the answers. And by God in heaven, she'd hit back before ghosts derailed her future.

September retrieved her phone, and searched for the number she'd not used since Chris died. Surely, it hadn't changed? She dialed, but only got voice mail. With hesitation, September left a message for Angela Day.

After the family gathering at Mom's, she'd pack for South Bend. Time to confront her past, and bury it once and for all.

Chapter 4

Angela opened the front door with a tight smile. "Thanks so much for coming over. You don't know how much this means to me." She shivered, and tried to steady her wavering voice. "Come on in, it's bitter outside."

"It's been too long. You sounded upset, but I couldn't get away during the week." The tall, imposing man scraped packed snow off his shoes before stepping into the front hall. "So sorry I couldn't attend Peter's memorial service." He pulled off heavy leather gloves and stuffed them into coat pockets before he shrugged off his coat and handed it to her. "That weekend we were on a tour of college campuses. Can you believe it? He's already a college freshman at Notre Dame."

She closed the closet door and motioned him into the living room. "Time flies. Seems only yesterday that Chris graduated alongside your oldest. For a while I thought they might make a go of it, until she chose law school and Chris dove into the police academy." Angela smiled sadly as she sat down on the edge of the sofa. "They made a cute couple." She caught herself twisting her wedding ring again, and instead crossed her arms.

He laughed, a high-pitched unexpected sound, but then wouldn't meet her eyes. "I wanted her to join the family business, but she's on track for great things at her Chicago law firm." He still hadn't taken a seat.

"Peter bragged on you, so happy that a kid he grew up with hit the big time." The small talk was making her queasy, and Angela wondered if she'd have the nerve to come out and tell him what she suspected. Part of her wanted to run before he asked her what this was about. "He always said you'd make us all proud."

"Don't know about that." He blinked quickly, and pulled off his glasses to polish them with a monogrammed handkerchief, which he then stuffed back into the pocket of his tailored suit. His buffed fingernails spoke of money and style. His smooth deep baritone voice instilled confidence. But his pacing suggested distraction. "Hard work all those years ago in Chicago helped before we decided to move home to South Bend. Gaining the respect of colleagues pays off. It's truly an honor to serve." He finally took a seat opposite her. He crossed and then uncrossed his legs, shifting in the chair. "So tell me about what's got you upset. Something you found that belonged to Chris?"

"I made coffee, would you like some?" Angela stood again, twisting her fingers.

He waved her back down. "I can't stay long, I'm on my way to a meeting with the mayor. Now Angela, tell me. I'll help if I can." He finally met her eyes.

She sank back onto the seat, but continued wringing her hands. Ever since she'd dropped the key in the mail, she'd second-guessed the decision to involve September. Yes, the young woman deserved the truth, but what could she do about it? Chris always wanted to protect September, to respect her privacy. But with his suspicious death, and the later attacks on his widow, the police should have the information. That would prompt questions—why hadn't Chris said something at the time? She couldn't have her son's reputation as a detective questioned. Nothing should taint his memory! This man, though, could figure out what to do—inform the authorities, but protect Chris.

Angela took a deep breath, rocking in place as she spoke. "Chris had a safety deposit box. I found the key when Peter died. He took care of things after Chris was…murdered." It had taken her many months to be able to say the word without breaking into tears. "Now it falls to me to take care of everything. I owe it to Peter, and to our son."

"Horrible time." The Judge leaned forward and patted her hand, stilling the nervous motion. His brow wrinkled. "Anything I can do to help, you know that I will. It's normal to feel sad, overwhelmed even, but you can't let it take over your life, Angela."

She pulled at the neck of her sweater then smoothed hands down her legs. Had she combed her hair today? Angela knew she'd let herself go lately. She surreptitiously checked to be sure her shoes matched and touched a hand to her lips. *Yes, she'd put on lip gloss.*

"Do you have other family around to support you? Church members? Close friends?"

She shook her head and whispered, fighting tears. "Some days I don't want to get out of bed. I miss Peter and Chris so much, sometimes I wish…" She stopped herself. She now had a purpose beyond vacuuming and dusting an already spotless house. She'd finish what her son had begun. "Don't you worry about me, I'll muddle through." She offered a weak smile. "I appreciate your support more than you can know."

"At least they caught the guy. He's in jail down in Texas somewhere." He laughed again, that odd high-pitched sound.

"That's the thing." Angela took a deep breath then the words came out in a rush. "I found research and notes in the safety deposit box about Chris's investigation."

"Investigation? What sort of notes?" He picked a spot of lint off his sleeve. "Angela, after all this time it must have been handled by the police department. They take losing a brother cop very seriously. Old notes can't matter anymore."

She hugged herself. "Maybe. But he'd been investigating a Chicago laboratory. A man named Detweiller worked there. Just before he died, Chris suspected he'd been falsifying results, maybe someone paying him off. I saw a recent news report about Detweiller that suggests the same thing. What if someone wanted to silence Chris and stop his investigation?"

He stiffened, straightened his tie, stumbling over quickly spoken words. "One man, a twisted fanatic obsessed with your son's wife, killed Chris. And he'll pay for his crime." He tugged at his collar, and stretched his neck, taking a long deep breath before he continued. "If Chris had information about illegal activity, the police already knew. He was a good cop, a great detective. He'd have kept the department informed."

"I know that. Of course he would." But her brow furrowed. If he'd told someone at the police department, wouldn't she have heard something about it? "It started as a personal matter about his wife that Chris wanted to keep private. I don't understand all the notes he left." She bit her lip.

He leaned forward again. One snow-damp shoe jittered for a moment before he set both feet firmly on the floor. "What else, Angela? What do you think he found? What do you want to do?"

"I'm not sure, and it kind of scares me. Should I take the files to the police? Or maybe I should forget I ever found that lockbox." If Chris had uncovered a hidden hornet's nest, poking it could get a lot of innocent people stung. Sure, September had a right to know about the contents of the box, but she wasn't the law and couldn't do anything about the information. Angela straightened. Chris would want her to do the right thing. "I want the police to know. If my son died because of what's in that damn box, I want to get Chris justice. Can you help me?"

He groaned and half smiled, condescending. "Angela, it doesn't work that way. I think your emotions have you seeing conspiracies." He held up his hands, palms up, when she opened her mouth to object. "But you've every right to be upset, losing Peter so suddenly then finding unexpected reminders of Chris's private business. He obviously wanted this to stay private though, and maybe you should respect that. Why don't you let me take a look before you involve anyone else? I'll put on my legal hat and we can keep things confidential—lawyer–client privilege." He smiled. "I can certainly talk to the police chief if need be, but I seriously doubt it'll come to that."

"Oh thank you! I knew I could count on you, George." She took a deep breath, and stretched her shoulders. Her back crackled, and she only then realized how tense she'd been.

"You've had enough bad news lately. We don't want to add to your depression." He smiled broadly.

A beep sounded and he checked his phone. "Must be your phone, Angela." He stood. "I need to run anyway. Let me take Chris's files with me and I'll review them tonight." He walked to the door and opened the coat closet.

She followed him. "Oh, I don't have the files here. I left them at the bank." Her phone beeped again from the small table by the door. "I'll get it later." Angela pulled out his coat and held it for him.

He frowned. "It's still early. We can get there before the bank closes at noon." He shrugged on the coat, pulled out his leather gloves and tugged them on.

"What about your meeting with the mayor? You've certainly got friends in high places!" She'd called the right person. If anyone could get to the bottom of Chris's suspicions, Peter's longtime buddy could take care of things.

"I can push back the meeting half an hour. But I've got a full workload leading up to Christmas. If I don't pick up your files to review now, it could be weeks before I get to it. You don't want to wait, do you?" He pulled out her coat and held it for her to don. A wire hanger jangled and fell to the floor; he stooped to scoop it up.

Her phone pinged, signaling a voice mail. "I'm sorry, George, but I don't have the key anymore." She supposed the bank would still let her in, though, with the proper identification, even if she didn't have the key. She ignored him, standing there holding her coat, to retrieve her phone from the table. "Hey, good timing! It's September. She must have gotten my note." She turned on the speaker to replay the message.

"This is September. Uhm, September Day? I just got your note, and the safety deposit key." Angela took a big breath then let it out in a rush. "Call this number so we can arrange to meet. You're right, Angela, it's time for answers, and…well, I'm sorry. So very sorry. For everything."

George's world tilted, and a weird buzzing drowned out the recorded message. Time slowed down, tick-ticking by, everything in herky-jerky stop action. He'd been dragged into a deal he couldn't refuse and tried to extricate himself more than twenty years ago. But as his influence grew he became more valuable to those who claimed his soul.

No one could ever know about that. His reputation, his career, his kids' futures were at stake. He hadn't killed Christopher Day but knew who had. Going to the bank tied him to the old investigation, even if he could satisfy Angela and make it disappear. If Christopher Day's investigation became public, his handler would clean house. George, and his whole family, would be at the top of the hit list.

He had no choice.

George swooped the coat hanger over Angela's head and twisted it tight, cutting off her breath. She dropped the phone to grapple the wire that cut into the soft flesh of her throat.

"Oh God, what am I doing?" His hands shook. He wasn't a killer! But he couldn't let go, couldn't relent. Nobody could know. Thank God Angela alerted him first.

George grunted and lifted Angela off the floor until she dangled from the garrote. Her legs flailed against his broad body, slowed, and finally hung loose. It took much longer than he expected. He held her, exerting pressure another endless moment, then dropped her without ceremony. He retrieved Angela's phone with shaking hands.

He'd message September to warn her off. Wait, no. He had to destroy the evidence in the safety deposit box. George stared at the phone, and then smiled as the analytical mind that brought him success weighed the options. He knew exactly what to do.

For now, September could wait. He had other loose ends to tie. Quickly he pocketed Angela's phone. Now to clean up the mess her death—no, her *suicide*—left behind.

By heaven, he'd protect his family. And he'd protect the dozens of innocents depending on him. Even if it meant destroying September Day.

Chapter 5

September pulled into her parents' driveway and sat for a long moment. She put the cards and the envelope with her wedding picture and key in the glove box, scooting them securely beneath the handgun.

She'd not returned to South Bend since burying her husband. Memory played tricks with paranoia born of the time before, but she knew her years with Chris and Dakota had healed the worst of her pain. It had taken two years for her to accept his proposal, and their almost five-year marriage flashed by like someone else's dream. He found her a mentor and got her a contract job as a dog handler for the Chicago P.D. When fear took too big a toll, he moved them to South Bend. Her career and confidence grew from Chris's love, and his faith in her.

In an instant, Victor stole everything away. And now two years later, ready to reinvent herself one more time, Angela Day's message blurred the edges of the clear picture she'd painted of her husband's murder.

Shadow danced on the back seat, eager to get out of the car. When she climbed out, Mom met her at the car.

"Honey, why don't you put it in the back yard next to the hot tub? It can dig and sniff and do whatever dogs do." She crossed her arms and shivered in the light December breeze. "I just vacuumed and don't want mud tracked in. You understand."

September opened the car door for Shadow and he hopped out and immediately sniffed the nearby grass. "*It* has a name. And you know Shadow stays with me." How many times had she had this same argument while living with her last summer? Before the argument could escalate, she threw Mom a bone. "Besides, he got a bath last night." *And he's better behaved than your grandkids.*

"Whatever you say. I guess he keeps you out of trouble?" Mom pursed her mouth, but gave September a quick hug. "Need help unloading?"

September smiled. "Thanks for asking."

Mom sniffed, taking in the abundance of festive packages. "Did you buy out the shopping center?" She grabbed up the first box filled with small packages, while September balanced another with several larger gifts.

"It's not a lot, mostly fun stuff for the kids." September shrugged. "I haven't been much of an aunt to them."

"You've had other priorities, like your health." Her tart tone softened as they walked to the door. "How are you?"

September forced a smile. "Best I've felt in years. But what about the rest of the family? I've felt out of the loop since we moved out. And I want to do better." September hesitated, then forced herself to continue. "What about Mark? I wasn't sure he'd make it with all the holiday stained glass orders. And losing Aaron." Her voice trailed off. "I know it's hard, believe me I know."

Mom remained pragmatic as always. "Some days are better than others. Staying busy helps." Her stoic expression hurt September's heart. When had Mom become so hard? "He says Aaron's brother took over the landscape business, so that will stay in their family." Three months ago, Mark's partner had succumbed to the same neurological illness that took Teddy's wife, and had stricken Combs's ex-wife and several others in the Heartland community.

September waited for her to juggle the door open. "Where's Dad?"

"Your father's putting a reinforced fastener on the gate to the hot tub, to make sure the kids aren't tempted. Prepare for bedlam, with everyone here. It'll be the first time since…"

"Since I turned sixteen, my going away party before the cello tour. Twelve years ago." September pulled off her cap, and finger-combed her hair into some semblance of decorum. Her pulse thrummed. Shadow pressed against September's side. She couldn't fool him.

"You're not the only one avoiding me." Mom didn't hide the hurt and bitterness. She'd wanted this family reunion for ages. Rose eyed her, up and down. "You do look good. Glad your hair finally has grown out, but you need a trim to style the mess. That white streak though, wish you'd do something about that." September cleared her throat, but knew arguing accomplished nothing. Mom reluctantly added, "I'm happy for you. Probably has something to do with a certain detective. Am I right?" Rather than disapproving, she sounded resigned. "Shame he couldn't join us. I'd think he'd make the effort, if you matter to him as much as he apparently means to you." She sniffed, turned, and led the way through the door.

Rolling her eyes, September followed into the house.

"Hello September."

The box of gifts tumbled from September's arms onto the floor. Her hands reflexively rushed to cover her mouth, and she struggled to form coherent words. "I-I-uh...didn't expect you to already be here." Shadow whined, and pressed hard against September's thigh. A strong wind would knock April's fragile figure over, but her sister's bright blue eyes didn't waver, steady and strong.

And sane.

"Here for the weekend. Mom insisted." April grinned, her blond hair and attitude a younger but less bitter version of their mother. Mom had moved behind April, a satisfied smirk on her face. "I made everyone promise not to say anything. I didn't want them to give you a reason to stay away."

With hesitation, and then more quickly, September crossed to her sister. They fell into each other's arms. The sisters held each other, hugging hard, no words necessary, as Shadow danced and whined about them.

They broke apart and April led September into the living room. "I want to thank you for everything. Saving Steven. And saving my life." She offered a rueful smile. "Steven's my miracle boy, because of you. He's helping his father in the back yard. But now I need another miracle, it seems."

Mom interjected, impatient. "For heaven's sake, April, go ahead and say it. After all, September owes you." When April wouldn't meet September's questioning expression, Mom clarified.

"September, your sister needs a kidney transplant. None of the others are a match, so it's down to you. And I know you'll be happy to donate, especially since it's your fault April got shot in the first place."

Chapter 6

Shadow whined and pawed September's calf. He sat beside her, sniffing the air with relish. A host of aromas from the nearby kitchen predicted a feast to come. Cheesy something. Turkey. And the bacon-smell that made a good-dog's mouth water. Would there be some for him?

He'd like that.

But only if September said so. Shadow pawed her leg again, and she dropped one hand to his brow. He leaned into the gentle touch, tail sweeping the floor when she stroked his cheek. Shadow gave her wrist a quick lick.

Salty. Acrid. The pungent taste shouted stress and his brow furrowed. He heard the stutter of September's pulse and braced his shoulder against her knee. She took several quick breaths in, and slow ones out. He knew the special breathing helped prevent the scary-gone spells that plagued her. Nobody told him, he just knew. Shadow was smart that way.

He also knew this place and how these people made September tiptoe around like Macy-cat during a thunderstorm. She spoke with whispery tremors in her voice. Although she tried hard to be strong, Shadow could tell. He yawned, to relieve his own tension, and remained alert.

In the long-ago time, he protected his-boy Steven because September wanted him to. She taught Shadow what to do by listening for her tongue-CLICK sound that meant he'd done something right. He'd first learned important words like *sit* and *down* and *wait* (he still didn't like that one). She showed him how to walk on a leash without surging ahead or dragging behind. Then Steven went away, and Shadow got to live with September all the time! At the thought his tail wagged harder. Now he did for September what she'd taught him to do for Steven—protect her and keep her safe. And he got to play fun games with September, like the *show-me* game that named important objects in his world. And how to *check-it-out* so no scary people lurked in hiding spots. He especially loved playing the *seek* game to find lost pets.

His most important lessons Shadow taught himself. He knew how to keep September safe from scary stuff a good-dog couldn't bite and chase away by connecting with his-person as only a good-dog could. Shadow held her still when invisible terrors made her shake and flail, and he led her away from inside-monsters that tormented her. And September stroked his face, snuggled him close, and promised he'd always be loved and safe. He belonged to September. She belonged to him. They'd chosen each other. Nothing could ever change that.

"Mom, please excuse us so April and I can talk." September spoke with a hurty-edged growl to her voice as if something choked her throat.

The Mom-lady shook her head. Her hands sliced the air, and her mouth spilled harsh words that made September flinch. Shadow didn't understand the words, but wanted to stop the anger. He stepped between September and the hard-eyed woman. Shadow stared back, tail held high, until she looked away. Her mouth closed into a tight line and without another word she disappeared into the next room.

Yawning once more he met September's eyes, looking for approval, and waved his tail when she yawned back in answer.

September smiled. "Good-dog, Shadow. I'm okay."

He didn't believe it, but shook himself hard to shrug off his own stress. That always made her laugh. September's scent changed as the thumpity-fast heart-rhythm slowed along with her breath. He wondered if Steven might join them, since his-boy lived with this other woman.

"April, I would help you any way I can. Please know that." September guided the other woman to the sofa, and they both sat down. "I tried to donate blood last year when you nearly died, but Doug—"

"My husband has a blind spot when it comes to you. But now he's desperate. We both are." She took a shuddering breath. "He's helping Dad with the hot tub fence. They couldn't stand the tension, waiting for you. I needed to talk to you alone anyway. I never thanked you properly for everything. I owe you so much and…I miss you, September." The two women hugged again.

Shadow woofed and paw-danced his concern but restrained the impulse to squeeze between and separate the pair. Dogs didn't hug, except to show each other who was boss, to fight, or sometimes with special-smelling girl dogs.

People hugged all the time. September and Combs hugged a lot. That worried him. A lot. He and September belonged together and Shadow hadn't figured out how Combs fit in. What if September liked Combs more than being with him? Sometimes he worried she wouldn't need him anymore. Shadow always felt relieved when Combs left. He preferred having September all to himself—the time she spent with Macy-cat felt different. As nice as cats smelled, and even if they shared treats, cats weren't the same as dogs. He guessed Macy couldn't help it, though. He'd learned to love September's hugs. He learned new things all the time, but people often confused him.

"Let me finish." September pulled away and caught April's hands in her own. "This isn't easy to tell you." She licked her lips and looked sideways, her voice soft as she finished in a rush. "When I tried to donate blood the doctors said you have a different type." Her voice shook. "I'm not a match, either."

Chapter 7

September pushed away from the dinner table, stacked empty plates and ferried them to the kitchen. Shadow tried to follow, but she gave him the palm-flat *wait* command, so he settled again under the table with an aggrieved whine. Mom barely tolerated his presence anywhere in the house. The kitchen was forbidden.

Muted conversation and occasional laughs traveled from the television room where the rest of the family gathered after the meal. She'd stayed behind to clear the dishes, wanting some alone time with Mom.

The last hour's stilted conversation and too careful small talk made September's jaw ache from its forced smile. Dad, Mark, and her sisters' families would pretend to enjoy family time for another twenty minutes, thirty at the most, before giving up the pretense and hitting the road.

"Go on, September, just set those down. Dishes can wait." Mom followed her into the large modern kitchen, stacking the last of the dinnerware on the butcher block island. She bustled here and there, unable to stay still. Her hands constantly smoothed her hair, or adjusted items on the counters, anything to avoid eye contact. The decorative stone mortar and pestle, rarely used, still held the yummy guacamole dip Mom made for every holiday gathering, but she lugged it to the sink to clean. "Wasn't this nice, the whole family together? Who knows when we'll have the chance again…" Her cheery tone contrasted with tear-polished blue eyes. She turned away to dab a linen handkerchief under her eyes, catching moisture before it ruined her makeup. As always, Rose January's perfectly coiffed hair and couture wardrobe could have stepped from the pages of a fashion magazine.

"Mom, I know you're disappointed and scared for April. So am I." She caught the woman's delicate shoulder and turned her around. "I could have told her months ago, if she'd said anything. You and Dad got tested, too?"

"Of course!" Rose looked away to the left, and fiddled with her wedding ring.

"Maybe I can help, now, to find another donor. It's not like I'm the last resort or anything." She forced another smile. "People manage for years on dialysis. Right? Don't they? Mom…"

Rose still wouldn't meet her eyes, but didn't pull away.

September stood a half a foot taller than her mother. Her three sisters took after Rose—blond hair, blue eyes, petite stature, and delicate features. But she and Mark had inherited Dad's tall, lanky frame, strong features, and dark hair. September tightened her lips, recognizing Mom's evasive expression. "There's something more. What else haven't you told me?"

Mom pulled away. "In the next few months, April testifies at that Baumgarten person's trial." Mom's voice soured on the name of the woman responsible for April's injury, and the death of so many others.

September knit her brow. What did Lizzie Baumgarten's trial for the Blizzard Murders have to do with anything? She'd happily testify, too. "I heard they petitioned to move up the court date."

Mom nodded. "For April's benefit. Just in case she's not well enough later, or…" She hiccupped a sobbed breath before she tamped down her emotions enough to continue. "April's been in and out of the hospital ever since. The treatments saved her life, but it damaged her kidneys. She's been on dialysis for nearly a year."

"What?" September fanned herself with a napkin, suddenly flushed and overheated. "Why am I only hearing this now?"

"She swore us to secrecy, didn't want you to blame yourself. And she convinced herself she'd get better." She shrugged. "You know April."

Yes, September knew April: so stubborn, so private, so secretive, and so very much like their mother. There'd been hints of her illness, of course, but September had been wrapped up in her own problems. "What about Doug?" April's husband didn't care for September, but at least he had more sense.

"Doug finally convinced April to reach out to family." She hesitated, then added, "Lysle wanted to tell you, too."

"Then why didn't Dad say something?"

"I wouldn't let him." She jutted out her chin, as if daring September to challenge Rose-Almighty's decision.

September fought to keep her tone civil. "I may struggle to be emotionally present but I'm still part of this family. I *do* care what happens." At her tone, Shadow padded to the kitchen doorway and peered inside.

Rose rounded on her, fierce with intensity. "But you were hurt, too. In the hospital after that awful man kidnapped you. Then you nearly drowned during the tornadoes." She swiped impatiently at her brimming eyes, smearing her makeup. "One crisis after another. Every time the phone rings, I'm scared you finally got yourself killed. Do you have a death wish, September?"

Her mouth fell open. "Mom, I didn't mean…" September couldn't remember Mom ever losing control. Not when Steven went missing. Not when April got shot. Shadow whined, and put one paw into the kitchen, then ignored previous commands and hurried to her side. She welcomed his warmth when he leaned against her thigh.

"I'm your mother. It's my job to protect *all* my children." Mom gulped, pacing from the sink to the kitchen island and back again, no longer stifling sobs. "I made horrible mistakes in the past. It's not fair for my children to pay for my sins."

"What are you talking about?" September braced herself against the counter. An eruption this intense, from a woman so stoic, had to be a release of years-long pain.

But Mom's words spilled over top of each other. "I prayed Lysle would be a donor match, or one of your sisters, or even Mark. Anyone but you, September."

The words stabbed because they confirmed September's exclusion. Mom didn't even consider her part of the family.

"Don't you see? All your pain, all your suffering. It's my fault." She grabbed September and hugged her close, as if she couldn't bear to see her face. The words rushed out even faster. "You were my brilliant, gifted little girl and I gave you away to a monster." Mom's grip on her neck nearly choked September. "I didn't think I had a choice, but I should have found a way. I understand why you stayed away, why you hide behind police friends and that dog of yours."

September jerked out of the embrace, shaking her head. She didn't hide, not anymore. Combs was more than that. And Shadow was her heart. She dropped one hand to his black fur, the contact countering sudden light-headedness. She'd overcome the abuse. With Shadow's help and the support of friends, she now had a future, and had broken the chains of the past.

"Forgive me?" Ruined makeup turned Rose's face into a tragic clown. "You don't know how much I want to remake the past."

September couldn't remember Mom ever accepting blame for anything. She struggled how to respond. Dirty water under the bridge. Besides, Victor no longer had any power to hurt, not from jail.

"I get that you wanted to protect me, Mom, but we can't change the past. This is now, today. I'm strong, I'm healthy again, and I make my own decisions. You should have told me about April." September couldn't mask her exasperation. She'd almost prefer Mom's steely control than to have to deal with this unfathomable brokenness. "I don't blame you, Mom." If she said it with enough conviction, maybe she'd convince herself, too, and forgive both her parents for handing her over to Victor.

"I didn't have a choice. But I should have known." The anguished words broke September's heart.

"Should have known what?"

Mom covered her mouth with both hands and ran from the room. Her stylish shoes clattered up the distant front stairs, headed to the master bedroom.

Shadow whined and nose-poked September's shaking hand. "Shadow? What just happened?"

September waited for a long moment, sighed, and found her coat. She had to pack and pick up Macy. To have any chance for a happy future, she must face the secrets Chris left behind in South Bend.

Chapter 8 (34 Years Ago)

Tana knew she'd go to hell for bashing in the agent's head—even though the *violador* deserved it. She couldn't go home, not when her torn dress and bloody underwear shouted what had happened. She'd lied to her parents, gone willingly to this stranger. She knew what they'd think. She might as well have invited his assault.

She wandered the streets for hours, ruined her beautiful white satin shoes and dragged the lacy dress in the oil-stained streets. She'd lost the blue sash. Exhausted, Tana finally took refuge in an alley behind a row of restaurants and fell asleep between two dumpsters that smelled of burned fish and rotten cabbage.

A rhinestone-covered shoe, worn by an exotic sloe-eyed beauty, nudged her awake the next morning. The woman, not much older than Tana herself, called her nasty names and threatened to call the cops. She only relented when Tana's story spilled out between sobs. The hysterical confession made the woman's eyes gleam.

The venomous tone turned silken, offering comfort and hope Tana welcomed. Kali had connections. Kali had solutions. Kali had ideas, perfect for a beautiful and obviously talented girl like Tana. Kali had no fear of the police, and her protection extended to her girls. She employed a handful of young women in similar circumstances in the many businesses Kali managed for mysterious Mr. Wong.

Tana knew Kali's help came with strings. When pressed for details, Kali scowled and threatened to withdraw the offer and call the cops after all. Tana had no choice. Her life was in ruins already and she didn't want to go to jail. Even more, she didn't want her parents to know.

She fought, at first. So Kali gave her drugs to make her compliant, and wielded the threat of a murder conviction like a club. The threat kept Tana in line better than the drugs.

After two months, on the eve of what would have been Tana's quinceañera, she won a victory of sorts. She couldn't risk taking the drugs anymore. Instead, she became what she'd yearned to be—a brilliant actress, performing to satisfy each client's fantasy. She earned most favorable status among the girls. Kali remained suspicious, but began to reserve Tana's talents for the high-dollar clientele who desired a pretense of class.

Meanwhile, Tana squirreled away cash favors, names, and faces. The day would come when she needed them to escape, to build a new life, with a new name. Because soon, she wouldn't be able to hide her pregnancy. Kali would not be pleased. Despite the baby's paternity, Tana loved it with a fervor beyond understanding. The child gave her back a reason to live.

Chapter 9 (Present Day)

September shut the wire pet barrier that sequestered the cargo area at the back of her SUV. She set the single small suitcase on one side and placed Macy's cat carrier on top. "Almost ready for the kitty-boy. I'll get Shadow settled." She looked over her shoulder to where the bigger dog played gently with Magic, Lia's police dog in training. Shadow allowed the puppy to chase him, bite his paws and tail, and bully him with impunity. Willie's terrier Kinsler watched from his crate, already worn out by his turn with the tireless youngster.

Lia had followed September to the car. She tossed her goldenrod hair over her shoulder. "Are you sure you need to take Macy, with his heart condition and all? I know you want to show him off, but still."

September busied herself, avoiding Lia's eyes. She'd texted Angela to expect her, but let Lia think the trip focused on meeting his breeder.

"He's no trouble. Macy even opens up his mouth to take meds like a treat, for heaven's sake." The younger woman handed September the canvas bag stuffed to overflowing with a collapsible litter box, litter, cat food, treats, and Macy's favorite toys. "It's the least I can do for all your help training the Magical-pup."

"He's a pleasure to train. Your new pup takes after his father. And his mom's no slouch either. You did a great job with Karma." September shoved the bag into its allotted spot.

Lia's hazel-green eyes welled. "I miss Karma. But she's where she's needed, partnering with a police officer. After five days in Chicago, she's already settled in. And Magic means I have a little bit of her still with me."

"I wondered how Karma would do, flying as cargo on the plane trip to Chicago." September knew how hard it must have been to send the Rottweiler away. But then, Lia had raised and trained Karma with that in mind from the beginning. "We love staying with you, Lia, and appreciate the hospitality. But it does get a tad crowded." Squeezing herself, Shadow, and Macy into the small quarters along with Lia's furry crew meant hectic schedules around the one bathroom and two tiny bedrooms. After the tornado nearly destroyed Corazon Boarding Kennels, Lia redesigned and renovated the facilities. In addition to upgrading the indoor-outdoor kennel runs, she'd added a second story with two small bedrooms and a living room/kitchen area. The second bathroom hadn't yet been finished—additional renovations of the living quarters wouldn't happen without the forthcoming holiday income. Fortunately, neither she nor Lia were much for primping.

"At least y'all are good roomies." Lia laughed, and adjusted the headband that kept flyaway hair at bay. "I guess flying with Shadow in cabin would be a problem?"

"Hard to find a last-minute flight with room for a German Shepherd. This time of year, they book pretty fast. It'd really be pushing it to get in-cabin for both Shadow and a Maine Coon on the plane. Fortunately Macy enjoys car rides almost as much as Shadow."

"Invite me on a road trip when I'm not booked solid. But it sounds like you need alone time anyway." Lia frowned in sympathy. Her ears probably still rang after getting an earful from September about Rose's meltdown.

September had used meeting Macy's breeder, something she'd wanted to do for years, as an excuse to visit South Bend. Nobody needed to know about the note and lockbox. She didn't talk about that part of her life to Lia or anyone else, not even Combs, although she had called him before she started packing. Not wanting to derail his vacation fun, she hadn't mentioned the latest family drama, or her travel plans. She'd only be gone a few days at most, and be home long before Combs returned. "Without Shadow to supervise, watch out that Magic doesn't tear the place down."

Lia laughed, and hugged herself in the afternoon breeze. "After playing so hard, I'm hoping the pup sleeps until tomorrow morning." They watched as the pair dashed in and out of the trees.

September opened the rear door and stowed another canvas bag filled with the rest of the pets' gear. Shadow's new bear-toy still sat on the back seat. As an afterthought, she had stuffed two baggies filled with Lia's homemade *Corazon Candy* pet treats into her coat pocket. Shadow and Macy both loved the stinky combination of liver and salmon. "Shadow, come! Let's go, baby-dog. Kennel up!"

Shadow play-bowed, tail up with front paws down, and then nose-poked the black Magical-puppy one more time for good measure. He whirled and bounded to September's side, then hopped into the back seat, turned around once, and settled his head on bear-toy with a sigh. "Shadow, wait. I'll go get Macy." September latched the door. He immediately sat up, and pawed the door with a whine, but stopped when she shook her head.

The puppy scampered around Lia's feet. She hooked the leash on his collar before they followed September back to the building. "Sort of weird that none of y'all, your brother or any of your sisters, are a match for April. What are the odds of that?"

"It happens." September had wondered that herself.

While Lia rinsed mud from puppy paws in the laundry room, September hurried to the apartment upstairs. When September moved in, they put up wall shelves and runways to accommodate Macy and Lia's rescue kitten Gizmo, who usually shadowed the older feline.

"Car ride, Macy! Ready for a car ride?" September sat on the bed and dangled the cat's jacket-halter in one hand. With an excited chirrup-trill the twenty-pound mocha-colored Maine Coon raced around the wall perches like a squirrel on speed until he finally plopped beside her on the bed. He rubbed against her with abandon, making it difficult to fit the green vest over his head. "Settle, Macy, we're going, just hold your mouses." She grinned, and scratched beneath his white chin, leaning down so they could press foreheads together. He thought every car ride ended up at the vet for petting and special attention, or one of the local fast food places that gave him chicky-yum nugget treats.

"Macy, sit." He plopped his luxurious tail onto the bed and waited patiently for her to clip on the halter's green leash that matched his eyes. He wore a collar, too, but only for identification, a just-in-case safety measure in addition to his microchip. On one side the tag had September's contact information and on the other an arrow pointing upwards to Macy's face with the note: Insert treat here.

In the best of all possible worlds, Macy could run and play in the great outdoors, with no restrictions. But local coyotes relished cats for meals. Besides, the big cat's heart condition meant she restricted his activity for his health's sake. The halter and leash were Macy's ticket to safely explore, and wouldn't slip over his head the way a collar might. "Let's go!"

He pounced off the bed, and with tail pointed high, led her quickly down the stairs to where Lia waited in the office. "Magic crashed. But he'll be missing Shadow when he wakes up. How long will y'all be gone?"

"Don't know. A few days. I can't drive straight through. I want to reach Springfield tonight, and start early tomorrow morning. It's two days on the road both ways. So maybe five or six days, a week tops." The sooner she could wrap up business with Angela, the better. She wanted to visit Chris's grave, too.

Lia's brow wrinkled as she looked around September. "Where's Gizmo? He's usually glued to Macy like a burr on fur."

September juggled the cat's leash as Macy impatiently meowed and wound around her ankles. "I didn't see him upstairs."

"Not again. Just shoot me." Lia jumped to her feet. "Could you wait while I check? Just in case the little door-dashing stinker got out again?"

September nodded, but pursed her lips with exasperation. "You need to teach that kitten some limits. You're a trainer. Set some boundaries."

Lia quickly reappeared, out of breath. "Gone again. Yes, my fault, all my fault. But please, before you go—"

"Of course. It's good tracking practice." September stood and gathered Macy's leash. "Paws crossed the baby hasn't left the building. Seriously, Lia, you've got to do something or you'll lose Gizmo for good."

Meekly, Lia nodded, and held out one of the kitten's favorite toys for a sniff-reference.

September took the toy and held it out to Macy, although he didn't really need it. "Why should Shadow get all the fun, eh? Want to play hide and seek? Where's Gizmo? The kitten, the pest. Macy, *seek Gizmo.*"

It had begun as an inside game to relieve the house-bound cat's frustration. Macy always watched Shadow sniff out hidden treasures, and had upon occasion (especially with treats), beaten the dog to the prize. At first September had laughed at the contest between the two. It shouldn't have surprised her, though, since a cat's sense of smell rivaled many dogs. Any cat had the equipment to track. A cat just needed the incentive.

He delicately sniffed the toy, pawed it once, and then began leading September. She followed him, grasping the leash securely but giving him slack to move. The big cat didn't sniff the floor the way Shadow did. He scented the air and once in a while nose-touched the baseboard as if following cheek-rub signposts. She followed him from the office to the laundry room that separated the office from the kennels at the rear. The tiny kitten could easily wiggle through the kennel runs' chain link fence, so September prayed Gizmo hadn't strayed that far.

Macy sniffed the edge of the doorway into the kennel, but turned around and focused on the opposite wall. He paced, a lion in magnificent miniature, toward the hamper filled to overflowing with soiled towels. With effortless grace, the big cat leaped from a standing start onto the top of the dryer and stared down into the hamper. Pawing one of the towels, Macy offered a soft trill.

The towel moved.

"Oh my gosh!" Lia pushed past September to reach into the fabric, and plucked out the damp kitten. "I just washed off the pup's feet and dumped that towel in there. Gizmo must have been in the basket the whole time." She cuddled the kitten beneath her chin and offered a finger to Macy to sniff. "Thank you, Macy, what a good boy." She turned to September. "When you get back, help me train this little troublemaker, will you?"

September laughed, and nodded. "Cats train the same as dogs. Well, there are some differences. Sure, when I get back we'll get you squared away on kitty training basics. Meanwhile, keep the doors latched!"

Six hours later, September pulled the car into the motel parking lot. In the back seat, Shadow stood and stretched, whining at the end of a luxurious yawn. "I know, baby-dog, it's been a long trip. You wait while I get us a room."

Macy trilled from the rear of the vehicle. Macy and Shadow had finally cemented their friendship, but the relationship often resembled that of siblings picking at each other, which made for interesting car travel companions. September had learned that having the pair loose in the car at once was a distraction.

Within twenty minutes all three had staked out their part of the king-size bed in the motel room. September pulled the heavy comforter up to her waist, sitting with pillows propping her back. Shadow lay atop the covers on the doggy spread she'd brought along just for that purpose. He snuggled hard against her thigh, holding his bear-toy in his jaws like a child with a blankie, squeaking it intermittently. Macy found a perch between her ankles, squirming until he balanced on his back, all four feet in the air—his favorite sleeping pose. The weight of the duo held her in place like a furry straight jacket, but September didn't mind. She would have felt bereft without the contact.

With luck, the long drive tomorrow would finish the journey by late afternoon—as long as they got an early start. On the bedside table, her charging cell phone beeped to announce an incoming text message. She smiled and grabbed up the phone, expecting a quick note from Combs.

Instead, the text came from Angela, suggesting they meet at the address of a law office the next day. September frowned, and Shadow stirred beside her, always able to sense her unease.

"I'm okay, baby-dog. That's weird, though." She re-read the text. "I never knew any attorney that kept office hours on a Sunday." She shrugged. The quicker they got this settled, the sooner she'd relax and head home. Besides, whatever Chris had hidden away in the safety deposit box had to wait until Monday when the bank opened.

September dreaded the awkward meeting, but how bad could it be? She'd already lived through, and survived, the worst life had to offer. With Shadow by her side, and Macy-cat draped across her shoulders, she had nothing to fear, not anymore.

She silenced her phone and curled up on the bed, blinking in the dark. Shadow pushed closer, and on the other side Macy readjusted to press into the curve behind her knees. But questions about what Chris had to say from beyond the grave played cat and mouse with her mind, and she'd barely slept by the time the sun rose.

Chapter 10

Shadow yawned and stretched, then hopped off of the bed. This tiny room smelled foreign, and he had had trouble sleeping soundly with strange noises outside. He nose-touched Macy—the big cat responded with a purr—before circling the bed to check on September.

She'd tossed and turned all night. But her disquiet hadn't alerted him to one of her scary-gone episodes. He knew she worried about many things a good-dog couldn't know. So he did his job—guarding her and Macy in this tiny smelly room, with bear-toy near for security—so she felt safe. He hoped they'd get in the car again soon and drive away. Shadow liked car rides, even if they didn't stop and get out to explore as much as he'd like.

He padded to the floor-to-ceiling window, hidden by large swaths of fabric, and nosed the curtain aside to stare outside. Shadow pressed against the glass, relishing the cold against his black fur. Streetlights pooled brightness across the dark pavement where their big car sat. He whined, needing to find a spot of grass and take-a-break.

As if the thought inspired him, Macy yawned, stretched, then leaped off the bed to pace into the adjoining bathroom. Shadow heard the cat scratching around in his litter box. He always worried when Macy posed to take-a-break inside the house. Good-dogs only left scent markings outside, but Shadow had never seen Macy do that even when on his halter and leash.

Shadow padded back to the bed and sat quietly beside September. He rested his chin on the pillow, so that he almost nose-touched her, and stared, willing her to understand his need. When her eyes opened it made him so happy his ears slicked back and he couldn't contain his wags and whines. He gave her a gentle nose-poke, first on her face then in the armpit, because it made her laugh. He pranced around the room when she sat up in bed.

"I'm up already. Sheesh, it's still dark out, Shadow." She yawned, stretched, and swung the covers off. "I know we need to start early, baby-dog. But we don't have to get up at the crack of dark-thirty."

He cocked his head at her, loving the sound of September's chiding voice. She wasn't really upset. He could tell. Shadow woofed, ran to the door, and sat patiently while September pulled on shoes and shrugged her puffy coat over her pajamas.

They hurried to the small grassy spot beside the parking lot, and September waited until he'd finished. The morning air made white puffs when he panted and Shadow raced back to wait at the door while September bagged his deposit. He didn't know why she did that. Other dogs would still know he'd been there from the scent he'd left. Shadow had rushed his morning ritual, as there were few interesting sniffs. Other dogs hadn't visited the grassy spot for many days and fresh smells always told him more. Besides, his breakfast awaited.

Once back inside the tiny room, Shadow sat and impatiently waited for September to serve his food. Usually she hid food-filled toys around their place at Lia's and put Macy's treat-toys on the high surfaces. Sometimes the cat knocked one of his treat-toys to the floor and Shadow got an extra munchy.

But today September filled two bowls with food and placed Macy's on the bedside table. The big cat padded quickly from the bathroom, mewing softly with excitement, to leap onto the bed. He held his mouth open for his special treat—"Pill time, Macy"— and then munched food that smelled stronger, yummier, than dog fare. Shadow licked his lips as September set his food down, but didn't eat until she gave him the release signal.

September started the water running in the bathroom. Shadow still didn't understand why people climbed into rain-boxes to get all wet and wash away all the lovely smells that identified them as individuals.

Macy paw-patted his bowl to the edge of the table. One final push and it tipped onto the floor.

Shadow woofed and ran to check out the unexpected bounty. He sniffed out and munched a dozen or so pieces of cat kibble scattered on the carpet. Macy stood on tiptoes, arched his back in a satisfied stretch, then reached down from his elevated perch to grab a good-dog's tail.

Growling happily, Shadow accepted the invitation. He nose-poked with an open-mouthed grin, braving the paw-pats until Macy danced away.

The cat grabbed bear-toy. With his powerful rear legs he launched himself from the bed to the desk, scattering notepads, pens, and September's small tote from the surface. A metal jangle of keys spilled from the tote and slalomed beneath the bed

Shadow galloped after, rescuing bear-toy from the cat thief and shaking the toy furiously for allowing itself to be swiped. Macy leaped back to the bed and Shadow raced around first one side and then the other, punctuating his excitement with happy barks. Macy teased him, pouncing around the bed, diving under pillows to spill them to the floor, only to paw-thwack Shadow's black muzzle. Something clattered off the bedside table, but they continued their play.

"What's going on in here?"

September's voice stopped the pair in mid-bark and thwack.

"I can't leave you two alone for even ten minutes for a shower? Settle, baby-dog. Macy, quit teasing the dog." She sat on the bed and toweled her hair and Macy pushed his massive frame into her lap. Shadow whined, but knew better than to demand attention until the cat vacated her lap. "Shadow, you should ignore him. You know Macy lives to get you in trouble."

He grinned and wagged, the placating expression meant to defuse her upset. Shadow wasn't sure what her words meant, but felt crestfallen at her tone of voice. He hated to disappoint her.

September set Macy aside and quickly gathered the scattered gear, stowing the bowls in the canvas bag. "Where's my phone?" She pulled a long wire from the wall that often leashed the small phone-box September liked so much.

Shadow tipped his head. Macy yawned and looked away.

"Come on, Shadow. Did you and Macy hide my phone?" She looked around the table, and made a sound of frustration, kneeling to reach behind the furniture. "What have I told you about roughhousing? Not that you pay attention." She continued to grumble and clambered back to her feet. "I know, you figured I needed exercise this morning before the car ride."

He woofed and wagged harder at the last two words.

She put on her coat and slung bags over both arms. Shadow could barely contain his excitement. At the door, September stopped him with a single, hated word. "Wait."

His tail fell and he growled but obeyed when the door swung open. He watched from the window as she carried her burdens to the nearby car then rummaged inside the smaller bag. September dropped the luggage and propped her purse on the hood of the car, searching for something. When she turned away from the car, a scowl drew deep furrows on her forehead and Shadow left the window to meet her at the door. She quickly entered and secured the barrier before Macy could dash out.

"Keys, Shadow. You know, from the *show-me* game? Keys."

He woofed, immediately picturing the metal jangle attached to a long ribbon.

"Keys, Shadow. *Seek.*"

He knew exactly where the keys hid. Macy liked to chase and bat them, but abandoned the keys when he tired of the game and Shadow often had to find them. Now he padded quickly to the foot of the bed, sniffed the narrow opening underneath and lay down, his signal for a find.

"Good-dog, Shadow, good find." September knelt and peered beneath the bed, then groaned. "I can't reach them. Maybe a coat hanger?" She got up to scrabble in the tiny closet and returned with something to reach far underneath, but grew even more frustrated.

Macy mewed from his perch on the desk and daintily washed one white paw.

September answered the cat. "I bet anything you knocked them under the bed, Macy. So you can just go get them out." She scooped him up and returned his nuzzle when he gave her cheek whisker-kisses. "No sucking up to me. Time to redeem yourself. And yes, treats are involved."

Macy trilled at the same time Shadow pushed forward at the sound of a favorite word. He'd fetch the keys for September, even without treats, but he couldn't fit underneath the low bed.

"Shadow, good-dog, you wait." She set Macy on the floor at the foot of the bed and pulled a small object from one coat pocket. "Macy, fetch!" She made a red dot light shine on the floor so it disappeared beneath the bed. Macy chirruped, and wriggled underneath to follow the beam. "That's a good kitty, what a smart boy, Macy. Fetch."

The cat returned dragging the fabric ribbon, the keys chiming in his wake. "Good boy, Macy! Good-dog, Shadow."

Shadow woofed happily and grabbed up bear-toy. He sat up in a beg position with the stuffed animal in his mouth, asking for a treat as well. September traded Shadow a treat for the stuffed bear and Macy a treat for the keys, her brow finally smooth. "Couldn't go too far without keys." She chose one key on the fob that looked different than the others. "And couldn't open that mysterious lockbox without the bank key either."

Chapter 11

George slouched over his desk, head propped between his fists. He blinked rapidly at Angela's cell phone on the desk before him, waiting for an answering text from September. Surely she'd received his note—or rather Angela's note—to meet later today?

He'd not slept. Then his constant fidgeting in the pew next to his wife had raised eyebrows from nearby friends, and dark looks from the priest. He prided himself on his honesty and fairness as a judge. So rather than fielding Roxanne's concern, and trying to lie about his distraction, he left early mass and headed to his office.

He had to figure out how to make things right, to protect himself, his reputation, and his family. He bit his lips, mouth dry, wishing for something stronger than coffee. Early in his career, ruthlessness paved the way to his current success. He'd only agreed to a couple of innocuous favors. The favors helped him win his first judgeship to the Appellate Court in Cook County. Finally, he could do some real good and make a difference in his district.

But after his ten-year term, facing reelection with ever-increasing demands from his *benefactor*, he decided to move back to Indiana. With his law degree from Notre Dame, and his Chicago experience, he'd easily won an appointment as a Superior Court justice and served two terms. From there, the Circuit Court became his home— for the past dozen years as his star continued to rise. The gubernatorial nominating commission just shortlisted him for consideration for the Court of Appeals. Nothing could get in the way of that appointment. He'd do anything to maintain the protective layer between his past transgressions and bright future.

He sat up in his chair, rubbing the back of his neck and loosening his collar. While awaiting September's response, he'd deal with Detweiller, the lab owner Angela mentioned. He knew of him from his early years in Chicago, and some of George's favors involved Clear Choice Labs. Bradley Detweiller's contract with the city meant both criminal and family law cases used his services. George didn't know or care exactly how Detweiller figured in Chris Day's investigation, but the fact his name came up raised all sorts of red flags.

He unlocked the lower drawer on the desk and pulled out a tiny notebook filled with scribbles only he could read. In this age of computer hacking and virtual forensic specialists, George relied on old-school paper he could destroy with the flick of a Bic. He coded any payments associated with his benefactor through a dozen bank accounts to avoid any appearance of a pattern.

Equally careful, his benefactor never answered the phone, but rather communicated through a series of carefully phrased and forwarded messages. Southgate thought for a moment how to construct his request. It couldn't be about protecting him. No, that wouldn't move the needle. His concern must specifically impact his benefactor's influence and business. He swallowed hard, trying to still the nausea, and carefully punched in the phone number of the answering service.

"I have a message for Kapu Enterprises from *Pono*." He used the code name assigned to him more than thirty years ago, when he made those first innocuous rulings favorable to the owner's business. Ever since, he'd fulfilled the company's requests—actually *demands*—without fail or argument, recognizing the value of his benefactor's behind the scenes influence. This message questioned the arrangement for the first time, and could rain down wrath unless played correctly. "With respect—be sure you say that," he told the operator. "With respect, I understand your fee has doubled, and I appreciate your efficient and welcome services. May I request a week's extension to fulfill this additional obligation demand from…?" He hesitated, not knowing the code name for the laboratory, and settled on, "…windy city's clearly chosen test partner."

George waited while the service read back his message, and once satisfied he disconnected. Suggesting that Chicago's Clear Choice Lab owner breached confidence by contacting George, and demanded kickbacks to stay quiet, stomped hard on dangerous toes. Mrs. Wong would not only punish Detweiller, she'd scrub clean all trace of the records that involved their scheme, including George's connection.

Reprisals came swiftly in this business, and he felt no more remorse than when sentencing a bad guy in his court. Southgate chose saving his own skin, and that of his family, over some lab rat overstepping his position. Kaliko Wong had a reputation for visiting punishments on entire families.

Chapter 12

September followed the directions dictated by her phone and parked at the entrance to the Niles Avenue Dog Park. The place had great reviews and stayed open 24 hours. Floodlights threw dark shadows here and there in the late afternoon gloom. Dark clouds hastened the twilight, and her headlights revealed a deserted field with nary a paw print marking the snowy ground. Lake effect snow continued to spit sandy particles against the windshield, a whispery spider sound she'd nearly forgotten. Nobody else wanted to brave the cold. They'd have the park to themselves.

Shadow needed a break, not just a doggy relief station, but somewhere to run and stretch his legs. After the almost ten-hour drive today, they both needed some exercise.

Shadow jittered in the back seat, paw-dancing his anticipation. "Give me a minute, baby-dog. Then we'll go for a run." He yawned, loud and long, turning the expression into a prolonged canine commentary on his enforced car incarceration.

September grinned, then quickly texted a note of apology to Angela. She'd already missed the proposed meeting at the attorney's office. She couldn't think straight after staring at endless highway for hours on end. Better to hit the bank early tomorrow when it opened, retrieve the lockbox contents, and meet Angela and her attorney later. After running Shadow for the next half hour or so, she'd want a hot shower, a light meal, a warm bed, and no conversation other than purrs and wags until morning. She hoped Angela understood.

September stepped out of the car, shrugging into her down-filled jacket. She dropped keys into one massive pocket that held her wallet and donned the bump cap to keep hair out of her eyes. She pulled up the hood over the cap and snugged the cord close to her throat. The tunnel-like vision kept wind and snow from blowing down her neck. She opened the back door for Shadow to hop out and quickly snicked the lead onto his collar.

Macy meowed, but had no interest in leaving his snug carrier. She'd let him race around once they got to their hotel.

September juggled to put on her gloves and grab one of Shadow's favorite tug toys, which she stuffed in one pocket. Her hands, already blue-white from the change in temperature, signaled an impending Reynaud's episode, and needed all the protection they could get. Shadow led the way to the fenced "big dog" area and September securely latched the gate before she unhooked his leash. He raced to the far corner before sniffing carefully and posing. She pulled out a plastic bag and followed.

Halfway across the space her phone buzzed with an incoming text. She struggled to fish the phone from her pocket without dropping it into the deepening snow. Before she was able to read Angela's text response, September recognized an incoming call and grinned.

"So how's Disney World treating you? Having fun yet?" Kids' voices in the background laughed and shrieked with excitement.

"Missing you." His low voice prompted shivers, this time of pleasure. "But yeah, the kids love it. Willie's all about the rides, the scarier the better. Melinda likes the shopping. I may need to buy another suitcase to get all the booty home."

"That's great. Glad y'all got this time away together, even if I miss you bunches, too." The icy wind threw snow against her face and September turned her back to its breath. Florida would be nice about now.

"So how's it going with you? You promised to tell me more about Christmas dinner with your folks. Did everyone show up?"

She made a face, but no way would she spoil his fun with the new dramas. Time enough to share when they were together again. "Oh, it went about as expected."

"That bad, eh?" He barked a short laugh. "Hold on a minute, honey."

Her face warmed at the endearment. She smothered a laugh at his next words of exasperation.

"Willie, stay where I can see you. Melinda, watch your brother, please? Can you give me five minutes?" He paused, then added for September's benefit, "We just watched the parade outside, and deciding where to go eat. Lots of people out and about, and a balmy 70 degrees. Supposed to get chillier this evening." His voice lowered, turned husky. "Good snuggling weather."

She laughed. "I could do with some snuggling about now. A cold front came through North Texas yesterday afternoon." True enough. She changed the subject before he asked questions she didn't want to answer. "So did you get me anything?"

He matched her teasing tone. "We've only been here a day. Don't worry, there'll be crap gifts a-plenty. Even got something planned for that big mutt of yours. Did I mention new luggage? Melinda's not the only one shopping."

She laughed as Shadow slalomed past, kicking up clouds of ice in a race around the perimeter. He barked, racing circles around her, playing zoomies like a puppy and shoving snow with his nose between play-bowing his invitation to chase.

"Are you outside with Shadow? I can hear him yelling at me." Combs's teasing turned a bit more serious. "He's jealous, you know. Doesn't like me around, wants you all to himself."

"Don't be silly. He likes you, too." She scooped up snow with her other hand, and lobbed it at the dog.

"He likes me, *too*? So you do like me? No fooling, Ms. September?" His voice dropped low again, gruff with promise.

Her breath caught. "No fooling, Detective Combs. Maybe even more than like."

She disconnected, still grinning, and wondered what crap gifts he'd find. September treasured the "Crappiocca Happens" cap he'd given her that Mom hated—perhaps another reason for Rose's bump cap replacement. September pocketed her phone, then picked up Shadow's creativity and disposed of the soiled baggy in the "doggy doo" bin. She made a mental note to find something equally silly for Combs.

September retrieved the large blue ball on a tug rope from her pocket. Shadow yelped with excitement as he bounded back and forth, churning the fresh snow into bulldoze tunnels thither and yon. She faced into the driving wind and threw the toy as far as she could.

Shadow raced after it, grappling the dark object by its rope. He had to arch his neck and hold it high to keep it from dragging, but quickly fetched it to September for a repeat of the game. She tossed it again and it fell into a deep drift of snow next to the fence. Shadow stared at her askance.

For a puzzled moment she stared, then understood and laughed out loud. He'd learned a bad habit from Karma. She'd put the behavior on cue and only allowed him to indulge when she gave permission. Shadow wanted his big ball, but wanted permission to indulge. "Go ahead, Shadow. It's okay, go get your ball. *Dig*, Shadow, *dig!*"

With joyful abandon, he dug out the toy. He scooped mounds of white with front paws, shoveling thick fountains of snow back between his rear legs.

After a dozen tosses, twice as many laps up and down the area, and as many recalls, she could no longer feel her face or fingers. Shadow would have played for hours, but dark had fallen in earnest.

At the park's gate September clipped the leash back on Shadow for the trip to the car. She opened the rear door. "Kennel up." He hopped back into the rear seat and settled with a happy sigh. She dropped his ball into the front seat, swapped it for the stuffie, and he settled happily with bear-toy clutched in his mouth.

September left her coat on as she slid into the driver's seat and cranked up the heat. She bit the fingertips of her sodden gloves to pull first one and then the other off. Flexing her hands didn't help. All ten fingers shined icy-white with blue-tinged nails. She held her hands before the vent, relishing the warmth as prickly-sensation returned.

Macy meowed.

"I know, I'm hungry, too. We all are. Let's find a place to spend the night and get settled." That reminded her to check the text that Combs's call interrupted.

Sure enough, Angela had answered.

>Forget hotel, plenty room here @ house. I'm at Martin's getting groceries. key in mailbox. let yourself in.

"That can't be safe, leaving a house key like that." Shadow whined as if in agreement. Maybe Angela had planned for September to stay with her all along. "I sure didn't want to talk about this tonight." They had things to say to each other, difficult things, before meeting with Angela's attorney.

She remembered Peter and Angela's address on White Oak Drive. The old but comfy home, conveniently near the Notre Dame campus, held happy memories of Chris. She wondered if his parents still decorated with the kitschy inflatable reindeer. "Guess we'll find out, huh?" She texted her acceptance and thanks. Shadow's tail thumped and he snuggled bear-toy close. Macy purred. She'd grab some food on the way.

George nodded with satisfaction and relief at September's text. That gave him time to put a few more details in place. Better she didn't come to his office. He could still fix this. Just a matter of tying up one more loose end.

Chapter 13

Charlie held her breath in her hiding place behind an ornate floor-to-ceiling cat tree. Intrigued as much as scared, purple bangs covering gray kohl-rimmed eyes, she eavesdropped on the angry conversation in the next room. When the war of words turned physical, she stuffed a tattooed finger into each ear, but she couldn't drown out Sissie Turpin's cries. Charlie shook, flinching with the sound of each relentless slap–slap–slap and with Sissie's counterpoint of rhythmic shrieks.

A pause. Gasping breaths. Charlie wanted to run, but couldn't move. She recognized his voice.

The quiet scared her more than the raised voices. Was he there for her? It didn't sound like it, so maybe if he didn't see her she was safe. She liked Sissie, but not enough to risk her own skin. At 110-pounds soaking wet, Charlie couldn't compete with him. She'd learned the hard way to choose battles, hide if possible, and run when you got the chance.

Licking beads of sweat off her lip, Charlie bit back a scream when Sissie yelled again. Sissie had rescued Charlie like a stray kitten, and now Charlie could do nothing to help her.

"Stop, please stop, I told you everything." Sissie's fear turned to desperation. "I'm just the bookkeeper. I've got lots of clients, lots I never even met. What Chicago records? I don't understand—" She shrieked again in anticipation of another slap. Either she truly knew nothing, or faked ignorance with an award-winning performance.

His persuasive tone wheedled but promised more pain. "Where do you keep your bookkeeping files? A computer? I won't ask again."

Oh God...he'd see her if he came into the cattery. Charlie peered around the cat tree at the computer desk across the room. A thumb drive with an attached lanyard poked out of one of the desktop ports.

Throat thick with tension, Charlie quickly sneaked forward and snatched it out of the computer—*screw you, Mr. Persuasion!*—then dived back into her hiding place. She never put the lights on to clean up each evening, so she wouldn't be seen unless he looked directly at her.

So far, out-thinking dangerous people had kept her alive. Charlie's eyes narrowed, her mind calculating, switching to survival mode. Something on the thumb drive must be worth a lot. That could come in handy. Too bad Sissie had problems, but her own survival trumped anyone else.

Two months ago, she had run away from her Indianapolis home and taken temporary refuge at a crowded cat show. Turned out Charlie liked cats better than people: cats were great mothers, they didn't lie, and they stood up to bullies with teeth bared and claws ready. When Sissie had heard her story, she offered Charlie a place to crash in exchange for help with the cats. Charlie didn't believe in fairy godmothers, but Sissie came close.

On cue, the orange and white Meriwether, the biggest of Sissie's Maine Coon cats, pawed the door open and Sissie stumbled into the room, weeping, probably tipsy from her nightly wine marathon. "Please don't hurt my cats!" The lights flicked on.

Charlie shrank farther behind the cat tree. He wore a mask. She still knew him.

The cats wound around Sissie's ankles. Meriwether jumped onto the desk to offer head butts. Sissie ignored the cat, booted up the desktop computer, typed in her password, and stepped away for Mr. Ski Mask to access the keyboard.

"Sit down and shut up, and just maybe you'll get out of this alive." He shoved Meriwether off the desk. The cat hissed.

The keyboard clacked as his gloved hands typed. Charlie peeked from behind the cat tree again. Sissie was perched on the edge of the rolling desk chair, face buried in Meriwether's orange and white fur, while another cat curled around her feet.

"Nothing here. What are you trying to pull?"

"Nothing, I promise. It's a new desktop. My cats crashed the laptop last week and I haven't had time to—"

"The files are on the laptop? Where is it?" Charlie heard him yank open file cabinet drawers, shuffling through the contents.

Sissie's voice trembled. "Trashed. The garbage truck came yesterday. I promise, it didn't work anymore." She shook uncontrollably, making the casters on the rolling chair clatter.

"But you have a backup. To load onto the new computer. Am I right?"

Charlie clutched the drive in one fist and showed her teeth, hissing under her breath. She wondered how much he'd pay to get it. It could mean she wouldn't have to rely on Sissie's plan, or look over her shoulder for him ever again. She'd take back control of her own life—and her body.

Sissie gasped when he slapped her again. "Yes, yes, I have a backup." Her voice scratched like fingernails on a blackboard. "It was right there in the desktop. Maybe the cats played with the cord and it's around here somewhere, if we look."

Another slap. "Don't be cute. I'm paid to collect the files and eliminate loose ends. No files to collect, no laptop, and you're the only loose end. Nothing personal." Another gasp, and then silence.

Charlie's breath caught. *Eliminate.* She looked at the thumb drive in her hand. Her breath returned, gasping, whimpering, and she put both hands over her mouth to stifle the sound. Thank God, he'd not noticed her.

He spoke into his phone. "Yes, I'm here. No files. Yeah, I think she tried to get rid of 'em like our friend says. Told me she trashed her old laptop—it's long gone—and the new computer appears clean." He paused. "Agreed, no loose ends. I'll make it look good."

An icy wet nose touched her cheek. Charlie squealed and flinched, jostling the tree. She looked up to see the emerald green eyes of Sherlock, a snow-white cat perched above her on the cat tree. He pawed her shoulder, asking to assume his favorite perch across her shoulders.

When he heard her, he strode quickly across the room, teeth bared. He recognized her and removed his mask, making sure she'd seen his familiar, expressionless face.

She knew what that meant. No more chances. She'd been warned.

Charlie bolted upright, braced herself, and pushed over the cat tree. It crashed on top of him.

Sherlock leaped from the falling tower and clutched her neck. Together they dashed from the room, leaving behind crying cats snuggled tight against the dying Sissie.

Chapter 14

Shadow snuggled close to September's side in the strange bed. His cat, Macy, purred softly from her other side. Shadow lifted his head, scanning the dark room from side to side. Fur bristled along his shoulders, making it hard for a good-dog to settle.

The deserted house held strange smells that spoke to him of sorrow, fear, and death. But September slept fitfully, unaware, her exhaustion holding her captive in dreams that echoed the danger she ignored. Now and again she stirred, whimpered, then fell silent. His job was to keep her safe, staying by September's side, anchoring her to reality should the nightmares drag her down.

But the house felt unsafe. She'd not asked him to check-it-out, to patrol the building before they'd chosen this room to rest. Instead, September just latched the door closed, as if that would protect them from the unseen threats even a cat felt.

Shadow carefully stood and hopped off the narrow bed. He waited until September settled again, before he padded to the door. Sniffing the base, he whined and pawed the wood, wanting out. How could he protect September and warn her of danger when cooped up in this tiny, second-floor room?

Macy stood and stretched, yawning wide, before joining Shadow at the door. The big cat rubbed his cheek against Shadow's neck, trilling a question.

Pawing the door again, Shadow's claws scrabbled the hard wood surface. He watched when Macy pushed between him and the barrier, then stood back, curious. Cats could do things with paws that dogs couldn't. And he knew Macy's prickly unease mirrored his own.

Macy stood on his rear legs and stretched high with both paws to reach and grab the lever door handle. His weight hung on the handle a moment, until a small "snick" sound unlatched the door.

Shadow pawed the door, inadvertently shoving it closed. He whined with frustration, and again allowed Macy to shoulder him aside. Watching with interest, he tipped his head when Macy grasped the lever handle, pulled down and released the catch. This time, the cat dropped to the floor, reached beneath the door with one paw, and pulled it farther open.

With a happy wag, Shadow nosed through the opening and padded out of the room. Macy stayed behind, a feline sentry in the bedroom doorway, bushy tail curved around to cover his paws.

Hurrying down the hallway, Shadow briefly sniffed and discounted the closed doors to other rooms. At the head of the stairs, he paused, cocking his head to listen. He quickly paced down the stairs, keeping quiet the better to listen.

At the front door to the house, he examined the floor. His hackles bristled even more. Shadow tracked the scent to the nearby closet, identifying the strongest smells emanating from inside. September's coat hung there, but something else, something *bad-scary-wrong*, left its invisible mark near this tiny room. He growled softly, committing the signature odors to memory.

A car passed by outside, slowed to a crawl, and stopped some distance from the house. The engine switched off. Shadow returned to the front door, peering out the murky glass sidelights, but couldn't see any motion. The porch light illuminated white, unmarked snow filling in a good-dog and September's footprints from hours before.

Shadow left the entry and worked his way around the house. He sniffed windows in each room, making sure nothing had come in that didn't belong. In the kitchen, more windows and two doors offered new places to search and guard.

No lights illuminated the rear of the house, but footsteps squeaking on fresh snow brought Shadow to full alert. His lips rose, curling over bright teeth in a silent warning snarl. A shadow entered through the back yard fence. He waited, watchful, as the intruder drew near.

The door lever into the kitchen moved. Metal grated in the lock as the key released the bolt. Shadow braced himself, low growl bubbling deep in his throat, louder and louder. The door creaked open, one inch at a time, revealing a gloved hand and booted foot when a tall, dark figure stepped inside. The intruder didn't turn on lights. His scent matched the unsettling odors near the coat closet.

Shadow exploded with alarm barks and fearsome snarls. The man's shouted exclamation morphed into a frightened scream when Shadow's teeth grappled his right shin and pulled him to the floor. Shadow bit harder, refusing to let go, even when fists rained blows down on a good-dog's head.

"What's going on?" September cried out, followed by quick thumping footsteps down the distant stairs.

Shadow released the intruder, but redoubled snarled warnings as the man scrambled to his feet and raced away out the door. He wanted to follow the man as he limped to the fence and grappled the gate open, slamming it shut behind him. But Shadow needed to protect September, so stayed to guard the open doorway. Icy wind blew snow into the room as September hurried into the kitchen and stood shivering in bare feet.

"Good dog, Shadow. Somebody tried to get in?" September peered out the open door, then slammed it shut and shot the bolt. "They're gone, baby-dog. You scared them off, what a good boy! Somebody else knows about Angela's house key." She switched on the yard lights, peering all around the fenced area. "He's gone now." She clicked on the kitchen lights.

He wagged and pressed hard against September's thigh. His fur still bristled, though. Shadow worried the stranger might return. He didn't like this empty house with fear-filled smells and strangers entering doors in the black of night.

"How'd you get out of the room? Never mind, just glad you did." She rubbed her eyes. "No more sleeping tonight. I better call the police. Hey, where's Angela? Didn't she ever come home?" She gasped and made a strange face. Shadow whined in reaction. "Oh crap. I hope you didn't just scare Angela half to death! Before we call the police, I better call to see that wasn't her, and she's okay."

George limped back to his car, breath white in the cold night air. He silently cursed his folly. He'd planned to catch September asleep and eliminate her as easily as Angela. Then he could stage the murder–suicide and wash his hands of the whole business.

The dog came out of nowhere. Thank God he got the fence gate closed, and locked from the outside, or the monster would've come after him.

He started the car and rubbed his bruised flesh as the heater roared. The boot had kept fangs from rending flesh, thankfully, but his ankle would swell. Now the damn woman would call the police, they'd find Angela's body, and, just damn! He'd given her his office address. If she shared that tidbit, he'd have more questions to answer.

His phone buzzed and he fumbled to get it from his pocket. But no call registered. George realized the noise came from Angela's cell, September calling. George smiled. Perhaps things could still be salvaged. He cleared his throat, and accepted the call.

George lowered his voice, turning it raspy and broken. "Hello? September? What time is it?" She'd expect Angela to be groggy, if awakened unexpectedly.

September sounded uncertain. "Is this Angela? You sound funny. Are you okay?"

He cleared his throat again, letting his words gargle. "Got a horrible case of laryngitis. Texting easier." He threw in a coughing fit, hoping to convince September, or at least allay suspicion. "Snow caught me, so I'm at a friend's. You got in the house okay?"

"Yes, just fine. But I worried when you didn't get home." She hesitated, then continued briskly. "Somebody tried to break into your house a little while ago. Shadow scared them away, but they must've had a key, and I was scared he'd gone after you. Anyway, I'll call the police shortly—"

"The police? Oh don't bother. Probably my maid service. They come early."

September's voice sharpened. "At this hour? Really? Through the kitchen door?"

He added more coughing. Damn! She was right, but now what could he say? "Neighbor lady's son. You know kids. Comes before work. Key only works for the kitchen door." He croaked the words, talking too fast, and hoping he hadn't dug a deeper hole.

She blew out an exasperated breath. "I shouldn't keep you

talking, Angela, that just makes laryngitis worse."

He added heavy breathing for effect, relieved. "Thanks. Will text you." He disconnected, thought for a moment, then smiled as he thumbed the message.

<Heard from housekeeper son, he's afraid of dogs. Sorry for scaring you. When bank opens, get lockbox info & meet at house?

He waited breathlessly for her reply.

>Okay.

George grinned but quickly sobered—he wouldn't risk the mutt's jaws again. His plan would work, but it meant reaching out to Mrs. Wong for help. She had little patience for mistakes, but he couldn't risk botching the job any further. Wong had resources. Very effective people. People he never wanted to meet.

He steeled his jaw, and dialed the special number again. With Angela and September both gone, he could bury that part of his life forever, and never worry about Kaliko Wong again.

Chapter 15

Charlie stumbled out of the house and nearly fell down the front steps, sliding in her threadbare canvas shoes. A pool of light spilled out of the door like a spotlight in the night. Snow sifted in powdery gusts and danced in the shaft of light like dust motes. Off to one side sat his car, a dark four-wheel-drive SUV well suited to the worsening weather.

She shuddered with adrenalin as much as the cold, jacket abandoned in the rush to escape. Why hadn't she grabbed the old woman's car keys from the desk? Was better than her own banged up beater, and for sure more valuable than the mysterious thumb drive.

Charlie felt for her pocketknife. She wanted to stab his tires, but couldn't risk the delay.

Sherlock clung to her neck like a furry stole, his weight making her top-heavy. Charlie still clutched Sissie's thumb drive and ran in an awkward shamble to reach the nearby storage building that sheltered her old car. She should've left Sherlock behind in Sissie's house—*oh God, Sissie!*—but she couldn't leave him behind, with that monster. Nobody had ever liked her…loved her…for herself until Sherlock. To free her hands, Charlie looped the lanyard over the big cat's fluffy white head and increased her pace.

She craned a quick look over one shoulder and nearly fell, breaths rasping and turning the air white. She froze for a lifetime, watched him stride out the front door, deliberate in his pursuit. Time stopped, then sped forward. She bolted.

Charlie slalomed the last few feet into the pitch-black storage building. In seconds she debated and rejected the option of hiding. Bags of cat litter towered in stacks nearly to the low ceiling. Between them, hay bales, grain barrels, and more unnamed containers jumbled like a child's giant building blocks. A one-time working hobby farm with chickens, goats, and a pony—Charlie had oohed and ahhed appropriately over pictures—Sissie still stored much of the feed and supplies although her passion now focused on her cats. No easy place to hide in there. Better to make a run for it.

Her heartbeat thrashed in her ears as she rushed to the battered car pointed nose-first into the debris. The rear car seats held three black garbage bags filled with all her worldly possessions, which she'd not bothered to unpack. Only cardboard covered the missing passenger-side window.

The car's rusty door hinges screamed when she yanked it open. She tossed Sherlock inside and slipped behind the wheel. The cat leaped from the passenger's seat and slunk immediately to the floorboards to begin sniffing. The floorboards were rusted through in places, held together with rubber mats covered with electrical tape.

Charlie moaned and whimpered, snagged keys from her pocket, and jabbed them into the ignition. The car growled and sputtered but refused to wake up. Hyperventilating, she twisted the key again and again, compulsively watching for her stalker to appear. His flashlight stabbed the darkness, sniffing after her, his figure a dark silhouette in the doorway. Charlie hit the steering wheel and screamed, "Turn over, damn you!"

As if understanding the threat in her voice, the car roared to life. Charlie shoved it into reverse and bald tires spun against frozen hard-packed dirt before grabbing purchase. Headlights, one skewed off plumb, lit up the storage building. The gas indicator barely registered, but with fingers crossed, it would get them away from immediate danger. The car backed out of the building, slid, and stopped for three heartbeats as she shifted into drive.

Black glove-covered fists smashed through the cardboard window cover. Charlie shrieked, not recognizing the primal scream from her own throat. She shrank from his clawing hands.

Sherlock crouched on the floorboards, green eyes glowing. He stared at the man's flailing arms, spit once, twice, and launched himself with a snarl.

Cursing, the man tried to yank his arm free. But Sherlock's claws hooked his sleeves, and the cat climbed up his arm, nearing his face. He flung the cat away, other arm still reaching through the open window. The white wraith lunged again, biting his glove, sharp teeth piercing leather and flesh.

She gunned the engine, swinging it around, dragging Sissie's killer. Her tires spun, and the car fish-tailed, until they caught the gravel beneath the powdery white.

He yanked himself free of the window, but Sherlock refused to back off. Ears slicked back, eyes dilated, a low keening growl grew to a scream. The cat leaped out the window, and raced after at the retreating man.

"No!" Charlie stomped the brakes. She watched the Maine Coon cat attack his leg, swarming upwards while adding vicious bites.

Sherlock's weight tripped him and he fell hard into the snow. The cat arched his back, fur bristled, stalking the man as he scrambled to his feet.

Charlie debated only a moment whether to go after Sherlock. He slept with her, loved to snuggle in her wet hair after a shower. She couldn't bear to think of him out here, in the weather. But his heavy fur equipped him for the cold. She could come back for him.

But only if she escaped. Because this time, it wouldn't end with a beating.

Sherlock crouched low, stalking, ready to launch another attack. When Charlie saw him point a gun at the cat, she screamed. Nostrils flared as she stomped the gas and honked the horn in a long, drawn-out blat. She aimed the car toward him. He would NOT shoot her cat!

He leaped aside into the growing drifts of white. Charlie cheered when Sherlock dodged away and raced back to the storage building. He'd be out of the weather until she could return and collect him. And the computer thumb drive was around his neck.

Charlie scrunched her head down between her shoulders, muscles so tense her whole body hurt. She pressed the accelerator, zoomed away from the isolated house, and slid onto the county road. Keeping one eye on the mirror, she switched off the headlights. Snow fell heavily, and lights made it harder to see, and also let the killer track her. Besides, the moon's reflection on the white gave more than enough illumination, as long as the road stayed deserted.

She'd have to wait until she was sure he'd left before circling back. He wouldn't expect her to go back. For years she'd taken whatever he dished out, but her mousy days were done. Plus, he didn't know Sherlock had the thumb drive, something he'd been paid to recover. Charlie knew about his so-called clients. They had no patience with failure. Maybe he'd be out of the picture for a while— or even for good! And once she retrieved the thumb drive, she'd call the cops—anonymously, of course—about what had happened to Sissie.

Then she'd figure out how to cash in. His clients didn't care who delivered the goods, just that the job got done.

Now that the adrenalin had waned, Charlie's bare fingers and face felt the full brunt of the icy wind pouring through the open passenger window. She fiddled with the heat. A lost cause. The heater hadn't worked in ages. She checked the gas gauge again, and bit her lip. Enough to get to town on fumes. She'd meant to fill up the tank from Sissie's car, siphon some out the way she'd done the past several weeks. Again, time got away from her. She'd grown complacent.

The snow clouded the windshield and her breath fogged the inside. She switched on the wipers, but without heat, ice formed under the blades. She leaned forward, rubbing the inside of the windshield to clear a spot.

Charlie gritted her teeth, concentrating on keeping her car in the middle of the two-lane. If the snow kept up, they'd close roads all over the county by morning. Good, that ought to slow him down, too. Hopefully Sherlock had found a nice cozy cubby in the shed and hunkered down.

Crash!

Her head smacked the windshield. A spider web pattern blossomed in the glass. Charlie clutched the steering wheel, eyes glued to the mirror.

His SUV bashed her a second time. Charlie yelped and whimpered. She didn't dare go faster. She couldn't outrun him on bald tires. But she couldn't stop and wait for him to shoot her, either.

They drove in tandem on the long uphill, him tap-bumping her battered car until eventually making constant contact, pushing, pushing faster and faster like a rhino bullying a puppy. They reached the crest of the gentle incline, and she cried out, face clammy and hands slick on the wheel. A steep, twisting slope led inexorably to the quaint bridge a quarter mile ahead. The water, frozen on top, wore the same sugar-white shroud that deepened by the moment.

His car paused as if relishing what was to come. He gunned the powerful engine, bashed her bumper hard, and followed close with repeated bangs down the slope.

Charlie knew she couldn't keep her car on the road. She was going too fast. She'd spin out. Go into the water. Drown. But if she could choose her spot, maybe she'd survive the crash.

The curve loomed near. *Now, commit to a choice. Pray for a soft landing...*

A big black and white dog, curled tail a bushy exclamation, dashed into the roadway. He stopped, well ahead of Charlie's planned crash site.

She stomped the brake. The car skidded into a tight 360-spin. Charlie covered her face. Jaw clenched, her stomach flip-flopped when the car launched off the road. Her teeth jarred. Salty blood filled her mouth when it landed, hit something solid, and flipped.

She came to seconds later. Pain radiated from her chest, her head. The car hiccupped and guttered in place. Her foot, still jammed against the gas, kept wheels spinning in the snow-clouded air. Hot liquid spilled from her nose and brow.

Boots squeaked on the snow, stopping near her head. Charlie squeezed her eyes half closed, peering through lashes, but couldn't stop the trembling of her chin and lips. She held her breath, playing possum.

He reached in through the passenger window and grabbed her hair. She screamed when he lifted her head. He let her go. Charlie's head clunked down again.

"Please." She hated the whimper in her voice. It echoed all those times before when she'd pleaded for mercy that never, ever came. When she ran away the last time, she'd told herself she'd never beg again. Staying with Sissie in South Bend—dear, sweet, clueless Sissie—made her hope things could be different. But now...

"Please!"

He smiled, and left without a word. She breathed again, at first thinking he'd shown her mercy. But then she realized he didn't need to shoot her. That would cause questions. And his employer hated questions.

The cold would kill her soon enough, if she didn't bleed out first.

Chapter 16

September yawned and flexed her shoulders while she waited at the stop light. She checked on Shadow in the mirror, and smiled when he copied her yawn with additional sound effects. "Maybe another trip to the dog park on the way home, and then nap this afternoon, what do you think?"

His tail thumped on the back seat. He settled his big head on his bear-toy with a groan.

The badge on his harness identified him as a working service dog. She rarely bothered with the gear—no law required he suit up—but it circumvented questions and opened doors more quickly especially when they visited business that didn't know them.

She circled the block before pulling into the parking lot. September checked the time. With slow morning work traffic, it had taken twenty minutes to arrive, but the bank doors should open any minute. Hopefully, she'd be in and out with the contents of the safety deposit box, and back to meet Angela by 10 o'clock. She'd left Macy dozing in the center of the guest bed, with the door securely latched, but didn't want to leave the big cat unattended for long. He had a nose for trouble, and she suspected he'd had a paw in Shadow's early morning escape.

An employee unlocked the door, and waved with a cheery smile. September waved back, and switched off the car. "Shadow, let's go."

September clipped on his leash and they walked briskly to the door. Snow still fell in fits and starts and had drifted overnight. At least the snow stayed dry in the bitter temperature, rather than becoming messy slush. Nevertheless, once inside the entry she told Shadow, "Paws." Shadow obliged, wiping first his front feet, and then kicking his rear paws against the floor mat. The lady holding the door for them looked duly impressed. Service dogs and their partners had a hard enough time maintaining necessary access, so she made sure Shadow acted like a poster dog for furry partners wherever they went.

At the desk she asked for access to the safety deposit box, and followed the attendant's direction. She kept credit cards, cash for their trip, and driver's license in a zippered flap inside one of her massive coat pockets. After producing proper identification and signing the log, she and Shadow settled into a small cubby with the metal box on the table.

She stared at the box for a long time, rubbing the back of her neck. Her stomach churned, and she unconsciously rocked in her seat. She started when Shadow pushed his head and shoulders into her lap. Taking a shuddery breath, September buried her face in his black fur, realizing how close she'd been to unraveling. It had been months since she'd suffered a panic attack. Reading messages from Chris, from beyond the grave, made her insides quiver.

This could change how she felt about her past, about Chris, and impact the future she hoped to share with Combs. Now faced with the uncertainty, September wanted to hide from the past. Again. She'd been doing that half of her life.

"Enough of that." She released Shadow and straightened in the chair. She'd run away and hidden from uncomfortable truths for far too long. According to Angela, the box held answers Chris wanted her to know. She could decide what to do about them, after she learned the truth they shared. She pulled out the wedding photo that Angela had sent and re-read the message on the back. *When you're ready, the answers are here.*

September opened the box and stared at an overwhelming pile of material. Chris had collected an enormous cache of file folders stuffed full of news clippings, notepads with Chris's familiar scrawl, and highlighted names and dates. It would take hours or maybe days to properly review everything. She needed to meet with Angela in less than an hour.

"Just a quick look. Then we'll head out."

Shadow woofed a soft agreement, but kept his sturdy weight pressed against her thigh to remind her: *I am here.*

She pulled the first file from the box, and opened it. Two newspaper clippings nested on top, both about a man named Brad Detweiller. September skimmed the first. Her heart skipped a beat to see Chris standing so strong and handsome in the picture beside the stranger. "Clear Choice Labs," she read aloud. "In Chicago."

Shadow whined and nudged her, and she smoothed his brow. "I lived in Chicago before I met Chris." *Back in the black days with Victor.* She shuddered and turned to the more recent clipping, this one from a week ago. Detweiller looked harried, with the headline stating he'd been indicted for falsified lab results. Angela must have added it to the material. "What does Detweiller and Clear Choice Labs have to do with me?"

She looked up the phone number, made a note of it on her phone, then gathered the research into a pile and stuffed it into a carryall she'd brought for that purpose. September thanked the attendant on her way out, and Shadow wagged when the woman complimented his manners. "Good-dog, Shadow. You made me proud, baby-dog, but you always do." He wagged harder, jumped up to press the door-bar to open the exit when asked, and led the way to the car.

Once back on the road, she thumbed her phone to dial the Chicago lab. A long shot, perhaps, but if caught off guard, maybe this Detweiller person would reveal the connection.

"Hello? Who's this?" A woman answered.

"Uh, is this Clear Choice Labs?"

"Yes, who is this?" Why did her voice sound familiar?

"I'd like to speak with Bradley Detweiller, the owner. Is he there? This is September Day." She slowed for a traffic light and waited impatiently as whispered conversation with others echoed from the other end of the line.

Finally, the woman came back. "We'd like to speak with him, too. Unfortunately, Mr. Detweiller killed himself."

September gasped and nearly went through the red light. She tromped on the brake and slid two feet into the intersection before stopping. Angry horns blared displeasure, but she ignored them, frowning at the phone. "Who is this? That's not funny."

"You're right, nothing about this is funny. What business did you have with the deceased? Oh, forgive me." She cleared her throat.

"I'm Officer Tee Teves. We met last summer in Texas. You helped train my K9 partner, Karma."

Macy yawned, stood, and stretched, flexing claws into the bedding that still held September's delightful scent. A distant sound had roused him from slumbers. After checking his food bowl—disappointingly empty—he padded to the latched bedroom door and meowed. When the request failed to bring the desired results, Macy stretched high to paw the lever handle himself, paw-pulled the bottom of the door, and then wound through the narrow opening.

He trotted to the top of the stairs to stare at the dark figure moving about the first floor. Macy's fur bristled, coffee-colored tail a bottle-brush of alarm. He cautiously sniffed the air, committing the stranger's signature scent to memory. He flattened himself against the wall and silently slunk down the stairway.

When he reached the bottom of the stairs he spied a glimmer peeking from beneath the closet door. Intrigued, he paw-patted the object, delighted to hear the jangle of metal. Rolling onto his side, he fished beneath the door and dragged the key fob into the entry. Macy sniffed it thoroughly: different than the intruder, but a familiar odor of someone who lived their life in the house. He pawed the keys again, liking the jangly sound. Macy grabbed the attached ribbon, lifted his head high with his prize, and continued to stalk the intruder. The jingle, so loud to cat ears, failed to alert the human's deficient hearing.

Invisible to the stranger, he paused beneath a chair to observe the man. Noisy. Clumsy, like most people. Angry smell, and the hint of a strange cat. Macy's whiskers pursed forward with interest piqued. When the tall stranger disappeared into the kitchen, Macy padded after him. When cold air whisper-touched his whiskers, he dropped his jangly new toy on the kitchen floor, creeping close to peer into the door left ajar.

The dank atmosphere made his nose twitch. A cold, silent car waited inside. Ultrasonic squeaks and rustles made his mouth water, and he crouched, instantly intrigued. He stalked over the threshold into the garage, closing on mousy prey one slow paw-step at a time.

Lights came on. Macy dove between nearby shelving, tail a quiver. From his hiding spot, he watched the man ratchet a metal ladder into place. The stranger climbed the ladder to reach the figure hanging over the cold car, swinging to-and-fro from an overhead fixture. He pressed a metal object into one of its dead hands so it made a POP sound.

Macy hissed and scrambled across the cement floor as far away from the scary sound and stranger as he could go.

"My day for cats. Here kitty-kitty-kitty." He made kissy noises, and Macy froze and hissed again. "You're just the bait I need. Nothing personal." The man took a step closer.

Macy spat and licked his lips, poised to dash away. The man shrugged off his coat and took another step. Macy growled, low and long, and flipped his tail, but the man ignored the warning. The coat swooped through the air. Fabric fell heavily on top of him.

Macy's growls exploded into screams and spits of surprise and fear. He flailed at the fabric, feeling the man's arms constrict around him to snug the coat into a suffocating bundle.

"Calm down, cat, I don't want to hurt you. I just don't want to get bit again."

When Macy shook off the heavy coat, the man's gloved hand captured his pistoning rear paws while curling his other hand through his collar.

With a final contortion, Macy chomped hard on the glove and felt satisfaction when the man yelled. Arching his body, Macy twisted and adjusted mid-air for a perfect four-paw landing as his break-away collar tore loose.

Macy dove beneath the nearby car and froze in place, poised, ready to attack should the threat come closer. The stranger stooped to recover his broken collar, then retreated back into the kitchen. The door slammed, locking Macy inside the garage with the dead body swinging overhead.

Chapter 17

Officer Pilikea "Tee" Teves disconnected and replaced the old-fashioned receiver in the cradle. She smoothed the soot-colored curly hair over both ears then rubbed her hazel eyes. The techs had already transported Detweiller's body and a team continued to investigate the apartment. It looked like suicide. But since his business dealings opened up questions, she and her partner had taken a look at his workspace at Clear Choice Labs. They found the place trashed—based on Detweiller's suicide note, he'd done the damage himself. But Tee took nothing at face value and was eager to sift through the mess.

After her Texas adventure, she'd taken a forced leave of absence. Once back full time, she'd barely left desk duty. Despite having seen and experienced more than her share of danger in her short tenure, she knew better than to hope for excitement, but boredom ate her nerves raw. So she'd been eager to take this call, despite Detective Redford's reluctance.

More than twice her age, a foot taller than her own five-feet-four inches, and double her weight, Detective Bobby Redford looked nothing like his namesake. He had another six months to make retirement with a full pension, and planned to coast these final months. So she'd been grateful he believed in the 'pairing and sharing' philosophy. By working with a detective on a criminal investigation, she'd learn on the job, get to network with other detectives, gain access to investigative resources, and further her future aspirations. Still, he kept her on a tight rein. Now she knew how Karma felt about her leash. She'd only had the police dog a week, but already felt like they'd been partners forever.

Why would a state-of-the-art lab like Clear Choice rely on an old-fashioned landline? They hadn't found Detweiller's cell phone at his apartment and thought it might be here, but nada. Its absence, along with September's call, added to her sense of unease.

"Interesting timing." Redford wore his faded winter coat open over a threadbare suit, with damp gloves stuffed in the pockets. "Sounded like you know 'em."

"Woman named September Day. I met her last summer during that human trafficking case. She helped train my dog." Tee rubbed tired eyes then fingered one of the tiny gold turtle earring studs. Her whole body ached. She blamed the icy weather. Ever since nearly dying when locked in the freezer, cold bit twice as hard. "September says she has information bearing on our case." Shivering, Tee prayed her sore joints wouldn't morph into the flu. She caught herself pining for the balmy temps of the Islands. To her, Lake Michigan paled in comparison to the ocean back home.

Redford groaned. "*Our case?* This isn't *your* case. You're just tagging along because you took the call and caught me in a weak moment. And we're shorthanded." She would have argued, but he cut her off. "I know you're itching to make Detective, but you won't get there faster by pushing so hard." He waved a hand at the debris. "Detweiller pretty much closed this case himself. Nothing says *guilty* like suicide."

"We…I mean, shouldn't *you* at least take a look at what September says she found?" Tee didn't know much about the woman, other than she trained dogs. "She found notes from some old police investigation by," she checked her notes, "… Detective Christopher Day."

"Chris Day? Hell, he's been dead for two or three years now." Sudden understanding lit his blue eyes. "Oh sure, I remember. The lady had a funny name, like the month. September, yeah, that's it. Must have been six or seven years ago, Day worked this weird kidnapping case. He ended up marrying the girl, and got murdered for his trouble." Redford pointed a finger at her. "There's a lesson. Keep business separate from personal."

"Murdered?" She made a mental note to find out more.

"Yeah, the cop-killing scumbag didn't take kindly to losing his girlfriend. By that time, Detective Day had moved to South Bend. He got shot outside a convenience store. Took a while, but they finally caught the shooter. He's waiting trial in Texas."

She wrinkled her nose. Not her favorite place. She'd learned a lot about herself while in Texas. Stretched professionally. And discovered relatives she could definitely live without. Of its own volition, her hand went into her pocket, cupping a half dozen seashells, fingering them like worry beads, the whispery shshsh-sound soothing.

But she gained a best friend with four feet, black fur, and a heart big enough to heal the ills of the world, especially her own hidden pain. The thought made her smile, and she dropped the shells back into her pocket. Karma had been a surprise gift from her half-sister, Lia Corazon. The paperwork was slowly working its way through channels to get Karma official as her K9 partner.

Redford took off his hat to scratch sparse strands of red hair, and reset the cap. "So Day's widow found something about one of his old investigations? How's it connected to Detweiller's death?"

Tee shrugged. "Don't know. September said the material includes the newspaper article about the recent Clear Choice Labs investigation and indictment, plus some older clippings." She waved one hand at the phone. "She called the number to find out."

"Long shot. Probably not worth much after six years." He shook his head, dismissive. "If it'll make you happy, I'll take a look when she brings it in."

"She called from South Bend."

"So she can scan and email it or something. With Detweiller dead, our timeline just opened up." He mopped his brow again. "Look, Tee, we got plenty to deal with already. I admire your energy and eagerness, but it's time to put this case to bed. No need to go snipe hunting for stuff you'll never catch. Besides, I got a date with the missus and my boy Zach, home for the holidays." He grinned. "His adoption-day celebration's bigger than Christmas and birthday combined. We got him a dog. He's always wanted a Border Collie." When he spoke of his son, Redford's face transformed from stoic cop to adoring, proud dad. "I've not had a dog since I was a kid. This one's a rescue, pretty calm for the breed, and mostly white, with a half-and-half face. Looks like an Oreo." He laughed. "Zach's gonna do cartwheels. He's asked for a dog every year since he was five.

This'll be the best Christmas ever."

Tee didn't want to think about Christmas. She couldn't visit her Aunty in California, or go home to the Islands, so Redford's happiness just left her hollow. "Come on, Redford. How many suicides call the cops in advance? Friends, maybe, or family. But the police? You don't find that odd?"

He shrugged. "When you've been around as long as I have, nothing surprises you. Suicidal people don't think straight, don't plan, it can be spur of the moment, especially when they got the means so handy."

She reflexively rubbed the light scars on her wrists, hidden under the long sleeves of her coat. She knew about that dark abyss that beckoned, and promised a relief to all the pain...Tee blinked rapidly. She'd got beyond that. She concentrated on the Detective's words.

"Detweiller stood to lose everything. Business, reputation. Not to mention an upcoming sensational trial and probably going away for a long time. Detweiller just filled up one of his syringes at work and took it home with him for a nightcap." Redford played with the zipper on his coat. "Once they found he falsified one test, every other result gets reviewed and probably tossed. Lawyers will have a field day. I already got Alderman Jacobs on my case to get this wound up tight."

She'd met Kelly Radcliff Jacobs III only once, late last year, working security at a function celebrating his son's seventeenth birthday. Tee found Jacobs pretentious, condescending, and entitled. He spent all evening bragging on his business success with his string of pharmacies.

"What's he complaining about now? He got his way." For the past year Jacobs had campaigned against aldermen being banned from outside employment. She held up her hands in surrender when Redford would have lectured her yet again on Chicago politics. Sometimes you had to make nice.

Nullifying lab results could impact a host of issues, from convictions to medical diagnoses, prescriptions, and treatments. Tee dreaded the pile of paperwork to come. The public believed cops chased bad guys, foiled conspiracies, and wrote irksome tickets. But she spent an inordinate amount of time filling out tedious reports.

"I got a gut feeling about September's information." She held up a hand again. "I know, you don't want to waste any time. So how about this. I've got a couple of days downtime saved up. I'll do it on my own, off the clock. Take a quick trip down to South Bend, pick up September Day's info, and poke around."

He stared at her, started to speak, then blew out a breath. "No, it'll be on the clock. Detweiller's bookkeeper is in South Bend, too, so that'll save me a trip. And it'll get you out of my hair for a couple of days. But clear it with the Captain first, and keep me informed."

"You won't be sorry." She turned away to hide a grin, thankful she kept a packed to-go bag handy. She'd need to buy a train ticket, and let September know. She wondered if Karma would remember September's dog, Shadow.

Chapter 18

Shudders wracked Charlie's body. Teeth chattered so hard she feared they'd break. Her car had finally stalled and stopped running during the night—not that it had provided much heat. One of the clothing-filled garbage bags in the back seat had burst on impact and the scattered fabric from random sweatshirts had cut the edge off the worst of the cold. She'd fallen in and out of consciousness all night, maybe even slept part of the time. At one point she'd dreamed Sherlock returned, his fur and hot body keeping her warm…Now the cooling engine tick-tick-ticked while sand-like snow peppered the shattered windshield. White drifted in through the open passenger window and piled up against the side of the car.

Her heart thudded when she became fully conscious. She might still survive. Something hurt deep inside, making it difficult to catch her to breath. Charlie swallowed. Her saliva tasted metallic. She spat, and her eyes widened at the crimson spatter now visible with the morning's light. Her breath quickened, and shallow quick gasps steamed from her numb lips.

With no seatbelt to stop the impact, Charlie left a second head-size dent in the windshield. The steering wheel bruised her chest, and maybe shattered a rib. She lifted a hand to feel the lump on her forehead. Charlie screamed when bone grated upon bone. Her shoulder unhinged in a bizarre way. Gasping, she squeezed shut her eyes, and bit her lip, riding the wave of pain until it eased from shriek-level to dull roar.

The space offered a wind-break that barely made a degree or two difference. Her thin clothing and other random attire did little to shield Charlie from the biting temperature. How long until she froze? Her light gray vehicle, coated with white, would fade to invisibility against the snowy field. Nobody would find her. Getting to the road offered only a slim chance for rescue, but it was better than none. She had to get out of the car.

Charlie slowly, carefully twisted her neck one way and then the other, braced for the next unexpected stab of pain. Her head throbbed, but she felt gratified something worked. She examined the tiny space. The car canted on one side, nearly upside down. The driver's side window pressed against spent corn stalks. The door, now a shivery surface upon which she rested, offered no way out. She'd landed on her left side with her arm pinned beneath her.

She had to get out! The open passenger window beckoned overhead, an impossible distance away. The remains of the cardboard cover blew to-and-fro in the wind, a monster's lip-smacking dare to breach the opening. Right arm useless, Charlie had to perform a one-arm push-up with her left, and somehow drag her battered body up and out.

Gingerly flexing her right leg produced a sickening grating sound as her pelvis shifted. Oddly, she felt no pain, and wondered if the cold finally worked in her favor, numbing her extremities. Her shivers had abated, but Charlie knew the car hadn't gotten warmer. Did shock make you stop shivering? If she lived, maybe she'd look it up. Right now, it didn't matter.

Bracing herself for the pain to come, Charlie held her injured right arm tight to her body, while she flexed her left leg and pressed up with the corresponding elbow. Any fitness instructor would be proud of the plank she managed. But Charlie held it barely a minute before she collapsed into a near seated position.

The tiny world inside the car spun, and Charlie struggled to stay conscious. Her effort brought renewed warmth to her body. Her stomach flip-flopped, suddenly queasy, and she fought the urge to vomit, fearing that would tear up her insides even worse. It was no use, with only one good arm she couldn't raise herself high enough to get out of the window. Even if she could, she doubted she could crawl the distance from her car to the road.

Snow completely covered the windshield. Charlie imagined the featureless lump of the car, a snowy speedbump in the field of white that wouldn't catch anyone's attention until long after the snow melted. She couldn't get out of the car, but how about making it more noticeable?

She squirmed to free her left arm and hand. Pins and needles enveloped the limb, and she moved it erratically, trying to regain the feeling. Her arm brushed and engaged the wipers, thanks to the key still on in the ignition.

Charlie gritted her teeth at the grating noise until she saw the icy blades clear away some of the damaged glass. She wanted to shout with success, but held back, conserving energy. Even out of gas the battery would last for a while. A car from the road would need to be traveling one direction to see the glint off the glass windshield. Still, she'd improved her odds exponentially. But she could do better.

The car looked like an abandoned wreck. People needed a clue she was inside. Charlie's movements had re-opened her head wound. She wiped her bleeding face and stared at her stained palm, then methodically painted the inside of the windshield bright red as far as she could reach. And every few minutes, Charlie switched the key on to engage the wipers and keep the red beacon free of snow.

That's when a black and white creature forced its broad head and snuffling maw into the open window.

Chapter 19

As September returned to Angela's house, Shadow made concentric nose prints on the rear window. He pawed at the door and woofed softly.

She knew he wanted the window rolled down. Shadow relished cold more than she did. "Okay, just a crack. I'm still cold and don't have fur like you."

He eagerly stuck his nose out the two-inch opening, drinking fresh air like a parched runner gulping Gatorade. He needed another run at the dog park, too, and she debated stopping now. Maybe after she met with Angela. And took a closer look at Chris's investigation before she picked up Tee from the train platform at South Bend Airport.

The bag of research on the front seat begged for attention. She'd agreed to turn over the material to the police, but wanted to read through Chris's research before Tee arrived this afternoon. Despite the continued snow, the roads weren't terrible. Indiana road crews knew how to manage the weather, but Tee planned to catch the 12:20 South Shore train and arrive at the South Bend airport about 4:00.

September took the same parking spot in front of Angela's house. She didn't see any fresh tracks in the drive. Where the hell was Angela? "She begged me to come visit, and now she's a ghost on the phone."

Shadow whined and thumped his tail, agreeing with anything she said. "You're just *hungry* for my breakfast sandwich." He licked his lips at the word and September laughed. She'd stopped at a drive-through after leaving the bank and had already eaten one sausage and egg croissant, but had saved the second to share with Shadow and Macy when they got home. A giant steaming container of coffee balanced in the cupholder.

She dropped the take-out food and her phone into the bag with Chris's research, and slung the bag over one shoulder, balancing the coffee in the other hand. Shadow leaped out as soon as his door opened and raced to the front door. September slowly followed, careful not to fall in the slick snow. She hesitated when she saw Shadow's hackles bristling, and his stiff-legged posture. He tipped his head from side to side, eyes glued to the door.

"Good dog, Shadow. Wait." Angela must have returned after all. Instead of unlocking the door for him to check-it-out and search the premises, she knocked first, then rang the bell. It wouldn't do for Shadow to scare her hostess before they'd reconnected. After waiting, and ringing a second time with no response, she called Angela's cell.

No answer. It again went to voice mail. "I don't know where you are, Angela, but I'm back from the bank and waiting at your house. I also found out that Brad Detweiller, the man mentioned in Chris's files, has killed himself." She didn't hide the exasperation in her voice, still shivering on the front steps in the icy temperatures. "I've had enough. I'm giving all the paperwork to the police this afternoon. So if you still want to meet up, call me back. Soon. Meanwhile, I'm packing to go home."

More than irked, September thrust the key in the lock and swung open the front door. Without being told, Shadow bounded into the first room and raced around the perimeter, his tail waving with excitement. He woofed as he returned to her, nose-touched her hand, then surged past into the next room.

She heard his thumping paws gallop up the stairs, and listened to his progress from room to room. September quickly shut the front door behind her, and dropped the bag of research next to the coat closet. "Good boy, Shadow. Hey baby-dog, good check-it-out. Where are you, boy?" She sipped her coffee, grimacing at the scalding temperature, and hurried up the stairs. Shadow met her at the top, whining, fur still bristled, but having found nothing.

The door to the guest bedroom stood open the width of a cat.

"Macy?" Crap, he could be anywhere in the house. At least he'd come when called, if she used the right enticement. "Hey Macy, want treats? I've got treats for Macy." She waited, listening for his eager meow and padding tread. Nothing.

She turned to Shadow. "Where's your cat? *Find Macy*."

He bounded past her back down the stairs and she followed more slowly to avoid spilling her coffee. Macy had already taken his heart medication this morning and acted fine. But his condition could blow up at any time. Stress could tip him over his threshold. She should have left him behind with Lia, safe and secure, rather than put him through the rigors of travel. She'd wanted to show him off to his breeder and alert her to HCM if she didn't already know about it. It often affected entire lines of Maine Coon cats. "Macy-cat, where are you, buddy?" *Please let him be safe!*

Shadow's claws clicked on the floor in the nearby kitchen and she hurried to join him. He'd searched every other room in the house.

Macy loved to open cupboard doors and lounge on top of refrigerators. The lever door handles proved irresistible and he had three to choose from in the small kitchen: a door to the garage, a walk-in pantry, and into the back yard. September held her breath as she scanned the room for evidence of the cat.

The back door stood open. "Oh no!" She'd closed and locked the door last night. Hadn't she? Had Angela's housekeeper returned?

Shadow pressed his nose to the base of the pantry door, paw-scratching the entry with a low bubbling growl deep in his throat. But September had already hurried to the open back door. A dark green ribbon of fabric the same color as the cat's eyes nested in the blowing snow on the back steps. Macy's collar.

"Oh no! Shadow, find Macy, *seek*!" She prayed he'd find Macy crouched and shivering under one of the snow-covered lawn chairs. At least the tiny back yard's tall fence would keep the cat safely confined.

But Shadow still whined at the pantry, probably eager for his food bag she'd left inside. Impatiently, she repeated the command. "Shadow, *seek*!" Her voice cracked with authority, and he obediently bounded out the back door to sniff the discarded cat collar.

A gloved hand reached past September, slammed shut the door, and trapped Shadow outside. He barked and snarled, throwing himself against the door.

September reflexively ducked and whirled away. Her knee cried out in protest. She gritted her teeth, hoping the old injury wouldn't betray her. A long, mournful *meow* sounded from the garage. Macy!

The silent man before her wore a ski mask. He produced a gun, silencer attached, with the dexterity of a magician.

"No!" September tore the lid from the coffee and threw the scalding liquid into his face.

He screamed with pain, struggled to strip off the scalding wet fabric.

September dodged towards the garage. Her foot kicked a jangle of keys as she pushed open the door and they spun through it. She slammed the garage door and leaned against it. Her mouth dropped open.

Angela hung from the rafters. Macy yowled below.

Chapter 20 (34 **Years Ago**)

She showed very little, but a client guessed Tana's secret and told. When Kali found out, she smiled that scary way that never reached her eyes. She paid a man to load Tana and another blond pregnant girl into the back of a camper. In the hours-long bumpy ride strangers became allies in shared misery. She and Rosalee whispered gruesome recaps of their lives and dire predictions of their fate to come. Each feared for her baby's safety.

When the camper stopped, the girls clung together until the door creaked open. The driver, a tall balding man in his early twenties, ordered them out. They blinked and squinted against the morning sun, shivering in the cold winter air. Neither had been allowed to bring extras with them, although Tana had managed to secrete her small stash of funds inside her bra.

A dumpling-soft woman appeared on the front porch of a rambling farmhouse, grinning and waving them near. The girls moved together, arms linked as if joined in some weird choreography. Tana stumbled, but the driver caught her other arm and kept her from falling. The kindness, so unexpected, brought her to tears. She managed the last several yards through blurred vision. Inside the house Tana discovered a commune-like atmosphere in which half a dozen pregnant women lived and worked.

In the weeks that followed, the dumpling-woman made sure they had plenty to eat and clean beds—with no visitors!—in which to sleep. Tana wondered how she'd ever taken such luxuries for granted. But she never let down her guard the way Rosalee and the other women did. She didn't trust this hell-to-heaven transformation. Kali had something more than altruism in mind.

Expectant mothers—some even younger than Tana—came, had their babies, and disappeared so quickly they became interchangeable. Even so, the nursery rarely had more than one or two infants at a time, and never for more than a week. The exception were tow-headed twins, about a year old, who didn't seem to belong to anyone. Had their mother abandoned them? What would become of the babies? In her motherly voice, the dumpling-woman sweetly suggested Tana keep questions to herself, or find another place to stay. So Tana bit her lip, but spent every spare moment with the twins, playing with them, feeding them, even changing their diapers.

She wondered about her own situation, but was afraid to ask. So she took every opportunity to eavesdrop conversations between the dumpling-woman and the nameless driver. The woman's tongue loosened after her nightly bottle of wine—a whole bottle!—and Tana finally learned what Kali expected in return for her generosity.

They'd already sold Rosalee and Tana's newborns, betting on the babies being as blond and blue-eyed as their mothers. Blond newborns brought the most money, older kids not so much.

Aghast, Tana confided in Rosalee, who confessed she'd been offered money and had no choice but to cooperate. She sounded guilty, but also relieved. Rosalee had no family or resources to help. Her baby would come any day now.

Tana wondered what would happen if she refused? Had that happened to the twins' mother? Would Tana disappear, too? Tana crossed her arms protectively over her stomach, and her baby kicked as if also rejecting the notion.

She couldn't risk staying here. She had to get away. She'd leave, change her name and appearance, start somewhere else. Somewhere far away, where nobody knew what she'd become, what she'd had to do to survive. She still had the funds gifted to her from former clients. Her baby could never know. Their future together would make up for all the pain and horror of Tana's past.

The driver controlled the ramshackle camper's keys. But it

couldn't be too different than the delivery truck her father had taught her to drive for her parents' restaurant. She'd steal the keys while the pair slept off their nightly wine. Tana stole a knife from the kitchen and added that to her stash. And she'd wait for the perfect opportunity. Tana had time, her baby wasn't due for three weeks.

But her baby didn't know about Tana's plan. Two days later, Tana's water broke. The dumpling-woman hustled her into the birthing room in time to see the driver pull a sheet over Rosalee's gray face, her deflated belly testament to a recent birth.

Tana screamed. She struggled to leave. They explained that Rosalee only slept deeply, an after-effect of the anesthesia. But Tana redoubled her screams when approached with a syringe filled with light yellow fluid.

The shot made the room go black. When Tana awoke many hours later, nauseated and groggy, her baby was gone.

Chapter 21 (Present Day)

September braced herself against the door behind her. She squeezed her eyes shut against the spectacle of Angela—*dead, how could she be dead?*—and concentrated on her escape. The man with the gun, his identity, the reasons for the attack, nothing mattered but protecting herself.

Shadow barked nonstop from the back yard. His frustrated yelps alternated with the thud, thud, thud rhythm of his body's impact against the closed kitchen door.

The scalding coffee wouldn't slow the intruder for long. Soon he'd burst through the door, gun blazing, and she'd be helpless.

She turned around, scrabbled at the door latch, saw no way to lock it, and backed away in quick, jerky steps until she bumped into the car. Nowhere to hide in the jumbled mess. He could simply shoot through the door.

At the thought, she dodged out of the potential line of fire. Her shoulders hunched, eyes wide as she frantically scanned the dim garage. Out, she needed out. She needed her keys, but if she could reach her car, she'd be safe.

She spied the garage door opener mounted on the wall; salvation! She scurried to the opener and pressed it, but nothing happened. September punched it again and again, whimpering under her breath when it wouldn't open. She flicked the nearby light switch. Nothing happened. He'd cut the power. Only the tiny skylight overhead offered dim illumination.

Another door on the back wall probably led into the back yard where Shadow barked. Stacks of gardening supplies blocked the exit. She scurried to the mountain of material, grabbed the nearest item and toppled it to one side. She couldn't even reach the doorknob. Seconds had passed—but felt like hours—he'd be upon her before she could uncover the exit.

Nostrils flaring, skin clammy, she wrestled the ladder away from Angela's dangling form. She grabbed it. Metal screeched against the cement floor, clanged when it crunched the side of the car. The dead woman's feet swayed overhead. September dodged them, biting her lip to contain whimpers threatening to grow into screams. She wedged the top of the ladder at an angle against the kitchen door and braced the ladder feet flush with the car's rear tire.

Just in time. He twisted the lever handle. When it wouldn't open, he bumped it. The ladder jarred and jangled. He bumped harder, it shifted still more, but held.

September whirled and raced back to the other exit. The ladder bought time for her to get through, to rejoin Shadow in the back yard. With him by her side, she could do anything. She'd puzzle out the whys later.

Shadow's barks grew more frantic. At September's feet, Macy mewed and wound about her ankles, wanting solace, but only managing to trip her.

The door pounding grew louder, more determined. The ladder jittered in place, shifting in increments as September clawed free and dragged aside bags of mulch, rakes, shovels. Finally uncovering the doorknob, she silently cheered as she grabbed and twisted.

Locked. No key in sight. She screamed, breathing in gulps, twisting to look everywhere for any other options.

He hit the door with a mighty crash. The ladder fell sideways.

Catching up a rake, September dashed to brace it alongside the falling ladder. She yelled, lying and praying he'd believe her. "I have a gun, too! Keep back, stay away from the door."

His pounding stopped, for the moment. Her gun, nested in the glove box of her distant car, offered no protection. And she couldn't call for help, with her phone in the bag of research by the front closet. She couldn't escape the garage. Maybe distract him, find out what he wanted, buy some time. Make enough noise to rouse the neighbors for help. She couldn't, she wouldn't give up!

September choked back a sob. "I just talked to her last night, she sent me a text. Why would Angela invite me here then kill herself? You killed her!"

Long pause, his voice flat. "I'm not that sloppy. I honestly don't care. I'm just the cleanup man." He rattled the door's handle. "So help me out. Give me what I came for and we part as friends." He paused again, nonchalant attitude in stark contrast to her racing pulse. She could hear his slow, steady breaths from the other side of the door. "I'll get in there eventually, and you'll tell me anyway. Then we won't be friends anymore." The words sounded practiced. He'd done this before. Many times.

The damn safety deposit box! *Oh my God—Chris, too? But Victor killed Chris. It couldn't be connected. Could it?*

He rattled the doorknob again, whispering against the door, voice measured and calm, but deadly steel beneath the words. "You've got nowhere to go. I'll turn the garage door and light back on long before the authorities finally come. Nothing personal."

Shadow's barks had stilled, as if he listened to their voices. Macy trilled, leaped onto the hood of the car, and from there hopped up to drape himself around September's shoulders. Her fingers dug deep into the cat's fur and he squeaked. She had to get them out of here. *Keep him talking.*

"Why are you doing this? Who are you? What's so important in those files?" Anything to delay the inevitable. He spouted empty promises. She wouldn't be allowed to walk away.

"Don't know. Don't care." Another of those long, deadly pauses before he continued. Had he yawned? "I suppose you could call me Mr. Bleak, because those are your chances. Give me what I need and I'll go away. Make me come after you and here's how my employer suggests it plays out." He cleared his throat and recited as if reading. "Angela Day blamed September for her son's death, so baited a trap to get her to South Bend. She killed September, then hanged herself out of remorse." He wiggled the doorknob again and waited.

September dug her nails into the palms of her hands. The walls began to close in. She shook her head, wanting to crumple to the ground. Black spots floated before her eyes—Shadow, she needed Shadow to ground her…Macy meowed again, and her trembling fingers clutched his fur harder.

"The clock's ticking. Cooperate, or I'll skin that mangy cat of yours, and shoot the damn dog." His weight hit the door. It jarred open half a foot, enough that he could peer into the garage.

He'd skinned off the ski mask. Blank nondescript brown eyes stared at her, blinking lizard-slow, scalded skin surrounding them already blistering and bright red. "Time's up." One gloved hand snaked through the opening to push at the ladder.

September screamed. She thwacked his arm with the rake. Macy swatted one clawed paw at the gloved hand.

He withdrew with a hiss. Stalemate. He couldn't get in. She couldn't get out. In the background, Shadow's barks again escalated.

His voice sharpened. "Tell me where you left the files. Do it now, or I'll shut up the dog permanently."

September clenched her jaw, teeth aching with pressure, and finally nodded to herself. He'd find the files anyway. She couldn't risk Shadow's life.

"In a bag. By the front door."

"Good girl. You sit tight and maybe I won't kill your dog."

Macy struggled in her arms and she let him go. He found something on the garage floor, batted it, then fetched the jingling object for her to toss.

"Not now, Macy." She looked down when he pushed it against her foot.

Macy dropped the car keys, sat, and pawed her leg again with a soft meow.

Chapter 22

People sometimes knew more than good-dogs. Shadow reluctantly obeyed when September ignored his warning. When the door slammed shut, locking him outside away from her, he couldn't reach September to protect her.

Hurling himself against the door didn't work, and barking made him more upset. Neither his paws nor teeth could grapple open the handle. He should have disobeyed and kept September safe. He'd failed!

The stranger yelled. A loud, hurt, surprised sound that made Shadow more intent on reaching September. He wailed, redoubling his alarm barks and paw-thumps. No way inside through the door. Maybe another way? A window.

Shadow ran up and down the back yard next to the house. The only window was in the door itself, far above a dog's paw-reach. He couldn't see inside, but the sounds of September's fear made his tummy hurt. He shook himself, closed his mouth, and took deep breaths. And looked around the enclosed square back yard.

He couldn't get back inside the kitchen, or the attached garage. A tall wooden fence enclosed the rest of the yard. Shadow ran the circuit of the tiny space, sniffed the fence gate where last night's intruder had entered. But it had no handle for him to grip.

Banging sounds erupted inside the garage, along with September's yells. He returned to the door, whimpering with frustration. September, so near—only a narrow door between them—but no way to get through. He barked hard and long, so September knew he'd soon come to protect her. He just had to figure out how.

The stranger also spoke with hard, loud words. Shadow had smelled the bitey scent of gunfire when they first entered the house. Guns could reach out and bite September from a distance. He whimpered again.

Shadow had to do his job. He had to get out of the small yard to stop the bad man from hurting her.

He turned his attention to fencing on two sides. No stacked storage boxes offered an easy escape. He knew how to climb ladders, the talent had come in handy more than once, but nothing offered a good-dog a paws up in the deserted back yard. Wind drifted snow high against one side of the fence, though. With interest, Shadow trotted to the area, paw-testing to see if the elevated white stuff might support his weight. He sank up to his shoulders and had to drag himself out, shaking the white from his black fur.

Backing away from the fence for a running start, Shadow galloped as fast as he could, aiming at the corner. He leaped high, reaching with forepaws to hook over the top, and scrabbled with rear claws for purchase. Ice nullified any traction. Only one paw reached the top and he clung for seconds, before falling back to the ground. Shadow tried again. He flailed and failed. All the while, mysterious and frightening noises and cries arose inside the garage, spurring him to try harder, to succeed, to get out, out, OUT and rejoin September!

Panting both in frustration and fatigue, Shadow searched for another way out. While one fence wall held mounds of drifted snow, the wind had swept clean the ground at the foot of the adjacent fence. Flowerbeds, now empty of anything but shriveled dead vegetation, offered another option. He couldn't go over the fence. But Shadow had claws for digging. September didn't like him to dig without permission. But this time, he'd disobey. Sometimes dogs knew better than people. He could go under the fence, escape the back yard, reunite with September.

He quickly padded to the expanse of nearly bare ground, scratch-testing a few likely spots. Icy dirt meant frozen soil for the first paw-digs. But he remembered the rose garden at their house, how garden soil gave way to digging more readily than the sunbaked dirt in the fields. Shadow excavated with determination, digging slowly at first, then more quickly when he reached softer ground.

Noises inside grew louder, more scary. Shouts and banging made Shadow whimper, but he concentrated on the hole. Soon, he'd enlarged the space enough to force his head and shoulders into the gap. He dug deep, and then pulled the loosened soil backward in piles between his rear feet. Over and over again, grunting and panting, no longer wasting breath on barks, Shadow struggled to widen the hole and reach the bottom of the fence.

With excitement, Shadow's paws dug below the wooden barrier. With whimpers of anticipation, he increased his tempo. He lay on his side, scooping with one paw, seeking to widen the gap beneath the wooden barrier. Another two paw-scoops of soil shuttled to one side would open the space for him to squeeze through.

Instead, he uncovered a wire and cement footing two feet under the soil. Impossible to breech.

Before he could regain his feet, the wall of the garage burst out toward him. A car crashed through. It barreled at Shadow, the rear eyelights glaring and angry.

Shadow flinched, backpedaled madly, tail pressed hard against the barrier of the fence. It bore down on him. He couldn't escape.

Chapter 23

The rear of the car crashed into Angela's back yard fence. September clung to the steering wheel. She wasted precious seconds scanning the yard for Shadow—no sign of the big dog—before shoving the gear shift into drive. If the garage door wouldn't open, she'd drive through it. Shadow must've found a way out of the yard. They'd meet up later. Now she had to escape.

Tires spun in the snow but finally caught. They propelled the car back through the splintered garage wall, and into the flimsy door. The car carried the accordion-fold barrier halfway down the driveway before it peeled off into the snowy roadway.

Macy yowled at the loud noises and abrupt acceleration. His claws clung to the passenger seat to keep from being flung back and forth. September braced herself when Macy launched himself onto the driver's side headrest, rear end riding the perch while forepaws clutched September's neck.

When the car zoomed toward him, Shadow shrank back into the small excavation. He shuddered, body freezing in place. The engine noise of the car over top of him made a good-dog's ears hurt.

It reversed, tires kicking up snow and dirt when it sped back the way it came. The car punched back into the hole in the garage wall and out the other side with a scream of metal on wood.

Shadow cautiously emerged, still shivering. He shook off the dirt and slush coating his fur and padded cautiously to the breach in the building. He stretched his neck forward to sniff the opening and stared into the dim garage. Oil. Blood. Fear. His fur bristled and a soft growl bubbled deep in his throat. He sniffed more thoroughly, detecting the familiar fresh scents of September and Macy. Maybe the crashing car carried them away.

She searched through the fogged windows for a streak of black fur against the precipitation. Dim streetlamps had stayed on in the murky daylight but offered little help in the heavy snow. The sound of the crash impacts prompted doors up and down the street to creak open. Silhouetted figures sneaked peeks through windows. The attacker's threat to target Shadow made her throat ache—now other people also were at risk.

Despite the worry for Shadow, her mind spun in dizzying circles. Angela dragged her into all of this, but Chris planted the seed years before. She couldn't believe Angela had killed herself, especially after what Mr. Bleak said. But without the files, how would they figure out why she'd been killed? And, dear lord, why Chris had died, too.

She had to call the police. Her attacker probably had her cell phone now, along with the files. She reached overhead to stroke Macy, only now feeling the Reynaud's tingling in her fingers. He head-butted her neck again. She looked out the windows, searching for Shadow. He had to be her priority.

Shadow wore his tracker collar all the time. But she needed her phone app to track him down. He had to know she drove the car out of the garage. He'd track her, too, if he could. She glanced at the clock on the dash. The weather would delay police response, but not by much. She had to find Shadow before the police arrived. They'd keep questioning her for hours, leaving Shadow unprotected and alone in this strange neighborhood.

He hesitated to climb through the opening, fearing a trap. The bad man in the house—he smelled his presence—had made September cry out in fear. But Shadow needed to find September, and his cat Macy, to protect them. That was his job. His ears swiveled, checking for danger. Finally, Shadow crept through the torn wall into the garage. He flinched when a squeak-sound overhead startled him and stared curiously up at the person swinging from the rafters. He whined. The death-smell came from her. She was beyond a good-dog's help.

A door into the house proper hung partly open, with a tall ladder spilled on the garage floor. Shadow drew near, still listening carefully. Someone rummaged inside the house. Shadow pushed through the door and padded past the kitchen to the front entry on silent paws until he could peer around the corner at the stranger. The man muttered to himself, while digging through a large canvas bag that puddled on the hardwood floor.

September's bag. Things she treasured and carried with her. They didn't belong to this stranger.

A low growl bubbled deep in Shadow's chest. The man had no right to paw through September's bag. Shadow stalked closer, the fur on his shoulders bristled. He growled louder.

The man froze, then slowly turned his head. He locked eyes with Shadow.

Shadow added snarls. He showed his teeth and stalked closer, stiff-legged, a hair away from rushing the interloper. Snarls warned the man to drop September's bag and go away.

Instead, the stranger stood in one smooth, fast motion, and swung the bag at Shadow's head. When Shadow ducked, the man spun and lunged for the front door.

Shadow roared. He sprang forward. Teeth scarred one booted foot, pulling the man off balance.

The man swung the bag again and again, thumping it against Shadow's head and neck until he loosened his teeth. With his other hand he unlatched the door, then backed out onto the icy front sidewalk, using the canvas satchel as a buffer against Shadow's threat.

Following close, Shadow fell silent, keeping wary eyes on the stranger's every move. Shadow could almost taste the greasy metal smell of a weapon. But as long as the man kept his hands busy clutching September's bag, he couldn't use the gun.

A car horn blared. Shadow's ears flicked in response, but neither he nor the bad man looked away. Sometimes September beeped the horn to call a good-dog to come for a ride. This didn't sound like her horn, though.

Beeeee-eeeeep! "Shadow! Baby-dog, come-a-pup. Please Shadow, where are you?"

This time, he couldn't help himself. Shadow hazarded a quick glance at the small car at the end of the block. The same one that punched holes in the garage.

When he broke eye contact, the man whirled and loped away.

Shadow bounded after, tackled him, and the canvas bag turned a slow somersault through the air, papers spilling across the snowy ground. The bag landed with a burst of white behind nearby shrubs.

The man reached inside his jacket. Shadow didn't wait for him to grab the gun. He'd done all he could. Now, he needed to rejoin September.

More strangers watched and murmured from nearby porches and stoops. Some gasped with surprise, pointing when Shadow rocketed past. The ice and snow hurt his paws, and he slipped twice, once going down on his tail, before righting himself.

Before he made it to September, though, a bigger car roared to life right behind him. It plowed down the street, clipping his tail. Shadow yelped more in surprise than pain. But the SUV never slowed, ignoring Shadow to target the little car that held September.

He barked a warning, and barked again. But the huge car continued its rush toward September. With a yelp of anguish, Shadow dashed after it, determined not to be left behind.

September rolled down the window, voice cracking as she yelled. "Shadow! Come-a-pup. Shadow, where are you?" Tears froze on her cheeks. She honked the horn once, twice, and a third long drawn out blat, praying he'd understand to come running, even though it sounded nothing like their own car.

More house lights switched on. Someone stepped out the front door of the house across the street, a child beside him.

An SUV revved behind her. Mr. Bleak! It gave chase, engine

snarling with hungry determination to ram her car and finish the job.

September gunned the gas, tires spun and finally caught purchase. She shouted out the window toward the neighboring looky-lous. "Call 911."

Murmurs and questions met her announcement. No time for explanations. She couldn't wait. Mr. Bleak didn't care about witnesses. She remembered his creepy, no nonsense comment: "Nothing personal." But this was very personal to her. Bleak's four-wheel-drive navigated more securely than Angela's lightweight car she'd borrowed. If she didn't move quickly, he'd run her down in front of bystanders. He didn't care, and probably wanted no witnesses. He'd maybe take them out as well.

More neighbors shrugged into coats and stood shivering with shared whispers at their open doorways as she sped away as fast as she dared, fish-tailing on the slippery road. Bleak's SUV panted after her, quickly riding the bumper of September's borrowed car in what became a slow-motion car chase.

She had to lead him away from Shadow. And pray the smart dog would know to follow.

Chapter 24

Tee disconnected the call to September after several rings went unanswered. She'd managed to take an earlier train, and spent the trip on her phone reading old news accounts to catch up on September's personal history.

Just as Redford said, trouble followed the woman. "We've got that in common," Tee muttered. They'd both been betrayed by those who should have protected them. Both turned to the police for healing. But whereas September married her cop savior, Tee became a cop to save herself.

Karma roused and pressed her wide black shoulder against Tee's leg. Tee smiled and smoothed the Rottweiler's rusty cheek patch, immediately feeling her tension drain away. Her headache still lingered, but she'd had worse. "I'm okay." *For I wish it to be so.*

She'd worried the young dog might not be allowed on the train. Sure, she could declare Karma as a service animal, but that meant labeling herself. She might be damaged goods, but refused to shout that fact to the world. She'd managed long before Karma came along, and could do without the dog if need be—not that she'd want to. Thankfully, trains allowed K9 officers on board without question, so showing her badge smoothed the way.

Redford hadn't been keen on Tee taking the dog with her everywhere, so she had to tread softly around him. Maybe that'd change, now he had his own dog. The more useful Karma proved herself, the more welcome they'd become as a team. Tee used every opportunity to teach Karma new things. Lia had drilled that lesson into Tee's head. So she counted the train ride as a teachable lesson for the dog. Besides, Tee had nobody she trusted to care for the dog if she had to spend days in South Bend.

Tee wondered again how Karma would react to Shadow. She'd read somewhere that wolves mated for life. September should know, as a dog expert. "Guess we'll find out, won't we, honey-girl?"

Karma woofed and wriggled her stump of a tail.

Tee had never been in love. Only ever loved one person, her Aunty. And now Karma. Probably never would find anyone to put up with her moods. She couldn't bring herself to open up enough to risk a relationship. But with Karma she felt safe, happier in the dog's presence. She leaned forward, resting her forehead against the dog's neck for a brief moment, and smiled when Karma slurped her face.

As the train pulled into the platform at South Bend Airport, Tee grabbed her duffel in one hand and gathered Karma's leash in the other. She followed the signs, walking the entire length of the small terminal to reach the car rental area.

Tee didn't like to drive in snow, but she had realized during the ride that she couldn't be at the mercy of civilians like September. The other woman's connection to Clear Choice Laboratories, however tenuous, might complicate the investigation. Tee needed to do things right, she needed her own wheels.

She managed to get an SUV. Tee gave Karma time to take care of personal needs at the doggy relief station nearby, stopped to buy them a muffin to share, and a steaming tumbler of chai. They walked the short distance to collect the ride. Tee pulled a towel out of her duffel and spread it on the back seat. "Kennel up." Karma leaped in and happily settled in the center, so she could stick her head between the front seats and monitor proceedings.

Tee climbed behind the wheel, stashed her bag on the floor, and adjusted the seat to her short legs. The cold made her knees and hips hurt worse. Lately she'd walked like a *kupuna* three times her age, not that a granny would appreciate the comparison. She sipped her hot chai.

"Sucks getting old, honey-girl." Karma whined as if in agreement. Tee shook out three extra-strength Advil and dry-swallowed them. The pain had abated behind her eyes, but a muzzy cloud remained, as if everything filtered through fog. "Shake it off,

Teves. You're a cop, for God's sake. Redford stuck his neck out for you." He'd put in a word for her with the Captain. She couldn't mess this up, refused to let a little headache and sore muscles stop her. Helping to clear this case made points on her path to becoming a detective.

Karma poked her blunt muzzle between the seats to nudge her arm, and Tee absently rubbed the dog's ear. "Okay, let's go talk to the bookkeeper. Shouldn't take long." Unless Sissie Turpin demanded a warrant. Redford could help with that, if need be, but it'd delay things and she'd have to stay in South Bend longer than the couple of days she'd planned. Innocent people bent over backwards to help investigators, or should. Tee didn't expect much, if any, delay. "We'll interview her, get the files, and be on our way."

Tee cranked up the heater, switched on her phone's driving directions, and wrinkled her nose at the mileage estimate. Turpin worked from her home northwest of the city proper. She'd be driving directly into lake-effect snow. She switched on the wipers, adjusted the heat to defrost, and drove slowly out of the rental lot.

The computerized woman's voice on the phone—why not a guy's voice?—and a dearth of traffic got her out of South Bend proper and onto the county road in record time. Street signs, hard to read even in the best of conditions, made Tee grateful for the smarmy phone voice prompting each turn. Each time it spoke, Karma tilted her head one way and then the other, intrigued by the electronic sound. But after twenty minutes even the dog lost interest and propped her rusty chin on the back of Tee's headrest.

The blowing white sizzled against the windshield. Intermittent gusts pushed and pulled at the car. Tee's shoulders hunched as she squinted to see through the reduced visibility. She held her breath and took her foot off the gas until the only car she'd seen in fifteen minutes, which materialized out of the storm like a ghost heading toward town, passed. Tee coasted to a near stop, catching her breath, second-guessing the wisdom of interviewing Turpin in this weather. It could wait a day, so she didn't end up in a drift.

She looked both ways, checked the mirror, and slouched in her seat. "We can't turn around." Empty pastures unrolled on each side of the road, with no houses, barns, or outbuildings visible. You couldn't see where the road and shoulder ended. She didn't want to end up in a ditch. "Guess we keep on, Karma."

At her name, the big dog stood up, woofed softly, and stared out the window. She balanced on the back seat like a surfer riding the waves, eyes attentive on the unrolling landscape beyond the windows. Tee knew she'd have to polish nose prints off the glass before returning the car, but didn't mind. Living with Karma made Tee more aware of her surroundings than ever before. The dog's hearing and scent sense pointed out wonders of the world she'd previously missed or ignored.

So ten minutes later when the big dog cold-nosed Tee's neck, she flinched, but paid attention. "What's up, honey-girl?"

Karma whined and clawed the rear passenger-side window, leaving paw-streaks on the steamed-up interior.

Tee hesitated. According to the phone, the Turpin house sat less than a mile ahead, just up the hill. She wanted to get this done. Also, stopping the car on the slick road might make it hard to get rolling again.

She compromised. Tee took her foot off the gas and coasted, rolling down the passenger window to better see past the swirling white.

The big dog jittered with increased excitement, whiffering scent carried by the breeze. Karma barked and stuck her blunt face into the wind.

Better not be a squirrel. Karma loved chasing the tree rats in the park near her Chicago apartment. This was different. They'd not been together very long, but Tee couldn't imagine the dog would alert in the car over something like that. Tee strained to see. The expanse of white remained unblemished except for a small mound off to one side. The closer they got to the mound, the more agitated Karma grew, until her whines mixed with gargled barks. Something there for sure. Worth the risk to get stuck?

Tee shook her head and rolled the window back up. "We'll stop on the way back. Police business first, downtime after." Decision made, she pressed gently on the gas to maintain momentum up the steep hill.

An explosion of snow erupted from the small mound in the field. A black and white dog dashed in front of the Tee's SUV, stopped, and barked.

Karma redoubled her own barks. Tee choked back a surprised scream. She reflexively stomped the brake, the car skidded sideways then turned in a slow circle. They ended up facing back the way they'd come, thankfully still on the county road. Tee breathed again, not realizing she'd held her breath.

"What the holy hell!" Tee shoved the car into park and ran hands through her short dark hair. Karma continued to harangue the dog that stood in the middle of the road to block their way. "That's enough already, Karma shush!" Her head wanted to explode and the barks didn't help. "Okay, I see the dog, yes I see." She half-turned in her seat, to get Karma's attention. The dog finally quieted, but still quivered with concern. "The dog's just fine, Karma, probably belongs to a local farm." The snow-covered mound might be a dog shelter for all she knew. But she wondered why the mostly white dog with his black, bear-like face—looked like an Akita—hung out in the middle of a deserted field?

Karma leaned in to slurp Tee across one cheek, then returned her gaze to the big dog guarding the road. It stood on the highway, preventing the car from moving. Karma pawed the window again.

The Rottie loved other dogs and probably missed having canine company. And Tee hated the thought of any animal being out unprotected in this weather. But the Akita had shelter. Once they left, surely it would go back into the dugout. They'd check on the way back to town, after interviewing the bookkeeper. Tee shuddered at the thought of Redford's scathing criticism, should she put police business on hold to rescue some mutt. Besides, with less than a mile to the destination, better to press on than postpone the interview.

The stray dog sat in the middle of the road. He watched Tee manipulate the car around, toward Turpin's house. She congratulated herself for keeping it on the road. With no traffic to speak of, she had the full two lanes to use. Tee decided to back up for a running start to get up the daunting hill.

Tee put the car back into gear, ignoring Karma's continuous whines, and gingerly built up speed. But before she'd traveled a third of the way up the slope, the Akita once again dashed directly in front of her car.

"Son-of-a—"

This time, she refrained from standing on the brake and the dog danced away before she connected. But the break in momentum proved enough to stop her climbing the rise, the car's tires spun without gaining purchase. Tee stopped before the car slid sideways into the ditch.

Karma woofed with excitement, and paw-danced on the back seat.

"Okay, dog, you win this round." Tee fumbled with her seat belt, adjusted her coat, pulled on gloves, and stepped out of the car. She left the car running, with the heater. No way she'd put a strange dog in the rental with Karma. But both dogs had been so insistent she stop. She remembered Lia telling her, "Always listen to your dog." So she'd listen and go check things out.

Before she got near the stray, he raced away, running back to the snowy hump in the field. Tee sighed and slogged after him. She winced when ice spilled over the tops of her boots when her feet sank into a foot and a half of white.

Behind her, Karma's barks and gargled invectives spilled out the partially open window, upset she'd been left locked up in the car. "Don't need you dashing off chasing your new buddy," Tee muttered, and then raised her voice, yelling over the susurration of the wind. "Hey *ilio*, what do you want? Don't tell me *Timmie's down the well.*"

He—or maybe a she, hard to tell—turned back only briefly, then hurried on to the shelter.

Tee didn't laugh at the joke. Her head hurt too much, and if this dog just wanted to play, she'd be royally pissed.

A cry—a human sound—answered.

"Oh my God!" Tee redoubled her efforts to reach the snow-covered mound. A car, on its side. The shattered windshield painted with frozen blood. Someone inside.

The dog again looked back at Tee, padded close to the car, and leaped lightly up onto the vehicle's exposed side. Carefully balanced like a tightrope walker, he paced to reach the open passenger window, peered inside, woofed, and waited for Tee to approach. Once she was abreast the window, the dog leaped off the car and dashed away, disappearing into the snow as if the storm conjured the hero Akita back to his cloudy guard post.

"Hey, you in the car, can you hear me?" Tee cleared away powdery snow from the windshield. A crumpled form, a young girl with purple hair and bruised eyes. The girl blinked, mouthed something, and Tee saw dried blood from her nose. "I'm afraid to move you. I'm a police officer and will get rescue out here to take care of you. Hang on."

No warmth came from the crashed car. It would become the girl's icy casket without quick intervention. Tee knew all about hypothermia. The cold killed quickly and efficiently.

Tee clambered back through the snow to reach her car. The warmth begged her to stay, and feeling guilty, she gave in to the invitation while she called for backup. She opened the rear door, and when Karma leaped out she collected the dog's blanket from the back seat, grabbed the still-warm tumbler of chai from her dash, and stumbled back to the accident.

Karma beat her to the car, intent on reaching the accident victim. The big dog had already mimicked the Akita's acrobatics and hopped up to peer inside. Tee pushed Karma aside. She had to stand on her toes to see into the angled window. "Hey, you. What's your name? Hey! Are you awake? Talk to me."

"Charlie." The girl answered softly, lips blue. "So c-c-cold. Why'd Bishop leave? Kept me warm. Licked my face, Bishop s-s-saved my life."

"Bishop? Is he your dog?" She didn't want the girl to know her dog disappeared. "Here's a blanket, get this wrapped over you. The emergency crew is on the way." She watched as the girl used one hand to pull the fabric close, then Tee carefully lowered the tumbler of warm chai. "Drink it slow. Should help warm you up."

"Not mine. Bishop just showed up. Tag on his collar had his name. Thought I dreamed him at first. He kept waking me up, wouldn't let me sleep, snuggled close. I don't even like dogs, he scared me at first. Cats are better but I lost my cat…" Her voice shook. Charlie looked around, suddenly frantic. "Did you catch him? Don't let him get me!"

"Bishop? The dog ran off." Tee's brow furrowed. Charlie's confusion could be from a concussion. Karma pushed her big square head next to Tee, breathing heavily and offering her best Rottie smile. "Oh, this is my police dog, Karma. She won't hurt you."

"Not the dog. A man. He ran me off the road." Charlie sniffled, throat catching in a sob. "I think he killed Sissie."

Chapter 25

She'd learned to drive in bad weather while living in Chicago and South Bend. September hated ice and snow, but thankfully muscle memory quickly returned. She gritted her teeth and prayed for no traffic as she blew through one stop sign after another in the residential area.

The car behind her bumped and then hit her harder. She nearly slid off the narrow street. Fewer stop signs appeared and she pressed harder on the gas, speeding up in tiny increments to stay in control of Angela's car.

Her attacker smashed into the rear of the car again. He grew bolder with fewer houses and witnesses. She managed to hold the car steady down the center of the street, but the next bump could spin her out of control. She had to head back to town proper, get to a more well-trafficked area.

Keeping one eye on the mirror, September took her foot off the gas, turned the wheel, and barely managed to hold the road. The SUV behind her overshot the turn, and took time to stop and reverse. September drove carefully, shoulders hunched, brow furrowed at the odd noises the car made from its crunched front and rear ends. She made another turn, heading back into the business section of South Bend and away from residential neighborhoods. She switched off her lights. They didn't help much in the driving snow, and only shined a beacon for Mr. Bleak to follow. If Angela's car stalled, she'd have to grab Macy and make a run for safety.

More lights ahead announced a larger intersection. But before she made it halfway down the street, the SUV appeared from a side street. He hit her broadside.

Macy screamed. His claws dug into September's shoulders to keep his perch. September's teeth clacked so hard she bit her tongue and grimaced at the salty blood flavor. Her temple smacked the driver's side window.

His engine growled. He bulldozed her car across the pavement and smacked it into a utility pole.

Macy clambered off of the headrest and head-butted her neck so hard, September thought she'd bruise. When the SUV backed away, then sat waiting an endless moment, she knew the next impact could end everything. September wound her arms around Macy's warm, solid body, snuggling and frantically zipping the purring cat inside her coat.

Mr. Bleak wanted them to run. He'd pick them off as they came out. She had no choice, had to take the only chance they had.

"Love you, Macy. Always remember I love you."

The SUV's engine roared. It barreled toward them.

Swinging open the door, she dove into the snow barely ahead of the impact. Her leg screamed in silent anguish when the SUV impact closed the car door on her thigh. He backed away again, ready to smash the car a third time. She had seconds to move, escape, hide...

September rolled, scrambled to her feet, and gambled precious seconds to slam the driver's door. Fogged windows hid the interior. He'd check inside before coming after them. That could buy them enough time.

She limped away in an unsteady crouch then ducked down a narrow alley crowded with dumpsters. Behind her, the SUV's third impact echoed. September increased her pace, running in a limping gait once around the corner at the end of the alley. She cradled Macy's bulk like a pregnant woman sheltering a child, and raced back the way she'd come. She had to find the police, Shadow, or both, before Mr. Bleak tracked them down.

Chapter 26

Tee called Karma from the doorway, and together they backed away from the macabre scene. Only then did the big orange and white cat stop hissing and growling. He guarded access to the room from his perch on the chair back, his paws kneading the top of Sissie Turpin's head.

Turpin's murder had been staged to look like a suicide. Even though she had been expecting it Tee shuddered, then fished out her phone. She dialed 911, waited for the operator, identified herself and reported the death. By rights she should sit on her hands until the locals arrived. Their county, their jurisdiction.

She set her jaw, and her eyes narrowed, taking in the details. While she waited for the locals to arrive, Tee carefully recorded the scene, taking pictures and video with her phone. She performed a careful, visual search of the room from the door. After enlarging the picture of the drug vial near the body, she dialed her phone.

Redford answered on the third ring. "Busy time here, Tee, what ya got? Make it snappy."

She quickly filled him in. "Whoever got to her staged a suicide. Looks like an overdose of midazolam after drinking heavily. The needle's still in her arm."

"How'd she get that drug? It's a controlled substance."

"She had a script from a veterinarian for one of her cats, to control epilepsy..." She crossed her arms. "The label's on the vial, clear as day. Makes me wonder about Detweiller's suicide."

He sighed. "Different drug, same M.O. In both cases, if it's the same do-er, he used whatever was at hand. Damn. That's cold. And takes planning. Goes a lot deeper than we suspected."

"Yeah." She nodded, her shoulders tightening, and craned her neck to relieve the tension. Karma leaned against Tee's thigh. She stroked the big dog's broad head, grateful for the company. "She's got a bunch of cats running loose. Locals are on the way and I asked for animal control. Can't get close to the computer. But from a distance, looks like the electronic files got trashed. Lucky for us— and her—the witness got away."

"You sure she's a witness, not the killer? Be a neat trick to point at some mysterious bad guy who disappears into the storm."

Tee scratched Karma's neck when the dog whined. "Possible, I guess. But Charlie truly seemed terrified. The girl's savvy, but young, but tries to seem older. I need to talk to her again."

"Okay, but get everyone to keep it quiet she survived. If she's a witness, she could be at risk." He spoke to somebody in the background before returning to the conversation. "What's her name again? Charlie Cider? Who is she, anyway? A relative of the vic?"

Tee wished she'd asked the girl more pointed questions. "Not clear. Purple hair, buzz cut above both ears, nose ring, tats on the fingers." She'd been more concerned about saving Charlie's life. Lucky for her, the furry Akita angel named Bishop decided to intervene and keep her warm.

"We'll run the name and description, see what we come up with from our end. Meanwhile, work with the locals. I'll reach out from here, see if I can light a fire. If you've got the same lake effect snow we're fighting, it could be a while." He paused before adding, "While you're waiting, anything you find out could save the locals time, doncha think? Probably be grateful for the help."

Tee grinned, then disconnected. Just what she wanted to hear. Redford had deniability if she screwed up, but she had a nod and wink to sniff around.

The guard cat hissed again when she disconnected the phone and made eye contact with her. The others milled around the dead owner's legs, while one sat in her lap. "Karma, I don't think the cats like us very much."

Karma whined and wriggled, her answer to a wag. As far as she knew, the dog's only experience with cats was raising Gizmo. Her imposing form and foreign smell probably scared these fancy show cats to death, but Tee wanted a quick look at the computer before the locals arrived.

"What would September do? She's the animal expert. Wish she'd answer her damn phone." At the thought, Tee texted the woman one more time, but didn't wait for an answer.

"Karma, let's go." Tee led the dog down the hall. Maybe if she moved the Rottie out of sight, the cats would calm enough to let her into the room. "*Down. Wait.*" The dog obediently dropped into a prone position. She whined but remained in place when Tee returned to the murder scene.

Before attempting to move anything, Tee took additional pictures of the position of the body, the toppled cat tree, and the open cabinet that contained several accordion file folders. She cocked her head to one side, noting the caster wheels on the office chair in which the victim sat. Cats continued to mew and circle the chair. If she could roll the chair away from the door…

Tee belatedly remembered Lia's caution about making eye contact with strange dogs. Hard stares meant a challenge and could escalate aggression and attack in dogs. Maybe the same held true for cats.

Karma whined, then yawned noisily from down the hall. "Karma, shush. Good girl. Wait." Tee knew the dog meant the cats no harm, but if they'd never been around a big dog, they wouldn't know that. Karma outweighed even these jumbo-size felines four to one. She'd never seen such fluffy, mammoth cats.

Tee spied a dust mop, still fuzzy with cat fur swept from the floor. She grabbed it, hefting the slight weight of the aluminum pole, and walked slowly through the door. Tee kept her eyes focused away from the cats, and turned sideways the way Lia and September had taught her to deal with strange dogs. She hoped it worked for these creatures, too.

The guard cat paused his kneading, stared hard at Tee, and growled. She froze and held her breath until the growl faded away. She extended the mop-end of the pole until it contacted one of the chair's casters. With gentle pressure, the chair rolled forward.

The cat hissed, but clung claws more tightly into the fabric of the chair back. He had no intention of abandoning Sissie.

With continued pressure, the chair rolled farther into the room. It swiveled three quarters around so that the woman's dead eyes no longer stared back at Tee. She sidled into the room, still clutching the dust mop in case the orange and white beauty launched an attack. But the distance seemed to have calmed the cat. Tee continued to avoid eye contact as she made her way into the office area.

Unfortunately, she'd moved the chair in front of the file cabinet. She had to get the cats completely away from the body. Maybe food? According to Charlie, she'd been chased from the house late last night, so the cats hadn't been fed in at least twelve hours. Karma loved bacon-flavor treats, and Tee had some in her kit. But did cats like the same thing? She doubted it.

Opposite the desk, a small refrigerator stood on the counter beside the large sink. Keeping one eye on the now silent cats, Tee opened the door, and found an open can of stinky cat food. *Yes!*

Two of the cats swiveled big-eyed faces in her direction when the refrigerator opened. One stood and meowed with anticipation. Tee grabbed the can of food and walked slowly past the toppled cat tree and into the cattery proper.

The open doors on each kennel held a name tag, probably identifying each resident cat. Clean empty food bowls sat in each. So Tee tipped out a finger-size portion of nasty wet food into each bowl. "Hey cats, dinner time. Hungry, are you hungry?" She entered the one floor-to-ceiling playpen on the opposite side of the aisle and closed the door, protection in case they decided to coordinate an attack like a campy horror movie. "Hey, kitty-kitty-kitty, which one of you is Sherlock? Where's Meriwether? Treats for the cats."

The magic "treat" word brought all running, each hopping up into respective kennels—all but the guard cat. Tee waited another thirty seconds before she slipped out the playpen door and closed the kennels of the resident felines. The two areas labeled for Sherlock and Meriwether remained empty.

The guard cat finally left his perch and stalked toward Tee. He held his tail straight up with just the tip waving. His ears continued to swivel to the side like airplane wings, but he chirruped and seemed interested in taking the chance on her—if treats were involved.

"Hey there, Sherlock?" He didn't respond. "Meriwether?"

The orange and white cat chirruped again, and his ears came forward. "Meriwether, good boy, cat. Sorry about your lady. Brave cat to protect her."

She didn't try to touch him. Tee set the nearly empty can on the floor of the playpen, and stood back until he entered. With a sigh of relief, and feeling accomplished, she latched the door. With all the cats safely confined, she could take a closer look at the files.

"*Mahalo*, Karma." At the release word, Karma hurried to join Tee and sat in the doorway. Karma would give her a head's up when the local police arrived. Until then, Tee quickly flipped through the paper files—some more than twenty years old. Other than cat pedigrees and show records, she found no outside bookkeeping records linked to Detweiller. One file held records of sales of the Maine Coon kittens, and when one name caught her eye, she looked closer.

At her shocked intake of breath, Karma whined. "This can't be a coincidence, honey-girl. Different last name, but I mean, how many people do you know named September?"

Chapter 27

When the surprising text arrived, Southgate knew it had been routed through several intermediaries. Not from Wong, but probably one of her minions. He'd already heard about Detweiller's demise.

>Coat hanger?! Clean up your own mess. Meet in ten, or you're done.

He slumped in the front seat of his car and dropped his face into gloved hands. He'd set up Angela's death to look like suicide, but slipped up somehow. He shook out an antacid, then two more, and chewed all three. *Delay. Deflect. Think*. He could still make this work. He had no time for this!

<Ten not possible. Tomorrow better.

Southgate stared through the fogged windshield at the entry into the gated community where he lived. Roxanne expected him for a holiday meal with her parents. They'd driven in special for an early Christmas celebration. Even the kids—Paul from Notre Dame and Sharon from her law job in Chicago—had set aside busy schedules for the rare family gathering.

>Clock's ticking. Cops on the way. Nine minutes.

"Damn!" Decisions from the past left indelible marks on the future. He didn't regret the path chosen. Those with weaker stomachs missed opportunities he'd embraced to get ahead. Look where it got him, successful beyond his parents' wildest dreams. He'd overcome every roadblock, helped make others wealthy along the way, and now Angela would derail everything from beyond the grave.

No.

Southgate took deep, pained breaths, and silently fumed. His face heated and his hands tightened on the leather-padded steering wheel. He imagined revenge scenarios before dismissing them out of hand for the indulgent fantasies they were. He couldn't touch Wong or her organization. She could have him swatted out of existence. But his message about Detweiller—actually a warning to her— granted him room to save his own life, and maybe his reputation. He texted back, lips curled in a snarl.

<Where?

He sucked in a breath when the reply came. Angela Day's house. Clear across town. No way could he get there anytime soon, especially with the weather. "What the hell, I'm screwed anyway." He dialed the number and expected to be ignored.

The phone picked up before the second ring. "Shut up and listen. Your faked suicide won't stand. You'll take the fall, and raise uncomfortable questions for our mutual employer. So fix it, or I will. Permanently." The voice, obscured by some sort of electronic masking, was quickly disconnected.

Southgate immediately redialed, but got a recording that the number had been disconnected.

He hit the dashboard with his fist. Hell! He wasn't a professional killer. What did they expect? He hadn't planned to hurt Angela. How was he supposed to fix things? Southgate shoved the car in gear and drove as quickly as he could without sliding off the road, mind spinning.

Nearly twenty minutes later, he arrived. Bright police lights strobed the snow, painting the ground bloody. Busy professionals trampled the front lawns and sidewalks of Angela's block, and rubber-necking neighbors huddled in coats on nearby porches. Southgate had to park a block away and limp in. The bruise from the dog's bite had left his leg tender. He composed his features as he hunched shoulders against the cold, mentally rehearsing a plausible story.

"Sir? Sir, stop, you can't go in there." The police officer stopped him, as expected.

Southgate raised his voice, wanting to be heard by those in

charge. "But this is Angela Day's house. She's my client, what happened? I was just here, did something happen to her?" He'd slipped up somehow, better to let them know they'd find innocent evidence of his presence. He allowed his voice to break. "Please tell me she's okay."

The police officer stood aside as the detective in charge stepped up. "Your client? And who are you, sir?"

"George Southgate." He stuck out his hand. "And you are…?"

"Detective Franklin Steele. Of course, I know who you are, Judge. What brings you out in this weather?" He gestured back at the house. "Someone you knew?"

"Oh no, what happened?" Southgate cleared his throat, his shaky voice no longer an act. Detective Steele had a reputation for clearing investigations that stymied others. "Angela Day is a family friend. Her late husband Peter and I knew each other for years." He blinked when he finally took in the state of the house. The splintered remains of the garage door gaped open, offering glimpses of the interior.

Steele registered Southgate's surprise, and indicated the battered building. "Somebody didn't bother opening the door. In a hurry to get away from the place." He grimaced. "I used to work with their son, Detective Chris Day, before he died. The whole department takes this personally. I'm sorry to tell you that Angela Day is dead."

Southgate let his jaw drop open, then turned away. He didn't want to overdo it. Steele would recognize theatrics. "How awful." His voice cracked all by itself.

"Looks like she hung herself. With a coat hanger—pretty bizarre. When did you see her? Recently, you say, as a client."

"More as a friend." He corrected the man, mind racing. Thanks to the texts, Southgate knew the suicide wouldn't stand. But Steele wouldn't know he had reason to doubt the obvious conclusion. Maybe best to play both sides. He took a big breath, and gave his prepared spiel. "Yes, she'd been depressed, but I didn't think to the point of suicide. Her husband died not long ago. And this week's the anniversary of her son's death. She seemed more angry than sad." He baited the hook, and waited.

"Angry? How so?"

"She called me for advice to deal with an unwelcome visitor. Her former daughter-in-law invited herself to visit, making trouble." He paused, as if debating whether to share, and concluded in a rush. "Angela blamed this woman for her son's death. They hadn't spoken in years, not since his funeral. Bad blood, there." He turned to look deliberately at the shattered garage door. "I wonder if she drove off in Angela's car. I'd like to ask her some questions myself."

"So would I. What kind of car, do you know?"

"It's a blue sedan, and it's wrapped around a utility pole three blocks over. Thank God you're here!"

Southgate whirled at the voice and squinted into the night. A dark-haired woman stumbled into view, cradling an oversize belly.

Steele brushed past Southgate to head her off. "And just who are you?"

One of the neighbors called out. "She's the one crashed Angela's car out of the garage. Told us to call 911."

Southgate gaped, then quickly recovered. "It's her! Detective, that's the woman I told you about, Angela's daughter-in-law. She must have done something. Why else did she run?" He shouted, pointing a shaking finger with outrage.

She ignored him, focused on the detective. Her arms shifted and a cat's face—a cat?!—poked out of the neck of her jacket. "I'm September Day, Detective Steele. We need to talk."

Steele looked nonplussed. The beginnings of a smile evaporated when a black flash of fur dodged past the outer circle of the police perimeter.

The detective drew his weapon. Nearby officers followed his lead, all taking aim at the German Shepherd pelting toward them.

Chapter 28

"Don't shoot him!" September lurched between the aimed guns and Shadow. Her arms reflexively tightened, and Macy struggled, meowing in protest. "My service dog won't hurt you. Shadow, *down.*"

Shadow dropped at her feet, whimpers and cries of happiness spilling from his throat. His tail swept a single angel-wing in the snow, and he pressed his cheek against September's ankle.

Detective Steele's aim didn't falter, but neither did he shoot. "Put it on a leash."

September shook her head. "Can't. Left his leash in my car." She nodded at the nearby SUV. "During the attack, we got separated. Thought I lost you again, baby-dog," she said, sotto voce, and then cleared her throat. "Now he's with me, he won't move from my side. Unless I tell him to." Her chin jutted out. "We're a package deal."

Steele grudgingly holstered his weapon and motioned the other officers to stand down as well. "Attack, huh? And you made it out, with a cat besides?" Steele pursed his lips and took in her bedraggled appearance, but to his benefit, he didn't roll his eyes. "That's a story I want to hear."

"Aren't you going to arrest her?" The tall stranger's face turned a mottled red. "That's her, Detective. She did something to Angela." He didn't shout, but spittle flew from his lips with the intensity of his accusations.

"All in good time, Judge." Steele tipped his head at the tall stranger. "We'll talk later."

September looked with surprise from the Detective to the Judge when Shadow growled and his body poised to spring at the stranger. She didn't recognize his voice. His face showed no signs of coffee scald, either. Her shoulders relaxed. She placed a gentle hand on Shadow's ruff. He looked up at her face, furred brow wrinkled with concern.

The Judge took a limping step toward September, gloved fist raised and shaking. Shadow growled louder, and stood, placing himself between her and the stranger.

"Judge Southgate. George." Steele sharpened his tone, finally breaking through to the upset man. "I'll get your official statement tomorrow. Thanks for your help. But I got my hands full here for the next several hours."

The Judge brushed snow from his wool coat as if shrugging off his outburst. He adjusted his hat and strode away.

He must be Angela's friend, maybe the lawyer they were supposed to meet. September didn't blame him. Finding out about Angela's death would be devastating to her friends. The circumstances made things worse. Adrenalin kept her own shock at bay, and Shadow wired, but would soon wear off. The vision of Angela's suspended body would haunt her forever. Without Shadow by her side—*thank God he'd returned to her!*—she'd melt into a puddle.

"It's horrible what happened to Angela. Is the Judge a friend of hers?" Macy mewed and struggle in her arms, probably overheated within the down-filled coat.

Steele nodded and narrowed his eyes. "What's your story? Were you with her when she died? Looks like a combat zone in there."

She shook her head. "She was gone when I found her. Hanging in the garage." She shuddered, her arms tightening again. Macy objected and dug his claws into her middle. "Can I put him in my car? Then we can talk without distraction."

"Sure, go ahead."

"Uhm, well…" September rocked from foot to foot. "See, I left my bag inside by the coat closet, with my car keys. That's why I had to take Angela's car to…to get away." Damn, it sounded like a graphic novel invented by teenagers high on energy drinks. "Can I get my keys? And my bag? Big ugly green canvas thing." She hesitated, then added, "There's a spare leash in the bag, too."

The idea of a leash seemed to convince Steele. He motioned to a nearby officer. "Look for a green canvas bag near the front door and bring it here." As the officer hurried into the house, Steele turned back to September. "We'll need to vet the contents first."

"Of course." With any luck, Mr. Bleak hadn't managed to take all of Chris's papers. Without them, she had no evidence to explain why Angela asked her to come.

Her eyes welled. Chris, Dakota, and now Angela. All felled by the curse she carried.

The officer quickly reappeared in the open front door of the house. She shook her head, holding out her empty gloved hands in a palm-up posture.

Steele stared at September with a hard smile, opened his mouth to say something, then thought better of it.

"Maybe he took my bag." Shadow whined and pushed against her thigh. Unconsciously, her hand dropped and clutched the ruff of black fur on his neck. She felt the dog relax and her own heart-rate slow.

"Who? Oh, the guy who ambushed you?" He forced a laugh. "What, did your bag match his outfit?"

She glared. "He wanted Chris's files from the bank lockbox. I had them in my bag." Disappointment made her throat ache. "Are you sure nobody could find car keys, or find my bag?"

Shadow stiffened and stood at attention. His neck arched with interest. September glanced down at him and he woofed softly as he stared up into her face. His tail waved, eager.

September nodded understanding, but tightened her grip on Shadow's fur. Without taking her eyes off of the dog, she spoke quietly. "Detective Steele, my dog thinks he can *find my bag*. It's still here somewhere. If not inside, then maybe dropped nearby. It could still have Chris's evidence…"

Steele crossed his arms, his eyebrows raised with mock surprise. "Your dog told you that? Read his mind, did you?" Sarcasm dripped, interspersed with impatience. "Sure, and my Barney and Milkdud will be the next big dog-and-cat winners on that big-assed TV talent show." He called to the police officer in the doorway. "Put Ms. September here in a car." His face tightened. "You can cool your heels until I've got time to debrief you. And, your dog damn well better not mess in the car."

When Steele turned away, September released her grip on Shadow's ruff. "*Find bag!*"

Steele yelled when Shadow leaped away. "What's he doing?" He put one hand on his gun, but thankfully didn't draw. "Call your dog. Dammit, I don't have time for this!"

September tried not to smile as she watched Shadow test the air for scent. "Shadow loves tracking games. If it's here, he'll find my bag. And maybe evidence about Angela's murder."

Shadow made a beeline toward the house next door where looky-lous gathered on the porch. They squealed and backed away when he bulldozed through white drifts to reach the holly shrub on one side of the front steps. The dog stuck his head into the snow beneath the plant first on one side and then on the other. His front half disappeared, until only Shadow's black haunches and wagging tail remained in sight. And then he backed out of the snowdrift, dragging the green canvas bag by the handle. Shadow dropped the handle momentarily, shook himself briskly, and then grabbed the strap once more and carried it proudly back to September.

"Good dog, Shadow." September motioned to Steele and watched as Shadow again picked up the bag, lugged it closer and deposited it at the detective's feet.

One of the porch gawkers, after a whispered conference with family members, called out to them. "We helped that other man collect the papers that spilled out. Was that okay?"

"Well, I'll be a swamp-toed nitpicker." Steele hooked a thumb for one of the police officers to take the neighbor's statement. He took off his glasses, polished them between the fingers of his gloves, but only managed to smear the lenses. He pocketed the glasses. "Neat trick. Don't suppose you staged that little demonstration?"

September bit back her retort. She'd be suspicious, too, given the circumstances. She fumed silently as he picked up her bag and fished inside to dig out the keys. Without a word, she allowed Steele to escort her to her car.

Shadow stayed glued to her side, keeping his body between September and the detective. Steele watched closely when she opened the rear of the car, carefully unzipped her coat, and unhooked the cat's claws from her sweater.

"Good boy, Macy-cat. You've been through a lot. Chill, big guy, and I'll be back soon." She spilled some dry kibble into his bowl. September closed the car door, satisfied Macy would relax and sleep off his adventure after finishing his meal. She cocked one eyebrow at the detective and his look of surprise. "Need to search my car, too,

I suppose? There's a gun in the glove box. I'm licensed to carry."

"Good to know." He eyed Shadow with suspicion. "You want to put up the dog, too, please." When she would have objected, he held out his hands. "Granted, he's well trained. I now remember your and Chris's dog was too. But meet me halfway. Put him on a leash, so he doesn't go dashing off and get himself shot."

She felt heat rise to her cheeks and nodded, accepting the short lead he found in her bag. Shadow happily slurped her cheek when she bent to hook him up.

"Tell me what happened. Someone ambushed you, and killed Angela?" The green bag hung from his hand.

"I don't know if the same man attacked Angela. He wore a ski mask. He'll have scald marks on his face where I threw hot coffee. And possibly cat bites through leather gloves. Macy tried to get him."

He smiled. "Resourceful. So noted."

"It bought me some time to get away. He called himself Mr. Bleak." She remembered what he'd said, about her taking the blame. "Angela invited me to visit, but we kept missing each other. It's all on the text messages on my phone. The cell phone's in the bag, too."

"Not the story that I heard. Interesting. Don't suppose you've got anything to support the invitation?"

She pointed to her bag, and he allowed her to dig inside to find her phone. When prompted, she gave him the code to unlock it.

He scrolled through the messages as she continued. "I'd left Macy—that's my cat—in the guest bedroom. When we returned, I sent Shadow to check-it-out. That is, to clear the house of intruders." The dog whined, his ears pricked, and he danced a jig, anticipating the action. She smiled, and put a calming hand on the white scar on his cheek.

September watched Steele's face as he perused the text messages. He poked a tongue into his cheek, and inhaled a long breath.

"Shadow alerted that something was wrong, but he got shut outside in the back yard when the man ambushed me. He said he'd kill me, and make it look like Angela did it and then hung herself." Tears finally threatened and she angrily dashed them away. "I didn't know she'd been hurt, and was … was dead … until I ran to hide in the garage and found her." She straightened her shoulders. "This Mr. Bleak ambushed me and shut off the power. I couldn't get the garage door open. So when I found Angela's car keys, I took the only way out."

"Drove a car through the garage." Steele shook his head in amazement, and handed her back the phone. "That's quite a story. But there's no text messages on your phone, not from Angela or anyone else."

"What?" She grabbed it from his hands and quickly scrolled the history. Everything had been deleted. "That makes no sense. Wait. You could recover deleted text messages, right?" She grabbed at her bag and he watched her shuffle through the contents. "Damn! He took Chris's files, too." Her cell phone rang, but before she could answer, Steele took it back. His brow furrowed when he read the caller I.D. "How do you know Officer Teves?"

"Tee? I helped train her police dog, Karma. Oh crap, I am supposed to pick her up at the airport." She reached for her phone again, but Steele held it beyond her reach and answered.

"Officer Teves, this is Detective Frank Steele of the South Bend P.D. I got a call from Detective Redford a little while ago, bringing me up to speed on your investigation." He listened, raising one eyebrow at September. "Yes, I'm looking at her right now. Yep, she's got a big ol' black German Shepherd dog with her. And a cat." He stifled a laugh. "So she's not a nut-case after all? She's legit? Wonders never cease." He handed September her phone. "I want you at the station tomorrow morning. We'll get your statement then."

She turned half away, whispered fiercely. "Tee? What'd you tell him? I've had a day from hell, and..."

Tee cut her off. "You and me both. Did you get Macy from a breeder named Sissie Turpin?"

September stopped, mouth open. What did that have to do with anything? "Macy was a gift from... Never mind." The big Maine Coon was the only good thing to come out of those horror-filled years with Victor. "Yes, he came from that cattery. Why?"

"Give your phone back to Detective Steele."

"C'mon, Tee, what's going on? I planned to visit the cattery sometime during my visit here. Before everything went to hell, that is. So what should I know?"

After a brief silence, Tee sighed loudly. "I think Turpin helped orchestrate a decades-long conspiracy. And the cats may hold the key."

Chapter 29

Shadow waited for September to unhook the short leash and stuff it in her pocket. He hopped into his usual backseat perch in September's car, next to where he'd left bear-toy, but watched anxiously until she climbed behind the wheel. Only then did he begin to relax. He whined softly, still anxious about all of the strangers milling around the house. Shadow rarely had reason to threaten and even fewer occasions to bite. But scary people made indelible impressions. He knew the man's scent, and the taste of his boot. Shadow swiveled his head, cocking his ears and huffing the cold air, ever watchful for the limping stranger.

There! Far in the distance, quickly walking away. He could see movement far away much more clearly than things closer to him. Shadow growled again and pawed the window button. He stuck his nose out when the glass scrolled down. The man's scent rode the wind, colored with anger and fear, and some murky emotion that spoke of dread. The man climbed into a distant car.

Some people like Steele naturally commanded authority, never needing more than tall posture and direct stares. Others, like the departing man, used words to mean one thing while their body said something else. Bad people demanded obedience with sticks, fists, and guns, lying to themselves about their worthiness.

Good-dogs could always tell the difference. Even when the tall detective pointed a gun at him, Shadow knew Steele didn't want to shoot. He just used the gun like a dog's warning snarl to say, *back off!* Shadow could tell Steele had no heart for blood-letting. Oh, he'd shoot, but only if necessary.

Not like the burn-faced man. Shadow whimpered under his breath. That bad-man didn't bluff the way dogs did, to avoid hurtful confrontations. No, he delivered on every threat. The scent of intent didn't lie.

"Shadow, you'll let out all the warm air." September sharpened her voice into a command. "*Window.*" His ears drooped but he pawed the button again at her direction, so the glass closed. September fiddled with something on her own door. "I wish the child locks were set-and-forget, so I don't have to remember each time. You're too smart."

He sighed. He learned from an early age to obey people, even if it made no sense to a good-dog. September knew much more than Shadow and could do wonderful, exciting things like make cars go fast, and create warm air gusts to thaw a dog's cold paws.

But sometimes dogs knew better than people, even than September. So Shadow paid careful attention to what September asked of him. He mostly did as she asked, because they loved each other and he trusted her. But sometimes he had to ignore her requests when it meant keeping her safe. He'd made a mistake today when he got locked in the yard away from her. He wouldn't let that happen again.

Crippled with a blind nose, and deaf to all but the loudest noises, September—really, most all humans—couldn't tell bad people from good ones, scary situations from safe. For a long time, to compensate for these deficits, September kept everyone at a cautious distance, even him. But the more she learned to trust Shadow, and special friends like Combs, the happier she became. Shadow wanted September happy, so she didn't suffer from any more terrifying *gone-times.* But the more she relaxed, the more Shadow's responsibility grew to keep them both safe.

His tummy growled.

"I heard that. We missed dinner, didn't we?" September half-turned in her seat, to reach back and gently rub his ear. "I think we all deserve some treats."

He thumped his tail and licked his lips. Macy, in the carrier in the rear cargo area, meerowed loud agreement at the *treat* word. Shadow leaned hard against her hand, grateful to have September's attention all to himself. He almost didn't care about the missed meal. Almost.

His paws ached from the snow. He licked and nibbled away the ice that crusted fur between his pads. Shadow enjoyed snow, but he'd been out in the weather far longer than usual.

"Detective Steele won't let us back into the house to get our stuff, at least not for a while. We'll figure something out for food."

Shadow tipped his head at the word, and licked his lips.

"Drive-through on the way to the dog park it is. We need to meet some old friends. You remember Karma?" She fiddled with something and the hot air rushed louder.

Arching his neck, Shadow leaped to his feet. He stared through first one side window and then the other, tail waving. Karma! Where? A burbled whine turned into a frustrated bark.

September laughed. "I guess you do remember your girlfriend. Settle down, Shadow." Her voice turned somber. "You and Karma can have a play date, while Tee explains what she means by a feline conspiracy."

Chapter 30

Southgate pulled up to his house in the exclusive neighborhood, grateful the snow had abated. Bright lights streamed from the windows and tasteful white sparkle lights in the shrubs and front trees created a holiday picture worthy of Hallmark.

He drove past his in-laws' sedan parked to one side on the massive driveway. Southgate punched the opener and the garage door rolled upwards, revealing his wife's car on one side. His son's sporty coupe fit neatly into the third slot, right next to the small sailboat temporarily in storage for the winter. He sat for a long quiet moment behind the wheel, listening to the tick-tick-tick of the engine cooling and the grating as the garage door closed. Already over an hour late, he'd need a good story.

"You can do this." He looked in the mirror, smoothed his hair and tested a couple of smiles. Roxanne would expect him to be pleasant, at the very least. Her parents wouldn't care, their mutual dislike set aside only for holiday appearances, but he couldn't disappoint Paul. He'd never seen his son in a bad mood. The young man's mere presence made others smile in delight. Southgate loved his daughter Sharon dearly, but Paul held his heart.

Now, as his world crumbled around him, Southgate struggled how to salvage the situation. He'd risked everything to keep his secrets hidden. He'd been careful, dammit! No matter what the voice on the phone insinuated, nothing but speculation and circumstantial evidence linked him to Angela's death. Southgate straightened his shoulders, unlatched the seatbelt, and climbed out of the car. He knew the law. And if worst came to worst, he had the resources to fund a legal battle, and the backing of respected people of power. He'd be fine. Hell, a little scandal these days gave one's reputation a certain patina.

Southgate limped through the garage door into the kitchen, still angry about his encounter with September's dog, and called with forced cheerfulness to announce his arrival. "Something smells marvelous, Roxanne! Hey Paul, what's new with you?" He congratulated himself on his jovial tone as he shrugged off his soaked overcoat and wiped his shoes on the mat.

His cell announced a text and he quickly scanned the message from Sharon.

>Running late with the storm.

The drive from Chicago could be treacherous. He quickly texted back, encouraging his daughter to find a hotel rather than risk driving.

>No, I'm already past the worst. C U in 20 min.

Argumentative. Always had to have the last word. Just like a lawyer. Yep, his daughter, all right.

The white floor tile and pale yellow walls shined in the overhead lights. Roxanne liked bright colors, and the matching yellow counter-top, edged with blue paisley tiles, could have been the cover of a high-dollar home decorating magazine. A number of liquor bottles, including Roxanne's favorite wine and Southgate's preferred sipping Haitian rum, shone on the kitchen island. He filled a squat glass with ice and poured a generous serving of Barbencourt, downing half the amber drink before topping it off once more.

A keening trill echoed in the room. An enormous black and white longhaired cat sidled into the kitchen, fur a-bristle and eyes dilated. She hissed and growled.

Southgate froze. What was wrong with the beast?

"Paul, come get your cat. Kahlua's gone nuts." The animal, usually quite friendly, would sometimes ignore everyone but Paul. Maybe the cat smelled the dog on him. "Paul? Something's wrong with your cat."

Paul didn't answer. For the first time, Southgate noticed the oppressive quiet of the house, not even the clink of cutlery breaking the silence. "Roxanne? Where is everyone?"

He edged around the room, pressing his back to the wall. Southgate clutched his drink like a talisman, but kept his focus on the Maine Coon cat that continued her low ululating whine. She rubbed against the yellow wall and her fur painted a red smear.

"Paul? Roxanne!" He ran from the kitchen into the adjoining formal dining room. And skidded to a stop.

The celebratory dinner still cooled on holiday serving platters. Southgate's family—Roxanne, her parents, a girl he didn't recognize, and Paul—*oh dear God in heaven, Paul!*—sat vacant-eyed and slack-jawed around the table, as if awaiting the guest of honor to take the last empty seat at the head of the table. None moved. Not a breath stirred the pine-scented candles burning in the centerpiece.

"Took you long enough. Take your seat. Yes, right there, next to your daughter." The stranger entered from the living room. Tall, nondescript. Red inflamed skin covered half his face. He wore a black knit watch cap that hid his hair, and large aviator sunglasses that covered most of his expression. A gun in one gloved hand leveled at George.

George looked around blindly, tears clouding his vision. His chin quivered. "Why?"

But he knew. He hadn't been able to clean up the mess. Kaliko Wong sent this man to finish the job. Southgate recognized his own gun in the man's grip and understood the story to be told—every murder–suicide demanded a narrative. This scalded-face puppet-master, the voice on his phone, forced his return to Angela's house. Detective Steele would find concrete evidence of Southgate's guilt. And that would be enough for the police, and the public, to buy into what came next.

"I said, sit down. Right there, by Sharon." He motioned with the gun.

George fell into his chair, the drink clunking on the table beside his plate. His hands clutched the pristine holiday tablecloth in front of him. He eyed the sterling place settings, used only during holidays, leaving his right hand near the knife. He couldn't catch his breath. The shock weighed his limbs, he moved through molasses.

"My son!" His voice broke. "He's only nineteen."

"Nothing personal. I don't question the targets: you, the wife, both kids, any additional witnesses." The man took a step closer. "Don't make this harder than it has to be. They felt nothing, never knew what happened." He offered the words like a gift.

The man's words finally pierced his brain fog: *Both kids*. But Sharon hadn't arrived. Yet.

His wife and son were dead. But Sharon would live, by God!

Southgate stood, chair toppled backwards into the wall. With one hand, he splashed rum down the hit man's front, and with the other tossed a lighted candle against the fabric. He never felt the bullet that ended his life.

Sharon Southgate parked in front of the big house, grateful the snow had abated. She'd managed to get past the worst of the weather before they closed major highways. Nothing new there. Regional snowstorms blew fast and furious, but the local road crews prepared in advance. When she and Paul were younger, they always crossed fingers any snowstorm lasted past midnight. If snow stopped earlier, the roads could be cleared in time for morning school buses.

She smiled at the memory. Hard to imagine Paul at Notre Dame. He'd skipped two grades in school, and had always worked hard, like he had limited time or something. Sharon looked forward to the annual Christmas dinner, one of the few times everyone could enjoy just hanging out. With her mother's volunteer schedule, father's workload, Paul's classes, and her new job demands, coordinating schedules required weeks of planning. She'd put in extra hours just so she could take the rest of the week off and spend time with family.

Sharon swung out of the car, grabbed the overnight case, and trudged to the door. The sidewalk had been swept clean earlier in the day, but fresh powder caked the pathway. Her bag left twin roller marks as she dragged it behind.

Snow on the front steps, though, curdled with a mess of footprints. Sharon squinted, and wrinkled her nose. Someone lost footing and slalomed off the top. She stifled another grin, betting that Paul and his visiting girlfriend missed a step. Wouldn't be the first time. She'd been surprised he had time to date. Sharon wondered if he'd warned Mom?

As a courtesy, she rang the doorbell before inserting her key. Her father's job over the years made him the target of the occasional crazy, so they always kept the door locked. So her eyebrows climbed when the unlatched door swung open without benefit of the key.

"Hello? Merry Christmas—early! I finally made it…" She

hesitated. A foul, burned-hair smell choked the air. "Where is everyone?"

Before she could step into the foyer, a twenty-pound flash of black and white fur leaped against her chest. Sharon reflexively caught the cat, the impact driving her two steps backwards onto the slick front steps. "Kahlua, what the hell?"

She struggled to keep her balance, but tumbled backwards, fall broken somewhat by one of the forsythia bushes beside the entry. Sharon scrambled upright, reaching to recapture Kahlua before she raced away. Paul would kill her if she lost his cat.

"Here kitty. Kahlua, don't do this to me." Sharon kept her voice soft, not wanting Paul to find out. With luck, she'd corral the intrepid feline, return her to the house, and Paul would never know. She sidled slowly toward the trembling feline, but as soon as she came close, Kahlua led her another half dozen steps away from the house.

The cat finally crouched in the snow and allowed Sharon to scoop her up. Sharon buried her face in Kahlua's long coat, nuzzling the beautiful black and white fur, but wrinkled her nose—again, that nasty smell. "Let's get you back inside."

She turned, hugging the cat in her arms. Only then did she recognize the sticky copper smell, and blood that stained Kahlua's fur. Before she'd taken two steps, the house exploded into a fireball.

Chapter 31 (34 Years Ago)

Tana struggled to shake off the effects of the anesthesia. Her body didn't work right. The bed shuddered as the camper sped up. She tried to speak, but her throat hurt and words wouldn't come. Her memory fragmented, she remembered nothing.

A baby cried.

She was going to have a baby soon, too. Tana felt for the familiar swelling. Gone. A foreign ridge of numb tissue, sutures bristling to hold it together, marked her bikini line beneath the smock. Her brow furled in concentration to make sense of the change.

The cries came again.

Had she already given birth? She couldn't remember. Tana whimpered and pulled herself into an awkward seated position. Her muscles wouldn't obey, and the weakness made Tana tilt and nearly fall sideways onto the floor. She squinted. Three car seats sat on the floor with an infant strapped securely in each. The twin girls slept, oblivious, but the tiny newborn screamed.

Her baby! Tana's eyes brimmed and an overwhelming joy bubbled from deep inside. Never mind she couldn't remember anything, she'd puzzle it out later. Right now, she needed to hold her baby.

Tana stumbled across the jouncing camper and fell to her knees. She clutched her abdomen. Something deep inside ached, muffled by the drugged fog. She marveled at the beautiful newborn. Unstrapped the infant, snuggled it close.

The camper stopped. Footsteps. The driver stood over her, surprised and then angry she'd awakened.

He wrestled her baby away and held the screaming infant beyond her reach. Told her lies. Said Tana's baby died. Said the newborn belonged to Rosalee, already signed away. Three sets of adoptive parents awaited. Tana must leave. Now.

She shook her head, tears streaming, arguing, pleading with him, offering anything. But he lifted her upright and dragged her to the exit. Tana grabbed hold of anything to impede his progress: the chair back, the kitchenette table, the door frame.

He unlatched and kicked open the door, then stepped down onto the dirt path. He dragged Tana after him.

Her hand grappled and found an empty wine bottle toppled off the table. In a repeat of the action that set her on this path, Tana hit him. He dropped like a stone.

Tana closed and locked the camper door, scrambled to reach the screaming baby. She crooned softly, smoothing the down-soft blond hair for only a moment. The doorknob rattled, followed by pounding. The flimsy lock wouldn't hold for long.

The other two babies awoke. The camper resounded with whimpers and sobs. Tana's own cries drowned out the infant chorus.

He'd left the keys in the ignition. She forced herself to strap the baby back in the carrier. Then Tana lurched into the driver's seat, shoved the camper into gear, and drove away, into her new life.

Chapter 32 (Present Day)

September pulled into the dog park beside the only other car. Tee raised a hand in a wave of acknowledgment before climbing out.

Shadow paced on the back seat, tail waving, and woofing under his breath. Tee opened her rear car door and the black Rottweiler hopped out. Shadow's soft whines morphed into gargled trills of excitement and he pawed the back window. It scrolled downward, the icy breath of wind splashing into the warm car.

"Hey, stop that. Shadow, wait!" Had she hit the wrong button on the key fob again? The new car's settings, different than her old vehicle, confused her. September fiddled with the door console, but stopped the action too late.

In delight, Shadow stuck his face out, breathing in the familiar scent. He puffed his cheeks with anticipation and leaped through the window. September sighed, and scrolled the window closed, before she joined Tee outside the car. After releasing them into the enclosed area, together they watched the dogs greet each other.

Karma transformed from serious police dog into a simpering coquette, spinning in the snow. The dogs took turns sniffing each other, offering play-bows and happy woofs interspersed with growls of joy.

"She's got some filling out to do, but looks good." September watched the pair race around the field. "Doing well? Training regularly, Tee?"

"It's only been a week. But she's doing great. Karma reminds me she wants to play her games so I don't forget." Tee rubbed her eyes. "The past two days I've let it slide."

September looked more closely at the woman's pale face. "You feeling okay? You look tired. Sorry I missed your calls about the change in plans. I kind of got sidetracked." She grimaced and rubbed the bruise on her thigh from escaping Angela's car.

"Headache I can't seem to shake, that's all. Life goes on. Can't let that get in the way." Tee squared her shoulders, a half smile turning her usually stoic expression softer as she watched the dogs' joyous interplay. "I hate snow. It's pretty, but messy. Nothing like the Islands." She nodded at the dogs dashing about, leaving blizzards in their wake. "But nothing dampens Karma's enthusiasm. Lia said not even her spay surgery slowed her down. How are her puppies?"

"Lia swears the Magical-Pup reads her mind—or vice versa. I'll show you pictures later. But for now—" September shivered, flexing her bare hands. "Can we get out of this weather? I'm not a fan of cold, either."

"I've got the file in my car. It's pretty sparse." The women hurried to Tee's rental and September climbed into the passenger seat, relishing the warm air blast from the dashboard. "It goes back more than twenty years and only has a few entries. Probably she kept digital files more recently, but her computer was clean."

"I don't understand why you're here, Tee. What does a cat breeder have to do with your investigation?" September kept one eye on the two dogs gamboling about the snow-covered area.

Tee pulled off her gloves to better access the accordion file. "Sissie Turpin kept the books for some sketchy folks, including that Detweiller character you asked about."

"Oh." She wished she'd looked closer at Chris's files before they were stolen. "Chris apparently investigated Detweiller several years ago. Detweiller got caught with some discrepancies in his lab results more recently. Is that why he killed himself? Does it have anything to do with Chris's notes from before?"

The inference was the lockbox files had everything to do with September, but she couldn't figure out any connection with Clear Choice Lab. She flexed her feet. The feeling had finally started to return, but her sopping wet socks and shoes weren't helping.

Tee leaned forward. "We've got no record that Detective Chris Day ever investigated Detweiller. That's brand-new intel and we have no way of knowing what he found out. With Detweiller's records destroyed, our best hope was his bookkeeper kept duplicates." She patted the thin accordion file of documents. "This has nothing to do with Detweiller, but there's some kind of connection. Both Detweiller and Turpin were staged to look like suicide."

Just like Angela, she thought.

"Detective Redford—that's my boss—said not to waste my time. But a name jumped out at me, so take a look. If you see what I suspect, it's worth a deeper look and maybe Detective Steele would give it an eyeball." She stared at September with rapt attention.

Curious, September took the file, balancing it on her lap, and shuffled through the various pockets. Each slot contained sales documents for a particular year. But rather than the dozens of annual kittens one would expect from an average size cattery, only one to three kittens were placed in any given year over the past thirty-odd years.

"It's the most recent file. Familiar name, don't you think?" Tee urged her to flip ahead, her eyes bright with anticipation, fairly bouncing in her seat. "Yes, that's the one."

September scanned the document, then slowly nodded. "Yes, that's me. Male kitten, registered name *Sissypurrz Amazing Amaretto.* That's my Macy."

"I knew it! So that's a second connection. Your husband investigated Detweiller because of you. And now the woman keeping Detweiller's secret books gave you a cat, too. But what does that mean?" She took out her phone and texted Redford with an update. Tee grimaced, breath hissing through her teeth at whatever response she received.

September didn't correct Tee. Victor arranged for Macy, not as a kindness, but as leverage. Abusers often threatened to hurt a beloved pet to keep victims in line. But Tee didn't know that detail of her history. Besides, September couldn't imagine what ancient kitten sales had to do with a corrupt laboratory operation.

Tee took back the file and shuffled further. "Here, looks like two cats were sold at about the same time seventeen years ago. What's up with the funny names? Sissypurrz Caramel Capucino, and Sissypurrz Karaoke Kahlua."

"*Sissypurrz* is the cattery name, a clever play on words with Turpin's first name. It can be a challenge to find a descriptive name that's not already in use. Catteries often incorporate funky spelling. The rest specifically identifies the individual cat, again often with unique spelling." September shrugged, and added, "Different registering organizations have specific requirements. For instance, there's a limit on the number of letters or characters in the name. And there's no rule about it, but to keep track over the years, some breeders name litters according to a particular theme. Like the months the babies are born, or musical terms." She waved at Shadow across the field, digging snow with his nose. "Some German Shepherd breeders use an alphabet system, so all the pups in a litter have registered names starting with the same letter. Shadow came from the "S" litter." She looked closer at the paperwork in her hands. "Catteries might do that, or name a particular litter according to a theme. In this case, it's drinks: Cappuccino, Kahlua." She answered absently, focused on the other information on the attached pedigrees. The two cats were littermates.

"She had nameplates on the cage doors for the cats, too, but they weren't long fancy ones. And there were more nameplates than cats. Guess it doesn't matter." Tee rubbed a spot of condensation clear on the window to better see where the two dogs played. They'd stopped chasing and now intently sniffed various spots along the fence. Shadow leg-lifted as she watched.

"Call names can be abbreviations of the registered names, or something entirely different. My a-MAZ-ing cat chose to respond to Macy." September smiled, knowing the explanation made little sense. "Dog registration names follow their own set of rules."

"With Turpin dead, what happens to her cats?"

September's stomach constricted at the thought. "Animal control for now. Responsible breeders take care of their cats, and of each other in the community. I can make some calls." She thumbed through the other years. "Macy is the youngest on this list. By now, many of the others have passed. I don't know what it means, though." She handed the file back to Tee.

"I'll dig deeper, now I know there's a real connection. Redford has to see that the cats are important."

"Yeah, Macy has always known he's important. That's part of being a cat." September smiled. "Keep me posted, will you?" She shivered again, and hugged herself. "I came to find out what Chris wanted me to know, and to say goodbye for the last time. So I can move on. We'll go home tomorrow, after I meet with Detective

Steele and give him my official statement." With the instant news hitting the internet, she needed to call Combs and bring him up to date before he heard it from colleagues. September dreaded that call. "I need a place to stay tonight that'll accept big dogs and a cat. We can't go back to Angela's—not that I'd want to."

Tee rubbed her eyes. "Share with me and Karma. I'll update the reservation." She grinned. "They already expect a police dog. What's another one, more or less?" She quickly made the call, and forwarded the confirmation numbers to September's phone. "Head there now, so you can get cleaned up. I'm supposed to share this info with Detective Steele. But he's at the hospital interviewing the hit-and-run victim." At September's puzzled look, she added, "A girl witnessed Turpin's murder and got run off the road for her troubles. The driver sounds an awful lot like the guy who attacked you and stole Chris's files."

September scowled. "Mr. Bleak got what he wanted. So at least we don't have to worry about seeing him again."

Mr. Bleak checked the scald marks around his eyes in the car's rear-view mirror. When Southgate lit the alcohol, the sunglasses had saved his eyes, but he looked like a hobo caught in the rain. Both cat-bitten hands sustained burns when his gloves caught fire, and his watch cap melted against his head. He'd peeled them away, taking flesh along with the fabric. Scooping and applying snow stopped the pain temporarily, but he worried the damage might be permanent when the flesh remained numb. He had taken a few moments to head back inside and turn on the gas fireplace to ensure all traces of his presence, and the blasted cat, were erased.

After changing clothes and donning a fresh paper cap that hid the worst of his injuries, nobody would question his presence. Never before in his long professional career had so many things gone awry. He took pride in providing the best cleanup service for his extraordinary clients. They rewarded him with generous paydays, and the leeway to improvise when needed. As a professional, he didn't know or care about his targets. Nothing personal.

Until now.

He hung a disabled card on the car mirror and parked in the closest spot to be ready for a quick departure. Once he adjusted the surgical mask over his face, Mr. Bleak climbed out and jogged into the hospital. Nobody gave his scrubs a second look. His detached attitude appeared focused on vital medical questions.

The girl witness saw his face, knew who he was, and too much more besides. He couldn't believe she'd survived the car crash when he got the call to finish her. He'd correct that situation first, then address his unfinished business with September Day.

Chapter 33

Tee pulled into the parking lot at the emergency entrance, surprised there weren't more vehicles. In Chicago a snowstorm meant more fender benders and worse, so the ER filled up fast and she'd been at her share of roadside tragedies. Maybe South Bend drivers played it smarter, rather than taking inclement weather for a macho dare.

In the back seat, Karma sat up straight and arched her neck. She offered a happy grumble-growl, wriggling in the seat, probably hoping to go inside, too. Tee met the dog's expressive brown eyes in the mirror, and shook her head. Immediately, Karma whined and stood up, pawing at the door in argument.

"You're still wet, honey-girl. And I don't think the hospital staff would appreciate paw-tracks muddying up the place. Next time, okay?" She'd like to take the dog with her. As a K9 officer, Karma would be accepted in many parts of the hospital. But Tee wanted staff to willingly cooperate and grant access, not antagonize them with an unwelcome dog, especially since the Rottie's protection skills weren't needed. Karma couldn't bite a virus, or guard against infection, after all.

Her knees protested as she left the car. Tee hurried to the entrance carrying the accordion file. At the information desk, Tee presented her credentials and asked for directions to Charlie's room. Prepared to argue, Tee had to bite back the sharp words ready on her tongue when she instead received directions. She punched the floor button, then leaned against the elevator wall, surprised the movement prompted the small space to spin. For a long moment after the doors opened, Tee stood with her eyes closed, willing herself to hang on. She hadn't eaten in a while. Just low blood sugar. She headed out of the elevator with purpose, but her steps faltered at Detective Steele's expression.

He met her at the ward desk. "What're you doing here? I got a call from your superior. You're supposed to be on your way back to Chicago."

Her headache flared, probably in response to a spike in blood pressure, but she kept her tone even. "First train in the morning. Detective Redford said I should give you these, first." She set the accordion file on the counter, then grabbed the edge to steady her balance. She nodded down the hallway. "Have you talked to her yet?" She leaned against the wall, surprised she needed the support.

"No, still waiting for them to bring Charlie back from X-rays for her head and arm. Hoping she's not too doped up to answer some questions." He stared at her flushed face. "You don't look so hot yourself."

She pushed away from the wall, determined to push through the dizzy spell. She couldn't appear weak, not in front of Steele. "I'm fine. Just need to eat something."

"What's that?" He eyed the file but didn't touch it.

"Records from Sissie Turpin's house. Your team left it behind, didn't think it pertained. But there's a connection." She filled him in.

He shook his head. "I don't get it. So what, Turpin sold a bunch of cats, and one happened to belong to your dog trainer friend. But that's from years ago, right?" His smile was condescending. "Sometimes a coincidence is just that." His phone rang, and he turned his back to answer.

Tee seethed, but tamped down her impulse to respond. She'd learned the hard way to choose her battles. She got it. Steele didn't care about decades-old history when he had two recent deaths to investigate. She comforted herself with the fact he believed—or at least wanted to hear more from—Charlie. Even without the coincidental cat placement, the connection begged a deeper look.

Down the hall, an orderly in a mask and a nurse wheeled a gurney into view. Tee straightened, bracing herself against the counter when the room threatened to spin. *Damn, maybe she picked up a bug.* "Hey,

Detective Steele, that's Charlie back from X-ray." She saw the small figure stir and raise one hand in feeble greeting before being wheeled into the distant room.

Steele turned back to her, still deep in conversation on the phone, but quickly disconnected. "I've got to go. Explosion and fire, looks like arson, over at a Judge Southgate's house." He scowled as the nurse and orderly exited Charlie's room. "I still need to talk to the girl, dammit." He gestured with the phone. "I got no choice, it's a command performance. The victims are friends of the mayor."

"I already have a rapport with Charlie. I can question her now and fill you in by phone. Or when you have the time." She bounced on her toes, then added quickly, "Sir." And waited

The nurse approached and looked up from her electronic tablet. She nodded to Detective Steele. "She's been sedated, so keep it short. She's got a concussion, bloody nose we cauterized, and a dislocated shoulder we reset. She needs rest."

Steele took off and polished his glasses, staring at Tee as the nurse walked away. "You want in on the investigation that bad?"

"That's why I'm here. Yes sir, absolutely." She smiled and leaned forward, but then killed the expression, not wanting him to think badly of her eagerness.

He checked his phone again and with a muffled curse stuck it back in his pocket. "Okay, Teves. I'll smooth things over with Redford for the delay, but then you're done. Find out what this girl knows, get a description of the guy, record anything she heard, and call me. Immediately. Got it?"

She nodded, but he'd already grabbed the accordion file and was quickly striding to the elevators. Tee almost ran to the room and knocked. Without waiting for an answer, Tee pushed into the room. "Charlie, feel like talking? I'm Officer Teves, the one who found you in the car."

The man in scrubs startled and backed slowly away from the girl's bed. The IV lines swayed when he released them and he adjusted his mask, but turned away before he spoke, voice gravelly. "She needs rest. Go away." He scribbled notes on the wipe-off board on the wall.

"The nurse down the hall said she could talk." Tee glanced at Charlie and raised one eyebrow.

Charlie blinked slowly, still groggy from sedation. A large purpling bruise colored her brow. They'd cleaned up most of her bloody nose and stitched up the laceration in her shoulder, but crusty rust marks trailed down her neck. "I can talk. I want to talk." Charlie twisted to answer the tall gowned figure, but he stood just out of her field of vision. "My arm doesn't hurt now. They gave me some good drugs before the X-ray, then popped it back into place. Really good drugs." She giggled. Her loopy smile and slurred words surely stemmed from the medication.

He didn't turn around, but nodded agreement. He continued to make notes.

"Excuse us, please. This is a police investigation." Tee straightened, surreptitiously bracing herself against the door frame when another dizzy spell threatened to take her to the floor. Her head pounded. "Any chance I could get some aspirin?"

He didn't pause on his way across the room, but she recoiled at his bright red complexion. She must have really gotten under his skin—literally. Maybe she'd ask at the nurse's station for aspirin before she left. Or coffee. Maybe both. Tee waited until he'd left the room before she pulled a small rolling chair to Charlie's bedside. "How're you feeling? Is there someone I can call?"

Charlie grinned again, but her eyes welled and lips trembled. "Like I said, the pain's not too bad. There's nobody to call. Not since Sissie's gone." She hiccupped before taking a steadying breath. "She treated me nice. Was going to help me with...with stuff."

The comment spoke volumes. Grabbing a tissue, Tee offered it to the girl. Charlie took it with her good hand. "I need to ask about what happened. Take your time, okay? I'm going to take some notes and also record your statement so there's no misunderstanding." When Charlie nodded, Tee set her phone on the nearby rolling tray and set it to record. "This is Officer Tee Teves, taking a statement from Charlie Cider..." She raised her eyebrows, prompting a response.

"Well, it's Charlotte, but nobody calls me that." She dabbed her eyes again.

"Okay, Charlie. What's your relationship to Sissie Turpin?"

Licking her lips, Charlie's eyes darted around before meeting Tee's. "I met her at a cat show. Sissie gave me a place to stay and I helped her out with the cats. That's all."

"So you're not related?"

"Heck, no." Charlie jutted her chin, defiant. "We helped each other, that's all. There's no law against that."

Tee smiled. "No law against friends helping each other." She guessed that Charlie's relatives, if any, didn't rate highly on the "nice" scale. They'd figure that out later. The traumatized girl witnessed a murder, survived an attack and wreck, and needed some space. Even so, Charlie seemed remarkably steady after all she'd been through. "So what happened last night? Tell me in your own words."

Charlie shrugged, then winced and clutched her injured shoulder with her good hand. "Like always, I cleaned out the cat area before going to bed. You know, scooped poop, picked up toys, swept up litter, and dished out food. They get special canned food at night. The cats love that. Anyway, I heard the doorbell ring. Sissie went to answer. At first I didn't pay any attention."

"When did you notice something was wrong?"

"Sissie yelled. An argument of some kind." Charlie wrinkled her nose. "I couldn't make out the words at first, but then she yelled again, told him to leave."

"What was the argument about?" Tee spoke softly, the way she'd talk to a spooked horse. Charlie seemed reluctant to share any details, either hiding information from fear or something else. "You're safe here, you know."

"Yeah, I've heard that before." Charlie muttered, then looked away before she continued. "Look, the argument made no sense. Something about computer records he wanted. She ran a bookkeeping business, did taxes, too. Personal and private information. So it wasn't hers to share, ya know?" She glared at Tee as though expecting an argument. "Sissie was a good person. She wanted to protect her clients. That's all. But he wouldn't listen." Her lip trembled again, and she cleared her throat.

"What happened? Charlie, you're not in any trouble." Tee leaned closer. "You wanted to help Sissie, right?"

Charlie nodded, and gulped back tears. "He slapped her around, but nothing serious. I couldn't see him, but I could tell, even through the door."

Tee's throat tightened. *Getting slapped around wasn't serious in Charlie's world.* Degrees of abuse. Yeah, she could relate.

Tee slammed shut the door on her own memories, suddenly wishing she'd brought Karma along. The dog kept the demons at bay. She stuck one hand in her pocket to finger the ever-present seashells. "You heard the guy pressuring Sissie to give up computer records?" Tee pressed her fingernails into her clenched fist, wishing she had something sharper to break the skin. Just a little, that's all.

"Yeah. Sissie's tough, though. She had a hard life, too, and knew how to survive. She wouldn't let a few slaps risk ruining her business." She hesitated, then added, "I mean, I don't know her clients, or anything. But word gets around. She gives up one customer and everyone else cuts her lose. Right?"

"Charlie, are you sure you don't know anything specific about Sissie's clients?" Tee yanked her hand out of her pocket to clutch the blanket on the edge of the bed, feeling dizzy again. "It's important."

The girl looked everywhere but at Tee. "It's my fault she's dead. All my fault. I didn't mean it." She whispered, "My family always said I was poison. Now look what happened."

Squaring her shoulders, Tee straightened in the chair. "I can't help you without knowing what happened, Charlie. But you didn't kill Sissie. And you couldn't stop it. You're not in trouble for that. I promise." She grasped the girl's hand. "Why do you think it's your fault?"

"Because I took the computer files, the thumb drive. Sissie finally told him about the backups so he'd stop hurting her. But I already took them, figured I'd hide them away and she'd thank me later. I didn't know he'd kill her!" She sobbed. "And then he came after me, and I had to run, and oh God poor Sherlock, he'll hate me now..."

Sherlock? "Charlie, slow down, I don't understand. You have the computer drives with the files?" Redford would be over the moon.

"One of Sissie's cats, that's Sherlock. He's kind of my special boy, my favorite, like a big white teddy bear." She blinked, pulling her hand away to wipe her eyes. "I hope he's okay. He's got the thumb drive." She wiped her eyes. "What'll happen to the cats? You've got to find Sherlock, he's not used to being outside, especially in all this snow."

"Wait. A cat has the computer files?" Tee stood so quickly, the wheeled chair spun across the floor and bounced off the wall. She remembered luring all the cats into their labeled spaces in the cattery, but didn't recall a white one—and Sherlock's kennel was empty.

"He grabbed onto my shoulders so I looped the string around his neck to keep it safe. But then Sherlock got scared and bolted out of my car." Charlie's sobs increased. "He saved me, he fought him off, maybe even bit him." She smiled through her tears at that, then blubbered. "I had to leave Sherlock behind."

"Calm down. Calm down, Charlie. Hey, it's okay." She looked

around, wondering what to do. "Wait, I'll call for help." Tee hurried to open the door, just in time to see the flush-faced nurse striding away down the hall. *Perfect, just when you need 'em, they leave.*

"Can you find him?" Charlie's sobs increased. "He trusted me, and I r-r-ran out on him." Her final words escalated into near hysterics, perhaps the shock finally registering.

Tee rushed back to Charlie's bedside and pressed the call button. She made soothing noises until someone came, before grabbing her phone and leaving the room. She rode the elevator back to the lobby and called Steele as she walked to the car.

"Cats again? Just shoot me already." Steele's disgust easily carried over the phone. "I'm tied up here for the foreseeable future. Southgate's daughter, Sharon, survived the fire, the rest are dead. It's a mess, and the mayor's calling for an all-hands investigation. I don't have the time or the resources to care about a stray cat."

Tee waited for him to breathe and spoke quickly into the breach. "I can find the cat." She lifted her face to the icy night air. It felt good against her pounding head.

"Right, you've got a K9 with you. Okay, good. Find the cat, recover the files. And check in with Redford, I've not had a chance to brief him. If he gives you grief, he can call me." He paused, then added gruffly, "You got a place to stay?"

"Yeah, no worries. Redford knows the trains won't run before morning anyway."

"Okay, call it a night. Then start early tomorrow. Once you find that cat, go home, back to Chicago. No argument." Steele disconnected without saying goodbye.

Tee smiled as she rejoined Karma in the car. The big Rottie hadn't been trained to track cats, but Steele didn't specify how to do it, just authorized her to find the thumb drive. Eyes glowing, she drove to the hotel to meet September and her pet-tracking dog.

Because of his scrubs, the clueless cop questioning the girl in the hospital room never questioned Mr. Bleak's presence. She had prevented him taking care of the girl. Time enough to eliminate her later. She couldn't tell them anything that could hurt him, and only knew one of his aliases, easily ditched for his next incarnation. He'd always been lucky that way.

This assignment was beginning to threaten his reputation. In his line of work, a misstep could be terminal. He'd mitigated his failure to clean up Angela's death by terminating the judge's family. Pleased at the outcome, his employer offered him the chance to recover the computer drive once he reported its existence, dangling a hefty bonus for delivery by morning, to sweeten the deal.

Failure wasn't an option. He didn't want to be on the wrong end of a clean-up operation. How long would it take to find the cat? He needed a few hours to rest, and let the plows get the roads cleared, before heading back to the bookkeeper's house.

The cops had impounded the bookkeeper's car, but he avoided parking in the empty spot. Instead, he parked his car in the empty slot in the storage building, so that anyone out and about wouldn't see. The lady cop wouldn't come before morning, so he had the night to search. But the time for subtlety had passed; he would find, preferably, or destroy the thumb drive before morning, even if it meant fire-bombing the place to kill the missing cat.

He'd never had a cat, but remembered reading somewhere they could see in the dark. Mr. Bleak smiled at the thought, then winced when the tugged flesh lit his scorched cheeks aflame. From his go-bag, he donned thermal-image goggles. Unlike night vision goggles that amplified existing light, these tracked anything giving off heat, and should easily flag the presence of the cat. He also readied his gun. The cat bite in the fleshy part of his left palm had swollen so much, he'd have to shoot with his other hand. Not a problem.

Until today Mr. Bleak hadn't particularly cared one way or another for cats, or dogs for that matter. Too unpredictable. But, after being threatened, bitten on both hands, and clawed, his ambivalence toward the creatures had become active dislike. Weak minded individuals relied on pets as an emotional crutch. He had no need of emotion, or crutches of any kind. Once located, a single shot would solve all his cat problems. Not out of vengeance. Nothing so petty as that. But simply expedience. Nothing personal.

Chapter 34

"Shadow, chill!" September knew by his flagged tail and happy expression that the visitor at the hotel room door posed no threat. She checked the view first anyway, then opened the door.

Karma raced into the room, Tee following more slowly. September closed the door behind the smaller woman, concerned. She really didn't look well. Practicing yoga earlier had helped her own physical and mental discomfort. "I already showered. Fresh towels on the vanity. Maybe that'll make you feel better."

Tee nodded. "Feeling rocky. I've fought a headache ever since Chicago." She sharpened her tone to address Karma when the big Rottie discovered Macy. The cat leaped to the top of the television cabinet and stared back, perfectly poised and probably enjoying the opportunity to tease a new dog. "Settle! No roughhousing. I don't want the department to pay for damages after they waived the pet deposit for us."

The dogs looked properly chastised. September backed up Tee's directive with a silent hand signal, pulled out her baggy of Corazon Candy, and offered a couple of treats to the two dogs and cat. Shadow hopped onto one of the two double beds and settled with a sigh. Karma immediately joined him, prompting his tail to thump the covers, and the pair spooned like an old married couple.

That made September ache to call Combs. He'd already left two messages. She'd replied with only brief texts, promising explanations soon. She wanted to wait to actually talk with him until it was truly over, so he didn't consider flying to her 'rescue'. He and the kids needed this time together, and there wasn't anything he could do anyway.

"How'd it go with Steele? Chris used to say he was a hard case." September propped a pillow against the headboard of the same bed as the two dogs, and leaned back. "He did have my stuff collected and delivered when I asked, though." She'd barely unpacked at Angela's, so they'd simply shut her overnight bag and dropped it off. Thankfully, she'd packed extra disposable litter boxes for Macy, which she'd set up in the bathroom. She'd left Shadow's bear-toy in the car, so the two dogs wouldn't argue over it. "We already ate burgers. I told Shadow and Macy not to get used to that." She smiled, but Tee didn't respond. The woman really looked bad. "I would've ordered you a veggie burrito, but didn't know how long you'd be, but you could order room service."

Tee grimaced, dropped her bag, and sank onto the other bed. "Please don't talk about food." She shivered. "Maybe I caught a bug. Nothing a shower and some sleep won't fix. We've got to be up bright and early." She smiled, but it looked forced. Freckles across her cheeks stood out in stark contrast to her pale olive skin.

"We?" September raised her eyebrows. "I'm hitting the road tomorrow as soon as I talk to Steele. I thought your boss recalled you to Chicago."

"He did. But Steele's giving me some latitude first. And I need your help. Actually, I need Shadow's help."

The dog thumped his tail again at mention of his name, but didn't move. His head rested on Karma's shoulder.

September's shoulders tensed. "Something Karma can't take care of? It takes two days driving to get back to Heartland." She rubbed her face. "With this weather, maybe longer. And I can't leave until Detective Steele releases me." She studied Tee's hopeful face, recognizing the eagerness to prove herself. "Okay, Tee. What do you need?"

The smaller woman pulled off first one boot and then the other, flexing her toes and rubbing her feet. "Oh, that's better." Tee skinned off soaked socks as she spoke. "I gave Steele the files at the hospital and pointed out the connection to Macy. He wasn't impressed." She glanced up at the big cat, now crouched like a miniature lion atop the cabinet. "No offense, cat."

"Macy doesn't take offense. Cats don't care about our opinions." September laughed. "Isn't that right, Macy?" She gestured, making a finger-beckoning motion, and he launched himself from his perch to land with a soft thump on the foot of the bed. He hopped over the dogs as he padded up to her lap and curled into the space between her knees.

"Steele went to the hospital to interview the girl I told you about. Charlie Cider."

September widened her eyes. "That's her real name? I thought my name was bad." September stroked the cat, relishing his rumbling purr.

"Who knows? We'll figure that out another time." Tee took a big breath, then spoke in a rush as if expecting September to cut her off. "Charlie said she hid the computer backup, a thumb drive, to keep it away from the attacker. I suspect other motives. Charlie's got a past, and probably not above a bit of larceny. Anyway," Tee paused, darting looks at September to gauge her interest, "she hid the thumb drive on a cat. Who does that?"

"Really? How original." September glanced at Shadow hiding a small smile. He'd been only nine months old when he protected another thumb drive. "So call up the animal control, or whoever took possession of her cats. You don't need me."

"No, you don't understand. The cat ran off, so it's somewhere out in the snow, hopefully still near Turpin's house."

"A show cat? Out in this weather?" September shivered, and scratched under Macy's chin. She'd nearly lost him once. Cats kept inside their whole life had no experience how to protect themselves in the great outdoors.

Tee leaned forward, whispering in hushed, excitable tones. "The cat got away by the garage or storage shed. That's quite a distance from the house proper." She wiggled her toes again, then sat cross-legged on the bed. "I promised Steele I'd recover the thumb drive by tracking the missing cat. But you saw how Karma acted around Macy. And one of Turpin's cats looked ready to take Karma's face off. Mine, too. Besides, I don't think Karma would know to track Sherlock. Not the way Shadow's been trained."

September frowned. Once a dog learned the joys of cat chasing, training the behavior away proved challenging. A police dog needed to be impervious to such distractions.

"You haven't seen these cats, September. They're huge." Her

oval, tilted eyes opened wide. "I had to put Karma in a down-stay in the next room before I could get close to them and get them into cages. They acted nuts, just having Karma there."

"Sherlock's the missing cat? Great name." September sighed. "Here's the problem, Tee. Those cats saw their owner killed. They went through hell, and then saw Karma shortly after. They may already identify dogs—any dog—as a *very-bad-thing.* Sherlock dumped out in a snowstorm elevates his stress. It could be tricky having even cat-friendly Shadow track him."

"Then I'm screwed." Tee flopped backwards onto the bed, and Karma jumped up across to join her. Tee pushed the dog away, dodging Karma's slurping tongue across her face. "Recovering the evidence is the only reason Steele kept me on the case. Oh damn, my head." She rolled over and cradled her face in a pillow.

Macy burpled and head-bumped September's cheeks. "Not so fast, Tee. I've worked with Macy to track missing animals, especially cats. He's not fully trained. It takes a long time to get reliable results. But so far, he's pretty good. No guarantees, but we could give it a shot."

Tee sat up, blinking hard. "Thanks. That's better than nothing." She rubbed her eyes again. "Hey, do you have any aspirin?"

September got off the bed and rummaged for the travel-size bottle, which she handed to Tee. "Did Charlie see her attacker? He ran her off the road with his car, right?" She settled again on the bed, and Macy stretched upward to cheek-rub September's face.

Tee shook out three pills and dry swallowed them. "She saw him only briefly. He wore a ski mask and gloves at first, but she got a good look when he left her for dead. Doesn't help much, though." She closed her eyes and repeated the girl's description. "Pasty-faced, brown eyes, thin lips, receding chin. In other words, he could be anyone. She couldn't even guess about height, because she only saw him from her perspective on the ground, with him standing over her. She might be able to identify his voice, though. She heard him clearly when he interrogated Turpin." She rubbed her neck again. "But dark clothes, dark SUV. Does that sound anything like your attacker? If it's the same do-er, and you both can I.D. his voice or looks, we're ahead of the game. That is, once we find him." She stood, strode to the bathroom, and turned on water in the shower.

September called to be heard over the running water. "I heard him, too, but didn't get a clear look. My guy also wore dark clothes, gloves, and ski mask. And drove a dark SUV. But with this weather, that could describe 80 percent of anyone brave enough to be out in the weather."

Tee shucked off all her clothes but underwear as she spoke. "Charlie said Sherlock attacked the guy, so there'll be bite or claw marks. If he's a hired professional, looking like Joe Shmoe from Idaho works in his favor. Bet we won't find fingerprints, he's too careful. Still, anything out of the ordinary that marks him builds our case."

"If it's the same man, look for burns. I threw coffee in his face. By the way, why'd Steele let you question Charlie?" September wrinkled her brow, noticing Tee's long slim legs and one side of her back had a bullseye-shaped rash before the woman ducked into the shower.

"Steele got called away to a fire. Some judge's house, friends of the mayor." She sighed. "Ah, yes, I needed this!"

September set Macy to one side and crossed to the open bathroom door. "Don't mean to pry, Tee, but you should get that rash looked at."

Tee didn't answer. Karma leaped from the bed, startling both September and Shadow. The big dog bulldozed her way into the bathroom, sticking her head into the shower. But her *Arooo* of warning proved too late to stop Tee crashing to the floor.

Chapter 35

Shadow's fur bristled with alarm when first Karma then September ran into the bathroom. She gave him the hand signal to *wait*, so he hung back, quivering with tension. He sat on September's bed next to Macy. The cat leaned against Shadow's neck, cheek-rubbing him, but that didn't calm him down.

"I'm okay, I'm fine. Just lost my balance." Tee's angry voice preceded her stumble out of the bathroom, clearly resenting September's support. "Long day, that's all. I'm fine. Don't fuss." She drew the damp towel more closely around her form.

Shadow stretched his neck to nose-touch Karma, but she ignored him, and took her place with Tee on the other bed.

September settled next to Shadow. He leaned against her. Her gentle hand on his shoulders immediately made him feel better. He could read her concern for the smaller woman, but she felt fine. Her calm voice kept him steady.

"How long have you had that rash? And the headaches?"

Tee shrugged. Karma whined and set her broad head across the woman's lap. "Doesn't itch or anything. Comes and goes. Guess I first noticed it back in the fall."

September's brow wrinkled, and Shadow nose-poked her to make the lines go away. He wished they'd stop talking and turn out the lights so a good-dog could sleep. A nap always made everything better. His tail thumped at the idea.

But the two kept talking and talking. Finally, Shadow hopped off the bed and trotted to the bedside table. Neither woman paid any attention, but Macy watched with interest. Sometimes, a dog knew best and had to decide for people. Shadow reached forward with his nose, found the button, and pressed down with his chin until the lights switched off.

Tee shouted with surprised delight. "Did you train him to do that?"

Laughing, September beckoned for Shadow to rejoin her on the bed. "He learned it from Macy. A hint, I think. Right, baby-dog?"

Shadow waited until Macy curled into the curve behind September's knees, and then took his own place snugged tight against her other side. Karma's quiet breathing morphed into soft snores, synchronized with Tee's breathing.

But he couldn't relax. September remained stiff, pretending to sleep. When she finally stirred hours later, and quietly rose from the bed, he whined with concern until she put a finger to her lips. She quickly dressed, scribbled something on paper by the bedside lights, and fit Macy with his tracking vest before placing the cat into his carrier.

Whines came in earnest. Shadow paw-danced despite himself when September cracked the door and they stepped into the hallway. He knew what the cat's tracking vest meant. His own gear lived in the car. He loved following scent to find the lost. Shadow couldn't wait to wear his own tracking harness.

"Stay with me, baby-dog. Don't wake Tee. She's so stubborn, but not invincible." September's worry filled her voice, even though Shadow didn't understand half the words. That didn't matter, as long as they stayed together. And he'd get to play his favorite tracking game again.

Once in the car, Shadow puffed his breath against the rear window, making nose smears on the glass. September turned up the heat, so the chill left the car. He hadn't slept so the warm air made a good-dog sleepy. The drive took them out of the city, and soon only the dim shine of moon glow played hide and seek in the clouds.

"Thank goodness the plows cleared the roads." September finally broke the silence, and Shadow roused from his doze as they drew near to a large house. "Now, let's hope for more luck to find the cat."

Shadow woofed and thumped his tail at the *find* word. He grew more excited when September climbed out the car. "Sorry, Shadow, this time Macy does the honors. Shadow *wait*." She walked around to the rear of the car, let Macy out of his carrier, and left Shadow shut inside.

He yelped. He ran to first one window and then the next to keep September and Macy in view. She left the front eyelights shining the snow to a white sheen, bathing the small outbuilding in a reflective glow. He watched her open the carrier's zipper webbing, and grasp Macy's leash, and barked his protest again. He wanted to play the tracking game! September always gave him something to sniff—a toy, or dog sweater, or cat brush—so he knew where to start. But she offered no sniff-suggestion to Macy, just set the big cat down in the icy tire tracks revealed by the lights. His brow furrowed. Maybe September didn't want Macy to track anything after all?

But after shaking himself hard to settle the fur beneath his jacket-harness, Macy padded quickly to the end of the leash September clutched. The big cat guided her forward, and September followed Macy's paw steps toward the small building.

Shadow barked again. September glared over one shoulder at him, putting one gloved finger to her lips. His ears fell. He licked his lips. With a whine, Shadow settled onto the rear seat, and watched.

Mr. Bleak remembered the white animal leaped from the girl's car, and figured it ran back to the house. But the police had secured all doors and windows, so he didn't need to waste time searching inside. He checked nearby trees—cats supposedly liked to climb trees—and viewed every angle of the roof. As he'd looked in each nook and cranny, his impatience grew. Surely it couldn't hide forever? He'd search the outbuilding last, and might have to torch the place after all. When a car's headlights speared the night, he stepped into the shadows to watch. He didn't feel angry at the miscalculation, simply made adjustments.

Huh. Not the baby cop after all. He recognized the black shepherd barking in the back seat. His research into the animal's owner told him all he needed to know about the dog's skills. What a weird-ass waste, to train a mutt to track lost animals, instead of something useful like to take down bad guys.

He sneered internally, but remained expressionless. The scalded skin felt so hot and tight on his face, it might split open if he blinked too hard. He settled in to wait. She'd come to him, so no need to track her down. Once she recovered the computer backup, he'd relish eliminating the cat, September Day, and her precious black dog.

Macy pulled against the leash, padding with dainty grace through the cold powdery white. He detested the snow, but enjoyed the games he played with September. The jacket vest signaled what game she intended, so he delicately sniffed the air as he drew near the building.

His ears twitched, detecting the ultrasonic squeak of vermin. Macy licked his lips, and the tip of his long dark tail twitched. He'd already eaten in his carrier, on the car trip here, so felt no urgent need to hunt. But still... the hardwired instinct challenged his focus, until September spoke one word.

"*Find.*" She urged him on, her voice soft, and rattled the baggy in her pocket. The promise of stinky fish treats trumped Macy's mousy temptation.

He tugged the leash again, eager to examine the scents that clung in the dips and hollows protected from the wind. Macy led September around the building, sniffing likely corners at cheek-rub height, seeking the signature territorial claim of another of his kind.

They reached the open doorway. Macy's nose twitched at two competing smells. The scary human scent bathed the large car that squatted in the middle of the building. He hissed, arched his back, and turned aside when September repeated the request once again. Macy understood the man-smell didn't matter in this quest. No, September only wanted to find a cat hiding nearby.

The missing cat's urine scent permeated the enclosure. *Male. Adult. Potent. Scared.* The height of its check-rub marks told him the cat's size, and more. He glanced up at September and mewed softly. She bent to stroke his cheeks—he loved that, and leaned hard into the caress. Macy understood she couldn't detect the smell evidence of the friendly intact male. He rubbed his cheeks against her hand, refreshing his scent-claim. September belonged to him.

He loved September, even if she lacked the discriminating skills of an intelligent cat. Macy appreciated other cats more than dogs, although he'd grown to like Shadow—once the dog had been properly schooled in cat appreciation. He had watched her show Shadow, and already knew what to do before September finally understood he wanted to play tracking games, too.

Sometimes, people took a very long time to learn things that cats quickly understood. Humans did know how to harvest the best treats, though.

Macy sniffed the sides of the doorway, then tugged September around the wall, sniffing only a couple more times to be sure. He stood on his hind legs, and leaped up to the top of a nearby stack of bags and boxes. Yes, the strange cat rested here for some time, but then fled, leaving behind fear-stink. Macy lifted his head higher and scented the air. He hopped down from the perch and tugged September deeper into the storage area, sniffing the bases of boxes and bags along the way.

The pee-mail deposit emanated from midway down the back wall of stacked materials. Macy liked the location. It offered options to escape from two directions, and clear sightlines to see approaching danger. He tugged harder, feeling the tension over his shoulders where the leash connected to his vest, and picked up his pace.

There! Under the table, back behind boxes, the freshest cat scent of all. Macy mewed, and pawed at the container. He scrunched down to stick his wide head farther inside, careful to test the opening by whisker-width.

In the far back corner, doing his best to shrink himself small, Macy spied the other cat. Bigger than Macy himself. But with his face turned into the corner. He shivered, not from cold—the strange cat's body heat warmed the small enclosed space. The pale cat had hidden himself in a fine place, one only other cats could access. Macy approved.

And Macy began to purr. *No threat, no threat, no threat…*

Slowly the strange white cat relaxed. His ears flicked, one turning toward Macy. He finally swiveled his face to see. Macy licked his nose as he turned his gaze aside. *No threat.* Macy's purrs rumbled louder in the still air, *no threat no threat no threat*, so loud even September's feeble hearing could detect them. But she didn't move or say a word. She waited as Macy continued his calming work.

The other cat's answering purr began, sub-vocal, something only another cat could detect. Macy backed away, shook cobwebs from his fur, then looked up at September and pawed her leg, confirming the find. She smiled and knelt beside Macy, stroking him and murmuring softly a strange word over and over.

"Sherlock. Sherlock. Here kitty, pretty boy, Sherlock, Sherlock." She opened the treat bag and gave Macy his reward of stinky dried fish flakes. She moved a box aside and peered into the cubbyhole, too, then tossed a couple of fishy treats to the white cat.

Sherlock stood, stretched and arched his back, and yawned wide. Macy backed away, also turning sideways, and head-butted September's arm to remind her he'd finished his treat and needed another. He trilled and rubbed the mahogany length of himself against her calf, showing the strange cat that she belonged to him— and that she also posed no threat.

Sherlock padded to the tossed treat, sniffed it, but left it in the dirt. With an answering trill of relief, he came out from under the shelter, and briefly nose-touched Macy. And he let himself be lifted into September's arms.

Macy licked his lips after finishing the second fishy treat, and accepted September's soft praise with pride. He led the way, tugging the leash harder and harder, anxious to get out of the snow and back to the comfort of his carrier.

Before he reached the doorway, Macy skidded to a stop when he heard Shadow's bark. September stopped, too. Macy heard her gasp when she peered out the doorway.

The wind puffed just right, carrying the scent of the scary man waiting for them just outside.

Chapter 36

September froze at the sound of Shadow's alarm barks. Macy's stiff-legged pose and bottle-brush tail confirmed the dog's long-distance warning. Someone waited outside the storage building.

The makeshift garage had no places large enough for her to hide. Even Sherlock had been hard-pressed to find a cubbyhole. She glanced inside Sissie Turpin's SUV parked in the middle of the space, hoping for car keys, and for the first time noticed snowy ice still coating the hood. September looked closer, and drew in a hard breath. The front grill carried scars from recent hit and run accidents. Not Turpin's car after all.

Mr. Bleak! He must have come looking for Turpin's thumb drive, although she wasn't sure how he knew about it.

Sherlock struggled a bit, before settling in her arms with a purr. September pulled the lanyard from around his neck and looped it over her own head, dropping the thumb drive down her front for safe keeping. She'd parked nearby, but with only one way out, Mr. Bleak could simply wait for her to leave.

Shadow's barks abruptly stopped and she imagined him silently tracking the man's movement. September guessed Mr. Bleak had moved away from her car, fearful Shadow would give him away. She hoped he didn't know he'd already been unmasked.

She couldn't make a run for it. She'd be tackled, or shot. Saddled with the two cats—no way would she leave either behind—she had few options. Even if she reached her car, he'd run her off the road. This time, he wouldn't leave her death to chance, like he did with Charlie. He'd end her.

Think, think! He couldn't see through the walls inside the building. Mr. Bleak hadn't found Sherlock, and maybe—probably!—waited for her to collect the cat for him. And he didn't know she'd already recovered the thumb drive. He'd wait until he knew September had it. She could use that.

She cleared her throat, and spoke with brisk authority, loud enough to be heard outside the building. "Good boy, Macy-cat, keep looking." As she spoke, she quickly fashioned a makeshift harness out of the end of Macy's extra-long tracking leash. She fitted it on Sherlock, then reattached the clip end to Macy's walking jacket. With the two cats connected and easy-going toward each other—*God bless show cats*—she'd have an easier time keeping them safely together. "That's right, Macy, go look up behind the boxes."

Macy stared at her, questioning her inane chatter. He crouched beside Sherlock. The pair exchanged polite sniffs, the white cat offered his head, and Macy agreeably began to groom his neck. September pulled out her treat bag and spilled the contents to keep them engaged. She knew Shadow also listened. Her conversation had no meaning to the killer, but when the time came, Shadow would know what to do.

"Good boy, Macy-cat, you checked the top of those boxes. Good kitty." She let the words pour out, buying time as she searched for something, anything to use as a weapon. Surely there'd be a knife somewhere, or scissors to open the cat litter bags. She needed something to puncture the tires.

"Yes, good kitty, you're getting warmer. I don't think our cat friend has left the building, keep looking." She kept one eye on Macy and his new friend, while scouring the small building for something sharp. Hanging on the wall, she found what she needed.

"Yes, that's the way. Just a bit longer, check the spot under the barrel." The cats ignored her, thank goodness, perhaps soothed by her calm voice. She prayed the nonsense also lulled the outside listener. She needed to work fast.

September lifted down the box hook that hung by a long strand of baling twine from a rusty nail. The dull hook wouldn't puncture the tough tires, but she could still slow the killer down. A chain would work better, but twine would have to do. She'd worked with bailing twine before, and knew all about its deceptive strength.

She cut free sections of the strands from several of the hay bales, using the twine itself to saw shorter lengths, then knotted them all together in a stout multi-strand rope. "Macy-cat, what a brilliant kitty, just one more place to look," she called, keeping her voice cheery. She looped the twine rope under the straps holding the last bale together, with the other end tied to the box hook. The square bale sat directly in front of Mr. Bleak's SUV. "Yes, that's right, under the car, good Macy, you're nearly done." She crawled beneath the SUV and hung the box hook over the front axle, connecting the bale to the car. The twine wouldn't hold for long, if at all, but the hundred-pound bale anchor should at least slow the car. She struggled back to her feet, grabbing armfuls of loose straw, and stuffing it behind the front tires of the car. The entire operation took less than three minutes.

Ready or not, here we go… September pulled out her car key fob, scooped a cat under each arm, and pressed the child lock release button. "Shadow, *window!*"

She heard the dog's thump when his paws hit the ground. A startled intake of breath came from the near side of the garage doorway, pinpointing Mr. Bleak's position. September ran, aiming for the other side of the opening, juggling the two cats in an awkward embrace. *"Hold him, Shadow!"* She didn't look. He'd either keep the killer at bay or they'd all die.

September thrust first one cat and then the other through the car window Shadow had opened, climbed behind the steering wheel, and shoved the running car into reverse. She ducked when a bullet starred the windshield, and floored the accelerator in reaction. Her car slalomed, but tires finally caught in the dirt driveway. She saw Mr. Bleak briefly in her car lights, crouched in a shooter's pose with some weird headgear, and swerved with a scream before bumping onto the highway.

"Shadow!" She screamed his name again and again, frantically searching in the gloom. Another starburst scored her windshield. And then she saw her dog, racing toward her. She quickly rolled down both the front and rear passenger windows to give him a best choice, paused to change into drive, and breathed with relief as Shadow vaulted into the vehicle.

She hazarded a glance back at the house. Lights blazed in the garage when he started his car. She didn't wait to see what happened, just pressed the gas and raced away.

Mr. Bleak tore the headgear off, half-blinded by the headlights, and rammed his car into reverse, cursing dogs, damning cats, and promising destruction to all difficult women. He hated everything about this assignment. How the hell had the dog got out of the car? His shot aimed at September went wild when the beast hit him behind the knees.

His car moved in an unexpected herky-jerky motion, and he cursed again, gunning the gas. It finally broke free, but something dragged underneath. He'd never catch them now. He stopped to clear the obstruction.

No worries, though. He always planned contingencies. He'd find the whole menagerie soon enough. He'd planted a tracking device on September's car.

Chapter 37 (34 **Years Ago**)

Time blurred for Tana. Every time she stopped the camper to care for the three squalling infants, she expected the police to show up. She had no plan. Tana simply drove to put as much distance between herself and the past as she could. She prayed the dumpling-woman wouldn't tell the police. She and the driver wouldn't want anyone to know about their black-market operation.

They might tell Kali. Being hunted by her worried Tana more than the police.

The driver left behind cash, credit card, a phone, and infant formula and diapers for what would have been a one-day delivery trip. She would run out of baby supplies quickly, and be forced to come out of hiding. At least she could feed her baby herself.

She couldn't ask anyone for help, not when she was wanted for murder. As long as Tana knew about Kali's operation, she'd be a threat. They'd want to find her, and silence Tana. And sell the babies. Her mind whirled, struggling for a way to keep the infants safe, and hide herself away. She couldn't do everything herself. And she slipped up. The driver found her three days later.

He wanted the babies, and threatened to kill her on the spot. His massive screw-up left Kali in a bind. She'd already relocated his sister's birthing operation out of state, and would kill the dumpling woman, unless he made things right.

By then, Tana had figured out what to do. She offered him— them both—a way out, to pay off Kali for the three babies. He grudgingly agreed, having no real choice. In exchange, he'd help her disappear. They'd keep each other's secrets, to protect themselves.

Tana made a call to her sister. Far from being relieved, her sister's shock and disbelief quickly became rage. Tana had stained the family name, shattered her parents' hearts. Tana agreed to a deal that would define the rest of her life. In exchange for a one-time fee, wired to a predetermined location, she'd disappear forever.

With the payoff satisfied, the driver fulfilled his part of the deal. Tana took the place of twenty-two-year-old Rosalee Dixon, and Latana Ojo would be found dead after giving birth. Nobody would look for her, ever again.

Chapter 38 (Present Day)

September drove too fast, risking a slide off the road but anxious to put distance between herself and the killer. The cats huddled on the floorboards behind her seat. Shadow rode shotgun in the front passenger spot, and reached out to paw her arm.

"I know, baby-dog." She tried a cheery tone, and failed. She couldn't stop the quaver in her voice, and unclenched one hand to stroke Shadow's broad brow. While in the middle of planning, and then escaping the garage, she'd held emotions at bay. But now, she couldn't still her shaking body. Her mouth tasted sour.

She'd planned to give Tee the thumb drive, but only a handful of people knew about the white cat. Detective Steele thought Tee would get Karma to track. Had Steele told Mr. Bleak about the cat? Or had he told someone else?

September yearned to call Combs, to talk it through with him. At this hour, a call would wake his kids, though, and spoil their time together. And wouldn't help, in the long run or the short term, other than selfishly make her feel better.

At the thought, September picked up her phone, and saw that Tee had texted her. Without bothering to read it, glancing every now and then in the mirror, she slowed her pace to a safer speed, and return Tee's call.

"Where the hell are you?" Tee shouted before September could get a word in, and then tempered her tone while Karma barked in the background. "I woke and you're gone. I thought we agreed to wait until morning."

"I'm sorry. But you needed the rest. If you've got Lyme disease, you need tests and probably hospitalization."

"Mind your own business. I can take care of myself. No time for wimping out over some stupid rash."

She scrubbed one hand over her face, and burst out with exasperation. "Who else knew about the cat, and the missing drives? The killer beat us there."

"What? At the house?" Tee nearly stuttered with surprise. "Are you okay? What happened? Did you find the cat and files?"

September's shoulders unclenched as they drove back into the city. The streetlamps turned the darkness into holiday cards. "I found Sherlock, and yep, I've got the thumb drive. Who knew I'd be out there?"

"Nobody." Tee answered immediately. "Only Detective Steele. He said to look tomorrow morning. That is, today, in a couple of hours."

September yawned. She hadn't had a good night's sleep since leaving Heartland. She wanted more than ever to be back on the road toward home. And Combs. "That's why the guy headed there in the middle of the night."

Tee's tone turned wary. "Don't even go there. My department tells stories about Detective Steele. He's a legend. I don't want to hear—"

"Okay, fine. So want me to drop off the thumb drive with Steele? He wanted to interview me anyway. Just as soon get that over with sooner rather than later." She checked the mirror. Still clear, thank goodness. "Will he even be there yet?"

Tee shushed Karma. September could hear the dog fussing in the background. "Just bring it here to me. It's barely five a.m. Steele won't come in until later. He was still dealing with the fire at Judge Southgate's house late last night."

"Fire?" September's throat clenched. Southgate? She wrinkled her brow. Where had she heard that name?

"Yeah, some kind of gas explosion they think. The whole family gathered for an early Christmas dinner, and everyone died. Well, except for a daughter who arrived late and discovered the fire."

September pulled into a nearby gas station and put the car in park. Her hands shook. She fingered the lanyard of the computer drive that hung around her neck. "Do you have a computer with you? So we could take a look at the thumb drive first, before we give it to Steele?" She'd left her own laptop at home, never thinking she'd need more than her phone on the short trip.

"No, sorry. The locals should have a team review and send digital copies to Redford in Chicago." Her voice sharpened. "Karma, will you please settle?" She sighed with exasperation. "I've got to take her outside. You have your key, so just let yourself back in. You sure you're okay? We'll have you file a report about the attack." She added, with disapproval. "You're not the police. I should have been with you for the search and recovery. Nobody wants any question about the chain of evidence."

"Yeah, right. I understand. Take your dog outside, Tee. I'll see you soon." September cut her off, not wanting to hear another word. Leaving it to the police sounded fine, until someone like Mr. Bleak turned up. She'd narrowly escaped him twice, and figured her luck wouldn't hold for another meeting.

She had to protect herself with information. September used her phone browser to access the local news and soon had file footage from the Southgate home. Engulfed in flame, it looked like a war zone. A reporter offered voice-over commentary, and then a picture of Judge George Southgate filled the phone screen.

"I knew that name sounded familiar." He'd been the angry man at Angela's house who wanted her arrested. He and Steele knew each other. She did another quick search and found his office address. It looked familiar, but with Angela's text messages deleted, she couldn't be sure he'd been the attorney they were to meet. Now, he'd been killed in an accidental fire?

"Accidental, my ass-ets. We need help." She whispered fiercely, Shadow and the two cats her only audience. The trio listened politely. Macy and the snow-white Sherlock had climbed into the back seat, and lay snuggled side by side—unheard of among strange cats, but September didn't question. She needed some luck. More than that, she needed a trusted sounding board. The unexpected stress and fear could tip her into a PTSD meltdown with little warning.

Tee was sick, whether she admitted it or not. Combs couldn't help long distance. And September didn't trust Steele, no matter his glowing reputation or his previously being Chris's colleague. She had to take precautions before turning over the evidence. Whoever ran this murder train wanted her tied to the tracks, too.

A dear friend helped her with a thumb drive once before. "Plan's changed, Shadow. We can't go home, not yet."

She retrieved his Christmas card from the glovebox, and looked at the return address. September knew she could count on Teddy Williams.

Chapter 39

Theodore "Teddy" Williams woke with a start. He looked around the small guest bedroom, at first disoriented, and then remembered. Despite visiting his son's family for the past three weeks, he still startled awake, expecting to view the familiar home he'd shared with Molly. He blinked hard, and his shoulders drooped. The disease took Molly's mind and memories long before she'd gone to her final rest.

After he sold their little house in Heartland, Texas—good riddance to the garden that poisoned her—Teddy traveled to Middlebury, Indiana to pick up his custom Coachman Nova. The compact motor home had everything a single senior citizen needed. For the first six months after Molly's death, he'd traveled in "Nellie-Nova" to all the places they'd planned to visit together. Finally, out of loneliness, boredom, and fear he'd lose his own marbles, Teddy came out of retirement.

With his custom computer and high-speed hot spot, he could work anywhere. He didn't need the money, but the extra would be a blessing to his kids when he finally rejoined Molly. When his latest contract brought him to South Bend, he accepted his son's invitation—insistence—he stay with them through the holidays.

He stared at the clock on the nightstand. 5:00 a.m. blinked back at him. He'd gotten four hours of shuteye, better than some nights. The older he got, the less sleep he required. It didn't bother him, he used to pull all-nighters all the time. Molly got aggravated, but Teddy always loved working at night. Nobody interrupted with phone calls, and even the birds shut their beaks.

"Might as well get a head start on the day." Lordy, how low he'd fallen, talking to himself. With a groan, he levered himself upright to swing his legs off the bed. "Getting old ain't for weenies," he muttered.

Teddy quickly dressed, picked up his phone and charger, and opened the bedroom door. Despite his caution, the hinge-squeak woke the giant dog sleeping at the end of the hall. He put a finger to his lips in a *quiet* signal, but that didn't stop the Great Dane from yawning as loud as a siren. Kismet belonged to the grandkids, but had taken an instant liking to Teddy. He'd always loved dogs, but had to keep his bedroom door shut or ended up with 120-pounds of lovin' pup crowding him off the bed.

Usually Kismet slept with one of the kids, but both girls were at sleep-overs to mark the beginning of their Christmas break. His daughter-in-law had left on a business trip yesterday. For the next few days, it was just Teddy, his son Theo Jr, and Kismet. They'd enjoy eating lots of unhealthy carryout and playing too many video games.

Teddy stroked the dog's massive dark neck and scratched beneath Kismet's chin. She leaned against him with a groan of enjoyment. He had to catch himself, bracing a hand on the wall, when she knocked him off balance. "Gotta go to work," he whispered. "Sorry, there's not room for you." While Nellie-Nova offered plenty of space for an aging white-hat hacker, a dog Kismet's size proved too much. One sweep of her tail cleared tabletops.

He didn't bother with a coat when he quietly left the house. Teddy hurried to the motor home parked in the drive. He walked carefully, belatedly wishing he'd donned boots. More snow had fallen after Theo last cleared the path. *Don't fall and break a hip.* Bad enough, Theo constantly pestered him about wearing one of those embarrassing Life Alert call buttons. He snorted. "I'm not *that* old."

As he unlocked the door, he felt his phone buzz, a reminder to switch it off silent mode. Teddy climbed into Nellie-Nova before glancing at the caller I.D. A grin nearly split his face. He shut and locked the door—Theo lived in a nice neighborhood, but Teddy always took precautions—and answered. "September, what a nice surprise. Guess you got my card? Merry Christmas, a week early."

"Merry Christmas to you, too. Sorry to wake you." She hesitated, and then rushed on. "I've missed you, Teddy. I loved your card. Are you okay? Visiting your son's family, you said." She sounded just as chipper as he remembered.

"You bet. Theo and his wife spoil me rotten with home-cooked meals. I usually just do take out, and reheat stuff. Gained a few pounds." He switched on the lights, and booted his computers, brow suddenly furrowing. "It's dang early to be calling. Are *you* okay? Not in any trouble again, are you?"

She sighed. "I need a favor."

Here we go. Trouble followed the young woman. He'd come to think of September as a daughter. She'd been there for him during Molly's illness and last days, and helped to punish the people responsible. "Tell me."

She told him about the thumb drive. "I've got no computer to see if there's anything on it. Then I remembered you're here in South Bend."

"Wait, you're here?" He pushed his glasses up his nose. "You left out that part. And why you're here. Sounds like more than a simple favor." September's life was anything but simple.

She laughed ruefully. "I'm parked just down the block. I didn't want to barge in unannounced. I can tell you the whole story, but I don't want to intrude if your son objects." He heard a woof, and smiled despite himself when she added, "Shadow wants to say hello. Macy's here, too, and… well, I owe you a bunch of hugs." Her hopeful tone proved irresistible.

He shook his head, and blew out his breath. "Don't go to the house. I'm in the motor home parked outside." Teddy couldn't help a thrill of anticipation. The contract job kept his brain going, but could wait until daylight. He needed something to get his blood pumping.

Teddy opened the door, grinning with pleasure when she arrived, big black shepherd in tow with a stuffed toy in his mouth. Teddy enfolded the tall, slim woman in a bear hug while Shadow whined and wagged at their feet. "Your puppy sure filled out. Looks like a macho dog, now, except for the stuffie. Reminds me of the shepherd Molly and I had years ago." He offered his hand and Shadow dropped his toy, and pressed his cheek into it. "Come on in. Nellie-Nova's small, but she's mine."

September unzipped and slipped off her parka, pulled off some sort of odd-looking knit cap, and sat on the twin bed on one side. She spread her coat beside her and invited Shadow to lay on it, as she looked around. "Sweet ride, Teddy. I'd really like to catch up with you, and hear all your stories. I enjoyed your cards and postcards from your travels."

"Time enough later. Sounds like you're in a time crunch." He took his place on the opposite bed that doubled as a couch, and pulled the mini table that contained one of his computer keyboards closer. "The thumb drive?"

She pulled a lanyard over her head, and handed it to him. "Déjà vu, right? But I don't know if this one's encrypted."

He grinned. "Like that matters?" Teddy plugged it into a port, typed on the keyboard, and the password page came up. Teddy swiveled a second computer screen around so that September could also see. "Piece of cake. I'll run it through my password-cracking software. Meanwhile, bring me up to date. What kind of files do you expect? You helping Combs on another case? Are y'all engaged yet?"

She shook her head, and blushed. "He's at Disney with his kids. His ex-wife isn't getting any better, and they needed a break."

He nodded. She'd been infected with the same poison that killed Molly.

"I used to live in South Bend. My former mother-in-law invited me to take care of family stuff. Her son—my husband—died two years ago tomorrow." She wrung her hands, and then stilled them when Shadow licked them.

"Oh." He knew she'd been married to a cop. Birthdays and wedding anniversaries ached your heart, but a death anniversary hurt the worst.

"Anyway, Angela found a bunch of Chris's investigation papers in a lockbox. She thought it had something to do with me, and that Chris wanted me to know. So she sent me the key. After I got the files, we planned to meet."

"So that's on the thumb drive. I thought you said papers."

She shook her head, and started to explain, when the name clicked. "Wait. *Angela Day*? The woman who just died? She was on the news." He took off his glasses and polished them on the hem of his sweater. "Somebody stole her car, drove it through the garage, and left her body swinging from the rafters. With a coat hanger." He shivered, and put the glasses back on.

She flinched. "That's her. We stayed in her house Sunday night but somebody came after us for Chris's papers." She leaned forward, elbows on her knees. "I only got a quick look at his notes, so I don't know how it involved me." She whispered, "But Chris always wanted to save me, to help me heal. Now his mother's been killed, and the attacker came after me, too. And oh, Teddy, if his old investigation was about me, maybe that's why Chris was killed. It's my fault."

"Hold your horses. Let's not get ahead of ourselves." He checked the computer. The software continued to work its magic. "Once we get this cracked, we'll learn what Chris knew. None of this is your fault, September."

She stroked Shadow's ears. "Oh, those records don't belong to Chris. They come from another murder victim."

He raised his eyebrows. "How long have you been in town? Already two victims—"

"Three. Almost four. That I know about." She jutted out her chin, and ticked names off, counting on the fingers of one hand. "Bradley Detweiller owned a Chicago lab. That's the one thing I learned from Chris's files. He committed suicide, and trashed all his records."

"Kind of a tenuous connection, especially if you don't have Chris's records anymore." Teddy fiddled with the keyboard.

"Maybe." She twisted her hands again. "The police tried to recover Detweiller's files by visiting his bookkeeper, a woman named Sissie Turpin here in South Bend. The Chicago police sent my friend Tee Teves to interview the bookkeeper. I told you about Tee last year when I helped with her police dog."

He nodded. "The cop from Hawaii, I remember. She came to Texas to investigate that trafficking ring." He watched the screen, and as soon as it clicked open, he began scrolling through the files. Sure enough, most were bookkeeping documents. "So this Detective Teves—"

"Officer Teves. She wants to make detective. I think that's part of why she pushed for this assignment. And why she won't slow down for anything." She nodded at the computer. "The thumb drive files belonged to the bookkeeper."

Great. A gung-ho young cop roped September into another skirt-the-rules situation. "So you've got Detweiller dead, Angela a suicide, and I'm guessing Turpin makes number three? Suicide again?"

"Right. Except we don't think any were suicides. Angela's doesn't make sense. And there's a witness to the bookkeeper's staged suicide, a young girl who nearly became the fourth victim." She smiled. "The girl, Charlie Cider, put the lanyard on one of Turpin's cats, so Macy tracked him down to recover the thumb drive." She rubbed her eyes. "The two cats are in my car."

Teddy looked up sharply. "Did you say *Macy* tracked the cat? Well, I'll be." He looked back at the screen. "Cats, huh? That explains some of these files. Pedigrees and sales records. So Turpin's not only a crooked bookkeeper, but also a cat breeder. Look at this." He pointed to the screen. "Some sales coincide with big cash transfers going back years and years." He squinted, and looked again. "Is that you listed as purchasing a cat?" He moved the cursor on the screen, to highlight a file.

She already knew, didn't need to look. "Macy came from Turpin's cattery. Victor got him for me." She blushed again.

He knew nightmare memories still haunted her, even if he didn't know all the details. But she had grown so much stronger than the fragile girl he'd first met. Much of that had to do with her cat Macy. And of course, with Shadow. "Victor's where he can't hurt you anymore," he offered softly. "Surely he'll come to trial soon."

"Oh, I'll be there to testify, and see Victor convicted." Her eyes shone with anger. "Anyway, Tee discovered the bookkeeper's body. She gave the paper records she found to Detective Steele. He's the local lead investigating Angela's death and the attack on Charlie." She hesitated. "Tee and I believe the same man attacked me at Angela's house yesterday, and at Turpin's a little while ago. So that's another connection that ties everything together." She put her face in her hands, and looked at him through a curtain of dark hair. "Teddy, it's a huge mess. I need your help to unravel it all, especially to figure out how Chris thought I'm involved."

He sat back, hands on his knees, and stared at her for a long moment. "You've got police departments in two states handling multiple suspicious deaths. This thumb drive holds answers. We can't interfere with an investigation—"

"We can turn it over later this morning, Teddy. Can't we make a copy or something? If it's about me, don't I have the right to know?"

He tried to interrupt her, but she bulldozed on, voice growing strident.

"I think Detective Steele might have his own agenda." Shadow tried to climb into her lap. She pushed him away, voice still rising. "I'm okay, baby-dog, just settle."

"What're you talking about?" She couldn't mean the police were involved.

"You know where he spent half the night? Do you?" She motioned to the computer. "Go ahead and look it up. The local news streamed the coverage. Steele got called to the fire that killed Judge Southgate and his family, just hours after Southgate tried to get him to arrest me for Angela's death. They're all involved, Teddy, it's all connected."

"Southgate? What the hell…" He returned to Turpin's records on the computer screen, clicked through a couple of files, and found the name. "There it is. George Southgate bought a cat from Sissie Turpin eighteen years ago. But he paid $25,000."

Chapter 40

September stared at the screen, and touched her throat, trying to digest the information. Turpin's cat sales record proved Judge Southgate's involvement. But in what? Overpriced cats?

"What? Why? That can't be right, $25,000 for a cat." Shadow tried to get in her lap again. She finally paid attention to him, took several deep breaths, and consciously lowered her voice. "Macy's priceless to me, but I've never heard of that kind of sale in the fancy. The paper files Tee gave to Steele mentioned no prices."

Teddy scrolled down the page to find the entry about Macy. "No dollar amount here for Macy. Just says, 'in exchange for services rendered,' whatever that means. But see," he used his mouse to point, "Others besides Southgate bought high-dollar cats. Looks like one every three or four years. See, there's $25K sales to K.R. Jacobs at the same time as G.W. Southgate. Those are the most recent. Others go back decades, ranging from $5,000-$25,000 payments."

Her mouth fell open and she grabbed Shadow's fur. She scanned row after row of kitten sales with large dollar amounts listed intermittently. "It's not every sale, though. Some fees fall in line with the norm for pet quality Maine Coon cats, or a few hundred more for show prospects. Those with the five-figure amounts—there's something else going on." Despite her excitement, September yawned as the lack of sleep combined with a post-adrenalin slump.

Teddy caught the yawn, and echoed it. He removed his glasses and rubbed his eyes. "We separate out the high-dollar outliers and see what else they have in common." He typed rapidly, and soon had a screen with more than twenty names spanning thirty years. "The dates are important, too. If I had to guess, Turpin used cat sales to hide or justify payoffs."

"That's it! Teddy, you're brilliant. The Clear Choice indictment accused Detweiller of falsifying lab results. I bet those dates coincide with high profile court cases." She yawned again, and flexed her neck.

He grinned. "Give me a couple of hours to dig deeper. By the way, how long do cats live?"

She wrinkled her nose. "Why? What does that matter?"

"Based on the dates, if actual real cats exchanged hands, it'd be good to know how many might still be around." He didn't look at her as he continued typing. The screen rearranged boxes and diagrams as he continued his research.

"Healthy cats live into their late teens, some into their twenties. Siamese live the longest, for some reason. Genetics and environment play into that, though. And there are lines of Maine Coons predisposed to hypertrophic cardiomyopathy, a heart condition. That reminds me, I need to give Macy his medication." She yawned and stretched again. "Would you mind if I brought the cats in here, Teddy? It's warmer than my car. I've got cat carriers in my car, and haven't had a chance to get them settled."

"Sure, why didn't you say so earlier? Even with lots of fur, bet it's chilly out there."

September hurried to collect Macy and his new buddy. She retrieved and unfolded the extra carrier, loaded the cats, and lugged them to Teddy's vehicle. Shadow followed, keeping watch in her wake. He stared down the road, ears pricked and neck arched. She didn't blame him. She still kept one eye over her shoulder and startled at the slightest unexpected sound.

Once inside, Macy willingly opened his mouth for his medication, and then pawed her arm impatiently for his treat. "Sorry, I left the treats in my car. Teddy, do you have anything?"

He hooked a thumb at the small refrigerator. "Does he like boiled eggs? I always keep a couple for a quick protein snack."

"Macy eats nearly anything." She removed the bowl with two shelled eggs, and set it on the counter. Shadow immediately sat, with a dramatic look of expectation. "Okay. Everyone gets a taste."

September cut one egg in small pieces. Macy gobbled up his portion, and licked his whiskers with appreciation. Shadow gulped his, and wagged for more. Sherlock sniffed, and turned away.

Teddy watched with interest. "Picky eater?" He nodded at the computer. "It's running a program."

"Likely the food's too cold. When it warms up a bit, he may eat it. Cats like their food body temperature. Like a mouse." She grinned when he made a face. "So, answers in an hour?"

"Probably more questions. But yes, the program should give us a road map." He tipped his head to one side, eyeing her. "I don't sleep much these days, but you look ready to fall over. Why not take a nap while we wait?"

She shook her head. "Thanks, but I want to visit Mount Pleasant Cemetery." She rubbed Shadow's ears when he pushed against her. "Once we take the information to the police, questioning takes hours. I need to pay my respects at Chris's grave, it's one reason I came." She blinked hard and wiped her eyes. "Now he's with his parents. He had no other family, just me."

Teddy rose and gave her a hard hug. "Of course. Go. Make your peace. Ya know, he'd be proud of how far you've come."

September shrugged into her parka and adjusted the cap to hold back her hair. "When we get back, I'll take the cats over to Tee's hotel room. Shadow, let's go, baby-dog." She opened the door and stepped out, waiting for him to prance down the steps. "Teddy, call me when you learn anything. We're so close!"

Once back in her SUV, she stuffed the baggies of treats into her pocket, and then pulled up the directions to the cemetery. Located only a few minutes from South Bend Airport, she fought the temptation to instead buy a plane ticket home. But she couldn't retreat, not now, with answers finally within her grasp. She owed it to herself, to Angela, and to the memory of Detective Christopher Day.

"You would've loved Chris," she told Shadow. "He's why I train dogs." All these years she'd blamed herself, and Victor, for his death. Once she found the truth, perhaps she'd also find peace—and open the doors on a future.

Mr. Bleak waited until she drove away with her devil dog. Only then did he approach the motor home. He knew of the old man by reputation, a brilliant hacker back in the day, and guessed she'd left the thumb drive with him. He fingered his scalded face, and flexed painful cat-bitten hands. They'd never find September, once he finished with her.

Chapter 41

Teddy watched September's car disappear down the street. Even though a safe, happy future beckoned with Combs—*a fine man*—September's survivor's guilt fueled her behavior to drop everything and come to South Bend. He couldn't make the past disappear. But perhaps he could help her understand, and then overcome, whatever ugliness shadowed her life.

The software program had compiled the list of names, dates, and amounts paid. The police needed a forensic accountant to get the whole picture, but even Teddy recognized patterns of inexplicable payments. He'd bet anything that few cats changed hands, and only served as a furry smokescreen, payment for secrets kept and favors granted. He had a bad feeling about how and why September's stalker, Victor, was connected to Sissie Turpin.

He started to close the door, and noticed Shadow's bear-toy had caught in the jam. Before he could retrieve it, one of the cats meowed. Teddy looked up, wondering which one wanted to talk. He'd never been much into cats. Molly loved them but they'd only kept dogs.

He crossed to the two cat carriers, nifty zippered duffels with pockets for leashes and whatnot. September had left her gloves behind. He stuffed them in his back pants pocket so he'd remember to return them, and peered inside. Macy blinked, yawned, and closed his eyes. But the white cat, Sherlock, meowed again, and pawed the webbing at the front.

"That's right, you didn't get your food, did you, Sherlock?" Teddy saw the remains of the boiled egg. "Picky cat, you like warm food, eh? We can fix that." He placed the bowl with the last shelled egg in the microwave and set it to 30 seconds. When it PINGED, he retrieved the bowl, turned—

The dark-clad man jerked open the door, and pointed a gun. Teddy froze.

"The thumb drive. Hand it to me. Now."

Teddy nodded toward the rear of the vehicle. "There, plugged in the port." He'd already saved a copy to his secure cloud. He didn't move. "May I get it for you?" He licked suddenly dry lips, but otherwise remained frozen as the man kicked away the dog's toy, and reached the computer, all the while keeping the gun trained on Teddy's mid-section.

The man with the scorched face hadn't bothered to wear a mask. That told Teddy he had moments to live. A sudden calm descended. He met the impassive gaze with stoic determination. He wasn't afraid, but he'd rather not rejoin Molly today.

Mr. Bleak broke eye contact to retrieve the thumb drive. As soon as his attention shifted, Teddy lobbed the microwaved egg at him and dodged the other direction to the door. His knees protested, and he fell the final step, just as an explosion jarred the inside of his RV.

Cats screamed. The man yelled.

Teddy scrambled to regain his feet. He slipped and slid on the icy drive. Another gunshot, this one muted compared to the first, coincided with a shriek of pain in his leg. Maybe he'd get to see Molly today, after all...

Porch lights blazed on. Theo stood silhouetted in the doorway. "Dad! What's going on?"

"Inside, get inside! Call 911!" Teddy tried to yell but his voice failed him. The dark man, now standing above his prone form, would kill him, and then Theo. He stared up at the merciless face weirdly clotted with bits of white and yellow.

A hundred-twenty pounds of Great Dane launched through the air. Kismet hit the killer hard, and Teddy heard the rush of air when together they struck the ground. Mr. Bleak cursed, and scrambled away, tripping over and squeaking the stuffed toy before escaping into the pre-dawn morning.

Theo knelt beside him, squeezing Teddy's hand. Begging him to hold on…hold on….

Teddy passed out with Kismet snuggled tight against his other side, crying and licking his face.

Chapter 42

The snow-dusted cemetery shined with an ethereal glow from the breaking dawn. Far from spooky, the place felt bathed in an other-worldly hush: expectant, quiet, almost holy.

September parked as near to the grave markers as she could. She'd only been here once, to bury her husband. Those days had blurred over time, the sharp pain that fueled her escape to Texas now a dull ache. But the location of his memorial was burned in her memory. Chris, as much as Angela, had called her back to South Bend, to finish what he'd started, for her. She needed to thank him, and say her final goodbye.

"Shadow, *wait*." He yelped in protest when she switched off the SUV and pocketed the keys next to her wallet. "I'll be right over there. I need to do this alone, baby-dog." She took her gun out of the glove box and carried it with her. She carefully set the child lock. He continued to fuss as she left the car.

She pulled the hood of her coat up over her knit cap, snugging the cord tight to keep wind off her neck. September trudged past several rows of headstones to reach the Day monument. They'd laid Chris next to places reserved for his parents. Slightly raised soil testified to the more recent interment of his father, Peter. Soon, Angela would join them both. September realized she'd need to make the arrangements for Angela, and her heart broke a little more.

With her bare hand, September traced his name. Christopher

Day loved her, a broken soiled doll he'd wanted to fix. Wanted to heal. And she'd loved him for caring for her, damage and all.

Through his work, Chris recognized the pain, anger, and emotional scars that led to the crimes he swore to prevent, or to solve. "Mr. Fix-It," she murmured. How their lives would have changed, had they never met. He'd be alive. Angela, too. She'd be dead, or behind bars. "How did it all come to this?"

Taking a deep breath, she knelt on the cold ground, and rested her forehead against the icy stone. "I'm sorry, Chris. I'm sorry I couldn't love you more, love you the way you deserved. Thank you for trying to save me. Thank you for Dakota. And I'm … oh God, I'm so sorry it got you killed." Her voice shuddered. Tears froze on her cheeks like sparkling contrails. "You should have told me, not hidden away what you found." She sighed, scrubbing her face. He knew how broken, how fragile she'd been, and wanted to protect her. "I'm stronger now. And it's because of you that I survived. I won't let you down, not again."

When her cell phone rang, she set the gun atop the Day headstone. At the same time she dug in her pocket to answer the call, the tenor of Shadow's barks changed. That's when the shovel hit the back of September's head.

The dog's screams in the distant car got on his last nerve. He'd take care of the mutt, after he finished with September.

Mr. Bleak stooped over September, scooped her up and slung her slight weight over one shoulder. He slogged back the way he'd come, shovel in his other hand. He had had to wait until the Uber driver left, explaining he wanted alone time in the cemetery to meditate. The freshly dug grave he'd passed on the walk gave him satisfaction. He'd always been lucky. After he finished here, he'd take September's car and leave it in an appropriate place. To the outside world, she'd simply disappear. He'd looked her up. September Day had a history of running away.

The tracker he'd put on her car paid off twice in one night. He recovered the thumb drive, and nailed the old man. He ran a gloved hand over his watch cap, still picking exploded bits of egg off his clothing and face. That had been a surprise, and so had the monster dog that interrupted him. When he finally finished this assignment, he never wanted to see a dog or a cat ever again.

At the fresh grave, Mr. Bleak dumped September face down beside the hole. He checked her pockets and collected her car keys. She moaned and moved. So he hit her a couple more times, grunting with effort at the thwack of the shovel blade on the back of her skull. When she stopped moving, he rolled her in.

Quickly he covered her body with scooped dirt from the nearby mound. To a cursory glance, the grave appeared empty. The poor slob's casket dropped on top of her would hide September for eternity.

Then he dialed the boss. "It's done. Got the computer records, eliminated witnesses, and terminated the September account." The girl, Charlie, didn't count, and he'd take care of her later. He stared down at the still mound of dirt in the bottom of the grave. "Wire payment to my account tonight." Once he received payment, he'd make arrangements for a new face.

"You need to settle two more outstanding accounts."

Two more people? This job had turned into whack-a-mole, with new targets multiplying with each elimination. "That's not in our agreement. I can't settle two more accounts until you clear the current balance. Immediately." This would be his last contract. He just had to figure out how to finish clean, and make sure that door stayed closed.

The voice on the other end of the line initially sounded female, but now changed timbre to a low bass. "I must check with my client. The organization appreciates your professionalism, but frowns on jobs left unfinished."

He smiled. The client believed the voice distortion software protected his identity. Fat chance. They all answered to higher power. And Mr. Bleak had a direct line to the highest echelon. Should this cretin try to stiff him, nothing would stop his retribution.

Nothing personal, of course. He simply had a reputation to protect. Additional fees, though, meant early retirement to the island retreat he'd picked out years ago. "Do what you need to do. Tell your client once I see the payment in my account, we can discuss additional jobs." He stabbed the shovel into the mound of dirt beside the grave.

The voice now mimicked the lisp of a young child. "Our end can terminate one loose end but need you to remove all September contract connections—do you understand? We'll double your fee to terminate the Latana Ojo account in Heartland, Texas."

He found it interesting how many ways one could discuss murder. You never knew who listened, or recorded conversations. Nobody could trace Bleak, though, and he preferred plain language. "I have a job to complete in Chicago first before deleting September's mother, and any related connections." When the man hissed at the blunt declaration, he added, "Yes. By tomorrow afternoon your troubles will be over. I'll terminate the Latana Ojo contract."

Pleased with the terms of the negotiations, he disconnected. Most flights from South Bend connected through Chicago O'Hare, a serendipitous convenience for him. He'd already agreed to remove the baby-voiced subcontractor to complete his assignment. The powers that be took house cleaning seriously.

Juggling the keys in one hand, and the shovel in the other, he strode back to September's car. If he wanted the police to believe she'd gone into hiding, the dog must disappear, too. Plenty of room in the grave to toss a dead dog. He'd make sure the authorities found September's car at the airport. The authorities always believed the obvious.

Chapter 43

Shadow barked so loud and long that his throat hurt. But he couldn't stop himself. He recognized the man's smell and his signature walk when the man followed September to where she knelt on the cold, frozen ground.

He needed to protect her but he couldn't get out of the car, however hard he tried. If he pawed the door just right, the windows scrolled down so he could leap out. But Shadow tried every window, and nothing worked.

The man stood up, carrying a slight form. Shadow howled. September, his person, swung like a limp bear-toy over the stranger's shoulder. He snarled until foamy saliva sprayed the windows. He leaped from the back seat to the front, around to the side passenger window, and back to the rear, so he wouldn't lose sight. But the stranger carried September out of view.

He had to get OUT and go to her! Barking didn't help. Scratching and paw-thumping doors only left his toes and claws bruised. Shadow sniffed each of the side panels, carefully examining the handles that somehow made doors swing open. If he couldn't get to September through windows, he'd chew his way out.

Shadow set to work, growling under his breath, but making satisfying headway on the armrest he chose. He gnawed the covering, appreciating the give beneath his teeth. At the same time, he kept ears cocked for any danger sign in case the dangerous stranger returned.

When the man did return, moving quickly, with purpose, Shadow still hadn't managed to breach the car door. He crouched low on the back seat. He didn't bother barking any longer. His lifted lips and silent snarl shouted a warning anyone of intelligence understood. His hackles bristled off his shoulders, doubling his size, and his tail stirred the still air in high jerking arcs.

Ignoring Shadow's threat, the killer drew closer and closer. Shadow increased the volume of his growls, and lunged halfway across the seat when the stranger stopped outside the window. The man brandished a gun in one hand, and something in the other.

Shadow whined. When the man pointed at him, he flinched, dodging to the far side of the car. But instead of the expected scary sound, the car made its normal beep-beep that announced the unlocking of the doors. The man opened the rear door and waved at Shadow.

"Go on, dog, get out." His voice wheedled. "I can't make you disappear with blood in the car. Get out, puppy, come on."

His unctuous tone didn't fool Shadow. The man's stink of violence shouted DANGER louder than any rabid snarl. Shadow shrank against the far side of the vehicle, then feinted toward the man, teeth bared in defense. This car belonged to September.

The man jabbed the shovel at him.

He bit the blade. Teeth clanked on the metal beneath the clotted soil. Shadow scented September on the blade, and roared. He dodged the poking metal, leaped past it, and attacked, bright teeth aimed at the man's face.

With a cry, the killer side-stepped. Shadow bounded by and escaped the car. He landed on the slick, snowy roadway, and whipped around, poised to renew his attack.

The shovel dropped to the roadway. The killer pointed the gun.

Shadow didn't wait. He'd done this before on September's command. This time, he knew what to do. He sprang high, compensating for the man's reaction, and nose-punched the gun. It flew out of his hand, landing in deep snow on the side of the road.

Cries silenced, the man caught up the shovel and swung it while he turned in a half-circle, to keep a good-dog's teeth at bay. Finally, he threw the shovel. When Shadow ducked, the man dove into September's car and slammed the door.

The car tires sputtered snow in his face as it drove away. Shadow didn't bother chasing. He had to find September.

Nose in the air, he scented deeply. He launched himself after the footsteps the killer left behind. The bad man's scent rose in scent-cones thick and bright as neon to a good-dog's nose. Within seconds, Shadow's measured tread became a jog and then a gallop. September needed him.

He came to the hole dug deep in the frozen ground, and slid to a stop, sniffing the dirt. The man spent many minutes here. Shadow snuffled beside the hole, where the disturbed snow marked September's last resting place. He whimpered. She felt near, she smelled close, but where? He lifted his head again, tasting the air, and cocked his head. Listening. In anguish, Shadow howled his fear and longing to the sky.

A moan. So very soft that only a good-dog could detect the sound… there! His head swiveled, eyes cast down into the dank, black hole. Fresh dirt below, speckling the snow with detritus. Again the moan. The dirt shifted.

Shadow leaped into the grave. Her scent surrounded him. Fear. Blood. Pain. He whimpered again, gently pawing the loose soil, then more eagerly, fiercely digging, digging, moving the wet earth off of her, finding the back of September's hood, pawing the way clear. He grasped the fabric of her hood, pulling it down to her neck, and clawed off the funny soft-hard hat she wore beneath. He nosed her dirt-clotted cheek, whining, crying loudly, licking at her face, cold-nosing her eyes, until September blinked and she coughed.

"Baby-dog. You found me, good-dog."

Her voice sounded funny, but he didn't care. He woofed, tail whisking the air with joy.

"Help me, Shadow. Dig, get my arms free." She struggled but couldn't move more than her face. The rest of her body remained encased in the wet muck. "That's right, Shadow, *dig*."

He clawed more and more of the dirt away from her shoulders to free her arms, until September could push herself up out of the dirt. Shadow stood back, tail still waving with excitement.

She began to weep, and he whimpered, too, and pushed himself into her lap. As September's arms hugged him tight, Shadow wagged his tail so hard it swept the dirt clear. He licked the tears from her face. They tasted like love.

Chapter 44

Tee steadied herself with one hand against the elevator wall. When the door dinged open Detective Steele stood in the hallway waiting for her. "We gotta stop meeting like this." He didn't smile. "When we couldn't reach the Day woman, Mr. Williams specifically asked for you. He refused to answer questions without you here." Steele glared at her.

"I've been up all night. The interview with Judge Southgate's daughter, Sharon, wrung me out. She had to watch her whole damn family burn to death." He took off his glasses, rubbing his eyes. "She clutched this big fluffy black and white cat the whole time, and wouldn't let it go. It belonged to her little brother. They got it when he was a baby. Now a friggin' blood-covered cat's all she's got left to remember him by."

"I'm sorry for the loss of your friend." Tee understood too well losing family members to violence.

"Friend? Not really. Doesn't have to be a friend to cut your soul in two. This whole case just makes me want to punch a wall." He sniffed and jammed the glasses back on his face. "Don't know what that means, but I've had it with everyone stepping all over my investigation. So you leave the questions to me, Teves. Got it?"

She nodded, and the room spun. She grabbed the wall. Damn, she didn't have time for some weird tick disease. Time enough when she got back to Chicago.

Tee followed Steele down the hallway to Teddy's room. A younger man waiting just inside the door introduced himself as Theo, and warned them to make it short. "My dad thinks he's a secret agent or superman or something. He's not. I'll chase you out after ten minutes."

"I don't need a babysitter." Teddy's quavery voice sounded weak, but determined. "I'm not dead yet, nor am I senile. I am perfectly capable of throwing 'em out myself, Theo."

Tee choked back a laugh at Steele's expression. No wonder September loved this guy.

He sat propped upright in the hospital bed, one leg wrapped and slightly elevated. Teddy whispered, eyes twinkling, "My son worries I'll fall and break a hip. Should've warned me about getting shot." The younger man rolled his eyes, face still etched with worry, but left the room.

Steele pulled up a rolling chair, and took out a tiny paper tablet. He licked the end of a pencil, poised to take notes the old-school way. "Tell us what happened, Mr. Williams. Start with when and why September Day contacted you."

Without drawing attention to herself, Tee set her phone to record, and propped herself against the wall. She bounced her left foot on the floor, trying to stem pins-and-needles. She must have slept wrong, or maybe the cold caused the numbness.

"I sent September a Christmas card. I've been staying with my son's family. That's the scowling young man guarding the door." He raised his voice, intentionally jabbing Theo's protectiveness. "September's been a friend for a couple of years. I helped her out when she needed my expertise."

"And just what is that?" Steele hadn't yet written a word.

"Anything with a computer." Teddy smiled. "Coding, tracking hackers, identifying and neutralizing viruses, un-ransoming system attacks. I'm sort of the Marshall Dillon of the 'Net." His smile faded and worry lines replaced it. "September needed help reviewing the contents of a thumb drive she recovered at the behest of the police." His veined hands played with the sheet, telltale nerves betraying his uncertainty. "Can you believe it? She told me her cat Macy tracked it down. Sounds like a spy movie, right?" He glanced over at Tee, making eye contact to ensure she paid attention. "Two cats are still in my motor home. We need to let September know. She'll worry."

Steele finally scribbled on his pad. "Tell me about the thumb drive." He glanced at Tee. "That's the one you promised to recover?"

Tee nodded. "It's the backup from Sissie Turpin's computer. September suspected a connection to her husband's investigation. We planned to turn it over to you this morning. But when I fell asleep, September took it over to Mr. Williams first." She raised her eyebrows at Teddy.

"She wanted a quick look, but no computer. She knew I've worked with law enforcement before and asked a favor." He smoothed the sheet, and met Steele's eyes. "September had every intention to surrender the materials. She'd already left when I got bushwhacked and the drive stolen."

Tee's stomach dropped. She should have known September might try to recover it on her own. But she'd been so damn tired. Now, Redford would never trust her again. Probably sabotaged any chance to become a detective.

"Don't look so stricken, Officer Teves." Teddy grinned. "The bad guy got the thumb drive. But I'd already saved a copy." Teddy's satisfaction warmed his voice and smoothed his brow. "Somebody hand me a cell phone, Detective Steele, and I can send the files wherever you need."

Steele smiled for the first time. "Terrific. I'll have our I.T. department coordinate with you." He made a note, licked the pencil lead again, and cocked his head. "I don't suppose you took a look at the files? Any thoughts?"

Teddy smoothed the sheet again. "You'll want a forensic accountant to review the files, I think. No time to run a thorough analysis—that got interrupted when the bad man showed up. But..." He scratched his head and adjusted his glasses, hemmed and hawed, then finally spoke again. "I saw files for a variety of clients. Maybe real names, maybe code names, but some did look familiar. The one that piqued September's interest had to do with Turpin's pedigreed cats."

Rolling his eyes, Steele slapped his notepad against his leg. "Seriously?" He glared at Tee. "What in the hell do cats have to do with my investigation?"

Tee glared back at Steele, but before she could answer, Teddy interjected.

"Everything, Detective Steele." He had their attention, and knew it, milking the moment like a bad actor hamming for applause. "Most of the records show nothing unusual. One significant placement, for instance, was September's own cat Macy, purchased by the man now awaiting trial for her kidnapping and attempted murder." He seemed to like the shock on Steele's face, and continued with relish. "But over the years, a significant number of cats sold at an exorbitant fee, $10,000 to $25,000 per animal."

Steele stared. "Go on." He wrote furiously.

"I'd just started running a program to cross-reference sales amounts with dates and purchasers. We—that is, September and I—believe the fees reflect payoffs for something else. Does that make sense?"

Tee started. "Detweiller's indictment cited fraudulent lab results. He had to have a reason to risk his business and rep. Somebody made it worth his while." Her headache took a back seat. She pushed away from the wall, numbness in her leg ignored. "Detweiller ended up dead. And his bookkeeper's death was staged to look like a suicide, which it clearly was not."

"We wouldn't know anything different, if the girl down the hall hadn't been a witness." Steele gnawed the eraser end of the pencil.

Tee spoke to Teddy. "If Karma and I hadn't found Charlie, she'd just be an anonymous hit and run victim."

"Well hold onto your hats, I'm just getting started." Teddy's face flushed with excitement. "Like I said, we'd just begun when a familiar name prompted me to run the program. And I'm pretty darn confident we'll discover a few more familiar names once your police guys get hold of the files." His grin faltered. "Did you hear about the fire at Judge Southgate's house tonight? Sad situation."

Steele looked up sharply. "What does that have to do…" He paused, spoke slowly. "I interviewed his daughter Sharon tonight. She had a cat with her."

Teddy winced. "Somebody named Southgate paid $25,000 for one of Turpin's cats eighteen years ago. Named Kahlua."

"Damn!" Steele didn't bother to write anything further. He stuffed the notepad and pencil back into his pocket. "Where is September? I've still got questions."

"She doesn't know what she knows," Teddy corrected. "She stirred up a hornet's nest when she came to visit her mother-in-law."

Steele furrowed his brow and shoved his sliding glasses back up his nose. "So Angela Day found her son's files, gave 'em to September, then they got stolen. What a mess, it has to be connected." He looked from Tee to Teddy, and back again. "Do either of you know where she'd go?"

"Well, yes." Teddy's sorrow filled the room. "I don't know how much you know about September's history. Today's December eighteenth, the anniversary of her escape from her kidnapper. It's also the day her husband died. She wanted to visit Christopher Day's grave."

"A cemetery before dawn? In the snow?" Steele shook his head and hummed a spooky "woo-woo" sound. "Okay, Mr. Computer Genius, thanks for all your help. I'll get my IT guys to reach out and collect the files. Don't leave town. We'll have more questions."

"Mr. Williams, what cemetery?" Tee turned to Steele. "Can't you get a team out there, make sure she's okay? She's not answering her phone."

Steele sighed. "She probably turned it off. You know, to pray and all." When she grimaced, he relented. "Okay, I'll make a call. But we're already stretched thin. South Bend ain't Chicago, ya know, and we got a rash of murders and fires, not to mention the usual fender benders and regular mayhem. She's supposed to meet me for questioning later today, anyway." He strode out of the room, phone at his ear.

Tee implored Teddy. "She saved my life. I owe her. Your attacker probably found you by following September. She's not safe."

He beckoned her close. "Steele's probably right about the phone. She's at Mount Pleasant." Teddy pointed to his pants, folded on a chair. "Those are September's gloves in my pants pocket, you might need these to track her. Be careful. The people at the top of this conspiracy have a long reach."

Chapter 45

It took September three tries to stand, and two attempts to claw her way out of the grave. The damp earth clung to her clothes, and she brushed it off as best she could. Shadow grabbed her cap, leaped out of the hole, shook himself, and licked his paws. His past bout with frostbite made him more susceptible to cold.

Her head hurt. She picked up the discarded bump cap. Her stomach flip-flopped when the cap crackled in her hands. She rubbed the growing goose egg on the back of her head, feeling shattered plastic clogging her hair, but the bump cap had saved her life. She'd also landed with her face pillowed on her arms, offering just enough trapped air to sustain her for the brief time she'd been buried. But if Shadow hadn't found her when he did, she would have suffocated. "What a good-dog, Shadow. You're so smart!"

Shadow grinned and leaned his shoulder against her, offering welcome support. She checked her pockets, grateful to find her wallet, but frustrated by the missing car keys and phone. She peered around the cemetery, still silent but no longer peaceful. Only grave markers and mute stone angels bore witness. She walked, Shadow beside her, and tried to think.

She'd been only semi-conscious, and remembered hearing something about eliminating witnesses. He'd mentioned Heartland…and her mother? What did Mom have to do with this?

Teddy! September gasped, and her gut clenched. Oh God, her fault, all her fault! Teddy wouldn't give up the thumb drive without an argument. What had she done? So stupid, so self-centered. She'd led Mr. Bleak to Teddy, a gentle man who never had the sense to say no to her schemes.

Why hadn't she listened to Tee? She should have simply waited to turn over the computer files to Detective Steele.

Detective Steele.

Steele knew Judge Southgate, the man who wanted her arrested. After demanding her arrest, Southgate and his whole family perished. Had Steele arranged to eliminate Southgate to hide the reason behind his $25,000 payoff? And Bleak had been at the bookkeeper's house, when only Steele knew about the thumb drive on the cat.

Was Steele targeting everyone on the payoff list? She hadn't paid for Macy, and Victor certainly never had that kind of money. What sort of favors would he have done instead? September gagged, bent over a nearby headstone, and threw up.

Only someone with insider information could manage this conspiracy. Someone able to stay one step ahead of the Chicago police investigation, manage killings in South Bend, and silence potential witnesses. Someone like Steele. His reputation for clearing difficult cases could be explained by insider collaboration, too. Even Southgate could influence the outcome of Steele's arrests. Or maybe Steele had yet another puppet master pulling strings.

She had to do something. The killer planned to travel to Heartland. If Southgate's whole family died, they wouldn't hesitate to target her whole family. Her parents. Brother and sisters. Combs. His kids.

No! September braced herself against the headstone, retching again. The cold granite bit into her bare hand. She wiped her mouth on her coat sleeve. She knew what to do.

Mr. Bleak reported her dead. Fine, she'd play dead. Even if she had a phone, she couldn't call Tee and risk her sharing with Steele. Even an honest cop could share information with the wrong party. September wouldn't take the chance, not when her family could pay the price.

She pushed off from the headstone, and picked up her pace down the road. The airport, five minutes by car, wouldn't take long to walk. She could beat the killer home, but she couldn't risk him seeing her.

Twenty-five minutes later she trudged into the airport parking lot. The small regional airport, mostly deserted at this hour, meant she wouldn't be seen by too many prying eyes, but she avoided the plane terminal and headed toward the train platform. She ducked into the first restroom she found and performed damage control as best she could.

Shadow never wore a vest. No law, not even the ADA, required official identification of service animals, but that didn't stop many people from expecting it. So he always wore an official-looking tag on his collar. The train couldn't turn away service animals. But she couldn't afford delays, or too much attention on this trip, so was thankful she still had the extra leash stuffed in one of her massive coat pockets.

She had an emergency stash of cash, a credit card, and driver's license in her pocket. She feared using the credit card in the ticket vending machine might be tracked. Whoever ran the show seemed to have unlimited resources. She could pay cash on the train. The South Shore ran three trains per day into Chicago, the two-hour trip costing under $20. Fortunately, the first train of the day was in less than an hour.

September bought food from a vending machine. She fortunately had stuffed two more baggies of the homemade dog treats Shadow loved into her pockets before she left Teddy's, and fed Shadow nearly a whole bag in lieu of a meal. Something else niggled the back of her mind from Mr. Bleak's conversation. The name, Latana Ojo, sounded familiar.

Chapter 46

Tee turned up the sound on her phone to better hear the computerized voice directing her to Mount Pleasant Cemetery. She didn't know exactly where to look for September. "That's where you come in, honey-girl."

Karma wriggled in the back seat, clearly up for anything. The dog's broad black brow wrinkled with interest, and she cocked her head with an endearing expression that never failed to make Tee smile.

Detective Steele had other priorities. She got that. Two suspicious deaths and the slaughter of a whole family demanded a team to collect and process evidence, interview witnesses, and put together each case. He'd said it'd be a couple of hours before anyone could check, and that dismissal of September's possible danger rankled.

The phone app led Tee directly to the cemetery entrance and the commemorative sign. Mount Pleasant, established in 1876, was an historic cemetery. She'd arrived via Lincoln Way West, but figured driving the perimeter—East Drive, to Edison Road, to Charles Street—offered the best chance of spotting September's car. Tee drove slowly, scanning the area, but only saw the top third of the tallest monuments poking out of the snow. After one circuit, she turned down side roads, back and forth, that divided sections of the old cemetery. Her tires squeaked as they passed over fresh, untouched snow. Clearly, September hadn't been here.

With frustration, Tee stopped her car, and called up Google on her phone for a map of the place. Even better, she located FindAGrave.com. Tee plugged in the Mount Pleasant name, Christopher Day's name, and his death date, and learned he'd been buried in the newer section. Within minutes, Tee found the proper area.

She got out, squinting in the dim light. Sunrise streaked the sky, but still revealed no car. The unplowed snowy roadway, though, showed multiple tracks, unlike the other sections she'd traveled. September had already come and gone. Tee dialed September's phone again.

Karma barked a sharp alarm.

Tee turned, surprised, still holding the ringing phone in one hand. The dog had been unusually quiet, although alert and interested in the view from the window. "What is it, honey-girl? Do you see something?"

Karma scratched at the back window, and whined. Tee unlatched the door, and before she could attach the tracking lead the big Rottweiler took off, dashing through the gravestones.

She chased after Karma, slowed by the nearly two feet of snow. Tee kept her phone to one ear, hoping September would answer. As they reached the mid-point of the large section, Karma slowed near one massive monument. Disturbed snow surrounded the granite marker. Someone had brushed clean the face to reveal Christopher Day's name.

Ready to disconnect the still-ringing phone, Tee paused, hearing the weird echo outside of her cell. Karma stuck her face neck-deep into the drifted white. She rooted beneath the snow, and came out with a ringing cell phone in her mouth. Tee disconnected her own line, and it stopped ringing.

Taking the phone from Karma's gentle grip, Tee wiped its face clean. No damage she could see. That explained September's silence. She might be on her way back to Teddy's place, unaware he'd been attacked. Tee attached the lead to Karma's collar, not wanting to risk losing the dog.

Karma continued to snuffle around the grave. The dog's hackles bristled, and a low growl bubbled from deep in her chest. Shoulders hunching, Tee scanned the area, and spied a dark object atop the monument. She reached gingerly for the gun, her heart skipping a beat. Did it belong to September or someone else? She didn't know if the woman carried, but wasn't surprised. Losing her phone in the snow made sense, but nobody brought protection and left it behind. Had she been surprised, and run?

She paid closer attention to Karma's behavior. Still learning to read the big dog's meaning, Tee recognized the police dog's arousal. The gloves Teddy gave her at the hospital would settle once and for all where September went from here. Tee pulled one of the gloves from her pocket, and called the dog to her, offering it to scent. Then Tee gave the German search command. "Karma *such*."

Karma sniffed deeply, and without hesitation, whirled and set off across the large cemetery. She had to bulldoze through deeper drifts, occasionally leaping over snowbanks. Tee stumbled after the dog, clinging to the tracking line, struggling to keep up and not slow Karma down. The blowing snow had only partially filled footprints. That made the trek easier. But without Karma, Tee wouldn't have seen September's path.

What made September leave her gun and phone behind? Why travel to another section of the cemetery, unless chased?

Karma stopped near a freshly-dug grave. The mound of dark earth, dusted with snow, contrasted against the white landscape. Tee caught her breath, reluctant to examine the hole. She used her phone's flashlight app for a better view, and breathed again to find it empty. Her brow furrowed when she saw the disturbance in the bottom of the pit. Karma's excitement continued, and she jumped into the hole, and back out again, all the while wagging her short tail.

"Good job, Karma." Tee put a hand on the dog's head, still examining the scene. She switched on the camera flash, and took several pictures with her phone. She recognized there'd been a struggle of some kind.

Karma whined, and walked away from the empty grave, tugging against the line. Tee called her back, still gathering evidence. "Let's go, Karma. Now, Karma, *mahalo*." She gave the release word, when Karma resisted. "That's enough. I need to see if Teddy's heard from September."

As they hurried back to her car, Tee's phone rang. She grimaced at the caller I.D., and let it ring several more times before answering. She opened the back door, waited for Karma to leap inside, and climbed into the driver's seat.

"This is Teves." She started the car, and switched on the heater.

"I planned to call you in a couple of hours. Didn't figure you'd be back in the station yet."

"Yeah, well you should've checked in last night." Redford's voice growled with aggravation. "Instead, right in the middle of Zach's party, I gotta hear from Detective Steele about you inserting yourself into his investigation."

"Wait, that's not what—"

"I don't want to hear it. You're done there, Teves. Pack up your kit and come back to Chicago. Let the locals handle their end, and we'll take care of the Detweiller case from Chicago. The departments will share anything pertinent. The way everything has blown up, Steele says South Bend has asked the FBI to take the lead with a multi-state task force. Just peachy." His voice dripped with sarcasm.

She closed her eyes, gritting her teeth. She tried again. "But September Day—she's one of the witnesses in this mess—"

"I know who she is. Hell, half the police agencies from Chicago to Texas know that name." He sighed. "Steele put a BOLO on her car, and they found it at the airport. Looks like she cut and ran back to Texas."

Tee stiffened. "But her stuff is still in my hotel room, and I found her phone and gun near her husband's grave. Looks like a struggle. Something else went down here, and—"

"What? I should look in my crystal ball?" He snorted. "Steele doesn't need your help. I expect you back here on duty ASAP. Don't disappoint me again, Officer, Teves." He hung up.

Tee clenched her phone in one hand and pounded the steering wheel with the other. It made no sense. Why would September leave her car at the airport? Hell, she left her cat behind. No, she would find a way to let Tee know. Or call Teddy Williams.

She didn't have his number. Quickly, she dialed the hospital. In the back seat, Karma whined and paced, still nosing the window and pawing to get out. "Settle down, Karma. *Mahalo*, just chill." The dog continued to react to Tee's tension. "Yes, please connect me with Theodore Williams. Room 432." She waited, until a groggy Teddy answered.

"They gave me good drugs, and I just got to sleep. Who the hell is this?"

"Sorry to wake you. This is Officer Teves, September's friend."

"Did you find her?" He came suddenly awake. Worry shook his voice.

"No, but Karma found her cell phone. And her gun." She rubbed her eyes. "I saw signs of a struggle, and her car isn't here." She paused. "I guess that means she didn't call you?"

"Don't be stupid." He cleared his throat. "Sorry, that's the drugs talking. But seriously, she has no phone, no gun, and how the hell should she call me? You've told the police, though, right?"

Tee paused. "Did you send the electronic files to Detective Steele?"

"Right after you left. Their team should be teasing out all the good stuff. You told him about September. Right? Officer Teves?"

She put the car in gear and headed out of the cemetery. "I've been called back to Chicago. And someone found September's car at the airport. Looks like she's gone home to Texas."

"What? Without telling me?" He chewed his words, and sounded furious.

Tee had to smile. "That's what I thought. It makes no sense. Steele hadn't even got her official statement. He should be spitting nails."

Teddy grunted, and then hissed as if he'd hurt himself. "Dammit, I got no time for an injury. You drive that car of yours back over to the hospital and pick me up."

"Mr. Williams, I don't think—"

"That's right, you don't think for me. I'm not gonna ask, I'm just discharging myself. Something's not right, and I'm not gonna lay around in the lap of luxury," he snorted again, "while September's in trouble. Now, I know you're a good cop, Officer Teves, like all law enforcement professionals I've worked with. But something stinks if Steele spun that bit of hogwash."

She agreed. But disobeying Redford's direct order locked the door on any chance to becoming a detective. "I understand the FBI will soon take the lead."

"Good. So you're gonna run back to Chicago and leave it all to me? Fine. I'll call an Uber."

"Wait!" She yelled, afraid he'd hang up, and Karma barked in answer. "I'll be at the hospital in fifteen minutes."

Chapter 47

Charlie sat up in the hospital bed, hugging her knees. "I feel fine. I'm ready to get out of here. See?" She stretched out both legs, uncovering her feet to wiggle her toes. "The doctor said no lasting damage."

The nurse smiled indulgently. "Glad you're feeling better, but frostbite's the least of your worries. It's not just about you, anymore." He made a notation on the chart, and left the room.

She stuck out her tongue at his retreating back, then gingerly fingered the tender swelling on her forehead. A concussion, hypothermia, bloody nose, dislocated and cut shoulder, and frostbite. She'd had worse.

Swinging her feet over the edge of the bed, Charlie grabbed the rolling IV pole and juggled the lines that wanted to tangle. She hadn't slept well since her admission. Granted, at first they'd kept waking her up because of her concussion. But she couldn't find a comfy position in the hospital bed. Her shoulder and arm ached after being forcibly put back in place, despite the pain meds and stabilizing sling. And she missed Sherlock snuggling under her chin at bedtime. She sure hoped the police lady found him, and Sherlock forgave her.

"How'm I supposed to pay for this?" She scowled, and a lump tightened her throat. She had no money, no friends to help, and no family she'd claim. She worried if her face got splashed around the news. If the wrong people heard about her she'd wish she'd died in the wreck.

Sissie tried to help, gave her a place to stay, and a ticket out of her situation. But with Sissie dead, Charlie had nowhere to go. Sissie's killer would come after her next, if she didn't get the hell away from here. She'd disappeared before. She'd change her looks, and her name, and do it again.

Charlie rolled the IV stand to the door, and cracked it open. She itched to pull out the needles studding her arm, and run. But they'd taken her clothes. She couldn't go anywhere without shoes in the sloppy sock-footies and ass-open gown.

Almost as if she'd willed his appearance, a nearby door swung open. Charlie ducked out of sight, but kept watch, intrigued by the white-haired man's sneaky behavior.

He checked both ways before limping out of his room. He braced a hand on the wall, grimacing as he made slow progress toward the elevator. He'd pass her room within moments. Charlie grinned, guessing that he also wanted to escape the hospital. Maybe they could help each other.

She waited until he'd reached her room before quietly stepping out and confronting him.

"Lord love a duck!" he whispered. "Girly, you nearly gave me a heart attack, sneaking around."

"Looks like you're the one sneaking."

"Shhh, keep your voice down." He flapped one hand at her, while glancing over his shoulder at the nursing station at the other end of the hall. "I'm discharging myself, that's all. Don't want to waste time arguing with a contrary-thinking medical person." He staggered another few steps, wincing with each one.

"Need some help?" Charlie rolled her IV stand closer, offering the stability. "What happened to you, mister?"

"I'm Teddy, the bad-ass. I got shot." He grinned. "Just a graze, really."

"Really?" She smiled, quite liking the old geezer. He must be ancient, like 40 or 50 years old.

Grasping the IV stand, they moved together, speaking in whispers, toward the elevator. "What's your name? This looks serious." He gestured at the IVs, and blinked at the bandage stuck to her forehead and her arm sling.

"I'm Charlie, another bad-ass. I survived a hit and run."

He stopped abruptly. "Wait, you're the girl with the cat?"

Charlie caught her breath, then she grabbed his arm. "Are you a cop? Did they find Sherlock?" She looked over her shoulder, noticing two nurses now at the station. "Can you get me out of here, too? They took my clothes."

Teddy shook his head. "From what I heard, you shouldn't even be out of bed, Charlie."

"Speak for yourself. I'm not the one with a bullet hole." She jutted her chin. "I gotta get out of here. I can help you with— whatever you're doing. You're working with the cops, right?"

They'd reached the bank of elevators, and Teddy punched the button. "You've already helped. In fact, Sherlock's over at my place. He's safe, and the police have the information. The best thing you can do is stay here and recover."

"No!" Her voice rose, and one of the nurses started down the hallway toward them. "Did they catch the man who shot you? He could come after me, too."

He didn't say anything. Teddy turned up the collar on his coat, keeping his back to the approaching nurse.

Charlie grabbed his arm, whispering urgently. "I know stuff. A lot more stuff I didn't tell the cops. I can help you, but you gotta get me out of here."

The elevator opened, and Teddy released the IV stand and stepped inside. "I'm sorry, Charlie, I've got to go." The doors shut, leaving her behind.

The nurse hurried to Charlie's side. "How did your grandpa get up here? It's not visiting hours. And I don't care how good you feel, you need to stay in your room." He grabbed the IV stand, rolling it down the hallway, and Charlie had no choice but to follow.

She didn't care what the nurse, doctor, or old man Teddy said. She had to get out of this place, and fast. Like the nurse said before, this wasn't just about her anymore. She had to stay safe. For her baby.

Ten minutes later, still pouting in the bed, the nurse returned carrying a bag from the hospital gift shop. Puzzled, Charlie waited until alone to open the package. Inside she found a set of stylin' sweatpants, a hoodie, rubber-soled house shoes, and a note from Teddy with two words.

"Be ready."

Chapter 48

"Swing by the airport, Tee," Teddy said as he tried to get comfortable in the passenger seat.

"Call me Officer Teves, Mr. Williams." She'd met him in the lobby, clearly angry, and hadn't said a word as she led him to her car. "I agreed to drive you home, not chauffeur you around to meddle in police business." She glared at him, face pale and lips tight. "You should've stayed in the hospital."

"Oh for Pete's sake. You said they found September's car at the airport. I know you want to follow up, so why delay? Hell, I'll even stay in the car while you sashay around to gather *clues*." He mocked her with air quotes on the final word, hoping for a smile, but she scowled. "Or instead, call up Steele. Surely he'll give you an update."

"Okay, fine." She made the turn onto the highway. "You're right, Steele won't share info with me. We'll take a look at the airport, but you stay in the car with Karma." Karma whined in the back seat at the tension in her voice, and she softened her tone. "How's your leg? That's gotta hurt."

"Just a flesh wound, doesn't hurt." He lied. The bullet had skimmed the muscle of his thigh, peeled off skin and luckily missed the bone. The pain medication helped some, but the pressure of sitting made the wound throb. They'd cleaned and packed the injury, and warned him to keep it elevated above his heart to reduce swelling. No way to do that in the car, of course.

She snorted. "You're lucky it didn't take off your leg."

He crossed his arms. He couldn't let a little limp sidetrack him. Besides, the pain meds worked fine. As long as he didn't walk.

The snowy streets still required careful navigation, but little traffic slowed their progress. Once at the small regional airport, they passed through the gate into the tiny parking lot. Only a handful of cars dotted the area. "Over there, isn't that her car?" He pointed.

The SUV sat in the front row, in a slot clearly labeled for the disabled. He wrinkled his brow as Tee drove her rental through the rows, and parked nearby. The impact of something—bullet holes?—starred the windshield. "Are you sure the police already checked out the car?" Pristine snow surrounded September's car. Only the immediate portion beside the driver's door looked disturbed, like the driver had left the vehicle.

"Stay here." Tee left the car running, and stepped out to get a closer look. She slowly circled the car, tried the doors—locked—and scrubbed clear a window to peer inside. She shook her head and shrugged, then turned to cross the narrow sidewalk and street into the terminal itself.

"Oh no, you don't." Teddy reached over, switched off the car engine, and struggled to get out of the car as he pocketed her keys. Karma roused from the back seat, and gave one loud bark of protest.

Halfway across the drive, Tee turned back, and held out her palm in a *stop* gesture. "I told you to wait."

"You're not the boss of me." He sounded childish and didn't care. "I may be older than God, but I'm not dead. And I'm not sitting on my hands waiting for you to decide what to tell me." He walked carefully, wincing with each step, until he reached her. "Give me your damn arm. I got a gunshot, ya know."

She stifled a grin, and he knew he'd won. She took back the keys, hurried back to the car to retrieve Karma, and together the three entered the plane terminal.

Tee kept the leashed dog close to her side. Teddy didn't think anyone would ask for I.D. The dog's patrol harness with collar badge clearly identified them as a working K9 unit.

He'd already checked the departure schedules on his phone. "There's only a couple of direct flights to Texas. Most connect through O'Hare in Chicago. People would remember if September boarded with a dog. Shadow's pretty memorable." He limped alongside her to the ticket counter.

Tee showed her badge, but surprised Teddy with her first question. "Have any police inquiries been made today regarding an abandoned car in the lot outside? Any calls about a dark-haired woman, September Day? She'd be accompanied by a black German Shepherd."

The ticket agent shook her head. "Not while I've been here, and I'm working a twelve-hour shift. I could ask security. Is she dangerous?" She looked at her co-workers along the counter, and they all shrugged.

Teddy's shoulders dropped. He followed when Tee grabbed his arm. He hadn't realized how hopeful he'd been that September had simply gone home. If she hadn't caught a flight, her car abandoned, but no sign of her or Shadow, he feared for her safety.

"I don't think she's here." Tee echoed his concern. "Only one set of tracks from her car. There should've been paw prints, too. You saw how Karma leaves a trail in the snow."

He nodded. "She wouldn't leave Shadow." He took off and polished his glasses. "They hadn't heard from the police, either. Wouldn't Detective Steele inform security, or put an impound notice on her car, or something?"

Tee's freckles stood out in stark contrast to her pale cheeks. She rolled her neck, and pulled at the bottom of her lip as she waited for the electronic doors to swish open. She hurried them back to her car. "Somebody came after September. She led them to you." She looked at him, raised one eyebrow.

Teddy struggled to limp in pace with her. "Agreed. He took the thumb drive, tried to kill me, and went after September."

She pushed hair out of her face, and nodded. "No sign of her or Shadow at the cemetery, but looked like a struggle. Then her car ends up at the airport. He wants us to think she ran. That's what the police think, anyway." Tee unlocked her rental, and helped Teddy climb back in. "Maybe she's okay. Shadow wouldn't let anyone hurt her."

He squinted, not wanting to consider the alternative—that they both could be dead. Teddy waited until she loaded Karma into the back seat, and Tee climbed behind the wheel to ask, "Who knew about the cemetery visit?"

"Detective Steele." Her expression icy, she started the car. "He talked to Redford about September's car being found here at the airport. Couldn't be Steele at the cemetery. He's been tied up with the fire at Southgate's place."

"Speaking of Judge Southgate, I found the connection there." Teddy shifted his weight to take the pressure off his wound. "Although I still don't understand what all this has to do with September." He paused, and added, "You can take me home now."

"So? What's the connection?" She started the car, pulled up to the exit, and paid the parking fee.

"Judge Southgate had kids, right?"

"Yes. Steele talked to his daughter, the only survivor of the fire. There was a younger son. Paul. Some kind of genius, started at Notre Dame a couple of years early."

Teddy pulled up the notes he'd made on his phone. "Okay, Southgate paid the cat adoption fee the same month as Paul's birthday."

"Okay. So they bought a high-dollar kitty as a birthday gift?"

"For an infant? And for that kind of money?" He winced, and adjusted his leg again. "That's not the only one. I tracked the last five sales. They're payoffs."

"For what?" She glanced at him. "How much farther to your house?"

"My son's house. Another five blocks. I'm camping in the driveway. Oh, Theo'll be so pissed off at me!" He laughed, feeling more alive than he had since Molly passed. "I looked up the names connected to the last five cat sales. They live all over the country, but have several things in common. The purchasers are well off. They're in positions of influence or authority—lawyers, politicians, business owners. And they each have at least one kid."

"And they like cats?" She arched an eyebrow. Karma barked at her irked tone.

"Just like Southgate, each of 'em bought a high-dollar kitty in the birth month of their child. September's only link, though, is Victor Grant and Macy."

Chapter 49

Rose January had put off calling September as long as she could, still embarrassed about losing control during their last encounter. Rose smiled sadly. Her youngest daughter had been a challenge from the start. If she'd had her way, Rose would have stopped with her first perfect child, beautiful April, who now lay dying in the hospital. The family dinner had been too much for her fragile health.

Rose had insisted that Lysle stay at the hospital to comfort Steven and be strong for April's husband. He'd let her know should something change. "My poor beautiful girl." She dabbed her eyes, careful not to disturb her makeup. Over the years, she'd perfected the art of hiding her emotions. Or of showing what emotions others expected. She'd survived the hard years, but at what cost?

This wasn't the life she'd envisioned, that she'd wished for. That she deserved. She gritted her jaw, and took a deep, cleansing breath. One made the best of choices thrust upon them. Dwelling on such things helped no one. You could let life crush you, or fight back and win the next round. And the next. Rose had always been a fighter. She fought for her kids, for all of them. Accidental families could be as fiercely loved as those planned.

Rose had fully expected September to call and apologize for upsetting her. September always apologized, even for things not her fault. They were so much alike, both deeply hurt, both having paid awful prices for Rose's damning mistakes. When September hadn't called, and April's situation worsened, Rose phoned several times. She hung up each time it went to voice mail. This conversation must be in person, not a message.

Rose squared her shoulders, and dialed again.

"Hello?"

Had she mis-dialed? "Who is this? I'm calling my daughter, September." Her brow furrowed.

"This is Officer Teves, of the Chicago police department. Do you know where your daughter is?"

What in the world had September done now? "Of course not." She snapped at the woman. "Why would I call her phone if I knew—" She cut herself off, bewildered. "Chicago? What's she doing in Chicago?"

"South Bend, actually. She's a friend of mine, and lost her phone. We haven't been able to find her, found her car at the airport."

Rose slowly sank to perch on the arm of the sofa. "I don't understand. South Bend?" September's circle of friends included all kinds of strange people, from police officers to ne'er do wells. Rose stiffened her spine. If September ran off on some police case rather than stay to support her sister, she'd never forgive her!

"Her husband left paperwork she needed to see."

"Husband? He's dead." None of this made sense. "I don't care why you dragged her off on some wild goose chase, Officer. But she's needed here. At home. Find her. Tell her she has to come home right away. Her sister April is in the hospital and… it's very serious." She couldn't bring herself to tell this stranger about her precious daughter, dying for want of a kidney match. She'd put off being tested, knew in her heart they couldn't be compatible—news that would destroy her family—and now…now, the results, even if good news, would come too late.

"I'll tell her. Please call this number if you hear from her first." Officer Teves hesitated, and then added, "Christopher Day's old investigation stirred up a hornet's nest stretching from Chicago to South Bend, and possibly further afield. We don't know how, but it involves September and Victor Grant."

She stiffened. One hand unconsciously rose to her throat. "He's in jail. He can't hurt us. I mean, hurt her—not anymore." She squeezed shut her eyes. She'd had no choice. How long would her children continue to pay for her sins? When would it end?

"If she contacts you, just tell her to be careful."

The phone disconnected. Rose sat for a long, silent moment, and then shakily accessed the phone's browser. She searched for South Bend, Indiana news, and began to read.

Horror grew.

The past had found her.

(29 Years Ago)

After five years, her new name and life felt more real than her previous fifteen years as Latana Ojo. Circumstances forced her to grow up fast, and what started as an act—pretending to be older to match her new persona—became reality.

At first, she'd lived frugally off the money left from her sister's grudging payoff. She never stopped looking over her shoulder, though. They moved every six months just in case someone from her past reappeared. Once she found a theater job she loved in Chicago, she started to relax. A little.

She lived for her girls. The twins, now six years old, loved school. Their golden-haired younger sister hated the regimentation, and begged to stay with Mom at the theater, trying on sequined costumes and performing for an empty house. When coworkers commented how alike they were, she just smiled with wistful longing.

Her dream of stardom died with Latana Ojo. Her face hadn't changed, after all, and she couldn't risk an audience member recognizing her. Now she supported other performers, helping with costumes, selling tickets, planning dinner theater meals—wearing a hairnet and dumpy apron like she'd previously scorned—so that someday Rosalee Dixon's little girl received all the applause Tana had missed.

Then he showed up again, a hornet circling to get in yet another sting. The one-time errand-boy driver professed to be an itinerant actor, pestering the house manager and director for auditions. She recognized him, of course, sure he still hustled for Kali.

She prayed he hadn't seen her, or if he had, didn't recognize her as the same skinny, sick, and desperate runaway. He couldn't hurt her without implicating himself. Still, she left work early to pack up her girls and run—where? Anywhere!

But he was waiting for her, already inside her tiny apartment, and not alone. An infant and a dark-haired toddler slept in two carryalls atop the sofa. He ranted about a business deal gone sour she must help him fix. And unless she agreed, he'd tell the cops everything.

Tana had no choice. She couldn't go to her sister again so she called her parents. And prayed they'd forgive her.

Chapter 50 (Present Day)

Teddy bustled to ready his RV for the road. They'd stopped by the hotel for Tee to check out and collect September's stuff, which Teddy would store.

"Help me get the cats situated. With two of them I will need to get more food and maybe another litter box, too." He turned around. "How long can a cat cross its legs? I think they've been locked up for too long. Should I let 'em out? I've only had dogs before."

Tee looked up from the phone. "I have no idea. Karma's my first dog, and I've never had cats, either." She gestured with the phone. "The call came to September's cell phone."

He stopped fussing. "Wait, what? Was that September? Is she okay?"

"No. Her mother called looking for her."

He made a face. "Rose January." She'd never struck him as the motherly type. September had a strained relationship with her.

"September's sister April is in the hospital." Tee rubbed her eyes. "Did they really name all their kids after their birth months?"

Teddy grunted as he moved one of the carriers across the RV. "A little help here? These cats ain't lightweights, ya know." He'd only met two of September's siblings. "She has a brother named Mark. Only the girls got those kitschy names. You can ask Rose why, the next time you talk." He grinned as she caught up the other cat carrier and set it beside the first.

"I doubt we'll be chatting. The woman sounded…odd, a little off, you know?" Tee sat on the tiny bed. She rubbed and flexed her leg.

He noticed. She'd done that a lot on the car ride. "Does it hurt?"

Tee shook her head. "Feels asleep. Needles and pins. I think it's the cold weather. It started a week ago. At least my headache's gone."

"Hope you get a doctor to check that out." Teddy checked his refrigerator. Empty. He limped to the front, and noted the gas tank also needed freshening.

Tee watched curiously. "What are you doing?"

He met her eyes. Maybe she'd help him out. He knew better than to ask his son. Theo would shut him down. "Time for me to go back to Texas. I gotta return these cats to September. You up for a drive? We can drop off your rental, and you and Karma can join my rolling ark."

"I can't. My boss called me back to Chicago, Teddy, I told you that. Besides, we don't know for sure September went home. She could be—" She bit her lip when his scowl silenced her.

"Don't you dare say it." Teddy refused to consider that September could be dead.

She bit her lip. "My boss gave me one job: to collect the records from Sissie Turpin." She hesitated, then pressed on. "You sent the electronic files on—"

"—but Steele may not be forthcoming." He nodded. "I know jurisdiction can get tangled, and delays won't help your cause. And you still want to make points with Redford. I get it." He'd seen that before, and didn't want Tee's efforts penalized for something out of her control. "I can send another copy to your Detective Redford, how's that? Get me a contact email, and how I should explain the message. I don't want to step on toes. Or get you cross-ways with your superiors."

She smiled with gratitude. September's phone buzzed again, startling them both. Tee showed the caller ID to Teddy. He limped toward her, holding out his hand to answer the call.

"This is Teddy Williams, answering September's phone for her. How're ya doing, Detective Combs?" He raised a hand, shushing Tee when she would have interjected. He switched it to speaker, and put a finger to his lips.

"Teddy? Are you back in Heartland? Good to hear from you."

Tee could hear loud festival sounds in the background, and

raised her eyebrows. Teddy shrugged. "Hard to hear you, Detective. You on a stakeout at a carnival?"

Combs laughed. "Didn't September tell you? I'm at the Magic Kingdom with the kids. She insisted we make it just the three of us." He paused. "Is September around? I got some news she'll want to hear."

"About her sister, April?" He hesitated. "September's away for the moment."

"April? No, what's up with her sister?" It sounded like he tried to block the phone with his hand to yell, "Willie, you do what your sister says. I'm not telling you again." Then he came back to the conversation. "Sorry. He's wired, wants to do the rides again but it's Melinda's turn to choose. Look, I've got to run. But tell September I got a call from the department. The news hasn't hit the networks yet, but they'll probably come to her for comments, and I don't want her blindsided." He didn't hide the satisfaction in his voice. "They found Victor Grant dead, hung in his cell. Just saved the taxpayers the cost of a trial. I'll call September later." The call disconnected.

Teddy felt his face drain of color. He sat down hard, and winced with the sore leg.

"His name's on the cat sale list. He got the cat for September. Right?"

"Macy." Teddy whispered the name, and the coffee-colored cat meowed back. "Victor Grant was a family friend. He did terrible things to September, and later tried to kill her." He pulled off his glasses, polishing them on the hem of his sweater, as he stared back at Tee. "How many does that make, Tee? A lot of people on that pricey cat list have died. Seems like someone's washing the slate clean."

Her face looked as pale as his felt. "September's on the list. If she's still alive—" Teddy scowled but she kept on, "—and I really want to believe that, then maybe she's keeping her head down. Could be she left the phone so nobody could track her." She stared pointedly at his computer set up. "If you can work magic with technology, she knows others can find her, too."

Teddy put his glasses back on. "She's changed. Not the same scared girl I first met. Before, she'd run and hide, but not anymore."

Tee zipped up her coat. "Redford expects me back in Chicago. Nice to meet you, Teddy, but I've got to go. Karma's waiting in the car, still upset I wouldn't let her in here with the cats." She paused, worried about him. "You shouldn't be driving anyway, especially not by yourself. Not with a bullet hole in you. Does your son even know you checked yourself out of the hospital?"

He shook his head. "And don't you tell him, either." He stuck out his hand. "Wish we'd met under different circumstances, Officer Teves. But a friend of September is a friend of mine. Call me with any updates, and I'll do the same."

Smiling, she shook his hand. "Email me the computer files so I can share them with Redford as soon as I get to Chicago. And don't try to drive to Texas by yourself!"

"You got it. You and September already have me coloring outside the lines." Teddy waited until Tee's car disappeared down the road before he quickly typed on his computer keyboard and sent her the bookkeeper's files. He checked that the cats were comfortable, then carefully backed up the motor home, and drove away from his son's house.

A quick stop at a neighborhood grocery provided cat food, and more sand to put in the litter box. Next he drove to his favorite taco place and ordered a to-go box with a dozen burritos and tacos. Finally, he topped off the tank at a gas station, and purchased energy drinks and candy bars. "Brain food," he told himself, just like when he pulled all-nighters back in his hacker days. From there, he tooled Nellie-Nova back to the hospital, and hobbled inside, wincing with each step.

The girl at the gift shop counter recognized him. "Did your granddaughter like her sweats outfit?"

He grinned back. "Guess I'll find out. I'm here to pick her up. While I'm waiting, could you give me a bottle of aspirin or something? Oh, and this is nice." He picked up a cane with an eye-buster metallic 3D design. He paid for his purchases, and took a seat in the lobby area, and made a quick call to the ward. "Ready if you are." He hung up.

Charlie emerged from the bank of elevators, hoodie covering her purple hair and most of her face. She didn't speak, and kept looking over her shoulder.

Teddy took her good arm, while testing his new cane with the other hand. They made their way back to his rolling home. She climbed inside, and exclaimed with happiness at the sight of Sherlock. He let her cuddle the white cat for only a couple of minutes before interrupting the reunion.

"Charlie, ever handled one of these RVs?"

She shrugged. "How hard could it be? Lots better than my junker." Charlie tipped her head to one side. It reminded him of Shadow puzzling out something new. "Road trip?" She kept the hoodie up, still hiding most of her expression. "Far away, I hope. Anywhere but here." She shivered, and hugged Sherlock.

"Right now, that's not important. But we made a deal. I got you out of the hospital, and even paid your bill." He hoped she hadn't blown smoke just to get his help.

She gasped. "You did that? For a stranger?" Charlie's tone changed to suspicion. She squeezed the cat so hard, Sherlock hissed. "What do you want from me?"

"Relax. Nothing bad. But I've got a friend in trouble. She's the one rescued your white cat." He nodded at the Maine Coon. "Tell me true. Did you lie just to get my help? About things you didn't share with the police?"

She crossed her arms, and hunched her shoulders as the cat snuggled in her lap. "I've got plenty to say. I just don't want to end up dead for talking to some old man."

He smiled, and put the RV into gear. "Buckle up, Charlie girl, we've a long drive ahead. Two days by myself, but only fifteen hours if we take turns and drive straight through. Plenty of time to tell your tale." He waited until she'd buckled her seat belt in the passenger side, pulled out of the parking lot, and eased into traffic. "How about you start with your real name? And what you really were up to at Sissie Turpin's house."

Chapter 51

More cars filled the airport parking lot. Tee circled the area once more, just to see if anything had changed with September's SUV. September's car sat in the short-term parking in a handicap space, with no handicap designation, an obvious way to gain quick attention (which also didn't make sense). But aside from a ticket under the wiper blade, the car looked no different than before. Nobody but she and Teddy had disturbed the car.

"So why'd Steele tell Redford the police checked it out?" In the back seat, Karma woofed impatiently. The dog had been cooped up in the rental for too long.

"You ready to go home, honey-girl?" Tee smiled, a bit light headed. "We gotta turn in our rental. And grab something to eat before we get on the train."

Once Tee turned in the car she walked Karma to the nearby pet relief station to *take a break*. Karma took more time than usual sniffing the area—interested in whatever pee-mail previous visitors had left—and Tee finally had to urge her to finish. They'd missed the early train, so the lunch run it would be. At least they'd gain an hour, with the time difference between South Bend and Chicago, and get in to the city a little after two o'clock. "Let's go, Karma."

They trotted past the single baggage claim—empty—and the ticket counters for the various airlines. The ticket agent waved when she recognized Karma again, and Tee waved back. They continued down the long corridor to the train platform, stopping at the South Bend Chocolate Cafe. She didn't want to risk the headache coming back. Tee ordered a coffee mocha and a cheese omelet bagel to go, with two plates and plenty of napkins. Karma licked her lips, and sniffed the bag. "Soon, we've got to hurry."

Tee stumbled. The numbness in her leg had progressed to include the bottom of her foot. Now that she'd probably be pulled from the case, she'd take time to check it out, once she got home and reported to Redford.

After Tee bought their ticket she carefully plated the egg and bagel sandwich; three-quarters for Karma and a quarter for her. The dog finished in two gulps, before Tee had taken her first bite. After three nibbles of her own, her stomach rebelled, and Tee gave the rest to a grateful Karma.

Only a handful of other passengers boarded the train. Tee settled with a relieved sigh, directing Karma to a place at her feet. Before the train began to move, a man clearly working for the South Shore line made his way down the aisle, taking tickets from some, and selling tickets to others. Tee forced herself to smile—her headache had returned, dammit—and produced both her ticket and her police identification.

He smiled. "Two in one day. How about that."

Tee stared up at him. "Two what?"

"Dogs. A German Shepherd rode with some woman on the earlier run."

Chapter 52

September murmured to Shadow, keeping him close to her side as she disembarked the train at the Van Buren Street Station, exiting to Michigan Avenue. She looked like a homeless person. Dirt from the cemetery still clotted her clothes. Without a phone, she'd have to check flights once she got to O'Hare. Now, she had a choice. She could walk to the Jackson Station Blue Line and buy a Ventra train card to take her to the airport. Or try to catch a cab. She'd have to use her credit card for the train card, and for the flight. The right cab would take cash. She needed to avoid using the credit card as long as possible.

She hugged herself, pinning her arms against her stomach. September ached to find out how Teddy fared, but couldn't risk a call. *Please God, don't let him die.* Let him live, so she could make it up to him. Somehow.

Shadow looked up, and whined. He pressed against her thigh. But the guilt continued to build.

Chris died because of her. The reason had changed, but the result hadn't. And now because of September, his mother had also paid with her life.

She ran her hand through her hair, smoothing it behind each ear but the white streak kept falling into her eyes. She kept her eyes down, staring at her feet as she walked north, and a block later turned left on Jackson to get to Dearborn Street and the Blue Line. The

South Shore train had been virtually empty. The same wouldn't be true now, or at the airport.

She needed to call Combs. Her chin quivered. With his support and love, she'd dared believe in a new beginning, in a happy future. Only his assurance that all would be well could assuage her pain. Four short days ago, she'd been in his arms, and wished she'd never left. She'd given up Disney for…this! She touched her lips, and imagined she could still feel the last kiss they'd shared: sweet, soft, but quick because of his nearby kids.

Kids she'd grown to love. Imagine that! September never dared think of herself as a mom, let alone a stepmother. If she'd learned anything, September knew that blood alone didn't create family; love forged bonds stronger than any familial relationship.

"Chosen family," she whispered. And oh dear God, she didn't want to risk losing any more family members. Her chest tightened.

September yearned to call Combs. But he couldn't get back home in time to make a difference. Willie and Melinda had to be his priority. No, she'd wait until closer to home so the local Texas cops would respond and not have time to check with South Bend and second guess her story.

How many times had she brought danger to those she loved? She'd made mistakes in the past, and owned that. But this time, September couldn't figure out what she'd done to set the deadly wheels in motion. So many deaths. It had to end.

The killer could strike from anywhere—Chicago, South Bend, Heartland. *Please God, not Disney World!* She'd remain a ghost, stay alive, and protect those she loved. Nobody else would die because of her.

At the station, just before she used her credit card for the train pass, a cab stopped to unload a passenger. September flagged it down. Cabs legally couldn't refuse a service dog and partner, and weren't allowed to charge more, but they did it anyway. September wasn't surprised when quoted three times the usual fare. She didn't quibble.

At the airport, she checked flight arrivals and departures, and headed for the ticket counter, Shadow glued to her side. The ticket agent's smile faded when she noticed the dog, taking in the service dog tag. September asked for the next available flight to Dallas, producing her driver's license and credit card. She knew advance notice was preferred, but not required. She also had Shadow's vaccination records with her, along with Macy's records, in one of her coat pockets. Although rarely enforced, most states required medical documentation when traveling across state lines with pets. Airlines could refuse service without them.

The ticket agent accessed flight availability. "I need to ask you some questions about your dog."

September nodded. She expected that.

"Thanks for understanding, Ms. Day." She read from a prepared card. "Is the dog a service animal required because of a disability?"

"Yes." She didn't blink. September had come to grips with her challenges. She'd improved, but could still suffer an episode at any time.

"What work or task has the dog been trained to perform?"

Swallowing hard, September placed one hand on Shadow's neck. "He alerts me to impending panic attacks."

The ticket agent smiled again, and put away the card. "Let's see if we can find you a flight. There's no charge for service animals, of course, but he's so big, we may have trouble finding space. He needs to fit at your feet, bulkhead would be most comfortable, but most of the earliest flights are full." She typed on her keyboard for several moments, frowning, and finally sighed. "The next flight with space available departs tomorrow evening. It gets you in to DFW at 11:30 p.m."

"Oh no, that won't work." September rubbed her eyes. Shadow whined and pressed against her.

"You could check him as baggage…"

"No!" September took a breath. "Sorry, but no thanks. Shadow isn't cargo, and I don't have his crate anyway. We'll find another way." She started to walk away, but the agent called after her.

"Maybe Amtrak? I think they have a route to Dallas."

Hopeful, September turned back. "Thank you. I lost my phone, and have no way to check. I hate to impose, but—"

The agent smiled again, typing quickly. "There's one scheduled to leave Union Station at about one-thirty. It would get you in a little after noon tomorrow." She made a face. "A long trip, but still faster than waiting on tomorrow's plane, and more comfortable, I'm sure. I'm a sucker for handsome, well-behaved good dogs."

"Thank you so much!" September waved, grateful for the kindness, and Shadow wagged at the woman's words.

They could sleep during the twenty-plus hour train trip.

September held out hope that Mr. Bleak's Chicago business would keep him there long enough for her to beat him back to Heartland. She had time to find fresh clothes before heading to the Amtrak station.

O'Hare had many shopping options. She quickly bought and donned fleece-lined sweatpants, matching sweatshirt, and thick warm socks. She also purchased a fluffy towel for Shadow to sleep on during the ride. September bundled up the soiled clothing in the shopping bag, but had to continue wearing tattered soaked shoes, and dingy overcoat. The dry, clean clothes felt amazing against her battered flesh.

Outside the terminal, she hailed another cab—this one didn't overcharge—for which she paid cash. Once at Union Station, she stopped at the first trash can she found and dumped the bag of dingy clothes inside.

Shadow whined, nudging her hand. "I know, baby-dog, I'll find us some food on the train." She'd been in a rush and should have gotten food at the airport. It had been years since she'd traveled by Amtrak, but remembered the train service offered snacks and sometimes meals. If worst came to worst, they'd sleep the whole way, and eat once they got back to Dallas.

September checked her pockets, gratified to still have the baggies of Lia's dog treats. Shadow wagged and munched as she fed him the remainder of the partial bag, reserving the other for emergencies. They hurried to the ticket counter, paid cash, then followed the instructions to the platform. While they waited, she rubbed down Shadow's fur with the towel, to the dog's immense enjoyment. She draped the towel around her neck when the train pulled up to the platform, anxious to board and relax.

She spread the towel on the floor by her feet, and Shadow settled with a grateful sigh. September wondered again just what Latana Ojo had done to attract the killer's attention. Whoever she might be, September's first priority was her mother. She prayed the train got her home in time.

Chapter 53

Tee gathered her duffle as the train rolled to a stop in Chicago. She'd spent the trip debating about who to inform regarding the news of the other dog on the train, and remained puzzled why September traveled to Chicago instead of taking a direct flight home. Redford didn't like her to guess or speculate. She needed facts, concrete answers, before presenting to him.

She wanted a shower. She wanted to sleep. And she wanted her laptop. The first two she'd defer long enough take a look at Teddy's digital file on her computer once she got home. But all three would have to be deferred until after she found September.

When the first several cabbies in line turned their backs at the sight of Karma, Tee impatiently pulled out her badge.

"No dogs. My car's new." One man stepped forward. "Just like I told that other lady."

"Other lady?" Tee stepped closer. "You had another fare today with a dog?"

He shook his head. "She wanted to go to O'Hare. I don't put no stinkin' dog in my cab, even if it's one of them handicap dogs. She sure didn't look handicapped, just raggedy. Maybe somebody else took her."

Tee gladly paid the driver extra to get her to O'Hare in a hurry, and promised more if he'd wait. She raced into the concourse with Karma trotting by her side, and skidded up to the first ticket counter she saw. Pulling out her badge, she asked again about a woman with a shepherd booking a flight. The ticket agent looked for September Day's name, but found nothing on any recent or forthcoming manifest. Tee turned to leave.

"Our day for dogs," said another ticket agent returning to her station. "She's a beauty. I've a soft spot for well-behaved dogs."

"You've seen another dog today? Did they book a flight?" Tee described September.

The agent made a face. "She looked desperate to get back to Dallas. But we had nothing available for a German Shepherd." She nodded at Karma. "She's big, too. Even if she's a K9 officer, there has to be room to fit in front of your feet. The earliest flight with space is tomorrow evening. Sorry."

Tee shook her head. "No, we don't need a flight. We're just trying to find the woman and her dog."

"Oh, I found her a train going into DFW from Union Station." She frowned again. "She looked like she needed some luck. I hope she's not in trouble?"

As soon as the cab dropped them at Union Station, Karma hit on a familiar scent. The Rottie tracked it to a nearby waste can, and alerted. Tee looked inside, and carefully reached in to pull out a shopping bag full of filthy clothes. Tee recognized the plastic baggy with a bright label that spelled out "Corazon Candies."

"Karma, *such*!" The dog whirled, and with authority guided Tee to one of the train platforms. She glanced at the departure board and saw that the train to Dallas left an hour ago. "Dammit!" She threw up her hands. At least September made it this far, with Shadow beside her.

Tee retraced her steps, gratified the cabbie once again waited as requested. He got her home to her tiny apartment in record time, despite new snow falling, and earned the bonus she gave.

Once inside, Tee helped Karma shed the K9 working harness. The dog shook herself long and hard, then slurped up most of a full bowl of water. Tee drank a water bottle herself. She booted up her laptop. Sure enough, the emailed zip file from Teddy waited in her in-box.

She called Redford to tell him about September and get protection assigned to the woman. And probably to her family. The call forwarded to Redford's desk at the precinct, and someone she didn't recognize answered. Weird. Probably the weather had wires crossed. She disconnected without speaking. She'd catch Redford later.

Instead, she called Teddy. She couldn't leave him worrying about September. She also wanted to thank him for sending the files.

"This is Theodore Williams. Who's this?"

"Teddy? It's me, Tee. Uhm, Officer Teves." She heard road noises and frowned. "Are you driving?"

"Glad you made it back to Chicago." He chuckled. "Yep, on the road and making good time. But don't worry about me. Charlie's driving."

"What the hell is she doing out of the hospital? Are you nuts, Teddy?"

"Never mind that, I'll explain later. Did you get the documents okay? What'd your boss think?"

She blew out a breath. "I just got in, and haven't been able to reach Redford yet. You were right about September." She filled him in on what they'd found at the train station.

"Thank God!" His relief quickly changed to aggravation. "Why the hell does she scare me like that?" He sighed. "It's not the first time, and I doubt it'll be the last. Trouble follows that girl like stink on a skunk."

She rubbed her nose, silently agreeing. "Her train arrives in Dallas at twelve-forty tomorrow and it'll take her some time to get home to Heartland. She must have a reason for keeping us in the dark. But I'd be a whole lot happier with the local PD knowing about the situation, especially since that Victor character offed himself in jail. That's way too convenient for my tastes."

"I'll call Combs back. He'll know who to contact, and can rally the Texas troops more quickly than either of us. Thanks for the call, Tee. We're driving in shifts, nonstop, but we started a bit late. With good traffic and clear roads, we'll get to Heartland shortly after September." He hesitated, then added, "Keep me posted with anything new. And I'll do the same."

Once they disconnected, Tee opened the zip file. She used her mouse to find the appropriate files they'd already perused. The "cat sales" file had today's date, with Teddy's notes and she hoped that wouldn't piss off Redford. Highlights pointed out all of the high-dollar cat sales documented over the past thirty-plus years. She pulled out a notepad to jot additional comments with purchaser's name and fees, along with the dates.

One entry from nineteen years ago made Tee sit back in her chair. For a moment, she couldn't breathe. She and Teddy suspected someone pulled strings from the inside. But this changed everything. She called Redford's direct line once again. She needed to give him a chance to explain, felt like she owed him that much. But it switched over immediately to another line.

This time, she spoke. "This is Officer Teves. I need to speak to Detective Redford."

"Teves? Where the hell have you been?"

Shocked that her lieutenant would answer Redford's phone, she heard muted conversation at the other end of the line. "I just got back from South Bend. The Captain signed off on sending me to work on the Detweiller case." Hadn't Redford updated him?

"Come in and make your report, Officer Teves. The Captain will debrief you."

Tee slumped in her chair. What had gone wrong? "I followed Detective Redford's direction, sir. May I please speak with him?" She really needed him to answer her questions. Tee looked up to him, she knew he was a good cop. He couldn't be part of this, could he? Her hand sought, and retrieved, the seashells and waited for their shushing to steady her nerves.

A long pause. "Earlier today, Redford tried to eat his gun."

Chapter 54

September awoke with a start when the train finally pulled into the last platform. They'd reached Dallas.

Shadow stood, stretched, and yawned noisily. He'd slept heavily, too, with paws twitching and even a few tail thumps in doggy dreams. Her own sleep had been fitful. Every time she dozed off, she felt dirt shoveled onto her back once more, and startled awake. September feared if she succumbed to sleep, she'd suffer a PTSD episode. She couldn't afford a meltdown now. She had no time to waste.

"Come on, Shadow, let's go." She stood, cracked her back, and gathered up his towel. Everything else resided in her coat pockets. She'd avoided using her credit card so far, but that wouldn't fly with the rental car. Still, she'd reach Heartland in less than twenty minutes from the station, so felt the risk worthwhile. Besides, she had no choice.

The agent took her credit card, and typed into the computer terminal. "Proof of insurance, please."

September blanched. "I don't have it with me." Her insurance was in her car, wherever Mr. Bleak had dumped it.

"You can call and have them fax you a copy. With no proof of insurance, you'll have to purchase ours." She eyed Shadow as he whined and leaned against her leg. "Is the dog riding with you? That's extra. Do you have a crate for it?"

"He's my service dog." September put a hand on Shadow's head. "Let me see your driver's license."

September stepped away from the counter, kicking herself. How had she not thought of that? "Someone stole my bag with my phone, and insurance information. I was fortunate the credit card was in my pocket."

"That's terrible. I'm so sorry, you look pretty frazzled. Do you want me to call the police?" Her kindness nearly brought September to tears.

"Very kind of you, but no." September thought a moment. She'd come this far without producing digital identification. She didn't want to drag anyone into danger, but surely Lia wouldn't be a target. They weren't related, not directly. "Can you call my roommate? Hopefully she can pick us up." September gave the woman Lia's number, and held her breath. This time of day, Lia usually ran kennel duty for boarding clients, or took her dog out to train.

A half hour later, September loaded Shadow into the rear of Lia's old vehicle, and climbed into the passenger's front seat. "Sorry for the short notice. Thanks for the ride."

Lia stared long and hard at September. "What's going on? Where's your car, September? And where's Macy?"

At the cat's name, September's throat clenched. "It's a long story." She prayed both Macy and Teddy survived the killer's attack. "Can I borrow your phone?"

"Really? No car, no cat, no phone. You just abandoned everything and jumped on a train?" Her brow furrowed, and sparks lit her eyes. "Folks called looking for you. I got two messages from Jeff Combs, and I just got a chewing out from your mother. I'm not moving this car without an explanation."

She couldn't call Combs, not yet. "Mom called? When?" *She's okay. For now.* "Is she at home? Drop me and Shadow off at her house." She'd call the police from there.

"Your mom didn't offer any details. But then, she rarely gives me the time of day. Just like Grandmother." Lia drove the car out of the parking lot, and headed back to Heartland. "We've got time for a long story, September. So talk." She glared at her. "You look all used up and wore out. Hungry?"

In the back seat, Shadow yelped at the word, and thumped his tail. September smiled ruefully. "Not much of an appetite. But Shadow could use some food." They'd shared a couple of sandwiches on the train, but nothing since late last night.

Lia grinned. "I've got some Corazon Candy dog treats in a baggy in the glove box. There's a couple of power bars in there, too, unless you want the treats. They're not bad, if you like dried liver and fish."

September opened the glove box. Next to the dog treats she saw Lia's handgun, the twin of the one she'd left behind in South Bend. She'd need to let the South Bend police know about her gun. She offered Shadow a handful of the liver treats, and took one of the power bars for herself. Fatigue made it hard to think. She could either go to protect Mom, or convince the police to do the same thing. She didn't have time to do both.

"So spill. What happened in South Bend? Look, I don't mean to pry…wait, yes I do. I'm dying of curiosity! I mean, you took off like some secret agent on a mission, and now you're back here without a ride, your phone, and you left Macy behind." She paused. "Are you in trouble?"

"Yes." September rubbed her arms, and stared out the window. "But there's no time to convince the police to help. I need you to trust me, okay?"

"I knew it! What can I do?" Lia pounded the steering wheel with excitement. "What's the plan?"

"Whoa, hold your horses. You're not a cop, Lia Corazon, not yet. And neither am I. But you go off halfcocked and you'll never be accepted into the police academy." *And, you could get us all killed.*

"I want to help. You called me for the ride, remember?" The younger woman huffed, clearly hurt. "So tell me what happened, and maybe I'll surprise you."

Even though they were half-sisters, and only a few months apart in age, Lia couldn't be more different than Tee. Where Tee's shyness and reticence made her seem older than her years, Lia's brash exuberance had the opposite effect. September consciously slowed her own breathing, using the technique to calm herself. It wouldn't help if she had a meltdown.

"I used to be married to a policeman." She rushed on, giving Lia the bare facts. "Chris's mother contacted me about an old investigation that had to do with my past. That's why he was murdered."

Lia whistled through her teeth. "Whoa, September. You sure are a lady with secrets." She turned onto the interstate and accelerated. "So the old case, is that why you're in trouble?" She cut her eyes sideways. "Er, what's in your past? Can you say?"

"No!" September softened her tone. "Sorry, but that's the problem. I don't know. I went to make peace with Angela, my former mother-in-law. But then somebody killed her, attacked me, stole the case files, and everything went to hell—"

"Wait. Somebody murdered your mother-in-law?" Lia nearly swerved off the road in surprise.

Now that she'd begun to explain, the words spilled faster and faster. "Asking questions sure lit a fire. I'm scared they might hurt my family or other people." She didn't have time to explain everything. This had to be enough.

"That's why you ditched your car and phone, didn't want to use a credit card. So they couldn't track you." Lia nodded understanding.

September hugged herself. "I couldn't tell anyone else and put a target on them, too. I never would have called you…" She blinked, hoping she'd not put the younger woman in danger.

Lia scoffed. "Don't be silly. I'm a nobody. Just ask Grandmother, she'll tell you." Her bitter laugh spoke of her own personal pain and betrayal. "We need to go to the police."

September knew Lia still blamed her Grandmother for many things, and hoped they'd find a path to mutual forgiveness. She'd learned from her own past trauma that blame only hurt the blamer. "I need to find my Mom first, make sure she's okay. Meanwhile, you need to bring the police." She rubbed her eyes. "There's someone else in danger, Latana Ojo. I don't know who that is, but the police can get out a protective order or something."

"Latana *Ojo*? Are you sure you heard right?" Lia turned into the neighborhood where September's parents lived. "I can drop you in front of the house. Are you sure you don't want me to stay with you?"

She shook her head. "Drop Shadow and me a block away. It's better that we go in on foot, in case…" *In case the killer beat her home.* She waited until the car slowed to a stop. "Do you know that name? Latana Ojo?" September climbed out of the car, and held the door for Shadow to hop out.

Lia rolled down her window. "No, I don't know anyone named Latana. That's Spanish for some kind of flower, I think. But Ojo—that's not a common surname. Grandmother's maiden name was Ojo." She cocked her head. "You do remember that your mother and my grandmother are sisters, right?"

Chapter 55

Teddy roused from his fitful doze, and sat up in the small bed. The hum of tires on pavement offered a hypnotic ambiance that lulled others to sleep. But he'd found, since hitting his mid-70s, sleep proved elusive even when he yearned for rest. He rarely needed the energy drinks and candy binges of his youth to fuel 24-plus hour computer marathons. Charlie, on the other hand, needed the help.

He rummaged in the small refrigerator for a beverage, grabbed an energy bar, and slowly gimped the length of the moving RV to the front passenger seat. "Here, thought you could use this." He popped the tab, and set the drink in the cup holder. "Need a break?"

"I'm fine, thanks." Charlie took the can, and drank nearly all of it in one long gulp. "Sweet ride. A whole lot nicer than my poor old tin can." She studiously kept her eyes on the road.

"You want this?" He offered the power bar, and when she shook her head, he peeled the wrapper and ate it himself. He'd given her space, but now felt an urgency to press her for details. Teddy felt sure the girl's association with Sissie Turpin hadn't been accidental. "You ready to talk?"

"Nothing much to say." Her lips tightened.

"Let's start with how you'll take care of that baby. Whoa!" He grabbed the armrest when the RV swerved. "Eyes on the road,

Charlie."

"How did you know?" One hand touched her still-flat stomach, and she glanced over at him, her glaring expression both hurt and defiant.

"I paid your hospital bill, remember? That little detail got flagged, probably because certain medications could hurt your baby." He patted her arm. "There's a rest stop up ahead. Pull in, we can take a break, and have a little talk. It's my turn to drive."

She pulled her arm away, sullen, but did as he asked. Instead of taking a turn in the restroom, Charlie busied herself with the two cats. "They need the break more than I do. Hey Sherlock, how's my big boy?" She crooned, snuggling the white cat before she let Macy out of his carrier.

Charlie complained again about the litter box he'd provided. "How do you expect Sherlock or..." She indicated the other cat. "I told you they need bigger facilities."

"Macy." He'd watched her situate the litter box, but the cats hadn't been productive the other times they'd stopped. He wrinkled his nose when this time Macy immediately hopped into the plastic square and posed. The cat enthusiastically pawed the litter over his creativity, getting as much outside the box as in. "Hey, he's making a mess."

Charlie smirked. "Like I said, he needs a bigger box." Sherlock, by comparison, ignored the litter even after Charlie cleaned away Macy's creativity. Instead, Sherlock purred, and wound around and around Charlie's ankles, getting in the way and nearly tripping her.

Macy jumped up onto Teddy's computer table once he was done with the litter box, and tried to plop down on the laptop. Teddy gently moved him off when he entered. Miffed, the cat stalked back to his carrier, turned around once, and settled.

"Macy is my friend September's cat. From Sissie Turpin's breeding, too." Teddy tried again to get Charlie to talk.

"Macy came from the cattery? So September's like me." Sherlock continued to rub her ankles until the girl sat on the opposite seat. He climbed into her lap, and pushed his face again and again into her neck, until Charlie had to set the big cat aside.

"What do you mean, she's like you?" Teddy took off his glasses and polished them on his sweater hem. "At the hospital, you told me you know a lot more stuff that you didn't share with the police." Teddy replaced his glasses and took his seat behind the computer table, ready to open the laptop and make notes. "I know you're scared. You're running, maybe hiding from some bad people, I get that. But unless you share what you know, I can't help you."

"How can you protect me?" She crossed her arms, but the white cat pushed beneath them, insisting on face-to-face contact. "What's wrong with you, kitty? Why so pushy?" She held him still in her lap, but he continued to fuss and struggle. "Teddy, I appreciate the ride, and I'll still drive with you to Texas. But after that, I'm better off on my own. Sissie pissed off the wrong people. They're after me, too."

"How so? C'mon, Charlie, work with me here." He narrowed his eyes. "I don't suppose this has to do with your baby's father?"

She shuddered. "Don't even go there!" She bared her teeth in a parody of a smile. "Someday I'll find him, and he'll pay for what he did to me. To us." One hand cradled her tummy. "At least Sissie wanted to give me a chance to start over. And give my baby a better life."

He nodded but said nothing. Sometimes, silence prompted more than questions.

Charlie pushed the white cat away from her face once again. "I come from a family of losers." Her bitter smile stopped him when Teddy would have argued. "You don't know, Teddy. I'm probably the pick of the litter, and look what a mess I am. I'd be no good for this baby anyway. It didn't ask to be born. And I sure as hell didn't ask to get pregnant."

"Hey, sometimes in the heat of romance, accidents happen." He remembered his grandmother telling him that nothing that took place in the back seat of a car didn't also happen in the rear of a buggy.

"Romance?" She nearly spat with anger. "My uncle raped me. My baby wasn't an accident, they wanted me pregnant. They had plans. So I ran." She seethed. "Sissie knew just what to do, how to find him or her a good home, get me enough money for a new start, and keep us away from *them*. I didn't even know whether to get pink or blue onesies. If I had money to get anything at all." Her anguish spilled from Charlie's tight throat, tears overflowing. She breathed heavily, and the cat again pushed his white cheeks against her face. "Dammit, Sherlock, get out of my face, just stop—"

Her eyes abruptly rolled up, and Charlie lurched to one side, falling heavily onto the small bed. Her legs and arms jerked in a grand mal seizure.

With a cry, Teddy rushed to her side, not sure what to do. It seemed to go on forever but probably lasted less than a minute. The white cat yowled, and pawed Charlie's face, ultimately snuggling into the bend of her neck.

While he waited for her to recover, Teddy made a long overdue call to Jeff Combs.

Chapter 56

September sat back in the truck as Lia made the call, then took the phone with trepidation. "Hello. Thank you for taking my call, Mrs. Corazon. I need some answers. About my mother. About my past." She waited a moment, and added, "You're on speakerphone. I think Lia should hear this, too."

Silence greeted her words. At first, September thought the woman had disconnected, but then detected ragged breathing on the other end of the line. Finally, Cornelia spoke. "I feared this day would come." Another pause. "I don't know much. I suspect more. But the time for secrets has passed. Ask your questions."

Now that she could ask, September's tongue stuck to the roof of her mouth. "Are you my aunt? Is my mother Rose your sister?"

"She was christened Latana. Yes, Lantana Ojo was my younger sister. Just before her fifteenth birthday, she ran away from home. To be a film star, or some such foolishness. Tana always had stars in her eyes and a volatile temper." Her voice steadied, grew strong, resigned. "She broke my parents' hearts when the police came knocking at the door saying she'd attacked some poor man. After that, she was dead to us."

"What?" *Rose January attacked someone?* "Did he press charges?"

"The man died, September. He was a talent agent or something. The police hounded my parents after that, trying to find Tana and arrest her. There's no statute of limitations on murder."

This couldn't be true! September clenched the phone so tightly her hand turned white. Shadow whined, and nose-touched her arm.

"They told us that they'd found Tana's body with her bastard child dead, too. That was a blessing in disguise. It stopped the police hounding." Cornelia waited for the next question.

Nothing could have prepared September for such news. "But Mom's maiden name was Dixon." She'd been a runaway teenager? Unwed mother? A murderer! Nothing squared that knowledge with the prim and proper Rose January who raised her.

"I don't know about that. Maybe she changed her name to hide her crimes." Cornelia sniffed. "Five years later she came out of hiding, trying to reach our parents. When I intercepted the call they had been dead a year, but she wanted money to bail her out of some new difficulty. I'd had enough. No reason to have her trashy lifestyle intruding on my own family."

September hunched her shoulders. "You turned her in? Your own sister, you didn't help her out?"

"Of course I helped her. And that's not the first time. I'm not a monster. Besides, killing that man happened long ago. I had my own family to protect, and couldn't have her crimes tarnish the Corazon name, too." Cornelia tut-tutted. "I sent her the funds she needed, but with the proviso she never contact me or our family again. Imagine my chagrin when she showed up a few years later in the next town over, married to that January fellow." She laughed, a humorless sound. "Suddenly she had a whole litter of offspring. God knows who all the fathers are."

Her face burning, September fought to keep control. She understood Lia's issues with her grandmother. "So you both kept your relationship secret. Out of the goodness of your heart." September didn't try to hide the sarcasm.

"I'll thank you to watch your tone with me. You've got your own closet of skeletons, missy. I only wanted to protect my family."

"And like you said, Latana Ojo had died, so Rose January didn't matter. I understand, I truly do. Thanks for your time, *Aunt* Cornelia." September disconnected. She had had only a few questions answered, but couldn't stomach continuing the conversation.

"So." Lia glanced over at her. "Help or hinder?"

September scrubbed her face, and forced a smile. "Doesn't matter. Once I get Mom to a safe place, we'll have the heart to heart we should've had years ago. I just wish she'd trusted me. Trusted her family." That gave her pause. Did dad know about Rose's past?

The phone rang almost as soon as she disconnected. September recognized Combs's number, and handed the phone back to Lia with a head shake, and finger to her lips. "It's safer for us both if he doesn't know I'm home yet."

Lia scowled, but nodded. "But I'm not lying for you." She let it go to voice mail, and they both listened.

"This is Jeff Combs. Again." She could hear the aggravation and something else in his voice. Fear? "September's brother called. Her sister April's in the hospital and I guess they're calling the whole family together. But now Rose isn't picking up the phone, either." He hesitated, and added, "Tell September that Teddy told me everything. Dammit, when will she trust me enough to share what's going on?" He blew out a breath. "Anyway, I called the local PD and my partner will swing by the January house. I can't get back any time soon. The connecting flights in Chicago are grounded with a snowstorm. Anyway, September—if you get this—call me, dammit. And I love you."

September squeezed shut her eyes. "He said Rose isn't answering her phone."

"Want me to take you to the hospital?"

"No. There's nothing I can do for April. I need to check on Mom.

(29 **Years Ago**)

For once, Victor proved true to his word. Documents he purchased signed by Judge Southgate proved her children's parentage. The final settlement Cornelia offered gave her enough to find a modest home, away from city life, so they could become a normal family.

The real estate agent made her laugh, and even better, he liked having a ready-made family. They joked that the two youngest looked like him. Six months later, Rose Dixon married Lysle January.

Chapter 57 (Present Day)

Shadow tipped his head side to side as he listened to September and Lia's conversation. Hearing Combs's voice on the phone made both women upset. He could always tell when September felt bad. While on the train, he'd worried for a while she might have one of her spells. She dozed and startled awake, over and over. He'd only slept a short while and tried to stay awake to do his job. He'd kept her safe on the strange noisy car-thing, and stood up tall and silently showed his teeth if anyone came too close. Not that he'd bite anyone. Shadow didn't like the taste of people, not even bad-people. But if need be, he'd show his teeth and warn them away.

He liked Lia. She understood dogs, and he especially liked staying where she lived with the other dogs and cats. But he preferred having September all to himself. So he'd enjoyed their trip together. Mostly. When she got scared, though, the fun disappeared. And this last part of their trip hadn't been fun at all.

He had whined with excitement mixed with more worry when Lia's car pulled to a stop far away from the front of the familiar house. Before they'd left, they'd visited people here that mattered deeply to September. They belonged to September the same way that Macy-cat belonged to Shadow. And the way Karma-dog belonged to him, too. They were family.

He knew Combs mattered to September, a lot, too. Almost like they belonged to each other. That worried him.

"Wait for us here. If it's safe, I'll bring Mom back." September left the car. "Shadow, let's go." He wagged his tail, ready to stretch his legs. September used her "serious business" voice, which meant fun work for him.

She didn't attach his leash. He knew the way to the front door, but she led them around to the back instead. They approached from the alley, and when September placed a hand on his neck, he could feel her tension. His anticipation grew.

"Shadow, *check-it-out*." She made a sweeping gesture with one hand, and he launched forward as though spring-loaded. The still, cool air offered perfect scenting conditions. He didn't need to stick his nose in the grass. Scent hung several feet above the ground, and he could move quickly through it, testing as he ran.

He stopped to more closely investigate areas where scent pooled; in the corner where the garage connected with the house; the cluster of garbage cans; a hollow beneath trimmed hedges. No cars sat in the driveway, and Shadow detected two vehicles, one still warm, waiting patiently behind the closed garage door. He sniffed the front steps, identifying the smell of the hard-brittle Rose-woman who so often upset September. Fainter smells reminded Shadow of the children, especially his-boy Steven. Only the brittle woman had passed this way today.

Abandoning the front area, Shadow continued to the rear of the house. More smells wove a more tantalizing story. The tall wooden fence sheltered a pool of warm water, hidden from canine view but the pungent chemical water tickled a good-dog's nose. Another familiar but frightening scent brought Shadow to alert. His ears swiveled, listening. A dragging sound combined with the scent of the bad-man from the cemetery. He didn't wonder how the bad-man followed them so far. Shadow only knew he must warn September.

Another smell—copper bright—clouded the air. Water splashed. The danger-man could hurt September. He had to protect her.

Shadow's whine escalated into whimpers of concern. He scratched the fence, leaped against it, and the gate squeaked open under his assault. He stalked inside, ears plastered flat and tail bristled, scanning back and forth, scenting for the danger. Steam billowed from the pool. Blood painted the water.

The gate swung shut, locking a good-dog inside.

Chapter 58

September slowly, cautiously opened the rear door of the house. She'd waited a long time for Shadow to finish his preliminary circuit of the house. His silence told her he'd found no overt threat. Combs would tell her to wait for the police, and she agreed in principle. But her heart screamed for her to run into the house, find Mom, and carry her away from the danger.

Why hadn't Shadow returned? She looked out the door, checking both directions, but heard and saw no sign of the big dog.

She scanned the room. At first nothing seemed amiss. Her mother kept an immaculate house. The room surfaces in the kitchen shined. September crossed to the butcher block island. The decorative mortar and pestle had been moved from its usual place. Mom might use something on the island, but always, without fail, replaced them, wanting everything tidy and in the right location.

The mortar held an open but empty pill bottle of pain medication scripted to her sister April. Curiously, September picked up the heavy stone pestle serving as paperweight on an old delicate lace handkerchief next to a yellow pad of paper. Mom's flowery script scrawled across the page, overlapping the lines with frantic loops and squiggles that screamed her alarm with a two-word repeated phrase:

I'm sorry. I'm sorry. I'm sorry!

"Mom? Mom!"

Outside, Shadow's alarm bark erupted, escalated to frantic

howls, and then fell silent. September whirled to run to her dog's aid.

Mr. Bleak stood in the doorway. "Why can't you stay dead?" He shut the door behind him.

Reflexively, September lobbed the stone pestle. It hit the side of his head with a satisfying *thunk*.

He grunted and took half a step back, then straightened. "This ends here."

"Mom! Shadow?" September screamed, and whirled. She raced through the kitchen toward the front door.

Bleak thundered after her. He tackled her in Mom's pristine living room.

September fell across the armchair, knocking it sideways to the floor. She scrabbled to crawl away, regain her feet.

But he fell on top of her. The breath burst from her lungs beneath his weight. Mr. Bleak straddled her, hands about September's throat. "This time, it is very personal." He squeezed.

She instinctively reached for his bare cat-bitten hands, each too swollen to fit inside gloves. She clawed at the constriction around her throat to no avail.

He continued to throttle her.

She had seconds before she lost consciousness. September fought panic. Remembered her self-defense class. She grabbed his left elbow with both hands, and pushed it up and sideways with all her strength. Nothing happened. He had too much control. So she quickly brought her left arm up on the inside of his right elbow and grabbed his shoulder. At the same time, she clutched his neck with her other hand, hugged him. And rolled.

The bridging move took him by surprise, but only momentarily. September struggled to regain her feet, gasping to catch her breath. She tripped twice on her way to the front door.

He came after her.

She yelled. Her voice made a choked broken-glass sound from his bruising grip. September grabbed a small lamp, one of the stained glass designs her brother made, and threw it at Mr. Bleak. He knocked it aside, hissing at the unexpected bruising weight that hit his wrist.

September reached for the front door handle.

Bleak casually stooped, grabbed up the entry rug, and yanked.

She flew sideways, arms outstretched to break her fall. September hit the floor, rolling. One hand closed on the brass lamp finial. Teeth bared, she held it like a dagger.

His kick drove the finial backwards, into her side. Pain blossomed. September fell into an abyss.

He didn't have time for this. He'd checked and the rest of the family remained conveniently tied up at the hospital. His information confirmed the mother's suicide made sense, and wouldn't be questioned once her secrets came to light.

But Mr. Bleak couldn't let September live, nor could he leave behind evidence of her death. That would prompt questions Mrs. Wong didn't want raised. No, this time he'd ensure September Day disappeared for good. He'd take care of the damn dog, too. A little blood wouldn't matter out by the hot tub. They'd just assume it came from the woman's nosebleed. Funny, what heatstroke could do to a body.

Mr. Bleak tidied the room. He reset the furniture, and balanced the lamp back onto the table, surprised the heavy glass hadn't broken. After he retraced his steps to the kitchen, he examined the pestle for evidence—it hadn't broken his skin—and placed it back on top of Rose's suicide note on the butcher block. He found plastic garbage bags he needed in one of the kitchen drawers. One would contain the mess of the dog. The other would take care of September.

He would do more than kill her. After what she'd put him through, she didn't merit a quick clean death.

So he slid the garbage bag over September's head and shoulders. Tape secured her arms at the elbow tight to her body beneath the plastic. For good measure, he taped her wrists together. She'd blackout in minutes, and would be dead in another five. Once loaded in the car for transport and disposal, he'd take care of the damn dog.

Chapter 59

Shadow stopped barking when he recognized the brittle-voiced woman in the pool of hot water. She sat neck-deep in the tub, outstretched arms floating while her head lolled backward. Red stained the water from her nose, and tainted the cold air with bitter copper. As Shadow watched, she slowly slid, slumped sideways, settling deeper into the wet.

He whined, and looked from the woman to the locked gate. The bad man—he still detected his pungent presence—lurked on the other side of the barrier. Shadow had to protect September, that was a good-dog's job! But this woman needed help now. September would want him to help her.

So he barked, and barked some more, but nobody came to help a good-dog. September would heed his warning if she could. Maybe she couldn't get past the barrier, either?

Padding closer to the unconscious woman, he nudged her neck. But that didn't rouse her. She just slipped farther into the hot water. He licked her face, and then ears—that always made September giggle and laugh—but the woman didn't react. She slid down again, and this time her face slipped beneath the coppery water.

Shadow reached down, under the water, to clamp strong teeth into her hair. And he backed up slowly, tugging her upward, grateful the water helped lift her high. After tugging for endless moments, Shadow let go, happy when she seemed to settle in place and stay still, head above the wet.

Red still slowly spilled down her face, though. The water tasted bad, too.

The tall wooden fence all around the steamy bath couldn't be climbed. Shadow knew that without trying. No rough edges offered paw purchase, and only cement he couldn't dig covered the ground when he investigated. Shadow yelped, urgency demanding he act, do something. But what?

September screamed.

Shadow threw himself at the wooden gate. But as he expected, it didn't give way. He spied a cart with wheels next to the far wall. It held several big bottles on the bottom, lined up side by side, with stacked plates and glasses on the top.

When September screamed again, Shadow didn't hesitate. From a standing start, he leaped upward to the top of the cart—scattering plates and glasses to shatter on the cement below—then up and over the fence, and raced to find September.

He pelted around the back fence. The rear kitchen door carried September's scent where she'd entered. He battered the closed door with his paws, but it wouldn't open. September had stopped yelling. But her cries came from the other side of the house, near the front door. So Shadow galloped the long way around to reach her.

As he skidded to a stop at the bottom of the steps, the front door swung open. The bad man had September slung over his shoulder, her head and chest covered in plastic cinched tight.

Bleak pulled out his gun, and aimed.

Reflexively, Shadow dodged one way, then feinted forward with teeth bared. The man's gun followed him. Shadow tensed for the gun's bite, knowing it could reach out however far away he might be. Bleak would be ready for his nose punch. So instead he lunged, with jaws wide, and clamped hard on the man's swollen wrist.

The gun spat once, twice. Shadow hung on, growling, shaking his head like he did with bear-toy. The gun fell.

The man kicked him, catching him hard in the ribs. Shadow yelped, and spun away, then came back again. He lunged at the man's other arm, holding September's legs tight against his shoulder. He made Bleak drop the gun. He'd make him drop September, too!

Instead, Bleak landed another kick, half spinning Shadow around. And he slammed the door in Shadow's face.

Shadow threw himself at the front door, anguished cries echoing in the still, cold air.

Chapter 60

Teddy's phone rang. He answered without taking his eyes off the road. "What is it, Tee? I'm five miles from Heartland, driving ten over the limit, and not in the mood to chat."

"Can you look something up for me? I need to be sure before I report to my Captain." Usually brash, at times full of false bravado, for the first time the young woman sounded shook.

"I'm driving. Can't it wait?" He glanced at Macy, perching in the passenger's seat, watching the road unfurl out the window.

Tee grew more insistent. "Have Charlie drive. I really need a confirmation. I can't make this accusation without more than a gut feeling."

"Charlie's gone. I'm driving by myself now." He'd been played the fool. Oh for sure, the girl had a seizure, no doubt about that. Maybe from the bump on the head she got in the hit and run. He'd wanted to stop at an urgent care to get her checked out but she refused.

"What do you mean, she's gone?" Tee's tone sharpened. "I knew that was a mistake! Are you okay, Teddy? She didn't hurt you, did she?"

He snorted. "Only my feelings. She disappeared about thirty minutes ago at the rest stop on Hwy. 75 at the Oklahoma/Texas border. Took that big white cat with her, and September's cell phone. And she swiped my snazzy new cane, probably so I wouldn't try to catch her." If he didn't know better, he'd say Sherlock tried to warn her about the seizure. He knew dogs did that, but cats? "She's terrified that Mr. Bleak will come after her. I think there's more to that than she's saying. Anyway, she's in the wind. Why, what does your Detective Redford say?"

"He's in the hospital. He tried to kill himself." She sounded stilted, maybe to control her emotion.

Teddy gasped. He took his foot off the gas in reaction, and the change in velocity made Macy stand up and meow. He reached out and chucked the cat under the chin, smoothing the fur to calm the cat.

"I don't believe them. Redford had this big celebration for his kid over the weekend. Got him a dog. A black and white Border Collie rescue named Oreo. He was so jazzed over that dog and his kid, he fairly glowed. Said the dog made friends with everyone, first time out of the car." She rambled, clearly unable to reconcile the idea of her mentor taking his own life.

"I'm sorry, Tee. That's got to be an awful shock." Macy head-butted Teddy's hand, and again settled in the shotgun position. He'd always been a dog man, but Macy kind of grew on him. "Sure have been a lot of suicides lately."

"My thoughts exactly." Her tone changed from mournful to speculative. "Redford was close to retirement. Before I left, he'd been getting grief from one of the Chicago Aldermen, Kelly Radcliff Jacobs. Wasn't there a Jacobs on the cat sale list?"

He passed the sign to the Heartland city limits and dropped his speed accordingly. Teddy had no intention of being sidetracked by a speeding ticket. "That's a pretty common name. You don't mean to accuse a Chicago Alderman of involvement? What kind of evidence do you have?"

"Only suspicions. I don't know what to think." She immediately backed away, as he figured she would. "He owns a bunch of pharmacies. Maybe drugs?"

"You're grasping at straws, Tee. That sounds like a bad television cop show." He followed the directions he'd memorized. "Once I get the chance, we can look closer at the dates, and then see if your Alderman had something coincide on that same date. Listen, I've got to go. I'm almost to the January house."

Tee couldn't hide her frustration. "Have you heard from September? You could be chasing the wind, Teddy."

He smiled. "I forgot to tell you. After I filled Combs in on everything, he got in touch with September's roommate. She's here. That is, they're both here, Lia and September. And if I know Combs, the Heartland police are on the way, too." He squinted, and pressed the brake. "I've got to go, will be in touch later."

Teddy disconnected, and pulled up behind Lia Corazon's shabby truck. Before either of them could get out, the sound of barking and gunshots split the air.

Chapter 61

The cold jolted September back to consciousness. It took several seconds to understand she hung upside-down. Her head pounded from blood rush. She couldn't move. Her arms ached, taped close to her body. A stabbing pulse throbbed in her side.

She couldn't see anything. Or catch her breath.

A door slammed. Barking, snarling. *Shadow?* Shadow! His cries grew fainter as someone carried her away.

Jostled, up and down, shifted roughly. Blinded? Big breath to scream—*no air…!*

Understanding flooded her mind. She inhaled, tasted plastic against her tongue, nose, her lips, stopping breath. Frantic, hungry for air, she kicked but it didn't help. September bucked, to make him drop her, escape… A car door *screed* open. He dumped her like garbage onto the back seat. The pain in her side flamed hot, but paled compared to *God help me breathe*, NO AIR!

Vibration and thrumming as the car started. Nothing mattered. Only air, sweet, fresh, fill-her-lungs-up air. She didn't care or worry what would happen when the car stopped again. She'd be dead by then.

Plastic starved her lungs…

She poked out her tongue to push the cloying material away, give space for breath. Strained her face side to side, her head up and down, swiveling her neck. Plastic clung, cloying, clutching, smothering, a deathly lover's kiss.

Arms bound to her sides, September's hands clenched and unclenched, straining to break the wrist tape free, to tear the constriction from her mouth. Bindings so tight to her torso meant only her elbows moved. She shrugged her shoulders, wriggled back and forth. She flapped elbows to loosen the bindings. A fish drowning in the back of a pine-scented rental car.

The garage door rolled up. The car moved forward.

The flailing of her right elbow drove the wreath-shaped lamp finial deeper into her side. September screamed, the pain a white-bright laser of momentary clarity. She had moments left before blacking out, and would never reawaken. She forced stillness, swallowed hard and held her breath. That hurt less than futile gasp-sucking of plastic. Gingerly, she pressed the inside of her elbow against the decorative brass piece, back and forth, until the metal still hung in the fabric of her coat loosened, and fell out.

She felt the scimitar shape, caught in the plastic just above her tape-bound hands. September clutched the brass piece, holding it tight through the plastic with the fingers of both hands—she couldn't drop it, had only one chance—and punched it through the flimsy plastic. Flexing her elbows brought the finial just high enough. She bent double, blessing her yoga flexibility. She brought her face as close to her hands as possible, and opened her mouth wide. September jabbed the sharp end of the brass wreath at the taut plastic covering her open mouth…

…and sucked in a sweet breath of fresh air.

She shuddered, afraid to make a sound. Afraid Mr. Bleak would hear, and shoot her.

The car continued to move. She held the butt end of the metal in her mouth, and used the sharp finial to cut the tape binding her wrists. She split the mouth hole wider and peeled plastic from her face.

"Damn dog!" His voice broke the spell.

She rose to her knees in the seat behind Mr. Bleak, clutching the finial. He goosed the accelerator, aiming for Shadow.

"You just made it personal." September stabbed him in the neck.

Chapter 62

His car swerved off the road, and smashed into a fire hydrant. A geyser of water spewed over the windshield.

Mr. Bleak roared, eyes wide and neck corded. He ignored the wound, felt no pain. His pulse pounded in his ears, and tunnel vision focused on September's figure stumbling away.

Mr. Bleak grabbed his phone with one swollen hand, collected his go-bag, and staggered from the disabled car. A block away, he saw a familiar RV parked next to an old, beat-up truck. He paused in the shadow of a nearby house as a crowd gathered. Pulling up his coat collar to hide his bloody neck, he walked with confidence through the throng. In less than a minute, he reached the battered SUV, climbed inside, and found keys still in the ignition. And a gun in the glove box, just like the one he'd picked up at the cemetery. He'd always been lucky that way.

For the first time in his long career, he ran.

After working for the Wong family for two decades, he'd survived by following orders, leaving no trail, appearing immediately when summoned, and disappearing just as quickly. This time, Wong wouldn't be happy. Instead of his usual clean job, he'd left a trail any wannabe CSI could follow. Nothing incriminated him, of course. But any extraneous link back to Wong wouldn't be forgiven.

He drove just under the speed limit to the Heartland city limits, and made a call. He'd never risked so much before, but those at the other end of the line offered his only hope for damage control. Judge Southgate had made a similar call, and triggered Bleak's activation. But Southgate had had no leverage, unlike himself. He literally knew where bodies were buried. Bleak only needed a buffer of a few hours delay to transfer his insurance—documentation only he controlled that protected him from contract termination—and the funds to put his retirement plan in place.

When the service answered, he recited his prepared spiel, waited for the voice to repeat the message, and disconnected. If successful, he'd know shortly.

Within minutes, he received a text with instructions. His relieved smile stretched painful burned skin, but he didn't care. Relief was within his grasp. Rather than the expected instructions to return to the airport, he drove north as directed. In forty minutes, Bleak pulled into the designated spot to wait. A new, unmarked car with untraceable credentials in the glove box would be delivered shortly.

While he waited for the final text confirmation, Bleak wiped down the steering wheel with one of the gloves that no longer fit his swollen hands. He exited the old car—it stank of dog, an odor he now despised—and visited the lavatory. The shiny metal that served as a mirror offered only a shadowy look at the stab wound in the side of his neck. It had begun to throb, but no longer bled. He set his phone on the lip of the sink, and pulled wads of paper towels from the rack, soaked them in cold water, then dabbed his sore face. He stuck his hands under the cold water stream. The backs of his hands carried blackened tissue courtesy of Southgate's final act. He'd since learned that Southgate's daughter escaped the blaze. He didn't know or care about the identity of the girl who died in her stead. Wrong place at the wrong time.

The door of the men's room squeaked open. Bleak looked up just in time to recognize the blurry image standing behind him, holding an iridescent neon cane. He grabbed for his gun, but his sausage-size fingers fumbled and it dropped to the tile floor.

Wrong place and very wrong time.

"Hello Uncle Danny."

Charlie's voice shook as she swung the cane again and again. She kept swinging until his teeth littered the bathroom and he lay still. She retrieved his gun, and hand shaking, finished the assignment. It was the only way Mrs. Wong agreed to help her.

Charlie texted a brief message on the phone she'd stolen from Teddy's RV, and the reply came immediately. It directed her to the promised car, complete with new identity and access to funds courtesy of Uncle Danny.

With Sherlock beside her, Charlie drove away, anxious to begin a new life.

Chapter 63

It had been a whirlwind ten days. September had insisted Combs finish his vacation, while she flew back to South Bend with Shadow to make the arrangements for Angela's burial. No funeral, but her memorial service would come later. She'd begun winding up the estate, and discovered Angela's will never got changed after Peter died, making September the beneficiary of the estate. It felt so wrong. She hadn't figured out what to do about that.

She'd also met with Detective Steele to answer his questions—and apologize for doubting him—and collected her car. The uneventful drive to Texas allowed September to move back into her house two days before Combs was due to return. She hadn't felt festive, but in her absence, Lia had enthusiastically decorated her renovated Victorian for Christmas as a surprise.

Now September held the champagne glass in one hand, while the other intertwined fingers with Combs. Shadow pressed his head against her foot, an anchor that made the moment real. The Christmas tree, a week past its use-by date, competed with tacky New Year's Eve decorations that Melinda and Willie plastered throughout the house. In thirty minutes, they'd ring in the new year.

She looked around the room, saddened at the tornado's lasting damage. She treasured the surviving pieces that much more: Harmony on the cello stand; her brother's stained glass lamp on a table; the Peaceable Kingdom engraving on the nearby wall; the stained glass table moved from the kitchen to serve as dining table; and her beat-up but still playable piano in the next room. What the tornado hadn't destroyed, rain and the elements had scarred. She'd replaced most of the furniture, and chosen to rebuild the old structure.

The renovated house still had a few screws to tighten and scrapes to patch, maybe like September herself. But she believed the chipped bricks and plaster scars added character—the face of a survivor. Many of the garden roses uprooted by the storm had sent up optimistic October sprouts—despite all the tradesmen tramping around—that, she dared hope, would survive the winter and bloom again come spring. She could do no less.

This night of nights, the old house rang with happy conversation, kid laughter, barks and meows, the sounds of absolute bedlam. September basked in the cacophony. Friends accomplished what deadbolts and fancy security systems failed to do. Her battle-scarred house on Rabbit Run Road no longer hid from the world. It shined with promise, and felt like home.

The feeling of déjà vu hearkened back to another New Year's Eve party when so much of her life took a detour for the better. Life continued to change, but she liked the view of the new road ahead. She squeezed Combs's hand, and he smiled, and moved to put an arm around her shoulders. Despite the latest revelations that once again disrupted September's entire family, Combs never wavered. He had her back. And her heart. Life would never be the same.

The front door opened, and Teddy bustled back into the house. "Combs, might want to check on your kids. Their dog's going nuts in the back garden. They say he found a squirrel."

Shadow raised his head with interest, and looked up at September, a hopeful gleam in his eyes. She smiled but shook her head, and he resettled his head with a sigh. "That explains why your new friend acted so hissy."

He nodded. "I'm new to cats. But Meriwether's all situated and seems happy in his new digs." He walked carefully into the room, hardly favoring his healing leg.

"When you asked about adopting, I asked Detective Steele if he could make it happen." September grinned, delighted the furry match-making worked, and would help relieve Teddy's loneliness. "I thought you two explorers were a good fit." The big orange and white Maine Coon would be a good traveler in Teddy's RV. And according to Tee, also guard the premises with tooth and claw.

More barks erupted from the back of the house, followed by kid squeals. Combs groaned and started to stand up. Lia stopped him. "You stay, I'll check on them." She handed a refilled champagne glass to Teddy, and hurried to join Melinda and Willie. Lia had promised them a sleep-over at Corazon Kennels, and a chance to play with Magic and Gizmo. They'd camp out in what used to be September's room, while September and Combs had the night alone in her refurbished house.

Teddy perched on the sofa, sipping his drink. "Combs, I thought your partner would be here."

"Gonzales and Mercedes had sick kids. It happens." He hugged September. "I'm just grateful he got to you in time, when I couldn't."

In time to save one life. But to lose another.

September blinked back tears. The note Rose left behind explained nothing, and only spoke of her regret. Had she really decided to kill herself, or been helped by the mysterious Mr. Bleak? Did that even matter now?

Rose had taken several of April's pills, but not a lethal dose. The temperature of the hot tub, though, had been ramped up to dangerous levels that caused heatstroke. She would have drowned had September not pulled her from the water, but she'd been beyond help. When the hospital pronounced her brain dead, they did the only thing they could. In life, Rose feared questions about her children's parentage. But in death, Rose's kidneys—both of them, because of possible damage from the heatstroke—proved her to be a perfect match for her daughter, April.

The same couldn't be said of September, or her other siblings. The truth had finally come out, none were the biological children of either Rose or Lysle; Lysle admitted to having adopted them all twenty-five years ago, but even he did not know that Rose was not their biological mother. September's oldest sisters had only fuzzy recollections of early life and no wish to dig deeper. Most of the family history had been re-imagined by Rose herself. They might never learn the truth, or know anything about the murder allegation. September kept that little tidbit to herself, since Aunt Cornelia had her own reasons for keeping such things quiet. Some secrets deserved to say buried. Chosen family didn't need blood to forge unbreakable bonds.

"What's the latest, Combs?" Teddy sipped his champagne. "Any progress?"

"Slow going." Combs shrugged. "It'll take time to unravel. Tee's team in Chicago, Detective Steele in South Bend, and Gonzales and I are part of a task force, with the FBI consulting." He shook his head with disgust. "Before Tee went into the hospital, she helped arrest Alderman Jacobs. We think he funded Mr. Bleak's killing spree, and probably pulled strings to eliminate Victor Grant in jail."

Teddy raised his glass in a silent toast. "Glad to know Redford's recovering."

Combs raised his glass, too, and the rest followed suit. "To Detective Redford. And to Oreo, a very brave dog." He drained his glass. He turned to September. "Tee said he'd just adopted the dog, when the Alderman stopped by his house intending to kill Redford. He'd asked too many questions. Then Mr. Bleak showed up, intent on eliminating the Alderman. There was some kind of a three-way struggle, and Oreo got in between the men…"

"Splitting behavior." September nodded. "To dogs, a hug or something like wrestling looks like a fight. A peacekeeper pooch splits the adversaries apart. You'll see dogs do that to people who dance, or hug, or sit too close, or…" She glanced at Combs from under her eyelashes, and then at Shadow.

"Splitting behavior, huh? That explains a lot." He grinned. "Tee said Oreo's a sweet, friendly dog, especially laidback for a Border Collie. So his splitting behavior skewed the gun's aim."

September nodded. "Border Collies are super smart and intuitive." Oreo would get a canine hero commendation. She stroked Shadow's neck. He didn't need a commendation for her to consider him a hero, every single day. "So Detective Redford got shot, and Mr. Bleak tried to stage it as another suicide, but got interrupted by Redford's son. Thank God the ambulance arrived in time."

Combs glanced over at Shadow. "Dogs know, right boy?" Shadow yawned and looked away. "September heard Mr. Bleak mention a job in Chicago. Somebody wanted Jacobs silenced."

Teddy shivered elaborately. "Somebody, indeed. Who is this Bleak character? He killed whole families."

Combs shrugged. "Somebody else pulled his strings."

"Tee says Redford needs rehab but will recover well enough to enjoy his retirement." September remembered Tee's complaints of migraines, body aches, and numb feelings. "I'm glad Tee's getting medical attention, too. I made arrangements for Karma to board at a kennel while she was hospitalized." *Dakota had come from that kennel.* Tee had only agreed to a week-long treatment, and swore she'd recovered from the tick-borne disease. The stubborn woman wouldn't admit she needed help. September guessed they had that in common.

Combs continued his recap. "Jacobs isn't talking. We don't believe he's the head of the snake. We've got him in protective custody, as well as his wife and son."

"Adopted son, right?" Teddy adjusted his glasses. "Jacobs comes from old money. I guess his old man's a piece of old-school work, too. Grandpa insisted on a male heir to carry on the family name. So Kelly Radcliff Jacobs III and his wife arranged to have a baby boy. Just ordered poor little Kelly Radcliff Jacobs IV up from the internet, and had to keep it a secret from Grandpa or get written out of the will. After that, the baby broker pulled the alderman's strings for the rest of his life."

September shook her head. "I can't believe this was all about selling babies. There are plenty of children needing homes, ready to be adopted. Why buy a child?" Combs squeezed her shoulders.

Teddy hazarded a guess. "These folks wanted a particular flavor of baby, made to order. Age, looks, sex, ethnicity. Makes your blood boil."

She leaned her head against Combs. "What about Judge Southgate? I feel for his daughter. Sharon Southgate lost her whole family. It's always the innocents who suffer the most."

Combs kissed her cheek. "Judge Southgate knew Peter and Angela Day for years. I think he and Peter went to school together. We found Southgate's fingerprints in Angela's house, and on the ladder in the garage. Circumstantial, but I like him for Angela's murder. You said Mr. Bleak claimed to be hired to clean up the scene, and frame you. He had no reason to deny Angela's death, when he took credit for others."

Teddy jumped in with more explanation. "We know more about Detweiller." He looked to Combs for permission, and at his nod, explained. "According to the bookkeeper's files, his Clear Choice Labs got all kinds of creative with payoffs. He took money and got favors to falsify paternity tests. He faked drug test results to terminate parental rights. That all played into the baby trade thirty years ago. But the baby sales dried up nearly twenty years ago."

"So anything more recent connects to a much more sophisticated organization, one leveraging influence on a broader scale." Combs took it one step farther. "Once somebody with influence—like a judge, or an alderman—steps over the line, the bad guys can use that to crack the whip and get all kinds of concessions."

"Any word about Charlie?" Teddy adjusted his glasses. "I worry about that girl. I hope she finds a safe place to have her baby. She claimed Sissie Turpin already had someone lined up to take him or her." He shuddered.

Combs shook his head. "We've got pictures circulating, but she could easily change her appearance and name. We're not sure she used her real name anyway. Besides, we're more focused on finding Bleak than a random runaway."

"A lot of runaways find themselves in precarious situations, through no fault of their own." September spoke softly, thinking of her mother. She knew Rose had done the best she could. And if Chris hadn't saved her, she wouldn't be here today, either. People made the best choice they could in the moment. Everyday heroes, some with two feet, and others with four, blessed the world like wingless angels in unexpected, miraculous ways.

As if he heard her, or at least felt her emotion, Shadow stirred, and pushed his muzzle against her knee. She leaned forward to smooth his brow and whispered in his ear. "You'll always be my hero, baby-dog." He thumped his tail, sighed, and settled his chin on her knee.

Combs smiled his agreement. "We tried. We pinged September's phone with no luck. But we did find Lia's truck at a rest stop on the Texas/Oklahoma border with no sign of Bleak."

Teddy choked on his drink, and they stared at him for a moment. He waved his hand dismissively. "I'm fine, really, something just went down the wrong way."

Combs stood up. "It's nearly midnight. Everyone have a beverage?"

Lia returned from the kitchen, herding the two kids into the room before her, and carrying a bottle to refill glasses.

Willie carefully closed the dog gate behind them. "Kinsler's paws are too muddy to come in, and we don't want to mess up September's new house. Texas snow gets dirty quick." He and his sister each had glasses filled with sparkling cider. "Dad, will ya give her the present already? Lia says we've got to leave soon."

September looked up at Combs, wrinkling her brow. They'd planned to exchange gifts later, privately. "You know I hate surprises." She smiled, the words teasing, finally able to trust enough to enjoy what he'd planned. Maybe an extra crap gift to make her laugh?

But he looked nervous. Combs, a decorated cop, a detective, looked scared. Everyone else in the room grinned, clearly in on the surprise.

"Okay, somebody tell me what's going on?" When she stood, Shadow bounded to his feet as well, woofing with excitement.

Lia stepped forward and nodded at Combs. "Go ahead. You got this."

Combs took a big breath, and then turned away from September. He went to one knee, to face Shadow. "Counting on you, Shadow. Like we planned, okay?" Shadow whined, and looked up at September.

What in the world?

"Shadow, *bring BEAR!*" Combs voice boomed, the authoritative tone familiar to his kids. And to dogs.

"Oh, but his bear-toy got left in South Bend with Kismet..." Her words faded and mouth dropped open as Shadow galloped away. She heard him thunder up the long front staircase, paw-thump down the hall to her bedroom, pounce onto the squeaky bed, and then return with a flourish. He carried a glossy stuffed Mickie Mouse, easily twice as big as his former bear-toy. Shadow laid it at September's feet.

She looked up at Combs, whose expression of relief made her laugh out loud. "Sweet! You got Shadow a new bear—I mean, a Mickie. Thank you."

"Straight from the Magic Kingdom. Plus a bit extra, September. Look closer." Teddy cackled, enjoying the show. The two kids giggled and punched each other.

"On the ribbon." Lia pointed.

September smiled, and reached for the toy. But Shadow picked it up again, and backed away, whining. He looked from Combs to September, tail lowered, ears pressed flat, and concerned. "Baby-dog, what's wrong? You don't want me to take Bear?"

Combs glared at Lia. "I told you this was a bad idea."

"Will somebody please explain what's going on?" September sat back down. Shadow gripped the toy, clearly worried. Everyone's smiles faded.

Clearing his throat, Combs took her hand. "I know that you and Shadow belong together. You're a package deal. So I know for it to work, for me—for us—to have a future, he's got to be on board. I wanted to try to make friends with Shadow, and sort of... Oh dammit, what was I thinking?"

It became clear. "You wanted Shadow's permission."

"We already said yes!" Willie shouted, and his sister punched and shushed him.

Her eyes filled, and she turned to the big black shepherd. And she knew, as surely as if he'd spoken.

Saw his notched ear, the mark of a bullet meant for her. Traced the white slash of fur he earned protecting her life. His steadfast presence, anchoring her to the here-and-now when horrors of the past dragged her into hell. "Oh, baby-dog, don't you know that nobody could ever take your place? More family—Combs, and the kids—it just means more to love."

He stared deep into her eyes, and a tentative wag grew wider, faster. She could read the ribbon message— "Please Adopt Me?" — And the emerald engagement ring it held that matched her eyes.

Shadow pranced forward, pressed the Mickie into her arms, and licked the happy tears from her eyes...*that tasted like love.*

The clock struck the hour on a new year.

The Story Continues...Read the first chapter of WIN OR LOSE

Chapter 1 – QUINN

Raised by murderers, on the run since age fifteen, Quinn Donovan hunted the wicked to redeem her soul. She relished the recent training that had honed her flaccid body into lithe strength, sharpened reflexes to whip-fast, and drilled innovative training until the skills became second nature—transforming her from prey to hunter. She'd proved herself four months ago, even before training, but knew she still had much to learn. Even with bare bones knowledge, the change offered new-found hope, and the possibility of a future where—eventually—she'd answer only to herself.

For now, though, she served as a weapon for another to aim and fire.

As a ghost, nobody would ever hurt her again. She had a new name, a new body, and a new purpose. No longer hiding in the shadows, Quinn operated in the light, and those in her sights got no quarter. She had no problem spilling the blood of bad guys. Like her bad-ass motorcycle-riding great-granny always said: *An eye for an eye*.

Quinn touched her newly toned tummy and made room for Tigger to settle on her lap. He immediately climbed to her shoulders, draping his large tabby-striped body around her neck, and kneading with claw-sheathed paws. By rights, she should have got rid of him. He tied Quinn to her past life, but had saved her sanity. So, like her, she'd changed his name and his appearance. She couldn't trust humans, but the cat never lied. She wouldn't admit it to anyone, but they needed each other. Neither of them had many more lives to spare.

The special phone buzzed. The text messages always came from different numbers. Her stomach fluttered. Another assignment so soon? She completed the most recent one in Mexico in record time by recruiting gullible students on spring break to mule the product over the border. Worked like a charm, and impressed the hell out of her benefactor by creating an ideal new revenue source. Hell, she'd already made all the right connections when she couldn't get what she needed any other way. She smiled. The contacts trusted her. In this business, that meant everything.

But when Quinn checked the text, her smile froze. The cat meowed and immediately head-butted her cheek. Quinn pushed him aside and sprang up with a soft curse. The text had two words:

>*Fix it*

It also contained a picture of a tall heavyset boy, pale dog at his side, sneaking off with a recognizable insulated thermos. Damn!

The cat head-butted her again. Quinn breathed deeply, willing her blood pressure to drop. She texted back a "thumbs up" emoji, gathered the cat into her arms, and buried her face in his short fur.

She'd given the party-hearty kids a chance to do good, instead of just hanging out and puking on the beach. If one boy went sideways, his friends might have followed his lead to line their own pockets. Served her right for going cheap and enlisting amateurs instead of hiring pros. He'd pay, though, for the betrayal.

No time to waste. She used her new skills to run one of the specialized searches on the laptop she'd prepared for just such an emergency. Quinn knew to plan backups and redundancies into everything. That had kept her alive this long, and there'd be less room for error working for the current Organization. As she waited for the report to percolate, Quinn stroked the cat until he had had enough and vaulted to the top of the motel television cabinet. Tigger always wanted to be on the highest perch.

Within minutes, the report spat out the bad news. Of the twenty couriers, sixteen delivered thermoses containing the product to Quinn's dummy recipients in south Texas. Once processed, the drugs continued up the distribution chain per her benefactor's requirement. Quinn's sole responsibility, to get the product across the border, failed. Her boss demanded 100 percent satisfaction. Or suffer the consequences.

Bad enough the delivery never happened. Even worse, the AWOL couriers knew her face and at least part of the enterprise. She'd need to change up her appearance again, and maybe her name, but felt grateful for the warning text. Another failure would earn worse.

How had she so misjudged them? She had to turn this around. *Eye for an eye, tooth for a tooth.* And maybe a bullet for betrayal.

She'd go after the first boy, recover the product, and explain to him the error of his ways. He'd tell her where to find the others, too. She'd learned a lot during her training about how to get answers. With this reprieve, she'd prove her worth once and for all to her boss. breath. She'd **fix it**, all right!

Staring at the disposable phone and the terse text she'd sent quickened Kali's breath. Two words. Enough to rattle the souls of those in her employ. Except this girl, too new to know better, had no clue what she'd set in motion. Her smile widened.

With care, she removed the SIM card. She placed it on a nearby battered butcher-block table stained with unmentionables and used a metal meat mallet to beat it into fragments. She brushed the fragments into a nearby ash tray, already filled to the brim with the remains of the imported cigars she favored. Dropping the phone, she crushed it beneath one elegant stiletto with a satisfying crunch, then kicked the debris into the corner. Her maid service would erase the clutter shortly.

When she beckoned, the man standing watch at the door reached her side in three long strides. He embodied her perfect mate. Much younger than her, biddable, with understated leonine strength she found more appealing than bullish bodyguards. He'd won her favor with his swift execution of each assignment. He never questioned. He followed direction. His stamina and appetite equaled her own. He deserved a reward, a tasty treat, to keep him coming back for more. Kali smiled. She had just the thing, and his fun would also clear the tedious roadblock that threatened her future.

She held out her hand. "Your phone." He handed it over, and she quickly found an online image and showed it to him. "Clarabelle lives in Heartland, Texas. Has all the young studs smitten." She liked that word, rolled it around on her tongue to say it again. "Smitten. She's not shy about sharing her favors. But I want her to be extra nice to one stud in particular, so very nice that young Studly won't say no to a favor. You understand?"

He nodded, eyes gleaming. "The favor?"

"All in due time." She handed back his phone. "Of course, use the Organization's air transport services to expedite the assignment. Make it happen. And once she asks the favor, and he delivers, you can have your fun with her." One of Kali's long, sharp green fingernails drew a line down his bare throat to the open collar of his shirt. "I've had a new identity prepared especially for this assignment. You answer to Mr. Casper Fright. Because you'll be an unfriendly ghost, and anyone who survives this should have nightmares remembering anything about you. Do you like that... Mr. Fright?"

He nodded again, breath quickening. Mr. Fright knew what came next.

"The usual arrangements apply. Success means rewards, and failure—well, you don't want to find out. And after taking care of Clarabelle, if you're still... hungry"—she looked him up and down, smiling at his obvious response—"I'll have more delectables for your exacting tastes."

Much later, after he'd satisfied her—for now—she dismissed Mr. Fright and his insatiable appetite. It made her itch to join him in the titillating up-close work that gave her the ultimate exquisite release, rather than delegating such jobs to inferiors. She couldn't indulge, though. Perhaps after cementing her control by eliminating her rival, she'd reward herself.

"This time, I win and you lose," she whispered. Between Quinn Donovan and Casper Fright, she'd created an unrelenting, indestructible, and unforgiving team to eliminate a certain gadfly named September Day.

Look for WIN OR LOSE #6 in your favorite book store!

FACT, FICTION & ACKNOWLEDGEMENTS

Thank you for reading HIT AND RUN, and I hope you enjoyed this fifth book in the September & Shadow thriller series. Interestingly, an accidental meeting between Rose and Cornelia in the fourth book FIGHT OR FLIGHT inspired this story. Weird how that happens. Now this latest installment gives me a jumping-off point for book six, **WIN OR LOSE.** Thank you for coming along with me on the adventure. There never would have been Thrillers With Bite without you, dear reader, adopting these books. (Can you hear my purrs and woofs of delight?)

After publishing 35+ nonfiction pet books, research fuels my curiosity. While in fiction I get to make up crappiocca, as September would say, much of my inspiration comes from news stories, past and present—the weirder, the better. For me, and I hope for you, the story becomes more engaging when built not just on "what if" but "it happened." So in each book, I like to include a Cliff's Notes version of what's real and what's made up.

As with the other books in the series, much of HIT AND RUN arises from science, especially dog and cat behavior and learning theory, the benefits of service dogs, and the horror and reality of black-market babies. By definition, thrillers include murder and mayhem, but as an animal advocate professional, I make a conscious choice to not show a pet's death in my books. All bets are off with the human characters, though.

I rely on a vast number of veterinarians, behaviorists, consultants, trainers, and pet-centric writers and readers, and rescue organizations that share their incredible resources and support to make my stories as believable as possible. Find out more information at IAABC.org, APDT.com, DWAA.org and CatWriters.com.

FACT: Anita Page, born Anita Evelyn Pomares in 1910, was a real person and star of the silent screen era. She was referred to as a "blond, blue-eyed Latin" and her grandfather hailed from Spain. She retired from acting in 1936, but returned to acting sixty years later, and appeared in four films in the 2000s. Page died at age 98 in 2008, so she and the fictional Tana certainly could have met thirty-odd years ago. Learn more about Anita Page here:

https://en.wikipedia.org/wiki/Anita_Page

FICTION: Any aspersions cast upon judges or Chicago alderman in the story are, of course, made up. However, there have been questions raised about whether or not Chicago aldermen should be allowed to hold outside employment is a thing, which inspired parts of the story:

https://news.wttw.com/2019/01/09/should-aldermen-be-banned-outside-employment-we-asked-them

FACT: Sadly, black market babies are a thing—more so in the past but also under the radar today. TLC's "Taken at Birth" shares untold stories of the "Hicks Babies," more than 200 newborn babies illegally sold or given away from the back steps of a small-town Georgia clinic run by Dr. Thomas J. Hicks during the 1950s and 1960s. The three-night special aired October 9-11, 2019. Here's a clip on YouTube: https://youtu.be/ESyhEzX7WNo

That's not the only example. From 1924-1950 more than 5000 children were stolen by Georgia Tann, and re-sold (adopted) with the help of a crooked local judge. Some children were adopted by celebrities including Joan Crawford and June Allyson. Other clients were Lana Turner, Pearl S. Buck and New York Gov. Herbert Lehman. Ric Flair, a future pro wrestler, was among Tann's abductees. Read more here: https://nypost.com/2017/06/17/this-woman-stole-children-from-the-poor-to-give-to-the-rich/

Think it doesn't happen in more contemporary times? Check out this 2017 story about children being sold:

https://www.cnn.com/2017/10/12/health/uganda-adoptions-investigation-ac360/index.html

FACT: Selective disobedience is vital in training service dogs. Whether trained as police K9 officers or for other kinds of service, the savvy dogs must learn to think for themselves. For instance, the guide dog must know to disobey his human partner's command to "forward" into car traffic, and canine heroes figure out when to follow the most important trail, or take a bullet to save their human handler.

FICTION: Midwives do not routinely work for baby-selling organizations. They are unlikely to have drugs at the ready without a licensed physician on the premises. Also, the drug midazolam (it's real) isn't the best one for use during birth, and it does cause memory loss. However, the midwife in the story probably doesn't care about the mother's safety, and has access to whatever drugs necessary with or without a medical license. Interestingly, midazolam also can be used to help control seizures in veterinary medicine, so that proved very convenient for my plot.

FICTION: Lab owners do not sell out their test results to the highest bidder—except in fiction stories like mine, and (wow!) occasionally in real life. That part of my story was inspired by 36-year-old Brandy Murrah's arrest for forging the results of drug tests performed by her A&J Lab, in Alabama. Investigators had to figure out how many parents may have lost jobs, custody of their children, or worse. Read about it here: https://www.theroot.com/lab-owner-arrested-for-falsifying-results-of-drug-tests-1834753568

FACT: Heat-detecting vision goggles do exist and are different than night-vision goggles that amplify existing light. Instead, these goggles detect heat from living creatures or from hot spots in fires. A better explanation of both can be found at this link: https://www.explainthatstuff.com/hownightvisionworks.html

FACT: I grew up in Northern Indiana. Mount Pleasant Cemetery is real and does have a historic marker as mentioned in the story. Several of the places mentioned in South Bend, like Notre Dame, are real. When Teddy needed a new ride, I found his "Nellie-Nova" made in the area. Pretty spiffy, huh? Here's a link: https://coachmenrv.com/class-b-motorhomes/nova

FICTION: I've lived in North Texas for more than twenty years and draw from the area in my fiction. But Heartland doesn't exist.

FACT: Boiled eggs really do explode when microwaved! Hey, voice of experience here (ahem). Also, learn more here: https://www.latimes.com/food/sns-dailymeal-1860438-healthy-eating-hard-boiled-eggs-explode-violently-microwaved-20171207-story.html

FACT: People have died from hot tubs overheating. https://www.sun-sentinel.com/news/fl-xpm-2000-04-01-0004010278-story.html

FACT: That bridging maneuver that September used to escape is real. Learn how here:
https://www.youtube.com/watch?v=kJcaRW1vkEI

FACT—sorta: Blood type inheritance can be complicated, and not only the type but also the genotype influences what the children inherit. Yes, kids can end up with a different blood type than parents. For example, the child of an AB dad and an OO mom could either be AO (blood type A) or BO (blood type B). Further, some blood types are considered universal kidney donors or kidney universal recipients—yet living donor transplants also can be complex. So for purposes of the story, I simply fudged a bit and never specified who had what blood type. Learn more about blood types, and living donors at these links:

https://genetics.thetech.org/ask-a-geneticist/parent-children-different-blood-type

https://transplantliving.org/living-donation/being-a-living-donor/tests/

FACT: Tick-borne pathogens can cause a variety of serious debilitating diseases in pets, and sometimes humans. Sometimes, people become infected with more than one pathogen, which can make symptoms, diagnosis, and treatment challenging. Lyme disease was first identified in 1975 when a cluster of childhood arthritis cases were reported in Lyme, Connecticut. It's caused by a spirochete, a type of bacteria named *Borrelia burgdorferi*, which occurs naturally in white-footed mice and deer. The organism is transmitted to people (and dogs) usually by deer ticks and is most common in the northeastern and Pacific coast states. But it does occur in Texas where it's carried by the black-legged tick. Typical symptoms in people include a bullseye-pattern rash, fever, headache, and fatigue, but the first sign in dogs usually is limping. If not treated early, Lyme disease infection can spread to your joints, heart, and nervous system, and cause long term problems.

A few years ago, I began to notice a pins-and-needles numbness on the lower left side of my back and abdomen. Within days, the sensation spread until my entire left leg and side, from my belly button down, felt numb. I thought "pinched nerve?" and visited my chiropractor for weeks, until he referred me to a neurologist when nothing improved. I spent nearly a week in the hospital, treated for a lesion on my spinal cord. Although I was tested for Lyme disease, we never got a definitive cause, and although most of the sensation in my left side returned, I still have numbness on the bottom of my left foot. I gave Tee the more typical signs, and a definitive diagnosis, but who knows if her treatment truly resolved the issue? Oh, and to allay concerns, dogs do NOT transmit tick-borne diseases to people (the ticks don't jump from one host to another). If you work outside in tick country, wear protective clothing, and keep your dogs protected with veterinarian-approved preventives. And if you notice signs, get help immediately.

FICTION: Shadow and Macy's viewpoint chapters are pure speculation, although I would love to be able to read doggy and kitty minds. However, every attempt has been made to base all animal characters' motivations and actions on what is known about canine and feline body language, scent discrimination, and the science behind the human-animal bond.

FACT: Cats can, indeed, do many of the same things as dogs, including sniffing out the missing or predicting seizures. Dogs have been trained to detect the smell of sweat from a patient seizing, and cat scenting ability can certainly detect these differences. In most instances, cats aren't easily trained, but instead they decide on their own with those with whom they share a strong bond.

Studies reported in the journal Applied Animal Behavior Science by Kristyn Vitale Shreve, and Monique Udell shine a new light on feline scent sense. Based on genetics, cats may be even better equipped than dogs at scent discrimination. Mammal scent detection relies on recognizing specialized proteins. Shreve, a researcher in Oregon State University's Department of Animal and Rangeland Sciences, says there are three families of receptor proteins in the scent detection organ of mammals: V1Rs, V2Rs and FPRs. She believes the number of V1R receptor gene variants predicts the mammal's ability to discriminate different odors. Dogs have nine, humans have two, but cats have around 30 V1Rs. You can access the study here:

https://www.sciencedirect.com/science/article/abs/pii/S0168 159116303501

Given cats' scenting prowess, and ability to access tiny spaces and heights, it follows that Macy-cat is a good fit for search and rescue operations. Kim Freeman, a specialist in finding lost cats, partners with Henry the black and white kitty to track down wayward cats. Learn more about her at LostCatFinder.com.

FACT: Real-life pets inspire some of the pet characters in HIT AND RUN. I've held a "Name That Dog/Name That Cat" contest for each of the novels thus far in the series. Since this thriller continues where FIGHT OR FLIGHT left off, some of those same pet names live on in future stories.

Some of you know that my heart-dog Magic inspired Shadow's character. We lost Magic in 2018, and I struggled with continuing the series. His best friend Karma-Kat mourned his GSD buddy and slept with Magic's collar for two weeks after he died. To honor their relationship, I included those names in the contest poll for FIGHT OR FLIGHT, and you—the readers—voted overwhelmingly to bless this and future stories with their names. For that reason, **Karma** the Rottweiler police dog (named after dog-loving-Karma-Kat) stars in this thriller. And the puppy-son of Shadow and Karma is named **Magic**, destined to share many future hero dog adventures. (Oh crap, now I'm crying…)

For HIT AND RUN, folks offered 158 cat names and 172 dog names, so many that I decided to include six hero pets in the story. I narrowed it down to sixteen each, and y'all voted 43,300 times to name the following winners:

Sherlock the white cat with green eyes was nominated by Lisa Mahoney. This loving cat enjoyed shoulder perching, snuggling in wet hair, and adored his big brother-cat Pie. I added the seizure-alerting behavior to Sherlock in the story, to better help his new friend Charlie.

Meriwether the orange and white cat was nominated by Kate Holly-Clark. Named after the explorer, Meriwether gets into everything, and is "a bit of an idiot and a real klutz." The Meriwether in this story certainly gets into everything and should be even more fun in future stories while partnered with Teddy.

Kahlua the black and white cat was nominated by Darla J. Taylor. She adopted Kahlua after a bad car accident. Kahlua became Darla's unofficial therapy cat, always able to relieve a bad mood. Kahlua in this story keeps Sharon from being hurt in the explosion, and will comfort and hopefully heal her emotionally, as she did in real life with Darla.

Bishop the black and white very large Akita was nominated by Cyn Clarke. He loves children, and adores the snow and cold weather, and like all Akitas, is known for bravery and loyalty. What a joy to add Bishop as a hero dog to save Charlie from freezing, and alert Tee to rescue the girl.

Kismet the very intelligent Great Dane was nominated by Robert Browning. Now eight years old, she's still very active, and loves all animals and wants to be your best partner and share the sofa with you. Even her name—Kismet—fits the story, as destiny brought Teddy together with this lovely Dane girl at the perfect moment.

Oreo the Border Collie was nominated by Sylvia Finch and was named by her granddaughter for her half black/white face. She's an extreme people lover and more laid back than many BCs. I hadn't planned for more than two hero dogs, so it took a while for Oreo to tell me where she fit in the story. But what a perfect adoption option for the retiring cop to bring a sweet cookie-of-a-dog into his son's life—and save his own.

For more about the winners, and pictures of some of the hero pets, visit the blog page here: https://amyshojai.com/hit-and-run-winners/. Congratulations and THANK YOU to all the winners. I think they all deserve treats. Maybe even bacon!

FACT: Therapy dogs can work wonders when partnered with autistic individuals. Emotional Support Animals (ESA) also partner with a variety of people, from children to adults, including those suffering from post-traumatic stress disorder (PTSD). Only dogs and guide horses for the blind can be *service animals* trained to perform a specific function for their human partner (usually three or more tasks), from becoming the ears for the deaf, eyes for the blind, support for other-abled and alert animals for health and physically challenged individuals. Of course, there are amazing people-pet partnerships that develop without any formal training—like Charlie's seizure-detecting cat Sherlock—and many animals like Shadow and Karma intuitively provide the support their humans need.

Learn about the differences and the benefits of pet-people partnerships at http://petpartners.org. You can also find out about "fake" credentialing services that hurt legitimate partnerships in this blog post: http://amyshojai.com/fake-service-dog-credentials/

FACT: This book would not have happened without an incredible support team of friends, family and accomplished colleagues. Special thanks to my fantastic editor Nicola Aquino of Spit & Polish Editing, who keeps me on track, catches the problems, suggests brilliant fixes, and deletes extraneous commas (I, love, commas, it seems *s*). I'm indebted to my first readers—Kristi, Bonnie, and Frank—for your eagle eyes, spot-on comments and unflagging encouragement and support. Wags and purrs to my Triple-A Team (Amy's Audacious Allies) for all your help sharing the word about all my books. Youse guyz rock!

I continue to be indebted to the International Thriller Writers organization, which launched my fiction career by welcoming me into the Debut Authors Program. Wow, just look, now I have five books in a series! The authors, readers and industry mavens who make up this organization are some of the most generous and supportive people I have ever met. Long live the bunny slippers with teeth (and the rhinestone #1-Bitch Pin).

Finally, I am grateful to all the cats and dogs I've met over the years who have shared my heart and oftentimes my pillow. Magical-Dawg (the inspiration for Shadow) and Seren-Kitty continue to live on in my heart. Brave Bravo my Bullmastiff, now a tripawed dog fighting osteosarcoma, inspires me every day along with his best buddy Karma-Kat. And newcomer Shadow-Pup (yes, named after the book's hero!) showed up when we needed him most. Read about Shadow here: https://amyshojai.com/shadow-of-hope-comfort-puppy/

I never would have been a reader and now a writer if not for my fantastic parents who instilled in me a love of the written word, and never looked askance when my stuffed animals and invisible talking wolf and flying cat friends told fantastical stories. And of course, my deepest thanks to my husband Mahmoud, who continues to support my writing passion, even when he doesn't always understand it.

I love hearing from you! Please drop me a line at my blog https://AmyShojai.com or my website https://shojai.com where you can subscribe to my PET PEEVES newsletter (and maybe win some pet books!). Follow me on twitter @amyshojai and like me on Facebook: http://www.facebook.com/amyshojai.cabc

ABOUT THE AUTHOR

Amy Shojai is a certified animal behavior consultant, and the award-winning author of more than 35 bestselling pet books that cover furry babies to old fogies, first aid to natural healing, and behavior/training to Chicken Soupicity. She has been featured as an expert in hundreds of print venues including The Wall Street Journal, New York Times, Reader's Digest, and Family Circle, as well as television networks such as CNN, and Animal Planet's DOGS 101 and CATS 101. Amy brings her unique pet-centric viewpoint to public appearances. She is also a playwright and co-author of STRAYS, THE MUSICAL and the author of the critically acclaimed THRILLERS WITH BITE pet-centric thriller series. Stay up to date with new books and appearances by visiting Shojai.com to subscribe to Amy's Pets Peeves newsletter.